Disinheritance

ALSO BY RUTH PRAWER JHABVALA

Three Continents
Travelers
Heat and Dust
Out of India: Selected Stories
Amrita
Get Ready for Battle
A Backward Place
Esmond in India
The Nature of Passion
Poet and Dancer
Shards of Memory
East Into Upper East
In Search of Love and Beauty
The Householder
My Nine Lives
A Lovesong for India
Like Birds, Like Fishes
A Stronger Climate
An Experience of India
How I Became a Holy Mother
At the End of the Century

Disinheritance

The Rediscovered Stories

RUTH PRAWER JHABVALA

Counterpoint | California

DISINHERITANCE

This is a work of fiction. All of the characters, organizations, and events portrayed in these stories are either products of the author's imagination or are used fictitiously.

Copyright © 2025 by Ruth Prawer Jhabvala

All rights reserved under domestic and international copyright. Outside of fair use (such as quoting within a book review), no part of this publication may be reproduced, stored in a retrieval system, or transmitted in any form or by any means, electronic, mechanical, photocopying, recording, or otherwise, without the written permission of the publisher. Additionally, no part of this book may be used or reproduced in any manner for the purpose of training artificial intelligence technologies or systems. For permissions, please contact the publisher.

First Counterpoint edition: 2025

Many of the stories in this selection were published originally by *The New Yorker*, *Kenyon Review*, *The London Magazine*, *Cosmopolitan*, *Blackwood's Magazine*, *Encounter*, and *Penguin Modern Stories 11*.

Library of Congress Cataloging-in-Publication Data
Names: Jhabvala, Ruth Prawer, 1927–2013 author
Title: Disinheritance : the rediscovered stories / Ruth Prawer Jhabvala.
Description: San Francisco : Counterpoint, 2025.
Identifiers: LCCN 2025034658 | ISBN 9781640097360 hardcover | ISBN 9781640097377 ebook
Subjects: LCGFT: Short stories
Classification: LCC PR9499.3.J5 D57 2025
LC record available at https://lccn.loc.gov/2025034658

Jacket design by Victoria Maxfield
Jacket image © British Library / Alamy Stock Photo
Book design by tracy danes

COUNTERPOINT
Los Angeles and San Francisco, CA
www.counterpointpress.com

Printed in the United States of America

1 3 5 7 9 10 8 6 4 2

Contents

Introduction: Disinheritance
  by Ruth Prawer Jhabvala ix

Lekha 3
Before the Wedding 23
Sixth Child 37
Better Than Dead 51
The Old Lady 69
The Elected 83
A Birthday in London 97
Wedding Preparations 113
In Love with a Beautiful Girl 129
An Indian Citizen 151
Foreign Wives 173
Day of Decision 187
An Intellectual Girl and an Eminent Artiste 209
A Very Special Fate 237
Commensurate Happiness 257
Grandmother 279
Aphrodisiac 301

Acknowledgments 321

Introduction

DISINHERITANCE

This introduction is taken from a 1979 lecture given by Ruth Prawer Jhabvala upon her receipt of the Neil Gunn International Fellowship by the Scottish Arts Council.

I FEEL GREATLY HONORED TO BE HERE TODAY TO speak to you as a writer in commemoration of your great Scottish novelist Neil Gunn. No two writers could, I suppose, be more different from each other than he and I; I mean, as far as background and experience are concerned. For he had everything, as man and writer, that I have lost. He had a heritage—an inheritance, whereas I have only disinheritance. You hardly need me to tell you about Neil Gunn's inheritance, by which I mean his rootedness in tradition, landscape, and that inexplicable region where childhood and ancestral memories merge; that ground of being from which all great writing comes.

But what I would like to talk to you about is my own disinheritance, my own lack of any such tradition, landscape, memory (either childhood or ancestral). Yes, as I shall explain in a moment, I feel disinherited even of my own childhood memories, so that I stand before you as a writer without any ground of being out of which to write: really blown about from country to country, culture to culture, till I feel—till I am—nothing. I'm not complaining—this is not a complaint, just a statement of fact. As it happens, I like it that way. It's made me into a cuckoo forever insinuating myself into others' nests. Or a chameleon hiding myself (if there were anything to hide) in false or borrowed clothes.

But don't let me slide off into metaphor but start concretely at my beginnings. I was born in 1927 in Germany. My father was Polish and had come to Germany during the First World War to escape military conscription in Poland. In Germany he met my mother, who was actually born in Germany—in Cologne, as I was. But her father had come from Russia—to escape military conscription there, probably. And her mother was born in Germany, in Berlin, though I don't know where *her* father—that is, my great-grandfather—came from. Probably again from Poland or Russia. Anyway, the point of all this is to show that whatever place we were in, we didn't go back into it very far. Not much rootedness—everyone having come from somewhere else, usually having run away from, or having been driven away from, somewhere else. Still, once there, once settled in a place and feeling some measure of security in it, I must say my family seem to have shown the same chameleon or cuckoo quality that I have already had to confess to in myself. And I was born into what seemed a very solidly based family who had identified with the Germany around them—had been through the 1914–18 war with them—had sung for Kaiser and fatherland. In fact, one of my mother's proudest memories was how she had been chosen to recite a poem on the occasion of her school's celebration of the Kaiser's birthday. She described the white frock she wore, the curtsy she made, the flowers she presented to whoever was the guest of honor of that memorable occasion. The school's name, by the way, was Kaiserin Augusta Schule—founded by the Empress herself, and full of pink-cheeked, blond little blue-eyed German girls. Yet it was my mother, whose name was Cohn, who had worn the white frock, presented the flowers, recited the poem in honor of the Kaiser.

My first memories then—that is, between 1927 and 1933—were of a well-integrated, solid, assimilated, German Jewish family. We couldn't, unlike other such families, forget the Jewish part, because my grandfather was the cantor in the biggest Jewish synagogue in Cologne. It wasn't an orthodox synagogue, nor was my grandfather an orthodox Jew. He prided himself on his friendship with Christian pastors—his identification with them insofar as they were all men of God, and our God was the same or at least as good as theirs (at that time). His Jewishness, his religion, was a profession—I don't mean of faith but the way a lawyer or doctor professes his profession. For the rest, he prided himself on being a German gentleman, a well-regarded citizen of Cologne. One of my family's proudest possessions forever afterward was a picture of the Cologne Rathaus presented to my grandfather in token of appreciation of his civic virtues. Most of all my grandfather prided himself on his beautiful baritone voice. And here I can come back to my most basic childhood memory (what should have been but never developed into my atom of delight*), and that is of my grandfather, a tall imposing bearded figure in a three-piece suit with a watch chain across him and wearing laced boots, standing by the piano, clearing his throat. At the piano my grandmother, who had studied at the Berlin Conservatory: small, rotund, wearing a dark-brown silk dress with a deep décolleté and pearls around her stout, manifolded neck, and her little round hands racing over the keys, her head swaying as she prepared to accompany my grandfather on his flight of song. Over the piano a picture of Rebecca at the Well, the sofa was velvet and so were the armchairs; the tablecloth tasseled, and in the corner a great porcelain stove reaching up to the celling, well stoked and heating the room to a temperature that

---

*   Neil M. Gunn's autobiography is called *The Atom of Delight* (1956).

I have ever since sought to recover (for a while I substituted the Delhi summers for it—but of that later). From the kitchen the delicate fragrance of a particular type of round little tea cakes that only my grandmother knew how to bake. There were aunts and uncles, all well settled, all German patriots, all life-loving, full of energy, bourgeois virtues and pleasures, celebrating every kind of festival—all the Jewish holidays, of course, but what they really liked was New Year's Eve and, especially, the annual Cologne carnival and masked ball. We all had costumes made for that every year; one year I was a chimney sweep, and another a Viennese pastry cook. All this would be in the early 1930s—up to, but not including, 1933.

I don't feel like talking much about 1933 and after. Everyone knows what happened to German Jews first and other European Jews after. Our family was no exception. One by one all the aunts and uncles emigrated—to France, Holland, what was then Palestine, and the United States. My grandfather died, so did my grandmother. I don't know what happened to the piano or the picture of Rebecca at the Well. I never saw them again. My immediate family—that is, my Polish father, my mother, my brother, and myself—were the last to emigrate, and also the only ones to go to England. That was in 1939.

I have slurred over the years 1933 to 1939, from when I was six to twelve. They should have been my most formative years; maybe they were, I don't know. Together with the early happy German Jewish bourgeois family years—1927 to 1933—they should be that profound well of memory and experience (childhood and ancestral) from which as a writer I should have drawn. I never have. I've never written about those years. To tell you the truth, until today I've never even mentioned them. Never spoken about them to anyone. I don't know why not. I suppose they are the beginning of my disinheritance—the way they are for other writers of their inheritance.

Anyway: England, 1939. My first entirely instinctive demonstration of my cuckoo or chameleon qualities, I took to England, and English, immediately. Up till then my language had been German. I haven't mentioned that I was writing furiously all through my childhood. It doesn't seem worth mentioning—one is just born that way: destined. One doesn't choose to become a writer. I started school at six and learned the alphabet, and then we were told to write our first composition. The subject: a hare—in German, *der Hase*. I wrote the title, "Der Hase." At once I was flooded with my destiny: only I didn't know that's what it was. I only remember my entire absorption, delight, in writing about—giving my impression of—*der Hase*. To think that such happiness could be! But this is an entirely different subject and I don't want to sidetrack myself. I'm talking about my disinheritance as a person and as a writer, not about the inheritance of my craftsman's tools. That's different, or at least I think it is. Because I have these tools—because they were given, gifted to me, happened to me—I have been a writer. The fact that I appear to have been disinherited of my "ground of being"—that is, my childhood and ancestral memories—doesn't, oddly enough, seem to have made any difference. I have plied my tools, regardless.

So this is what happened when we went to England in 1939; I at once, within a week, I think—started to write in English. I didn't have all that much English—only what I'd learned at school in Germany—but once in England I did learn fast. And not only did I then write in the English language but also—and this is where the chameleon or cuckoo quality really came in—about English subjects. I mean, all the English life I saw around me, first in the Midlands. I first went to Coventry, then was evacuated to Leamington Spa to two maiden sisters and their caretaker father; and from there I went to London, in 1940, to rejoin my parents, who had bought a house in a London suburb and sent me to the local grammar school. And I got to know the English there and wrote about them in the stories, plays, unfinished novels that I turned out in a relentless stream all through those school years. Nothing very good, of course—at that age one's just learning one's craft. Anyway, I was. I wasn't very precocious.

By the time I had acquired enough skill to finish some of those unfinished novels, round off those formless stories, I no longer wrote about England. I never went back—either to write or to live there. But before I go on to talk about where I did live and write, I must record some of my experience of England. Which is my debt to England. England opened out the world of literature for me; what other writers have experienced and set down. Not really having a world of my own, I made up for my disinheritance by absorbing the world of others. The more regional, the more deeply rooted a writer was, the more I loved them: George Eliot, Thomas Hardy, Charles Dickens. Their landscapes, their childhood memories became mine. I adopted them passionately. But I was equally passionate to adopt, for instance, the landscape of Marcel Proust, of James Joyce, of Henry James, of the great Russians—Tolstoy, Dostoevsky, Turgenev, Chekhov (that noble roll call). Whatever author I read last, I was ready to become a figure in that particular landscape. It was as if I had no sense of my own—besides no country of my own—but only theirs. This was the great gift, the inheritance, that England gave me: my education, which became my tradition—the only tradition I had: that of European literature. It became my equipment, my baggage for the journey I didn't know I had to make: the journey to India.

Unlike so many British people—and I'm sure many of you here today—I had no connections with India: no Scottish grandfather who had built the Grand Trunk Road, or opened up canals in the Punjab, or played the bagpipes at the Relief of Lucknow. I didn't know anything about that. I'd read *Kim* and *A Passage to India*, as literature; neither made me want to go to India nor became anything more than another literary landscape to be enjoyed. Nor was I in the least attracted to anything else India-like, for instance, the spiritual scene. I knew nothing about it and if I had done, I wouldn't have cared. I went to India, as it were, blind. If my husband had happened to live in Africa, I'd have gone there equally blindly; asking no questions and in fact fearing no fears. Maybe going there like that, with no preconceptions of any kind, was better than anything, insofar as it kept me completely open to receive whatever there was to receive—that is, India.

I still can't talk about the first impact India made on my innocent—meaning blank and unprepared—mind and sense. To try to express it would make me stutter. Perhaps the best way to put it would be to compare it with the effect the scenery made on Neil Gunn in his childhood: the moors, the crofts, the sea, landing the salmon and cracking the hazelnuts. Stunning, overwhelming, beyond words. I entered a world of sensuous delights that perhaps children—other children—enter. I remember nothing of it from *my* childhood. That way India was remains till today my childhood (though I was twenty-four when I went there). I don't know why this was so. Was it in reaction to the bleakness and deprivations of my own childhood—Nazi Germany and then wartime-blitzed London (those nights and days spent in damp air-raid shelters, and queueing for matches and margarine)? Or did it go farther, and was it that whatever was Oriental within me—I mean, through my being Jewish—was opening up to buried ancestral memory? I don't know, but whatever it was, it was very strong and lasted for years. I won't go into detail. I can't; as I said, it would make me stutter. The smells and sights and sounds of India—the mango and jasmine on hot nights—the rich spiced food—the vast sky—the sight of dawn and dusk—the birds flying about—the ruins—the music—I've tried to write about it; I've spent years writing about it. At that time I loved everything there: yes—to my shame I have to say—even the beggars, the poverty, they didn't bother me then; they seemed right somehow, a part of life that had been taken out of the West (like death, which was also always present in India, carried on a bier in front of my window down to the burning ghats, or the vultures swooping over something indescribable in a ditch). It was life as one read about it in the Bible: whole, I thought; pure, I thought.

I felt like that for ten years. I didn't feel like going back to Europe—and in fact, didn't. I didn't ever *know* any Europeans. I just lived there in my house in India, with my family; but really lived. All the time I was writing those early books and stories of mine. They were all about India—set in India and all the characters Indian. I was pretending to be writing as an insider, as if I didn't know anything else. As if I wasn't a European at all, had never heard of such a place. I don't know how I had the impudence to write like that—in English, in my careful precise (maybe even prissy) prose style learned in England via English literature classes—about people who didn't ever think in English, let alone speak it. But I pretended I knew them—no, more, I pretended I was them. For instance, I was always fond of writing about great big beautiful sensual Indian women, full of passion and instinct; the very opposite of myself, physically and in every other way. And yet I wrote about them, was them, wanted to be them. All this is quite inexplicable to me: those ten years of delight and immersion and more (much more) than acceptance.

What followed is more explicable. I wouldn't call it disillusionment. I don't think it was that; it was more the process of becoming myself again. Becoming European again. The turn my life—my feelings—took is reflected in my writing. I still wrote about India but now seen from a European point of view. I became a European sensibility again, and now I saw everything as perhaps I should have seen it from the beginning. I was no longer immersed in sensuous delight but had to struggle against all the things people do have to struggle against in India: the tide of poverty, disease and squalor rising all around; the heat—the frayed nerves; the strange, alien, often inexplicable, often maddening Indian character. All the things that make Europeans into sahibs and (worse) memsahibs out there, make them close up and shrink into themselves, and then again shrink; making them tight, prim, self-righteous. As I said, closed-up. I became like that. I've written about that too.

Perhaps I should be a bit more specific. Let me talk about my attitude to the spiritual scene in India, or I should say the spirituality of India. I never doubted it was there—why, it was there for me in the sight of the sky. I'd never been so aware of the sky—of there actually being a heaven with stars in it and a moon that was sometimes huge and blown and orange, like a sun, and sometimes the most delicate silver sliver. Maybe it had always been too cold in England to look up at the sky, but here I slept under it all night (those great drenched Indian nights) and that made a difference. So that was another dimension, actually, physically: the world extended upward and much farther than I had thought. Then in the morning—in fact, at dawn, and what lovelier time is there—I could hear all the holy men on the banks of the Jumna singing their morning hymns, and the temple bells ringing. All that was very real: the spiritual and the physical all mixed up, all one sensuous delight. And then I loved people's simple faith: the way they could see God in a cow—let alone in a cow, in a clod of earth, in some misshapen little idol made of clay and costing a couple of pennies. And their belief in swamis and gurus and human beings actually being holy. This was the more touching when I thought of all the bad experience everyone had of human nature—like the grasping landlord, the pitiless money lender, the evil mother-in-law who tortured the little daughter-in-law (aged fourteen) for not bringing enough dowry from her father's house. All these were facts of everyday life to be lived with: one's neighbors, one's fellow human beings; and yet one could still think of human beings as being good, even perfectible, godlike. In fact, the worse the people one came into contact with, the more acceptable the notion of the holy man: a man so good he was holy. I wanted to believe in such a man too. Whenever opportunity came to visit a swami, I did so. I loved to think I was near someone holy, within the range of such wonderful vibrations.

Of course here was the richest soil for disillusionment, and I reaped that harvest in plenty. I couldn't stand those swamis anymore; far from embodying human perfectibility, they embodied its corruption, degradation, lies, I loathed them. And yet at the same time always wishing: if only it could be. And those hymns still sounded so pure and beautiful (as did all Indian music, touching eternal chords); and there was absolutely no doubt about the sky being beautiful with all those stars and the moon, not to speak of the monsoon clouds and all that. It was all still there. But those terrible swamis and their terrible followers. I hated them for being what they were and not what they pretended to be, and what I wanted them to be.

I wrote a lot about that spiritual scene. I saw a lot of Western girls come to India for that. They wore saris and walked around on bare feet (and got hookworm) and took dancing lessons and meditated on the holy mantra given to them by their guru. They became vegetarians; they bathed in the holy river; they got jaundice and became very pale and worn away physically and as people, in their personalities. They had given up their personalities (as tough, thinking, fighting European or, more often, American girls). Their eyes and thoughts and souls were only for their guru. I deplored them; I wrote about them, disparagingly. I laughed at, even despised, them; but also envied them—for thinking they had found, or maybe—who am I to judge?—they had found, what I had longed to find and never could and I guess never would now.

It became time to leave India. I had spent twenty-four years there, and the last twelve or so were a perpetual struggle with India: not to love it too much and not to hate it too much, one could say; but that would make it too simple. I could also say to keep my own personality and not become immersed, drowned in India; to remain European—and yet at the same time to remain open to India and not close up and wither away. Too difficult for me. I couldn't make it, not at that stage, for there was something else too—a terrible hunger of homesickness that I cannot describe, it was so terrible, so consuming. Not for any specific home; I didn't have one. England wasn't it, Germany wasn't, Poland wasn't—but for Europe: to live in Europe again among people who spoke, thought, looked—it makes a difference, that—the way I did. Who were immersed in the same traditions—the same books and music and morals, I suppose one could say; moral assumptions—whose soul was the same color as mine. I wanted desperately to go.

Before I go on to what is, up to date, my last journey—exile—or disinheritance—or search for a home—or what is it?—before I come to that, I'd like to mention those cuckoo or chameleon qualities that seem to be part of my heritage and how they came into play in India. I've already mentioned how as soon as I got to India I did just the same thing as I had done the moment I got to England: that is, write as if I were from within that society, part of it. Later, when I began to alienate myself and to write from outside Indian society, as a European, it wasn't as the sort of person I really was myself but again adopting another alien civilization. In fact, I identified myself as an Anglo-Saxon: I took over, that is, *your* heritage—the Scots grandfather who built bridges, canals, railways. My last novel written in India—about

India—*Heat and Dust*, has come from within a double pretense: two chameleons, two cuckoos. On the one hand, as far as the Indian characters and their society and thoughts and values were concerned, I pretended to be of them; on the other hand, when I wrote about the Anglo-Indian (that is, British) characters and their traditions, I pretended to be of them. So I exited from India on a double lie—one it took me twenty-four years to manufacture.

Someone once told me that, whatever project you have in your life, whatever central concern or task or duty you set yourself (or is set to you), you should give yourself twenty years in which to bring it to its maturity and, hopefully, fruition. I consider my work—or rather, experience—in India as this twenty-year task. But I also consider the twenty years up and the task over. I'm now committed to a new twenty-year program—in fact, I began it four years ago when I left India and also at the same time stopped writing about it.

I said that during my last years in India I became desperately homesick for Europe. Finally it got so bad that I just had to go and live there and start again—adapt myself again—leaving India behind me as I had left Germany and then England; find a new nest or world both as a person and a writer (it is no longer possible for me really to disentangle the two). And feeling so homesick for Europe, longing for it so intensely, I went to live in New York. This is not as paradoxical as it may sound, as I'll try and explain. I find myself doing a lot of explaining on this score—people are always asking me, "But why New York? Why America? Why not England or some other country in Europe?" I've had to explain myself so often that perhaps I've become a bit pat in my reply. Anyway, I've had to think it out, and whether the conclusion I've come to is a true one or one I've slightly manufactured to justify and explain myself, I'm really not quite sure. It might only be self-justification—perhaps I'm just fickle by nature and get tired of countries the way other women do of husbands or lovers; and then, like them, hiding my fickleness behind a screen of too many good reasons. Anyway, here are my good reasons for going to live in New York.

In a way I consider it as the place for which—like so many twentieth-century European refugees or exiles—I was destined. Certainly when I first went there, in 1966, I felt a sense of homecoming. It is the most European city I can think of, with every kind of pocket of Europe inside it—German, Czech, Polish, Italian. There are whole sections given over to these nationalities, with their languages and foods (of course there are Chinese and Indians and Puerto Ricans as well, but I was in search of Europe). And literally I met the people who should have remained in my life—people I went to school with in Cologne, with exactly the same background as my own, same heritage, same parentage. Now here they were living in New York, as Americans, in old West Side apartments, with high ceilings and heavy furniture, just like the ones we grew up in in our Continental cities (as blissfully overheated as my grandparents' flat in Cologne), and with the delicatessen at the corner selling those very potato salads and pickled cucumbers and marinated herrings that our grandmothers used to make. In fact, I haven't had these childhood tastes on my tongue since I left Germany in 1939—the exact, memory-stirring, awakening, madeleine taste that magically opens the door into one's personal and ancestral past.

But not only in New York. Wherever one goes in America, there are these pockets of Europe, of those settlers, whether they were Czech, Hungarian, Polish, Italian, who have become American and yet at the same time—in their cast of features, their physique, their food, their family structures, in all the most intimate details of their lives—have retained their origins. You can find small towns and villages with small churches and cemeteries where the names are all Dutch and so are the houses in their neatness and incredible cleanliness and the people in their square good-natured faces and bodies. The accent of the tongue may be American, but the accent of the soul has retained the intonation of the European past. And for me, and maybe for others like me, this Europe that we find in America is what I can only describe as clean and wholesome. It is untouched by the events of the 1930s and '40s—an idyllic, bucolic Europe reaching far back into earlier generations, no longer to be found in Europe itself but in the pretty white houses with green shutters in (for instance) Pennsylvania or Connecticut; set in a landscape that again recalls an earlier Europe, with rivers and lakes and boys fishing in them in the summer and skating on them in the winter, and acres of pastureland with cows and waterfalls and not a house in sight, and in the distance hills and clumps of forest with a church spire sticking up on the horizon. There is all the simplicity of a childhood landscape that perhaps I never even knew but only dreamed or read about in German fairy tales.

And yet another good reason why New York, why America. Although my longing was for Europe, can I after all these years and all this immersion into India really ever consider myself totally European again? Is there no trace of India left? I can't believe it. Certainly I find myself stirred by certain aspects of New York that are not unlike India. I can't speak about this too much as yet—it's what I want to write about, so I'm still groping in the dark—but there is something bizarre about New York that appeals to me as strongly as did the bizarre in India. It might even be the cruelty of both places—the abyss forever open. In India it is there in the dreadful poverty and physical disease, and New York too has dreadful poverty. You see sights as horrifying there as you do in India—the down-and-outs, the drunks, the drug addicts lying in the gutters or scrabbling in the trash cans, and the derelict houses in the derelict areas of New York with the boarded-up windows, and hopeless figures shuffling over the littered pavements, and miserable little shops as bankrupt and abandoned as their owners. That's in New York everywhere; and also everywhere in New York the wrecked people: talking to themselves, waving their arms in frantic gesture, tomorrow's suicides, mumbling in the deep abyss of mental sickness—everywhere as continuous a pointing to the frailty of the human condition as there is in India. You can't forget death and despair in New York any more than you can in Calcutta. And the fear everywhere—not as in India the cruelties of nature, but those of man: the muggers and the murderers that make people lock and double-lock their doors and keep their distance from strangers in the street and scuttle home at nightfall and keep clear of certain areas as though they were infested by those thugs that throttled wayfarers in the deserts of Rajasthan or the ravines of Madhya Pradesh.

And again one more—last—good reason why America. After India, can one ever really be satisfied with a country that is anything less than a continent? The way I usually put it is this: If you have for many years lived on a diet of hot spicy curries, how are you going to get used to boiled cabbage again? And as with one's sense of taste, so with all one's other senses and faculties, mental as well as physical. They become coarsened, sensationalized: you need the violent stimulation that only a big coarse country with terrible things happening in it can give you. So, after India, I find only America really big and coarse and bizarre and desperate enough.

But, as I say, all this may really only be excuses: too many good reasons for being promiscuous. Perhaps if you've been faithless once, you can never be faithful again but are committed to a life of promiscuity. Perhaps after my first disinheritance—and my calm acceptance of it, of so cheerfully pretending to be English, and then Indian, and then Anglo-Indian, changing color as I changed countries—maybe I will just have to go on doing it, changing countries like lovers. But always totally, with total abandonment and identification, like Chekhov's "darling," who, you may remember, when married to a theater manager talked of nothing but the bad taste of the theater public who wanted to see only clowns, and when married to a timber merchant became very knowledgeable on all aspects of wood, seasoned and unseasoned, and when she had an affair with a veterinary surgeon was entirely preoccupied by the problem of epidemics caused by the lack of veterinary inspection. Her thoughts and life were filled only by her love for a man, but always a different man; mine just so by a country, but always a different country.

Does one grow too old for this sort of thing? When I went to India, I was twenty-four—plenty of time for that twenty-year stretch one has to give oneself. But now? I've only just started on my new twenty-year stretch, and it's no use pretending I don't hear time's winged chariot drawing near. But I think perhaps one mustn't hear it; one must just go on pretending at the end of each twenty-year stretch that there is plenty of time for the next one, or at least start off on it as if there were. That's how I feel about America. I don't know if I'll finish my twenty years there, but that shouldn't make any difference to starting it. There's a saying, and I can't (characteristically enough) remember whether it is a Jewish, or a Muslim, or a Hindu, or a Buddhist one: "It is forbidden to grow old." I take that to mean that one just has to go on—learning, being—throughout however many twenty-year stretches in however many different countries or places—actual physical ones of countries of the mind—to which one may be called.

Disinheritance

Lekha

THE HEAD OF OUR DEPARTMENT—MY HUSBAND'S DEpartment, that is—in the Ministry of Valuation was a widower for a long time, but three years ago, when he came back home to Delhi from his yearly holiday in Bombay, he was married. We were all very much surprised. We had thought that he was happy living alone in his government hostel; he had such a nice room there, and a good bearer, whom I myself had selected for him, and, of course, all we wives did our best to make him comfortable, often sending special dishes to him or arranging little dinner parties. We were a happy group—he and the other senior officers of the department and their wives—and there was a close feeling of friendship among us all. Of course, we did have a bit of friction sometimes; for instance, I often found myself cross with Mrs. Nayyar, because I felt she was pushing herself forward too much in order to get into the Head's favor. She invited him far too often to her house, and that time he had jaundice, she went around at least twice a day to visit him. I do not like to see a lady being so forward. I truly think that the Head favored me and appreciated all the little things I was able to do for him, since he knew that I did not do them because he was my husband's superior officer—I am not that sort of person, doing things only for my own interest, though I'm afraid that Mrs. Nayyar may be rather inclined that way—but only because I have always genuinely liked him and esteemed him for his good qualities.

When we heard that he was married, we all realized that things would be different, but we hoped that our friendly relations with him would continue. Naturally, we were very eager to meet his new wife. At last, we were invited for dinner, and I must admit I was rather nervous at the prospect. So much depended on this lady and whether she would like me. It can be very awkward if the wife of your husband's superior officer does not like you. In the car on our way to the dinner, my husband gave me a look out of the corner of his eye and said, "I see you have made yourself very elegant to meet her."

That annoyed me a little, so I told him, "I don't know what you mean. Certainly I always like to look my best when people invite me out to dinner." He did not say anything, and after a while I continued, "You need not think that I am going to put myself out much for her. If she likes me, very well, I shall be happy. But if she is going to expect me to go down on my hands and knees to her, I'm sorry—I'm afraid I have too much pride for that."

But as soon as I saw Lekha, I knew at once that it was going to be all right. She was young—about twenty—but not really pretty. Only her eyes were nice—very large eyes, which seemed to take up all her face. She was terribly nervous, and when I realized this, I at once stopped being nervous myself. I said to her, "We have all been so eager to meet you," in a kind and confident way. She giggled (and her voice trembled so at the same time that it was almost as if she were crying) and said, "Oh, thank you, thank you!" She bit her lip, and a last strangled giggle came out, and then she was very serious.

Mrs. Nayyar, who was already sitting there on the settee with a glass of pineapple juice in her hand, cried out to me, "Just think, she used to go to school in Bombay with my cousin!"

"Oh?" I said.

"They were in the same class. Isn't it a coincidence?" She sounded triumphant. "We have already found a *lot* to talk about!"

Lekha did not say anything for a moment, but then suddenly she said, in the same trembling way as before, "Yes, isn't it? Isn't it a coincidence?" But she seemed to be thinking of something quite different while she was saying it. Her eyes kept straying around the room, and she looked lost and unhappy about something. I have had enough experience to recognize that look; there was something wrong with the dinner. Poor little thing, I thought. I felt very protective toward her because of her inexperience, and I did not like to see Mrs. Nayyar being already so possessive about her. When she went into the next room, I followed her and said, "May I help you, please?"

"Thank you, no," she said. "Please stay comfortably with the others." But then she glanced up at my face and suddenly threw her head against my shoulder and began to cry. I patted her gently.

"Oh, I don't know what to do!" she cried, wiping her eyes. "Nothing is ready for the dinner, and it looks so terrible! How will anybody ever eat it?" Without another word, I walked into the kitchen. I could see at once what sort of cook she had got. But I soon showed him that I was not a person to stand for any nonsense, so he bestirred himself as best he could, and under my directions the dinner was soon made ready. It was not a good dinner, but at least we got it served, and everybody sat down to eat.

SO THAT WAS how I became Lekha's best friend, right from the beginning. She came to see me the very next day, and sat in my drawing room, drinking coffee and eating my homemade biscuits, and talked and talked. I had never heard anyone talk the way she did. She told me all about herself and her father and the house she came from, and she told me that she loved Indian classical music and dancing and to go walking late, late at night on the beach at Bombay, and how she was sometimes very happy and sometimes so unhappy that she did not want to live any more. "I have always been like that, since I was a child," she said.

"But you are still a child," I said, smiling.

"Oh, no," she said. "You do not know how very serious I am inside me." And she sighed and ate another biscuit. Of course, she was very sweet, but I could not help feeling that she was hardly suitable to be the Head's wife. A little later, she told me that what she had first liked about her husband was that he was so serious.

"He is a very fine administrative officer," I told her.

"Yes," she said rather slowly. And then, more cheerfully, although it seemed to be an effort, she added, "Yes, I am sure he must be." They had been married then about five months.

After that, Lekha and I used to meet several times a week. I was the only person she ever came to see; I don't think she knew anyone else in Delhi. She never visited the wives of the other officers, though I know Mrs. Nayyar tried very hard to become friendly with her. But Lekha had taken a dislike to her right from the beginning. "She is like her cousin," she explained to me.

"Why, what is wrong with her cousin?" I asked.

Lekha turned away and said, "Please don't let us talk about her," and her lips went tight.

"Why?" I asked. "What has she done to you?"

"It is nothing she has done to me. It's only what she is." Suddenly, she turned to face me, and her big eyes were flashing. "I *hate* that sort of person!" she cried. "A person with a cold heart." I could see that she was really filled with hate, and it quite frightened me. I myself disapprove of Mrs. Nayyar's nature, but I certainly do not hate her. It is wicked to hate people. But the next moment Lekha's face was its usual sweet, childish self again. She came close to me and rubbed her cheek against mine. "I told you we shouldn't talk about her," she said. "What have you and I to do with such people? You have such a dear, warm nature. I am so happy you are my friend."

What worried me the most as I grew to know Lekha better was the fact that she did not care about her house. Mrs. Nayyar and I and all the other ladies take great pride in making our homes dainty and nice to look at. We hang up ruffled curtains and paint our own flower vases and embroider cushions and table runners. Of course, I wanted to help Lekha to make her home nice, too. At first, she was quite enthusiastic, and we went out to buy material for curtains, but then she lost interest and never even bothered to have the curtains made. In the end, I brought my own tailor and had the curtains stitched, and I hung them up with my own hands. Lekha was very grateful to me and kept saying how nice they looked, but she never took them down to have them washed. They just hung there, limp and full of dust and showing a missing curtain ring in one place.

The real trouble with Lekha was that she was not modern. She simply did not understand the new trends we have in India today. Of course, we are all very proud of being Indian, but all the same we do realize that there are some things we can learn from the West. The Western way of doing up a house and living in it, for example, is more attractive and advanced than ours. But Lekha kept to the old Indian ways. When she was alone, she never sat down to eat properly at a table but squatted on the floor and had her food brought to her on a round brass tray, and then ate it with her fingers. That may be the traditional Indian way, but it is my opinion that it would be better for India if everyone learned to eat in the way people do in the West. I also didn't like the way Lekha always had incense burning in her house; that smell always reminds me of the dirty shops in the bazaars. It was not as if she were orthodox—I have never known her to go to the temple. And yet she would often observe some fast day, all the way from sunset to sunset. On the day of the Spring Festival, she would wear only yellow, just like the peasants, and once, when there was an eclipse, she even went down to the Jumna to bathe, with all the crowd. Some of our old customs are very pretty, I know—the lighting of little lamps on Diwali, for instance, which we always do because the children like it so much—but no modern person observes as many of them as Lekha did. And, as if there were not enough Hindu festivals, she would keep the Muslim ones also, such as Mohurrum and Bakri-Id, when she had some goat meat cooked and sent to our house. When I asked her about this, she said, "Oh, you know, I love festivals so much that it doesn't matter whether they are Hindu or Muslim. And anyway I think there is bound to be some Muslim strain in all of us, so it is only right that we should keep their holy days." The only festival she would not keep was Christmas. I think Christmas is such a nice festival; we always have a turkey dinner with plum pudding and so do all our friends. But Lekha said she did not like Christmas, because it is not religious. She said it is only social and only for Englishmen. When I pointed out to her that, on the contrary, Christmas is very religious because it is the day on which the God of the Christians was born, she said yes, she liked Jesus Christ, but she did not like Christians or their Christmas. What can you make of a person like that?

    It surprised me that the Head allowed her to carry on with all these fads. He himself has always been very correct in his behavior, and one would have thought that he was the last person to allow his wife to go in for practices that were so unsuitable to a high social and official position. But apparently he made no objections and let her do whatever she pleased. I think he had grown very fond of Lekha. I could detect a change in him, something in his face that had not been there before and that showed he was—I don't know quite how to say it—perhaps satisfied is what I mean, or perhaps just happy.

Lekha didn't enjoy the little dinner parties we gave. She came once or twice to dinners at Mrs. Nayyar's house or Mrs. Kaul's or one of the other wives', but it was quite evident that she did not enjoy herself. She would just sit there with her head bowed, not joining in the conversation, and play with her bangles. Then, one day when Mrs. Nayyar was giving a dinner party, the Head telephoned her in the afternoon to say that his wife was ill and therefore they could not come. I went to see Lekha straightaway next morning, but when I asked her what was the matter, she laughed out loud. "Only Mrs. Nayyar's party was the matter!" she said. "No, I have had enough now of these little dinner parties. I have done my duty."

"Lekha, are you telling me that you are not coming to *any* of our parties again?" I said. I was quite shocked, for I myself was giving a party the following week.

"I will come to your house," she said, "but to nobody else's. Why should I sit there and die with boredom while everyone talks stupid things? I will sit at home and think my own stupid things."

I ALWAYS FEEL rather nervous before my dinner parties, so you can imagine that I was not at all pleased when Govind suddenly appeared at my house half an hour before the guests were due to arrive. Govind is my husband's younger brother, but he is as unlike my husband as can be. He finished his studies at the university, but after that he never made any attempts to get into government service or into any proper job at all. He only sits in coffeehouses all day, with other loafers like himself; sometimes he does a little something for films or radio—I do not know what. He associates a great deal with musicians and dancers and such people. I did not even pretend to be pleased to see him. "I didn't know you were in Delhi," I said.

"I have been here for three weeks," he said, and laughed. (He laughs a great deal.)

"And only now you come to see your elder brother."

"But you are never happy to see me," he said. That was true, but I didn't think it was right for him to say it. Just then, my husband came in, and the two of them greeted one another. My husband is quite fond of his brother, although, of course, he disapproves strongly of his ways. While the two brothers talked, I thought desperately about how I could possibly fit Govind into my dinner party. He was entirely unsuitable to meet the Head and all the other officers, who are serious and important government servants. Even his clothes were unsuitable; the others would all be coming in evening dress, but he was wearing his usual wide white pajama trousers, with a loose and very fine Lucknow kurta on top. He keeps his hair rather too long, and this gives him a not quite respectable appearance.

But it turned out that I need not have worried after all. Govind knows how to behave himself when he wants to, and that evening he really acquitted himself very well. He took an interest in the office affairs the gentlemen were discussing, and asked some quite intelligent questions, which the Head answered for him in a clear, precise way, and he was very polite and attentive to the ladies. Indeed, I could see at once that Mrs. Nayyar felt flattered by the way he got fruit juice and nuts for her and found her handbag when she mislaid it. A little later, after the buffet dinner had been served, I noticed Govind talking animatedly to Lekha. He was sitting on the arm of her chair, holding his plate and swinging one foot, and she was looking up to him. If Lekha had not happened to be the Head's wife, I would have felt embarrassed for her appearance. She was wearing an orange cotton sari—*cotton* for a dinner party!—and, as usual, no lipstick. She had the Hindu tikka mark on her forehead, and she had stained the palms of her hands and bottoms of her feet with henna to make them bright orange, which I think is really a dirty habit, even though it may be an old Hindu tradition. Her big, big eyes appeared even bigger, because she had underlined them with kohl. She and Govind seemed to have a lot to talk about, and I must say they fitted well together—both of them so odd in their appearance and so different from the rest of us. They looked like a couple out of Hindu mythology—the sort of Krishna and Radha couple you see on calendars or in historical films.

THE DAY AFTER my party, Sita, my eldest child, got measles, and after that my son got it, too, and finally the baby. It was a very hectic time for me, and it was three weeks before I could leave the house again. I had many errands to do that first day, but in the afternoon I happened to be passing near Lekha's house, and, because I still felt responsible for her, I decided to drop in. The servant showed me straight into the drawing room, where I found Lekha sitting on the floor. Lying beside her, with his head in her lap, was Govind. She was stroking his hair. They started up when they saw me, and Lekha came flying to meet me. She embraced me with great fervor and said, "I am so happy to see you, so happy!" Really, I have never known anyone to sound so happy.

I sat down and said quite formally, "How are you, Lekha?" I felt terribly shaken, and my heart was like a cold, dead weight inside me. Govind lay down on the floor again and rested his head on his hand. I didn't want to look at him, but I could not help myself, and I saw he was smiling. Lekha was also smiling, and laughing, and she kept talking all the time. I was so upset, and she was talking so fast that I couldn't take in half of what she was saying. She asked after Sita and the two other children and my husband, and asked what we had been doing, but she never waited for a reply, and all the time she didn't really seem to be asking those questions, because her voice was full of something else. Govind did not say anything, but sometimes he would laugh at something she said, and then she would cry, "No, you must not laugh at me! Tell him not to laugh at me!" But she laughed, too. I told her I had to go—I made up a lie and said I had an appointment with the dentist—and I went out without saying anything at all to Govind. Lekha saw me to the door, and there she embraced me again. "I will come and see you tomorrow," she said. "I have so much to tell you!" Suddenly, she kissed me on the neck; her lips and breath were very hot.

When I got home, I lay down on the bed and shut my eyes. But I could not get rid of the picture of the two of them together as I had seen them when I came in, or the sound of the laughter between them. I was shocked not only because it was Lekha and Govind, though that in itself was bad enough and would get worse when I grew calm enough to think about it. But to see two people behaving like that, a man and a woman together! Oh, it was nothing really that they did; it was only the understanding between them, and something else, which I cannot describe—something that had come rising out of them and filled the room. I have been married now for ten years, and I am fond of my husband and we have three children, but there has never been anything between us like what I felt between Govind and Lekha that afternoon. I pressed my face into my pillow and suddenly I began to cry. I do not know why I cried, but I cried bitterly.

By the time Lekha came to see me the next morning, I was quite calm and collected. I had not told my husband anything about what I had discovered. I did not want to worry him—he has enough worries in his office—and also I felt shy about telling him. I did not know how to put it into words for him. So I determined to deal with this thing myself. I would talk to Lekha very strictly, and, speaking as an older married friend, I would make her see her folly. But when she came, it was she who did all the talking. She came running into the house with her arms full of toys for the children. "How are they?" she cried. "How is my Sita?" And when they came, she embraced them and kissed them—something she had never done before—and they were extremely pleased with the toys. There was a great change in her; she had become beautiful. Her movements had always been a little awkward, but now they were light and graceful. She tossed back her hair, stretched out her arms, and walked up and down—she could not sit still for a minute—and her bangles jingled, her eyes sparkled, and she was laughing, laughing all the time.

"I am so happy!" she said to me. "You don't know how happy!" Here I should have started telling her what I had meant to tell her, but she would not give me time. "I didn't know there was anyone so wonderful as he in the world!" she said. I wanted to protest—I had known Govind a good deal longer than she, and there was no one who knew his worth (or, rather, lack of it) better than I—but she went on again immediately. "There is such depth in him, such greatness! Oh, I know, he hasn't done anything great yet, but he will. Only wait and you'll see! He will astonish the world!"

If the situation hadn't been so serious, I could have burst out laughing at the idea of Govind astonishing the world. If sitting idly in coffeehouses will astonish the world, then he certainly will do it, but not otherwise.

"I feel so privileged to be allowed to know him," she said, and added, in a whisper, "And to be loved by him."

"Lekha," I said.

"You don't know what happiness he gives me, what a paradise he has made for me. He is like a god."

"Lekha," I said, "are you in your senses?"

"Oh, no, no! I have taken leave of my senses! I have no mind anymore—only a body and a soul! He has awakened both for me. You can't know."

I said, quietly and sternly, "And your husband?"

"Please don't!" she cried and put up her hands to cover her ears. "Why do you talk of him? What has he to do with this?"

I was aghast at such total irresponsibility, but I managed to say quite calmly, "I should have thought your husband had a great deal to do with it."

"Nothing! Believe me, this is different. Oh, believe me . . ." She stood still and put both her arms up to her head to stroke back her hair, and her eyes shone more brightly than ever. I felt embarrassed to look at her. "He is good and kind, I know—" she began.

"The Head is an excellent man in every way," I interrupted, taking her up rather severely.

"I know, I know!" she cried. "But being good and kind is so little—it is nothing. You cannot touch another person's soul by being only good and kind. I was not alive before. Nobody could show me what there was in me until he came."

Then I only wanted her to go away. But she wouldn't go; she kept talking on and on about herself and Govind. I sat quite still and tried not to listen, but I couldn't help listening. There was something burning and fierce about her, like fire.

After that, she often came to see me, and every time it was the same. She talked, and I had to sit and listen to things that should never be spoken. She had no shame at all. She talked to me of the beauty of Govind and how she, too, had learned to feel herself as beautiful. It was painful for me even to look at her, and after a time I began to avoid her. I would go out of the house at the times I knew she would be coming to visit me. I did not care where I went, as long as I didn't have to see her and listen to her. Mostly, I went to Mrs. Nayyar, where we would sit and talk quietly and normally about normal things, like the children's schooling and the high price of vegetables and the lovely new Benares saris that had come in at the Cottage

Industries Emporium. These conversations with Mrs. Nayyar were soothing to me, yet whenever I got home I would find myself thinking of Lekha and Govind again. I became very irritable, especially with my husband; somehow I had a feeling of dissatisfaction about him.

Some time later, it came my turn again to give a dinner party, and, of course, I had to invite the Head and Lekha. When the guests were all assembled, Govind walked in. I knew who had told him to come, but with all those people there was nothing I could do but pretend to be pleased to see him and make him welcome. He was perfectly free and smiling, and not in the least embarrassed. This was the first time I had seen him since that day in Lekha's house, and I looked at him curiously, for I had wondered how Lekha could possibly find him handsome and "like a god." But now I saw that there was something about him that might strike an impressionable person like Lekha. His complexion is rather too dark—my husband, thank God, is much fairer—and against this dark skin his strong and healthy teeth and the whites of his eyes shine quite brilliantly. He has strong shoulders, and because he always wears such thin, transparent kurtas one can see exactly how they are formed and how the muscles move. His hair is really far too long, but it is very curly and shines with oil. He always wears a fine gold chain around his neck. There is something strange about him, something that is more like an animal than like a man, though perhaps it is a sin to say that.

I watched the two of them anxiously, but I must say their behavior was quite good. I never intercepted as much as a glance between them, and they talked together very little. Lekha was more lively than she usually is at parties, for which I suppose I ought to have been grateful. The Head seemed pleased to see her enjoying herself, and I noticed that he still looked at her with an expression of satisfaction.

The talk turned to a celebrated South Indian dancer who had given a recital in Delhi the week before, and from there a discussion arose about the various styles of dancing and their exponents. Govind talked intelligently and managed to impress the other guests with his knowledge of Indian classical music and dancing. Mrs. Nayyar, I could see, was thrilled by all he was telling us, and the Head, too, listened with interest. Then, suddenly, the Head said, "You know, my wife is quite a competent exponent of Bharata Natyam," and he smiled in a deprecating but rather proud manner.

"Oh, yes? How interesting," said Govind, and he looked around as if he were not quite sure who the Head's wife was. Really!

"Oh, but why does she not dance for us!" cried Mrs. Nayyar, clapping her hands together. She always likes to be lively at parties, and now, of course, she was being especially lively, for Govind's benefit. So then everybody looked at Lekha.

"Should I?" she said, with a smile. She was not at all shy or embarrassed.

"It would be a great pleasure for all of us," Govind said.

"Yes, wouldn't it?" I said quickly. "But there are no ankle bells and no music. What a pity!"

"Couldn't she borrow Sita's ankle bells?" Govind suggested. "And you have a *dholak*, I think?"

"What are we waiting for?" cried Mrs. Nayyar.

I looked at the Head; I was sure he would not allow it. But he smiled and rubbed his chin and said, "Well, Government is always telling us that we must preserve and foster our cultural heritage..."

I hoped that Sita's ankle bells would be too small for Lekha, but, of course, they weren't. Her limbs were as thin and fragile as a child's. Govind sat on the floor by the *dholak* and began to beat it with his fingers and sing while Lekha danced. He sang:

> Bring, oh, bring my beloved unto me!
> Oh, what ecstasy shall I know with him always on the couch strewn with flowers, in the white radiance of the moon.
> O my friend, beautiful as a bird! I languish with love for my Lord.
> What is this happening to me? Come, O friend!
> Ask my Lord to come to me, so that flower-adorned I may dance, sing, and play with him. Why this delay!

And that was what Lekha danced. She really was quite a good dancer. Her hand gestures were very suggestive, and so was her smile, and the way she rolled her eyes and swayed her head from her neck. "I languish with love for my Lord," said her fingers. "What is this happening to me?" said her eyes and her lips. The ankle bells rang out as she stamped her feet: "Come, O friend!" Govind flung back his head as he sang, so that one could see the movement in his throat. His long brown fingers danced on the drum, his whole body swayed, and he smiled with flashing eyes and teeth. "Like a god," Lekha had said of him, and now she was worshipping him with her dance. Mrs. Nayyar sat with her hands clasped before her and a smile of rapture on her face. The Head was also smiling a little and he looked very proud. As I looked at the Head, I thought how good he is—how true, how affectionate, and how stupid!

A WEEK LATER, Govind went away to Bombay—I think on some film work. When he had gone, Lekha began coming to see me every day. If I was out, as I often tried to be, she would sit and wait for me, and the moment I came in, she would begin to talk about herself and Govind. His absence did not seem to make her at all sad. "You see, he has not gone away from me," she told me. "He is with me here." And she clasped her hand to her bosom in such a passionate gesture that I had to look at the floor. "He is with me all the time, all the time." Another day, she said, "You remember when Krishna went away from Radha? How she thought she could hear his flute playing, even when he was not there? Well, it is like that with me. I can feel him playing in my heart." She had told him to send letters to her at my house. "Because I know you are my friend," she explained to me. But there were never any letters. Every day she came with a trembling air of expectation, but every day there was nothing. After a week or so, I could see the look of disappointment and pain more and more clearly in her face, and the smile with which she tried to cover it. "There is no need for him to write," she explained once. "He knows how near we are together, even when we are apart." I think she was writing to him every day.

The days went by, and Lekha stopped coming to see me so often, and when she did come, she did not talk as much. She sat quite quietly in my drawing room, playing with the bangles on her arms. She was thinner and her lips were pale, and it became hard for me to imagine how I had ever managed to think of her as beautiful. Now it was I who did most of the talking, but she never seemed to take any interest in what I was telling her. I couldn't help thinking that Lekha was rather a dull girl, but all the same I began to feel protective toward her again and to like her as I had in the beginning.

Then a whole week went by with no visit from her, and I became worried, and went to see her one morning. I found her sitting in her drawing room, on the floor, with her knees drawn up and her arms clasped around them. Although it was after eleven o'clock, she had not yet had her bath or dressed, and her hair straggled over her shoulder in a very untidy manner. The room smelled of stale incense, and I could see at once that it had not been dusted or made neat for many days. She did not move, and hardly even smiled, when I came in.

"Hallo, Lekha!" I called, in a loud voice. I was trying to cheer her up, and besides I felt fresh and vigorous after my morning bath, in my crisp, clean sari and with my household duties all ordered and done. But Lekha only looked at me out of her big, sad eyes, and lifted one hand to brush a strand of hair from her forehead. I wanted to shake her and shout, "Come on, Lekha! Up and doing!" I wanted to fling open all the windows and call in the servant to give the room a good scrubbing and cleaning and then bring fresh flowers to arrange on the mantelpiece and a clean starched cloth to put on the table. But I realized that my first duty was to give Lekha a good talking-to, so I sat down on the settee just behind her, with my hand laid affectionately on her shoulder.

I did not know how I was going to start, but the words came of themselves—all the words I had been wanting to say for many weeks but which she had never given me an opportunity to say. First, I talked to her about her husband—about what a fine, good, conscientious man he was and what she owed to him as his wife. And after that I told her what a worthless loafer Govind was. I explained, in a very understanding, womanly way, how he was the kind of man who might impress a young woman who didn't know his background and his association with people who were not respectable. I even gave her a very small hint of the rumors I had heard about his behavior with a certain type of woman in Bombay. I talked for a long time. She sat quite still, with her head bowed, and the only movement she made was once when she shrugged the shoulder on which I had laid my hand. I thought it might be making her feel hot—it was rather sticky that morning—so I took it away. She did not see me to the door when I left but remained sitting there on the floor. I felt pleased and contented all the rest of the day, for I knew I had done my duty, and in the evening I made my husband take me to a cinema.

I telephoned to her the next day, but the servant said she was out; the day after that it was the same, and the day after. I was rather surprised, so I went to her house to see her. When I entered at the gate, I saw her sitting on the veranda, but she got up at once and went indoors. I thought she had not seen me, and I was about to follow her when the servant came running out, calling, in a loud voice, "Memsahib has gone out!"

I realized then that Lekha didn't wish to see me anymore. I went home and I sat in my bedroom and cried. But I didn't cry long, for I knew that I had acted rightly in every way, and that if Lekha had been a person of principle, she would have understood that and felt grateful toward me. At any rate, I had nothing to reproach myself with. It was not my fault that Lekha chose to take this attitude. I had only done my duty.

ONE MORNING, SHORTLY afterward, I finished my shopping a little earlier than usual, so there was just time to drop in at Mrs. Nayyar's for a chat and perhaps a cup of coffee (though the coffee she serves is never very good). I came by the veranda, and I was just going to enter the drawing room through the open glass doors when I heard a voice say, "I don't know how it is, sometimes I am so happy, so happy—and sometimes I am so sad that I don't want to live anymore." I stood quite still and then I looked through the door, and, yes, there was Lekha, curled up on a rug in Mrs. Nayyar's drawing room, talking with great animation and nibbling homemade biscuits. I wanted to go away, but unfortunately Mrs. Nayyar caught sight of me and called out, "Hallo, there! What a surprise!"

Lekha got up at once and said, "I must go." She had averted her head from me and was playing with her bangles.

"So soon?" said Mrs. Nayyar, and she put her arm round Lekha's shoulders to walk with her to the door. I heard them whispering together outside, and then I think they kissed each other goodbye.

"Poor Lekha!" said Mrs. Nayyar, coming back into the drawing room wearing her big, pleased smile. "She is such a shy little thing. Whenever anybody comes, she rushes off at once. A cup of coffee?" She poured the coffee and then sat on the settee, stirring the sugar in her cup. "Yes," she said, "Lekha is very shy before others. But when we are alone together, she sits and talks and talks for hours. She tells me everything. Everything," she said again, stirring, and looking as if she had a big secret. I also stirred. After a while she leaned close to me and continued in a low voice, "You know, she has had a great love affair with an Artist." I kept looking down into my coffee cup. "They were terribly in love," Mrs. Nayyar went on, and her eyes shone. "But then Lekha sent him away. Because of the Head. She says she couldn't do anything to hurt the Head. How fine," she said in a voice full of feeling. "How noble." I sipped the coffee, which was, as I had expected, of a rather inferior quality.

The only times I ever see Lekha nowadays are at one of Mrs. Nayyar's dinner parties. She won't come to any of our other parties, and at Mrs. Nayyar's she only sits there and plays with her bangles. She never as much as looks at me. Mrs. Nayyar has told me in confidence that Lekha has told her she does not like me because I am a person with a cold heart. I think that is a very unfair and unkind thing to say about me, especially after I have been such a good friend to her. But what distresses me most is that because of Lekha's attitude toward me we can no longer have any social relations with the Head. I know it will not make any difference in the end, because he is really too fair-minded a person to let personal considerations stand in the way of his official reports. But I am sorry to have lost contact with him, because I have always had a genuine liking for him. He is such a good man. Often I can't help thinking that it is a pity he could not have married a wife who would do more credit to his office. After all, being the wife of the head of a department carries a lot of responsibilities, and if my husband ever attains such a high position, I certainly shall not shirk them as Lekha has done.

(1957)

Before the Wedding

ALTHOUGH PREPARATIONS HAD BEEN GOING ON FOR weeks, what convinced Maya that her parents were really serious about her wedding was the arrival of Uncle Mohan Lal from Allahabad. He came early one morning, marched straight into the drawing room, pointed to the biggest armchair, and asked to have it drawn into the middle of the room. Placing his umbrella, his turban, and his slippers beside the chair, he sat down in it with his legs tucked under him. After that, the two jewelers who were to make Maya's wedding jewelry were led into the room, and, sitting on a white sheet spread on the carpet in front of him, they began their work.

Uncle Mohan Lal remained in the drawing room, in just that position, for most of the next three weeks. Many times a day, tumblers of sweet, milky tea and platefuls of freshly fried fritters were brought in to him, and occasionally he would ask for hot coals for his hookah. But all the while his attention never wavered from the two jewelers. That was what he was there for—to watch them and make sure that they did not misappropriate any of the precious stones given to them for their work. A dishonest jeweler would have had little chance against Uncle Mohan Lal, for watching jewelers might have been said to be his profession. He spent a great deal of his time in the drawing rooms of families with whom he was distantly connected, supervising the making of their wedding jewelry. He enjoyed a position of high respect, which he carried with some dignity; he was not unaware of his own importance.

Maya knew that Uncle Mohan Lal didn't like people to come into the drawing room to watch, but today she persuaded herself to brave his displeasure and the disapproving noises he would make at her in drinking his tea. Walking in softly, she took up a position directly behind the jewelers. They were setting diamonds into a necklace, and her fingers began to play around her throat as she imagined how she would arrange the finished necklace there. On the sheet beside the jewelers were the matching earrings, nestled in cotton wool—long pendant earrings, golden and set with diamonds, incredibly beautiful. Reverently, she picked one up and pushed it into her ear lobe. But before she could even turn to the mirror Uncle Mohan Lal said, in an authoritative voice, "Run away, girl. Don't come here to disturb the work." Regretfully, she replaced the earring in the cotton wool and left the room.

Outside, she muttered indignantly, "It is *my* wedding." Nobody was acting as if it were. In the dining room, her mother and aunts were choosing materials for her wedding wardrobe. Yesterday her mother had asked, quite absent-mindedly, "You like this, Maya?"—holding out a heavy purple sari of Bangalore silk with a vast golden border.

"I like this one better," Maya had replied, fingering a very light Mysore silk of pale, pale blue.

"You don't know what is right for you to like," her mother had said casually, passing on to another pile of saris.

She had not even noticed the look of annoyance on Maya's face. But one of the aunts, who had been watching her, said, "You are a silly girl. Flimsy saris are only for everyday occasions. For weddings, you must have heavy ones." When Maya left the room, the others had not even glanced up, they were so busy exclaiming over a hideous museum piece of golden-threaded silk, which Maya promised herself she would never let herself be seen in, wedding or no wedding.

It was strange, she thought, but really she had had a better time before her sister Didi's wedding than now, before her own. Then everything had been most marvelously exciting. But now she was piqued, because she should be at the center of it all and they wouldn't let her be. She was even annoyed with her little brother, Munna, for enjoying himself so much. He skipped excitedly from one room to another, and when they pushed him out of the way, he didn't mind at all but skipped off to watch somewhere else. How silly he was, just a child. She was eighteen, an important person—the bride-to-be.

So, to console herself, she went upstairs to her parents' room and telephoned her closest friend. "Oh, Nita," she said as soon as she heard the answering voice, "you don't know what a rush everything is."

Nita, whose marriage had not yet been arranged—indeed, she had not even been betrothed—said in a sensible, adult way, "Of course. It always is on these occasions."

"It's very exciting," Maya went on, speaking more slowly this time. "They are setting a most marvelous diamond necklace."

"Diamonds? How nice. Of course, you know what a weakness I have for pearls."

"There are some pearls also. Oh, Nita, I wish you could be here!" This wasn't true at all; she wouldn't care to have Nita see what an unimportant role she was playing in her own wedding preparations. "A lady is coming from Bombay specially to do my hair. She will do it in the style of the Maurya period."

"Maurya? But it couldn't possibly be Maurya."

"Perhaps I mean Gupta," Maya said. "I'm so confused. So much is happening. Nita, I *do* wish you could come and talk to me."

"Out of the question, my dear. I have all my lecture notes to write up, you know."

"You are such a scholar," Maya said handsomely. She could afford to say this, since she knew Nita went to graduate class only because her parents had not yet found anyone for her to marry.

"Well, I have to run," Nita said.

"Then I won't be seeing you before the wedding? But you *are* coming?"

"Of course."

After this unsatisfactory conversation, Maya walked downstairs and was delighted to see her sister Didi just coming in by the front veranda. Didi was touching up her hair at the back with one hand, rather casually. She looked very elegant.

"Didi, how glad I am you've come!" Maya said as she went to meet her. "Everything is in such confusion, and everyone is so busy and cross!"

Didi only laughed. "Of course. What else did you expect at a time like this?"

Maya had hoped for something more satisfactory from *her*. "And Munna is being so silly."

"Oh, Munna. Where is Mama?"

Maya led Didi to the dining room—triumphantly, for she was sure Didi would support her taste against that of their mother and aunts.

"No," Didi said as soon as she began to examine the selected saris. "This purple one is quite impossible."

"Then what do you think?" her mother asked, frowning and scratching her hair.

Maya was pleased, but at the same time a little resentful because Didi's opinion was so deferentially listened to. Thinking it might be wise to assert herself a little, she said, "I still like the pale-blue one best."

"Don't be silly," Didi said, digging busily into the pile of materials. After a while, she cried "Just look at this one!" and drew out a glowing orange silk.

"You like it?" Mama asked and began to finger it. The aunts also fingered it, and said, "Very nice."

"It's exactly right," said Didi with authority. "We must have a big golden border on it."

"But I can't wear orange!" Maya cried. "It doesn't suit me at all."

Didi transferred the orange sari to the pile of accepted saris and turned her attention to the blouse pieces.

"And I hate big borders," Maya said desperately.

"Darling, just leave everything to us," Didi said.

"Maya," her mother said, "why must you get in the way so?"

MAYA WENT UPSTAIRS to her room and lay down on the bed. She particularly resented Didi's attitude; after all, Didi was only three years older than she and had been married hardly two years. Yet she was acting in such a knowledgeable and superior way. Before Didi's own wedding, it had been very different. Then she had looked on Maya as her closest confidante. She had lain here on Maya's bed with tears rolling down her face, turning her head from side to side in anguish. "What is the use of it all?" she had demanded. "They are preparing for my funeral. Marriage will be a living death to me." Maya had been very impressed. "Oh, Raj, Raj," Didi had moaned. Raj was the boy she had fallen in love with at college. When his parents married him to another girl, Didi had been heartbroken and had allowed her parents to arrange her marriage with anyone they chose. "It is all the same now," she had said tragically. "All a living death." Yet it had not turned out to be a living death at all.

Maya thought it was time she, too, had tragic thoughts. But thoughts of that nature were difficult without a confidante, and she had none. Nita had been thoroughly unsympathetic;

her married friends were all busy with their new husbands and their new social life, and besides they had all become superior, even patronizing, like Didi. Marriage seemed to make everyone like that. The only exception she knew was a girl who had had an unhappy marriage and had been separated from her husband after only eight months. But it would be no use to confide in her; she would only talk about herself and her husband, who drank.

And really, Maya thought, she had nothing very important to confide. She had never been in love with anyone except her English teacher at college, and she had forgotten him months ago. She did not even have any objections to the boy she was to marry. On the contrary, she thought him rather nice. She had seen him first about three months earlier, when his uncle brought him to tea. When her father called her into the drawing room that day, she had been very shy and embarrassed. But everyone had been nice, the uncle had told some very funny anecdotes, and there had been chocolate cake for tea. She and the boy had had a few words together; he had told her that he often went hunting and had already shot a tiger and a bison. A few weeks afterward, her parents had taken her to his house, which was exactly like her own—large, with lots of carpets, ivory elephants, and servants in white uniforms. His parents were more or less like hers: his mother short and stout, and with a sharp eye on the servants; his father, who was a Supreme Court judge (her father was a Minister in the government), important, good-humored, wearing gold-rimmed spectacles.

Two days after this visit, her father had called her into his study and asked her very seriously if she had any objection to the marriage. "I want to do nothing against your wishes," he had said. He was always like that—scrupulous and considerate. She had thought for a while, and then answered no, she did not think she had an objection. "You can see the boy again, if you like," he had offered. "We could arrange to have you see a cinema show together."

Since she always liked the cinema, she had agreed to this, but in the end nothing had come of it, because the boy had had to go to Allahabad to finish his law examination. Now she would not see him again until the marriage ceremony. She would be led in, her head and face covered, to sit beside him in front of the sacred fire and listen to the pandit chant religious verses.

Munna came into her room suddenly. "Why are you here?" he asked.

"Go away. I am thinking."

"You know how many cases of Coca-Cola they have ordered?"

"Go *away*."

"Two hundred. You know how many bottles of Coca-Cola that is?" He shuffled the pack of cards he always carried on the off chance that someone would play flush with him. "Four thousand eight hundred. Four thousand eight hundred bottles of Coca-Cola." His eyes gleamed with excitement.

"This is a terrible time for me," Maya said. She really did feel a great longing to talk to someone. She rolled her head from side to side on the pillow, the way she remembered Didi had done, and tried to look anguished. "You do not know what thoughts are going on in my head."

"You have a pain?" he inquired, not without sympathy; he had always been a good-hearted boy.

"Oh, Munna, a new life is starting for me. What will it bring?"

"Perhaps you would care for a game of flush?" he asked—casually, so as not to appear too eager.

"You had much better go away," she said, and wearily shut her eyes.

But after he was gone, she felt quite bored. Perhaps she should have played cards with him after all. She got up and went downstairs to find him. And there, standing in the entrance hall, was Subramanyam, her father's Personal Assistant. He held his briefcase tightly under his arm and told her, "The Minister will not be home for lunch today. Some American technologists are coming to see him." She felt sorry for her father, who so hated missing his lunchtime at home and the nap in his study afterward.

"Shall I tell them to give you some tea?" she asked Subramanyam, and then remembered he was a South Indian and would probably prefer coffee. But it appeared he was too busy to want anything; there were the technicians coming to see the Minister, and the Indonesian Trade Commissioner had made an appointment for the afternoon. Oh, they were very busy men, he and the Minister. Maya listened to this for a while, then said, "Of course, you are coming to my wedding?" Subramanyam looked down in embarrassment and simpered, "Oh, thank you. Thank you very much."

She noticed for the first time that he was quite good-looking. Why had she not noticed this before? It would have been so romantic to fall in love with her father's Personal Assistant. And certainly her position now would have been much more satisfactory. She could have lain on the bed and moaned, "Oh, Subramanyam, Subramanyam." But it had never occurred to her to fall in love with him. Perhaps that was because he was a South Indian Brahman; she would not care to marry a South Indian Brahman. His family, she was sure, were terribly orthodox and would never sit down to eat with her, a non-Brahman. And all they would ever eat would be rice—morning, noon, and night—with that horrible gravy. They would be squatting on the floor in cotton saris and dhotis and digging their hands into their bowls so that the gravy would run out between their fingers. She remembered with some satisfaction her future mother-in-law pouring tea in the drawing room and saying, "Won't you have another slice of cake?"

THE THREE SWEETMEAT-MAKERS, who were to start work next morning, had brought their vats and pestles into the courtyard, and they and the servants were gathered about Maya's grandmother. She was telling them of all the different kinds of sweetmeats that had been made at her wedding, sixty years ago. The sweetmeat-makers, standing at a respectful distance from the bed on which she was sitting, countered by telling her about the sweetmeats they had made at weddings in other families. It was an animated conversation that everybody seemed to be enjoying very much, including the servants, who from time to time would make some contribution of their own. Munna sat at Grandmother's feet, his eyes, as he listened, huge in wonder, and his hands mechanically shuffling his cards. Grandmother was not at all like other people's grandmothers, who sat in the courtyard all day and gossiped with the servants; she always wore beautiful silk saris, and her fingers were covered with rings. The only thing about her that was not elegant was her complete lack of teeth. She had a set of false teeth, but they were not comfortable, so she kept them in a drawer, wearing them only when there were special visitors.

Maya waited until the sweetmeat-makers had gone and the servants were beginning to disperse, and then she said, "Dadiji, what is it like to be married?" For who was there more suitable for this kind of conversation than a girl's own grandmother?

Grandmother immediately reacted in the right way—assuming a very serious expression and swaying her head from side to side. "Ah, to be married..."

"Is it very different?"

"You see, child," Grandmother said, "in Life there are four stages." As soon as Grandmother said "Life" in that way, Maya's heart sank. But the servants, sensing the beginning of the kind of conversation they loved, crowded around again; the cook brought the dish in which he was stirring eggs, and continued stirring. "First, there is childhood, carefree and gay," said Grandmother.

The servants nodded, and the cook said, "What could be more free from care and anxiety than the life of a child?"

"In childhood, the heart is like a bird," Grandmother said, and they all nodded again while the cook explained, "It sings with joy like a bird, and is free like the bird also." The ayah brought a cup of tea for Grandmother. Maya knew that it would take Grandmother at least an hour to get through the four stages of Life. Soon she would be telling fables from the Panchatantra for illustration, and the cook would bring in apposite quotations from the Gita.

"The bird and the heart of the child are both near to God," Grandmother said.

Maya murmured, "Mama is calling me," and started into the house.

Only Munna noticed her departure. "Now I am playing solo," he called after her, which was his way of again inviting her to a game of flush.

When Maya reentered the house, she heard voices in her father's office. It was her mother arguing with the Caterer. He was a big, fat man, and wore a thin shirt through which his undervest and the folds of his stomach could be clearly seen. Every day he came and every day Mama shouted at him. They were trying to decide on the food to be served the wedding guests. Mama would agree with the Caterer's suggestions one day, but by the next she would have changed her mind. The Caterer would listen patiently to Mama's new suggestions, saying "Very good—*shami* kebabs, excellent," and then he would make his own suggestions, which were quite different from hers, and most of which she finally accepted, though at the same time shouting at him that it was a pity he did not know his job after so many years in the catering business.

Maya entered the office just as Mama and the Caterer were coming to a temporary agreement, though Mama still looked very doubtful. "Cheese and pea curry," the Caterer rolled richly from his tongue. "Oven-baked chicken, roasted fish, *seekh* kebab, fried rice." Maya remembered all the wedding feasts she had attended: the multitude of tiny electric lights lacing the front of the house in an elaborate pattern; the red-and-orange striped marquee; the rows of long tables at which the guests sat side by side under colored streamers and banana plants and Chinese lanterns; the bearers passing around with loaded dishes, heaping the huge plantain leaves used for plates with mounds of spicy, steaming food. But at her own wedding she would be sitting in a little room by herself, dressed in her crimson wedding sari; each of the lady guests would come to talk to her for a few minutes, but all the time they would be straining to be away to where the food was, and the laughter, and the band. She might faintly hear the laughter and the band, but she would not be able to as much as smell the food. Really, one's own wedding was the dullest of all.

LATER, WHEN MAMA told Didi what she had arranged with the Caterer, Didi clicked her tongue and said, "No, really, Mama!"

"Not good?" Mama asked, anxiously looking up into Didi's face.

"Oh dear." Didi sighed and sank into a chair.

"But they are the traditional dishes for weddings," Mama said.

Didi bridled at once. "That is the trouble! Tradition, tradition, tradition—that is all one hears in this country! Nobody ever realizes that the world is progressing!" Maya listened with shining eyes. "This is the twentieth century," Didi continued heatedly, "but to listen to all of you nobody would ever think it!"

Mama said, quite humbly, "We are still the older generation; it is different for you young people."

Oh, yes, Maya thought with joy, it is very different for young people. But when she thought "young people," she did not think of herself—only of Didi and other young married women like her. They led marvelous lives. So modern, so very fashionable. They lived in small flats done up in bright colors, with wrought-iron furniture, hand-loomed textiles, and enormous Naga hats for lampshades. They wore their hair cut short, and their saris were printed over in bold, bright designs. They laughed a lot and called one another "darling" and went to cocktail parties and the Army Horse Show. Photographs of them enjoying themselves at parties—hugely smiling, with eyes shut against the flashbulbs—appeared in the weekly social magazines.

Maya thought, I shall be married soon, and then I shall be one of them. She realized that all the things that had been making her feel so dissatisfied did not matter at all, because soon everything would be very different. Soon she would be as smart and modern as Didi—and then Mama and all of them would listen deferentially to her opinion. She thought of Uncle Mohan Lal in the drawing room—how self-important he was, bubbling at his hookah, drinking his tea with a loud sucking noise. But all he was doing was to insure that the jewelry being made for *her* should be quite perfect—the diamond necklace and matching earrings, the string of pearls, the opal ring, the long earrings set with nine different stones, the golden bangles. He sat there so that she should be able to shine and be beautiful in these things. So then she wanted only that the wedding be finished quickly, the old life be over and done with; she wanted to be married, and have jewelry and a husband and a flat and a telephone of her own, and so live happy and grown-up forever.

(1957)

Sixth Child

THE PAINS STARTED EARLY IN THE MORNING, AND AT once the house was full of busy women. It was amazing how quickly they came—some of them all the way from the other side of the town. Babu Ram never could understand how women managed to get news so quickly; a deathbed, a lying-in, a sickness, an accident, any sudden blow of fortune or misfortune, and all the female relations were there without delay. The men always tended to fall into the background on these occasions—especially, of course, at a lying-in. Never did Babu Ram feel so awkward, useless, unwanted, and embarrassed as he did in his own house every time his wife had a new baby.

Now he wandered around aimlessly, with sad eyes and an apologetic smile, trying to keep out of the way of the women, who rushed around full of purpose and determination. He would have liked to talk to his little girls, but a squad of women had taken charge of them and were washing, brushing, scrubbing, feeding, and dressing them prior to pushing them off to someone else's house, where they were to stay till it was all over and the baby safely born. Babu Ram felt as sorry for his little girls as he did for himself. The five of them looked so subdued, with their faces scrubbed terribly clean, their hair oiled and pulled tight from their foreheads. They kept quite still, their eyes huge with wonder, whereas usually they were as quick and twittering as birds. Babu Ram wanted to throw them some word of encouragement but was himself feeling too subdued and discouraged to do so. All he could manage was a very shy smile as they were bundled out of the house; they looked back at him with big, silent eyes.

At last, one of the women deigned to notice him—his mother's cousin, a short, square old woman who was always very prominent on these occasions, waddling around with her elbows stuck out and a pleased, busy look on her face. "Now then," she said to him, "what are you still doing here? Be off with you!" "Yes," he said, passing his hand over his balding head, "yes, it is time I went to the shop." Another woman called out, "Don't let us see your face again too quickly! Your work is done—now it is our turn!" He simpered and shifted uneasily from one leg to the other. "Come back tonight and see what we have for you," said his mother's cousin, and brushed past him into the room where his wife lay groaning on a string bed.

He put on his little round hat and walked slowly down the stairs. Plump and neat, with his dhoti falling in tidy folds around his legs and exposing his fat, smooth calves above his highly polished black shoes, he looked as comfortable as he did every morning when he left thus, clean and breakfasted, for the shop. But he did not feel comfortable at all. He was worrying about his little girls and about himself, all driven out of the house so unceremoniously; and also about something else, which he did not dare think about much. Downstairs, he met the first-floor tenant, who said to him, "So it has started," and then, "Well, let us hope this time . . ."

"Yes," said Babu Ram, lifting his hat from his head with both hands and then settling it back again. "Yes," he said, and couldn't say anything further, because he hoped so much that he trembled when he thought about it. He stood on the bottom step, with his head lowered, and looking, in spite of his comfortable, confident paunch, almost humble.

"God will be good to you," said his neighbor, himself the

father of four sons. "He knows five daughters is enough for anyone." And he laughed with the easy heartiness of a man to whom the topic doesn't matter much. Babu Ram also tried to laugh, but he could not do so at all heartily.

HIS YOUNGER BROTHER, Siri Ram, had already opened the shop, as he did every morning, and sat inside eating his breakfast from a leaf, which he held in the hollow of his hand. Babu Ram stepped out of his shoes and into the shop. He hung up his hat on the appointed nail and sat down on a white sheet spread on the floor, with his legs tucked underneath him. Quickly his eyes ranged to the right, to the left, and behind him, up the shelves piled with bolts of cloth, row upon row, up to the roof of his little hut of a shop. Tomorrow he would have to take down the pink-and-green muslin from Kanpur, which had not sold at all well and was getting faded, to make room for a consignment of flowered white lawn he was expecting from Bombay.

Siri Ram licked his fingers, all ten, one after another, and asked, "How is it going?" Babu Ram replied by shrugging one shoulder and looking resigned.

"It always takes time," said Siri Ram, speaking with authority, for though he was still a very young man, he already had four children of his own.

Babu Ram grunted, then said, "See that you have all this month's sales-tax vouchers. Otherwise, those Government people will come sitting on my head again." He spoke in a brisk business voice, for he did not want Siri Ram to know how much he was thinking about the baby.

It was a morning like every morning—quiet, with not many people in the bazaar, and the shopkeepers sitting cross-legged in their shops, some smoking their hookahs and some saying their prayers and some writing business letters and some doing the

"Win 10,000 Rupees" crossword puzzle. Tall glasses of buttermilk, frothing with cream, arrived from Lal Singh's Milkshop of Lahore, and hot fritters with chutney from the Peshawar Famous Hotel. There was a little desultory conversation across the narrow lanes that ran between the rows of shops, and a few hawkers walked about calling digestive powders or elastic—though not very lustily, because there weren't many customers about. Babu Ram did his accounts, sitting on the floor with his big ledger in front of him and his spectacles perched on the end of his nose, and moving his hand up and down his paunch, which flowed gently over his thighs. Now and again, a customer came, and Siri Ram brought down bolt after bolt of cloth, until the floor of the shop was covered with a flood of shining new materials; after the customer had gone, Siri Ram patiently rolled them all up again.

Though Babu Ram tried to concentrate on his accounts, he could not help thinking of the son he was hoping for so much. It was the sixth time he had hoped this way, and he was afraid of being disappointed for the sixth time. Not that he did not love his five little daughters. His heart turned over every time he thought of them—quick, skinny, demure in their wide trousers with the flowered shirts over them, their hair neat in thin pigtails, their huge eyes full of wonder and shyness, their piping voices that always sounded excited. But he longed for a son. There were all the obvious reasons he must have a son (Who, otherwise, would preside over his funeral obsequies and pour the ghee to feed the cremating fire? Who would carry on the shop, the properties?), but there were also other reasons—less obvious, and closer to his heart.

Perhaps what he really wanted was to have, like the other shopkeepers, a little boy to sit with him in the shop. It was in the evenings that he most felt this lack. The bazaar became very busy in the evenings: shoppers thronged the narrow lanes between the shops; there was buying and selling and haggling; hawkers cried their wares, and beggars whined for alms. But inside the shops it remained private and cozy. When one walked through the bazaar, each shop, with its completely open front, was like a photograph of a family group exposed to view in one big square of electric light: one could see the shopkeeper and his assistants (who were, of course, members of the family—a younger brother, an impoverished uncle, a nephew) talking to their customers, who sat on a narrow bench and looked critically at the goods shown to them. Here the bargaining was quieter and interspersed now with gossip and now with philosophy; glasses of cool water were offered; everything was calm, leisured, very polite. And always, in almost every shop, there was a little boy. He sat at the edge of the shop, with his legs dangling over. Sometimes he did his homework or ate dried peas out of a paper cone. It was obvious—perhaps from the fearless, even arrogant way he looked at the passersby and the customers—that he was quite at home and at ease here; that he knew himself to have every right to be here; that it was, in short, his father's shop.

With little girls, it was different. They had to stay at home with the women of the family, where they became as familiar with the life of kitchen and courtyard as the boys did with that of the shop. They learned to imitate the ways of grandmother, mother, and aunts, and pretended to wear saris and to pound spices and sift rice and scold servants. How often Babu Ram had watched them at their games, chuckling to himself, his heart all glowing with love! Yet at the same time there was always a trace of regret, because he felt that there should also be a little boy, to play at doing as the father did—to wear a dhoti and a little round hat, and to pretend to be a shopkeeper. He could almost see this little boy following him down the stairs of the house on their way to the shop, treading in his footsteps and trying to look just like him—tucking in his chin, frowning as he adjusted his hat, clearing his throat in a proud parody of his father's manner.

Babu Ram, sitting in his shop, stroking his belly, and seemingly intent on his accounts, felt himself ache with wanting. Siri Ram sat at the other side of the shop with his knees drawn up, looking out with vacant eyes and picking his nose. Babu Ram could not talk to him. Yet he wanted terribly to unburden himself to someone and have him share his weight of anxiety. Perhaps not share, though; what he really wanted was for someone to relieve him of it—someone to come and say, "Don't worry anymore. This time you will have a son." But who could say that to him, except perhaps God?

Of course, he believed in God and did all the things that he knew were required to please Him. Thus he had accompanied his wife several times on the daily visits she made to the temple during her pregnancy, had made his offerings of flowers and sweetmeats, and had vowed to feast five hundred Brahmins if his prayers were granted. But all the same, he could not help feeling now that there was something more he should do. Prayers and offerings were too remote and impersonal; they were what one did, as a duty, on all occasions. Now he wanted to please God with something more direct, more spontaneous, more personal—something exceptional, to prove himself worthy of the great favor he was asking.

A boy arrived from Lal Singh's Milkshop with tumblers of buttermilk. Siri Ram began to drink, making loud noises of relish from behind his tumbler. "Ah!" said Siri Ram. "Hah!" But Babu Ram hardly noticed himself drinking; he was thinking how unworthy he was and how presumptuous it was for him to expect God to favor him. He felt that in his present sinful state he did not deserve a son, and that, to become worthy in the sight of God, he had somehow to cleanse and purify himself.

When he thought of his past sins and imperfections, his mind went at once to a certain incident. God knew there were plenty more (after all, in business life one could not always think of others as much as it was perhaps right to do, and with his many dependents he had to put his family and its interests above all else), but none of them disturbed his conscience the way this one did. He could still see the old man's face, with its expression of patience and resignation, and himself shouting abuses, his face swollen with rage. Oh, yes, he had been right to shout abuses and to turn the old man out of the house. Everybody in the family said he had been right. Everybody had abused the old man because of the way he had stolen from Babu Ram, who was his cousin, and who had kept him for many years in his own house and had taken him into the shop and had always been so kind to him. "Ungrateful devil!" they shouted at him. "Thief, liar, cheat!" Babu Ram shouted loudest of all; he felt rage throttling him until it was difficult for him to get the words out, and then in his fury he even slapped the old man—*one! two!* across the face—the way he might have slapped Siri Ram or some other younger brother over whom he had been set in authority. "Quite right!" the others all said. "With shoes he should be beaten!" The old man stood quite silent and patient, as if he were actually waiting for Babu Ram to take off his slipper and start beating him with it. This silence infuriated Babu Ram more than ever: there was something like innocence and martyrdom in it, although it was quite clear that the old man had stolen from the shop—consistently and unscrupulously and, moreover, in surprisingly large amounts. "Get out!" Babu Ram screamed, his hands twitching so that he was almost afraid of his own anger. The old man quietly rolled up his things. Babu Ram could still see him walking away with slow steps and eyes downcast, the little bundle of his possessions under his arm.

Now he drank the last of his buttermilk, holding the glass with one hand and shutting his account book with the other. He shut it with a pop, to make clear to himself the finality of his resolution. He would go and get the old man back. Now, at once.

He got up, adjusted his dhoti, and took his hat down from its nail. Siri Ram looked up at him in surprise. "I am going out," Babu Ram said sternly. "If that man comes from Sita Mills, you can tell him to come back tomorrow. Today I have urgent work."

"You are going home?" Siri Ram asked. "To see about the baby? But it will be many hours until . . ."

"What concern is it of yours where I am going?" Babu Ram said, frowning with terrible authority. He didn't want anyone to know. They would all know soon enough; they would be angry with him and say he was a fool. "Perhaps we have not enough mouths to feed in this house?" his wife would say reproachfully. But Babu Ram wanted the old man back: to wipe out that moment when he had been angry, and the old man had stood patient and silent—to make himself worthy of a son.

BABU RAM KNEW that the old man had gone to live with another group of relatives, who were only remotely connected with his own branch of the family. He climbed into a cycle rickshaw and had himself taken straight there. The house was behind a temple, hedged in by many little stalls selling flower garlands and sweetmeats and plaster-of-Paris images of the gods. Pilgrims sat resting by the side of the road, and there were clusters of ascetics in orange robes on the steps of the temple, and, just down the road, a few dirty gray cows walking about and two pariah dogs snuffling in the gutter for refuse. Babu Ram haggled for a while with the rickshaw driver and then went into the house, calling in a hesitant voice, "Is anyone here?" But the house was quite silent, sunk in midday heat and sleep. All the men were probably out, and the women and servants resting in cool rooms after their meal. Babu Ram stood in the passage, scratching his head under his little round hat and not quite knowing what to do. He did not want to go farther, for fear of intruding into the women's quarter. Yet it was in the women's quarter that he would be most likely to find the old man, who had always had a predilection for sitting there—so strong a predilection that the family had called him, in his younger days, "the eunuch." But the old man had his reasons: in the women's quarter he could be close to his only two real interests in life—food and children. He ate enormously, and he could amuse children as no one else could. Babu Ram's five little girls had loved him; they had clustered around him, clambered on his back, on his knees, and up his arms, crying in shrill voices, "Uncle, tell us a story!" "Uncle, make us a kite!" "Uncle, be a train with a engine!" And the old man had laughed and tried to defend himself, saying, "But wait a minute, just one minute!" For the first few weeks after he left the house, they had often asked after him and had to be promised that he would come back soon. Now, of course, they had almost forgotten him; children were like that.

Babu Ram cleared his throat and called again, "Is anyone here?" Suddenly from the temple, bursting into the still, hot afternoon with an air of great joyousness, came the sound of chanting accompanied by the tinkling of tiny cymbals. Now, too, there was a faint stirring from inside the house. Babu Ram heard a woman's voice, heavy with sleep, in some inner room, and a jingling of keys and bangles, and then the woman came shuffling out on naked feet. She was a young, fat, healthy woman, and she was rubbing her eyes, which were still full of sleep; she must have washed her hair before lying down, for it hung down her back in damp, glistening waves, all the way to her waist. "Every time we sleep, they wake us with their prayers," she muttered crossly, standing in the doorway, scratching her elbow and looking at Babu Ram with bleary eyes. The chanting continued, loud and joyful. Babu Ram joined his palms together in greeting and said, "How are you, sister?" She blinked at him a few times, leaning her heavy weight against the doorframe, and then recognized him. "So you have come," she said.

She turned and he followed her. They crossed the courtyard, and Babu Ram saw the old man. He was lying on a low bed in the covered part of the courtyard. In front of him, on the ground, sat a little boy. The old man was saying, "The hunter was so ugly that the birds all flew away at sight of him. His eyes were bloodshot, and he was flat of hand and foot and he carried a big, big club with spikes on it . . ." The little boy sat quite still, his hands laid folded on his bare knees, and he was looking up into the old man's face with his eyes stretched wide and his teeth biting into his lower lip. Babu Ram stood still and looked at them, and his heart beat faster. "O Ram, O great Ram!" came triumphant voices from the temple; the cymbals danced and jingled. "O Ram, O great Ram!" Suddenly Babu Ram knew that God would give him a son—perhaps had already given him one—who would sit like this little boy and listen to the old man telling stories. Waves of happiness passed over him, and he trembled.

The woman, seeing him look at the old man, also stopped, with her hand on her hip, and said, "That is all he is good for—to lie all day on a bed and fill the heads of children with nonsense."

"Like a tiger he came," the old man was saying, "very, very softly, and he held his terrible club in his hand, and his teeth, which were very sharp, were bared like a tiger's." He demonstrated the bared teeth, and the little boy watched him.

"And to eat," said the woman. "How he can eat! O my God and fathers, how he can eat!" and she put up her hands to clutch her head. The chanting stopped, and, after one last joyous tinkle, so did the cymbals. Now the house seemed very still, with only the drone of the old man's voice telling his story.

Another woman appeared out of an inner room—an older woman, very short and very broad and waddling from side to side as she walked. She also said to Babu Ram, "So you have come," and he again joined his palms in greeting and said, "How are you, sister?"

"I hear your wife is having her sixth," she said. "Well, let us hope this time . . ." The younger woman put her hand in front of her mouth and laughed from behind it. Babu Ram put on the weak, self-deprecating smile he always used when people laughed at him for having nothing but daughters. "Though there is the example of my sister's brother-in-law's wife—Shantidevi, we call her," the older woman went on. "She had nine daughters before she had a son."

"Oh, no," Babu Ram said, lifting his hand with an instinctive gesture of defense. He knew this could not happen to him. He knew that his wife was about to give birth or had already given birth to a boy. God had spoken to him and promised him, through the chanting in the temple and the tinkling of tiny cymbals.

"One can never tell," said the older woman. "These things are in the hands of God. To some He gives and to some He does not give. It is so in life." She sighed.

To some He gives, thought Babu Ram, and felt himself swelling with triumph. And now he wanted to hurry home with the old man to see how God had given to him.

"Like a great king he is lying there," said the older woman, jerking her head toward the old man. "The good-for-nothing."

"Yesterday he ate up all the *halwa* again," said the younger woman. "What is it he has inside him—a pit or a stomach?"

"A curse on him!" said the older woman.

The women had spoken loud enough for the old man to hear, but he went on droning his story with no change of expression: "His terrible net was spread, and there he crouched, club in hand, and with a wicked, vicious look on his wicked, vicious face." Babu Ram remembered how it had been the same in his own house—the women had cursed and the old man had calmly carried on, eating, sleeping, telling stories, as if he didn't hear them. He had been a poor relation all his life and had learned how to live as one.

Babu Ram turned to him now and said, "You are coming?"

The old man gave no indication of having heard and continued to tell his story to the little boy, whose eyes had never left his face. Babu Ram sat down and watched them, which gave him a deep pleasure. It was as if he were looking into the future and seeing his own son sitting thus and listening to the old man. The two women continued to talk—about how necessary it was for a man to have a son, and about Shantidevi with her nine daughters, and about how much the old man ate and how lazy he was and good for nothing—but Babu Ram hardly heard them. With his head inclined to one side and a tender smile on his face, he sat watching the old man and the boy.

At last the story was finished, and the boy asked "That is all?" and the old man answered "That is all." Then he got up from his bed, removed the rug on which he had been lying, pulled out a bundle from under the bed, and wrapped it in the rug. He was ready.

Babu Ram jumped up. He was in such a hurry to get home that his farewells to the women were rather perfunctory. "Well," said the older woman, "you have taken a great burden from our backs." "Like a deliverer you have come," said the younger woman. The old man, his bundle under his arm, quietly followed Babu Ram out of the house. He had some difficulty keeping up with him, for Babu Ram was almost skipping on his plump legs. They found a cycle rickshaw at last, and sat down in the seat at the back. "Quickly!" Babu Ram told the driver. "Go quickly!" He couldn't wait to get home and hold his son in his arms. The smile with which he had watched the old man and the boy was still on his face. "Go faster," he said from time to time. The rickshaw driver clenched his teeth and put all his weight on the pedals of the cycle; perspiration trickled down his neck into his torn and dirty vest. The old man sat holding his bundle on his knees, enjoying the drive.

WHEN THEY REACHED the house, Babu Ram's haste left him, and he walked up the stairs very slowly. All his elation, all his certainty had gone; now he felt only rather afraid and would even have liked to go away. There were no more busy women rushing about, so he knew it was all finished. Subdued voices came from the room where the birth had taken place. Beckoning to the old man to follow him, he went in, softly and timidly. A group of women were squatting on the floor, eating out of brass bowls; a few others were sitting on the edge of the bed, on which his wife lay asleep with her head turned sidewise and her hair straggling loose on the pillow. Next to the bed stood the cradle. Nobody said anything, so he knew it was another girl.

At last, one of the women got up and took the baby out of the cradle and put it into his arms. Another woman said, "We must welcome what God has given us," and sighed, and then several others sighed and said, "It is a gift from God." Babu Ram looked down at his new baby. It was turning its head from side to side, with the mouth round and open like a little bird's; its neck was scraggy like a little bird's, too. The old man bent forward and smiled a wide, toothless smile at the baby and clicked his fingers at it and made tender noises with his tongue. Then he looked at Babu Ram and smiled some more and nodded. So Babu Ram also smiled, and began to rock the baby to and fro on his hands. "Careful! What are you doing?" the women shouted, but the old man wagged his head and cackled with approval.

(1958)

Better Than Dead

WHAT MADE ME FIRST CARE FOR MY HUSBAND WAS that he was so kind to me. It was a very difficult time for me; I think it is a difficult time for every girl when she is first married and taken away from her own home to go and live with her husband's family. I had been happy and excited when my parents arranged my marriage for me, because, like every girl, I was eager to be a bride. But when the marriage festivities were over, and it was time for me to be sent away with the stranger who was now my husband, then I was very much frightened. I was thirteen years old at the time, and I had never been out of the village where my father had his land. But now I had to go all the way to Delhi and live with my husband's family in a house in the middle of the city. Everything there was so different from my own home, and I longed for my mother and my younger sisters and our courtyard, where we sat together doing our household work. I had not known before how happy I had been at home. Outside the house where we lived, there was a big old tree, to which one of my brothers had tied a swing for us; we sat on this swing and swung up high among the leaves of the tree, and we laughed, and sometimes we sang songs. I think we were laughing and singing most of the time. In my husband's house, there was also a lot of laughing, but it was different. Everybody there was so big. There were my husband's brothers—five of them—and they were all taller than anyone I had ever seen before, and their shoulders were broader and their chests wider and their voices louder. Their wives also were big and with loud voices, and so were my mother-in-law and my sisters-in-law. All were tall and big, and all ate a lot and shouted; sometimes their shouting was in fun and sometimes it was in anger, but to me it always sounded the same, and it always frightened me. I was frightened most of the time. I sat in a corner and hoped nobody would see me or speak to me. They were never unkind to me, but, all the same, I was frightened. I felt so small and weak that I thought if they wanted to they could crush me and I would be dead.

My husband was not as big as the others. His hands—even though he is a carpenter and works with them all the time—are like a woman's, and so are his feet; his voice is low and gentle. But at that time—seven years ago, when we were first married—I was frightened of him, too. Perhaps I was even more afraid of him than of the others, because he was my husband and therefore my master, and could do with me what he liked. I had always been told that a woman's husband is her god, and that she must worship him and obey him in everything. I knew that some husbands were very bad to their wives, so I was afraid of what he might do to me. When he spoke to me, I trembled and my heart beat loudly and I could never answer him. "What is it?" he would say. "What is the matter? Please tell me." But I could never speak. And what to tell him? How could I tell him, "I am frightened and unhappy; please send me home again"? He might be angry with me; they might all be angry with me, and then what would I do? So I sat quiet and said nothing, though he said, over and over again, "Please tell me what is the matter." His voice was sweet and gentle as he spoke to me, and so was his face as he looked at me, but I never realized this, because I was so frightened that I could hear only the beating of my heart and a rushing in my ears.

Once he really was angry—not with me but with the others. "What are you all doing to her," he said, "to make her sit day and night like this in a corner?" Then they all shouted with their loud voices—my mother-in-law and my sisters-in-law. "What do we do?" they shouted. "All day we beg her to come and sit with us, come and eat with us, but never can we get her out of her corner!" It was true; they did try to make me come to them, but I felt safe only by myself, as far away from them as possible.

"You are frightening her!" my husband shouted. It was the first time I had heard him shout, for he was usually very quiet.

"Son," cried my mother-in-law, "I swear to you"—and she beat her fist against her heart so hard I thought surely she must have hurt herself—"swear to you we try to be kind to her!" My sisters-in-law, too, shouted, and then my brothers-in-law joined in—all of them standing there facing one another and roaring like lions. I thought at any moment they would turn and tear me to pieces, and I was so frightened that I began to scream. I hid my face behind my hands and I screamed. I couldn't help myself. My husband lifted me up and carried me and laid me on a bed. Then I was so tired I went to sleep; I think he stayed sitting on the bed, looking at me, but I can't be sure. Anyway, when I woke up next morning he was no longer sitting there.

It was a few days after this that he came home one evening from his work and said to me, "Pack up your things." I got up and I wrapped my things into a bundle, and we left the house together. I thought he was taking me home to my parents' house, and though that was what I had wanted most ever since my marriage, now I felt hurt and ashamed. I knew it was the greatest shame a woman can endure to be sent back to her parents' house. But soon I noticed that he was not taking me to the railway station. I knew the station was near the house, but now we seemed to be walking a much longer way. We walked through many narrow roads, all crowded with shops and people, and there were bullock carts and cycle rickshaws going down the middle of the road, and sometimes also cars came, hooting loudly, so that I had to walk close to the wall. My husband went in front of me, clearing a path for me through the crowd; I kept my eyes fixed on his back, for I was afraid of losing him. What would happen to me if I lost him or if he decided to abandon me now in the street? I would never be able to find my way back to the house, and I would be quite alone and forsaken in Delhi, where I knew no one except my husband and his family. So I kept as close behind him as I could; he was like a friend to me in all that crowd of strangers. Once he stopped at a sweetmeat shop and bought a few sweetmeats for me. I ate them as I walked behind him.

At last, he went into a doorway beside a tailor's shop, and I followed him up a very dark and narrow staircase. Once I stumbled, and he put out his hand to me; I held it, and then it was easier for me to climb the stairs. We stopped at one door, and he took out a key and opened the door, and we walked into a room. There were two beds in that room, and in one corner there was a place to make a fire for cooking, and a few cooking utensils, which were shining and new. My husband said, "This is where we shall live. Only you and I." He saw that I did not understand him, so he made me sit down and he talked to me for a long time. He talked about how he believed that husband and wife should be alone, away from their families, and how they should make their own life and be free and happy. But though I did not understand most of what he was saying, I noticed he was talking in a gentle, kind way, so I was not at all afraid of him. And I began to think that perhaps he would be good to me and that it might be possible for me to be happy living with him.

HE WENT TO his work every morning and came home at night, and I cooked for him and cleaned our room. At first, it was very strange for me to be alone, without a family; in my own home there had always been so many of us—my grandmother and my parents and uncles and brothers and sisters—and in my husband's house there had been his brothers and their families. But after a time I became used to being alone with my husband, and I even began to like it. My husband gave me money for our food, and I went out and bought a little store of rice and flour and lentils; and sometimes I went to buy vegetables at the bazaar, where I bargained with the shopkeepers and kept a sharp lookout to make sure that they gave me only fresh things and weighed them right. And I swept out our room and rolled up our bedding neatly in a corner and made everything sweet and nice.

There was a water tap in the courtyard, where all the women in the house came to get water. Often they quarreled about who would fill her bucket first. I always let everyone else go before me, so that they could not quarrel with me, for I was rather afraid of all the shouting and abuse. But when I was alone, cooking my husband's food or cleaning out our room, then I sang the way I had sung in my father's house. Only it was different from my father's house, because all the time I was waiting, impatient and waiting, for night to come; and when I heard his step on the stairs, my heart beat loudly, but now it was no longer beating in fear.

I remember the time I was expecting my first child. Though it was such a happy time for me, when I think back on it now I begin to cry. I cry most of the time now; my children look at me, and I know it hurts them that I am crying, but I can't help it—my tears won't stop flowing. But at that time, during my first pregnancy, I was always happy and laughing. And, looking at me, my husband, though he was usually quiet and serious, would also begin to laugh, and we were like two children together. Yes, at that time I could still make him laugh, and call him away from his serious thoughts and his books. Even then, he was often reading and thinking. He had learned to read in a school in the city, and I had never known anyone to sit so much with a book as he did. He wanted me to learn to read and write, too, and even tried to teach me. But when he was being my teacher and sitting close to me, my thoughts always turned away from the lesson, and I would begin to stroke the back of his hand or touch his cheek gently with my fingertip. At first, he would frown and say, "No, you must learn," but soon he would not be able to resist my caresses, and he would love me.

When my baby was to be born, he took me home to my parents; and when he was first shown our baby, and held it, I could see that there were tears in his eyes. Afterward, he sat by my bed and talked to me for a long time. He said many things, most of which I did not understand. But I was used to his talking strange things; he often made me sit and listen while he talked about—I don't know what. About God and the world and people and being happy and not being happy—all things like that, which I think he must have read about in his books. But when he talked that way after the baby came, I could hear my sisters talking and laughing outside, and I was impatient for him to finish so that I could call to them and join in their talk and laugh with them. In the end, I could not bear it anymore; I had to call to them, "Why don't you come in?" Then they came running, still laughing, and they stood round my bed, and we all talked together and were so merry. Only my husband was quiet, and after a time he got up and went away.

ELEVEN MONTHS LATER, I had another child, and the year after that I was pregnant once again. But that time my husband did not take me to my home, because my mother had died in the meantime and my sisters had all been married and my brothers had brought in their new wives, so it wasn't home for me anymore. I did not like to go to my husband's family, for though I was no longer so much afraid of them, I always felt shy and could never love them. So I stayed at home in our own room and had the child there. But something went wrong and that child died, and I nearly died, too. But the next year I had another child, and that one lived. I had become weak after the third child, and after the fourth I felt so bad that I could hardly stand. But I could never rest, because there was so much work to do—looking after the children and cooking and washing and cleaning and carrying the water up the stairs. My husband was also working very hard, to bring money home for us. We always had enough food, and in the winter I could make warm clothes for the children, and if they were sick, I had money to pay for medicine. Often, too, he brought little toys and sweetmeats, and, for me, colored glass bangles. He played with our children and told them stories, so that they loved him very much and waited at night for him to come home. I was always glad when he was home, though I was usually too tired to speak much with him. It had been a long time since he tried to teach me to read and write, but he still liked to sit and talk to me about what he read in his books and the thoughts that were in his head. He would talk and I would try to listen, but I was always so tired, and I could not really understand what he was saying. There were many other things I had to think about, such as why our store of rice was finishing too quickly this month—was it because the grocer had not given me the right weight, or had someone come and stolen some out of the stone jar in which I stored it? And then I thought about whether I would be able to buy a piece of cloth to make a shirt for my eldest child, or would it not be better to make one for my husband instead, because his was getting very frayed. But most of all, I thought about the water tap in the courtyard. My thoughts were always very bitter about this, because the older women pushed us younger ones out of the way and quarreled with one another about who would take the water first, so that there was shouting and abuse almost every day.

Once or twice I tried to tell my husband. But he would not listen to me. All he said was "Why quarrel with people? Why fight?" and then he went on talking the way he liked to talk. I think he must have noticed that I was not really listening to him. Once he became quite impatient, and he said, "You never even try to understand." When he spoke like that, I began to cry, and then he was sorry and was gentle with me again. But he spoke with me less after that; instead, he would read his books or only sit silent, with his cheek on his hand.

But we would have been happy together again. Perhaps one day there would have been less work, and then I need not have been so tired, and we would have laughed together again and been happy, the way we were when we first came to live in this house. It could have happened like that. But now Fatima has come, and my husband is different and everything is different. Fatima came six months ago. She rented a room downstairs and came to live there with her two brothers. She has no husband; at first I thought that perhaps she was a widow, but later I found out that she had been divorced. Fatima is a Muslim, and it is very easy for Muslims to get a divorce; they only have to go to their priest and say three times that they want a divorce, and then it is all finished. So now Fatima lived with her two brothers and cooked for them and washed their clothes. We saw her when she came down into the courtyard to get water, but she never talked to any of us. She was very different from the other women living in the house. Of course, she was a Muslim and we were all Hindus, but it was not only that. She was different in every way— the way she moved and looked. She seemed so proud, somehow. She wore a burka, as all Muslim women do to hide their faces and bodies. But she always had the front of the burka open, so that her face could be seen. How fair her face seemed, looking out from the black burka! But her eyes were very dark and long, and they always seemed to be moving, as if she wanted to see everything; and really it was as if she saw everything and knew everything. But she never spoke to us—not because she was shy, of that we were sure, but perhaps because she was too proud. We did not like her at all, but no one ever quarreled with her—not even about the water—for there was something about her that made one a little afraid of her. And though we did not like her, we could not help seeing that she was beautiful. She never showed herself in anything except her black burka, which covered her from head to foot, with only her face looking out. But when she moved there was a jingling sound, as of earrings and many bracelets, so that one had to think that under her burka she wore the costliest ornaments of gold, and perhaps also thin, fine silken clothes. We could not help thinking that, even though we knew she was poor like the rest of us. Her brothers were tailors who did not even have their own shop.

ONE DAY MY youngest child was sick with fever, and I was very worried. I did not like to leave him alone, even for a moment, but I had to go down quickly to get the water. It seemed I was lucky, for most of the women had already taken their water and there remained only a few of us waiting. When I thought it was my turn, I placed my bucket under the tap, but suddenly it was kicked aside, and someone pushed my shoulder and said, "Get out, you! It's my turn!" I looked and saw it was the old woman who lived in the room on the top floor; she lived there with her four sons, none of whom ever did any decent work, so that she was always scolding them. The whole house could hear how she screamed at them, and sometimes we could hear her beating them, too. She was a terrible old woman. Any other time, I would have picked up my bucket quietly and waited for her to fill hers, but that day I was so worried about my child's fever that I said, "Please let me. My child—the littlest one—he is sick." Then she screamed again, "Get out!" so I knew I would have to wait. But just as I was stooping to pick up my bucket, Fatima said, "Let her go first." She spoke in a low voice, but everyone heard her at once. The old woman was very much surprised, and for a moment she said nothing. Fatima took my bucket and placed it under the tap again and stood by it while it was filling. She never moved at all—not even when the old woman began to shout abuses at her. When my bucket was full, she said to me, "Go," and she moved aside to let me pick it up. I hurried away with it as fast as I could. I don't know what happened between Fatima and the old woman after I had gone.

My child's fever went higher in the evening, and I sat by him with my hand on his forehead. I was very worried, yet I also kept thinking about what had happened at the tap. I wondered why Fatima should have done this thing for me. I was glad and grateful for what she had done, but I wished also that she had been friendly to me. She had never even looked at me, and when she said "Go," her voice, even though it was such a sweet voice, had not sounded friendly. I felt that she had done this thing for me not as she would have done it for a friend or a person for whom she had regard but as for anyone who was weaker than she was, even for a dog or a cat. I felt that I was no more to her than a dog or a cat, and I was hurt.

When my husband came home, he also sat down by the sick child, and he rubbed his hair and softly sang to him. The other children came in from playing, and I gave them their food. I would have liked to tell my husband about what had happened at the tap, but I was afraid that he would think I had quarreled, so I said nothing. We were sitting like that, my husband quietly singing to the sick child and I feeding the two other children, when Fatima came into the room. She was not at all shy or embarrassed, the way other people are when they come for the first time to a strange home. She looked round the room, her large black eyes moving quickly, the way they always did, so that I knew she was seeing everything: the tin trunk in which we kept our valuables; our two sitting beds, one of which had lost a leg and was supported on an old kerosene tin; the piece of carpet on which the two elder children slept, and which I had washed so often that the edges had frayed and the color had faded; the little statues of Vishnu and Ganesa, made out of plaster of Paris; and the gilded picture of Siva and Parvati, in front of which we said our prayers and did all our ceremonies. I knew she saw all that, and more—she saw and knew us all and everything about us. I lowered my eyes and felt shy and even a little ashamed. But Fatima took no notice of me. She said to my husband "Your child is sick?" and, without waiting for an answer, went straight to the bed. My husband moved aside without a word. We all watched her in silence while she looked at the child. She laid her hand first on his forehead and then on his chest, and then she pulled up the lids of his eyes. After a while, she said, "I will give you medicine. He will be well in a day or two." None of us spoke; we only stood and looked at her. It was so strange to see her in our room, in her black burka, with her beautiful, fair face looking out of it, and to hear the gentle rustling and jingling sound she made every time she moved.

Suddenly she laughed. How her eyes and teeth sparkled when she laughed! "Why are you surprised?" she said to my husband, and her voice sounded sweeter than ever, for though it was mocking, it was also tender. She smiled and looked at him closely, so that he had to smile, too, though I could see he was shy. "Why are you surprised?" she said again, and she moved nearer to him and looked into his eyes. He looked back at her, and at that moment I knew what was going to happen between them, and my heart began to pound in fear. "You think I am a witch?" she said to him and laughed. "No," she went on. "I have only taught myself a little homeopathy, that is all. I will make up some powders, and you may come and fetch them."

"You are kind," my husband said.

"Yes, I am very kind," she said, and she looked at him, and her eyes were bright with laughter. Later, he went down to her room to fetch the powders. I could not think of anything to say that would stop him. When he came back, he never said a word to me. He gave the child the medicine, and then he lay down on his bed. But I knew he did not go to sleep, for I, too, lay awake for a long time, and I could hear him moving.

FROM THAT DAY on, Fatima often came to our room in the evenings. My husband began to come home earlier, but he no longer sat with his books, as he used to do, nor did he play with the children or try to teach them. He was impatient and waiting, and it was strange for me to see him like that, for he had always been gentle and calm and full of rest. But now he could not stay still, and his hands touched everything but took up nothing; if the children asked him to play with them, he answered them impatiently. When she came, his face changed and all his impatience left him. She came in, jingling and rustling, her eyes bright, her mouth smiling. She would clap her hands at the children and cry "Who will have the most today?" and then she would throw a handful of little sweets onto the floor, scattering them all over, so that the children, shouting and laughing, had to look for them. Sometimes she would help to pick them up, and she would say "Just see, I am quicker than any of you!" and really she was—she was quick, like a bird. And she would also make my husband get down on the floor to play, and they would all be laughing, she and the children, and my husband, too, while he looked and looked into her face, and I stood and looked into his. When she was tired of playing, she would say, "Now, enough," and she would sit down by the little low window that looked out over the street. Suddenly she was very still and calm, sitting there on the floor by the window. Even the children knew that when she said "Now, enough" like that, the game really was finished. My husband sat beside her, and both had their backs half turned to the room as they looked out of the window. There was nothing very much to see from that window—only horse tongas and cycle rickshaws passing up and down, a man with a little wooden barrow who sold slices of watermelon, and, just opposite our house, a row of open stalls occupied, from one end to the other, by a vendor of gold-embroidered slippers, a man who sold sweetmeats freshly prepared in pure ghee, and a doctor who pulled teeth at one rupee each. My husband and Fatima sat and looked out, and he talked to her in a very low voice. He went on and on, talking the way he had once talked to me, and sometimes she answered him, also in a low voice, or questioned him. They talked about all those strange things that I had never understood. Fatima always seemed to be listening with great interest. Only sometimes she was in a mood where she would not listen. Then she would laugh at everything he said, and tease him, and finally she would jump up and call to the children again, "Who is playing with me?" How gay she would be as she played, her bangles jingling like music! The children loved her; they followed her like slaves, like dogs, and I knew that she had no more feeling for them than she would have had for slaves or dogs—that she had no more feeling for them than she had for me. My husband would remain sitting on the floor, and his eyes were very sad as they followed her round the room. I felt sorry for him and would have liked to go to him and to lay my hand on his cheek, the way I had always done when he was sad. But

Fatima never even looked at him, she was so busy laughing and playing with the children, though sometimes she passed very close to him.

I did not like to see all this, but where could I go? If it had been summer, it would have been easier, for in the summer we lived mostly in the courtyard or on the roof of the house. But in the winter we had to stay in our room, and I had to be close to them and see everything. There was nothing I could do or say. Once, though, I did stay close by the door, just as she was going out, and I said to her, "Why do you come into my home?" But I said it in such a low voice that it was easy for her to pretend she had not heard. I could not speak to my husband, either. What was there I could say to him? And I could see he did not wish me to speak to him. When we were alone together, he kept his head lowered and avoided my eyes and sat in silence, and as soon as he could, he would lie down on the bed and pretend to be sleeping. It was as if he were afraid I would speak to him.

On two days a week, I began to notice, my husband did not come home till late in the night. I soon discovered that on those two days Fatima's brothers worked late, and so he could spend that time in her room. Our room seemed very quiet on those nights. The children, after waiting for their father and Fatima, fell asleep disappointed. And I sat alone, waiting and thinking. But it was even worse than when they were there in front of me, for it was so still that I felt I would be alone forever and ever while they were together down in her room. I thought about what they were doing there, and I cried, quietly, so as not to disturb the children. At last, when I heard my husband's step on the stairs, I would run quickly to my bed and pretend to be sleeping. But one night I could bear it no longer, and I crept down the stairs, softly in the dark, till I stood before Fatima's door. I looked through the crack and I saw them. The pain was so great for me that I sank to my knees and leaned my head against the door. Suddenly a voice screamed, "Yes, look at them! Look at them! See what they are doing—your husband and your friend!" I started to my feet and saw the old woman from upstairs. "Have you seen?" she screamed into my face. I whispered, "Please be quiet," and even tried to put my hand over her mouth, but she struck it aside and laughed and screamed. Other doors opened, and people came and looked at us. Only Fatima's door remained shut. I ran stumbling up the stairs, putting my hands over my ears, so as not to have to hear the old woman shouting and laughing. I woke up the children and dressed them. I was crying all the time; the children looked at me, but they never said a word and did whatever I told them. I carried the youngest child, and we ran through the dark streets a long way, till we came to the house where my husband's mother and his brothers lived. I knew of nowhere else to go.

It was very late when we got there, and everybody was asleep. My mother-in-law always slept alone in the place they used for cooking, so I crept quietly round to her and touched her on the shoulder. I was still sobbing. She started up and cried, "Who is it?" I told her, and when she saw me there with the children and heard me sobbing, she suddenly cried, "My son is dead!" The words were like a knife to me; I caught her hand and whispered, "No. Oh, no!" She was sitting up on her bed, with her hand clutched to her heart, and she was breathing heavily in fright. I, too, was very frightened, and I kept whispering, "No, no." My mother-in-law called in a weak voice to my eldest sister-in-law, who woke up at once and came to see what was the matter. "Oh, my God," my mother-in-law moaned. "God, my God."

"No," I said. "No, he is not dead."

I could hardly speak the word "dead," it frightened me so.

My sister-in-law lit a kerosene lamp, and said, "First put the children to sleep." We laid them to sleep, and then I told the women why I had come. It was difficult for me to tell, for I had never yet told anyone one word of it all, though it was many weeks now since my husband first saw Fatima. My mother-in-law only said, "Thank God." She was still trembling at the thought that something had happened to him. My sister-in-law began to laugh. "And is it only the first time?" she asked. She sat cross-legged on the bed, her head thrown back on her big neck, and laughed. I was afraid that she would wake the others with her laughter, and that they would all get up and she would shout out to them what I had told her. I could see them all standing round me—the men and the women, all of them big and strong, like giants—shaking with loud laughter. I crept quietly into the corner where my children were sleeping, and I lay down beside them. I kept hearing the way my mother-in-law had cried, "My son is dead!" I thought of him dead, and it was worse than thinking of him with Fatima.

I left early in the morning. I awakened my children and dressed them very quietly, so as not to wake the others, and walked home. The streets through which I had to pass were crowded with men pushing barrows piled with vegetables, and others sitting by the roadside selling eggs out of baskets, and milkmen cycling back to their villages with empty cans. There were also people who had come out early to buy the day's provisions—women like myself with babies on their hips and their money tied into the end of their saris, and old men sent out to the bazaar by their daughters-in-law, and little girls carefully carrying earthenware pots full of curds, and the servants of the rich come out to buy meat and fish and fruits. I carried my youngest child and made the two elder ones hold tight to my sari on each side of me, for there was much pushing and jostling, and every few moments someone would shout "Mind yourself!" from behind us, and we would have to move aside to let a piled-up barrow pass, or a man carrying firewood in a basket on his head. I thought of the first time I had come from my mother-in-law's house to my own home, and how my husband had walked in front of me, clearing a way, so that it was easy and safe for me to walk. Now there was no one to walk before me, and I had to look after myself and my children. But he was not dead; I would see him again. I would still every day see him move, and hear him speak with his gentle voice, and in the night listen to him breathing on the bed next to me. What cause was there for me to be unhappy? If he had been dead, there would have been cause, but he was not dead.

When I got home, I at once began to work very hard. I swept out our room and washed the floor with water; I cleaned the window, the door, and our two beds; I scrubbed our pots till they shone. Then I began to cook; I cooked rice and a curry made of curds, which was my husband's favorite dish. Afterward, I went down to the tap and carried up more water, and I gave all three children a bath. Then I bathed myself and combed out my hair and put oil on it. I opened our big tin trunk and took from it the new sari with the red border that my husband had given me seven months before, which I had never yet worn. I sent the eldest child to go out and buy a fresh flower garland to hang round the picture of Siva and Parvati, and then I made the children sit in front of this picture, and I said a prayer. I was calm now and almost happy, waiting for him to come home.

When he came, I gave him the food I had cooked for him, but I don't think he noticed that it was his favorite dish. I wondered if he was angry that I had gone away in the night, but he did not look angry; he looked only impatient and waiting, the way he did every night when she had not yet come. The children asked him to play with them, but he said, "Later, later," as if he were thinking of something else. It became quite late, and still she had not come. The children, too, were waiting for her, and my husband began to walk up and down the room. I sat still in a corner, content that he was there with me in the room and not dead. Suddenly he stopped walking and he cried, "But why are you staring at me like that? What harm have I done you?" I looked at him, and the tears came welling out of my eyes, for I saw that he was looking at me the way one looks at someone one does not like. "Always tears!" he said, and his voice was not like his at all, but shrill and loud, like that of an angry stranger. "Wherever I go, there are your tears!" he said. I covered my face so that he would not see them. There was a step on the stairs, and then a jingling and rustling, and the children cried, "At last she has come!"

(1958)

The Old Lady

SHE WOKE UP, AS SHE DID EVERY MORNING, EARLY and very happy. The sky was still gray, and only here and there a bird stirred in a tree and gave its first, fresh twitter. She stood on her veranda and looked out at this quiet dawn breaking over Delhi, and she smiled with happiness. She was strong and calm and at peace. Still smiling, she turned back into her bedroom and sat on the floor before the little table on which stood a small brass image of Vishnu and an incense holder and a framed photograph of her guru. She sat there with her legs crossed under her and her hands laid palm upward on her knees. She sat like that for quite a long time, though she did not know for how long, because she was too happy to be aware of any time.

Then the bearer came in with her morning tea set out on her silver tray, and she smiled and was happy at that, too, because she always enjoyed her morning tea. Munni, her small granddaughter, came with her tumbler of milk, and they sat drinking together. Munni told her dream; she had a dream every night, and this time it was about how a big white horse had come for her and carried her off to a blue cloud. "How beautiful!" said her grandmother admiringly, and Munni, in a complacently offhand way, said yes, it was. Sometimes Munni's dreams were beautiful and fantastic, and sometimes they were very stern and tragic, as when she dreamed that both her parents had been condemned to be hanged, and she had watched the execution. Her grandmother was always the first person to be informed of these dreams, and afterward she and Munni sat together and discussed them. Nobody else in the house would listen to Munni's dreams, but her grandmother told her they were serious and important.

Satish, the old lady's elder son, had already left for his office; her younger son Bobo and her daughter Leila were still asleep. So the old lady had time to go around and see that everything was being properly cleaned and dusted. The whole house was alive with cleaning; marble floors were being wiped, brass ornaments rubbed, rugs beaten, cushions shaken, door handles polished, fresh flowers put in vases. The old lady walked around sprinkling rose water from a long-handled silver sprinkler. She sang as she did this, she was feeling so happy and lighthearted. Like a bird, she thought—she felt just like a bird singing from green trees and lawns on a dewy morning.

But Leila was feeling cross when she got up at last. She suffered from some stomach trouble, and that always made her irritable in the mornings. She had consulted many doctors, but they had all said that there was nothing wrong. "It is nerves," they all told her. So now Leila often referred to her nerves.

"I can't bear it" was the first thing she said on this particular morning, and her mother, full of sympathy, asked, "What, Daughter?" Leila's face was an unhealthy color, and it was screwed up with irritation. Looking at her, the old lady was a little ashamed that she herself was feeling so fresh and gay.

"Not today," said Leila, shutting her eyes. "I can't bear it today. He will talk, and we will all talk, and what will be the good of it?"

"Krishna?" asked her mother. Leila nodded, her eyes still painfully shut. Her mother clicked her tongue in sympathy, but offered, "It will be nice to see him." Leila laughed hollowly.

Munni, who had just entered the room, asked, "Daddy is coming today?"

"Go away and play," Leila told her. Munni saw that her mother was in her morning mood, so she went without comment.

"And it will be nice to see him eat," the old lady said, a trifle sadly. She never could help feeling sorry for her son-in-law. "I don't know *what* they give him in that hotel." She added "Poor boy," and could not suppress a very gentle sigh.

"Oh, Mother!" said Leila in exasperation.

"I know, I know," said the old lady. "It is not your fault." Now she felt sorry for both of them—for Krishna and for Leila. How sad it was for people to be unhappy in their marriage. She sighed, and picked up a plate of biscuits. She took the plate into the drawing room and put it on a table beside her son Bobo, who lay stretched out on the sofa, reading an art magazine. She enjoyed feeding biscuits to Bobo—she had baked them herself, with such love—but she wished he were not getting so fat. His stomach bulged through his silk shirt; his cheeks were round and puffed. It was not a healthy fatness, and one could see that he often had pimples and boils.

The old lady hurried out into the garden. She had to hurry because she felt waves of happiness passing over her—not really *happiness*, but that was what she called it to herself, because she knew no other word for it. She stood in the garden, sheltered from the morning sun by the tall old trees, and the birds' twittering trickled like water, and the gardener's hose gurgled softly in the grass, and she could hear the gardener snipping with his shears. She stood there with her eyes shut, seeing nothing, yet feeling everything, while ecstasy held her and carried her. She did not mind the gardener's seeing her like this, though she did mind it when her children saw. That was why she always hurried away from them when she felt her happiness coming over her. She did not want them to know about it. Perhaps it was because she felt guilty for having something so precious and not being able to share it with them.

Munni came running across the lawn with her doll pushed carelessly under her arm; one finger was stuck in her mouth, and she was warbling a war song. She ran straight into her grandmother and, clasping her arms round the old lady's legs, buried her face in the sari, which smelled of jasmine scent and camphor. The old lady laughed happily. Once, the descent from her states of ecstasy to ordinary everyday being had been very difficult for her, but now it was easy and effortless. Everything now was easy and effortless. Gay as a young girl, she went back to the house and into the kitchen, where the cook was squatting on the floor, vigorously grinding spices on his stone. "Quickly now!" the old lady cried in her bright voice. "Cut up the onions!" And she began to melt fat in a pan, deftly shaking it round with sharp little jerks. She had always loved cooking.

The cook let his knife slice through an onion with precision, his head laid critically to one side. "Have you heard?" he said. "Yesterday they killed a snake outside Mathur Sahib's bungalow."

"A snake!" she cried.

"A cobra," he said with enthusiasm, handing her the cut-up onion, which she slid into the fat while clicking her tongue over the cobra. "It was so long," he told her, showing her with his hands. He pursed his mouth and said, in a judicious voice, "It must have been some evil spirit."

"Yes," she said. "It is difficult to know in what shape an evil spirit may not come to visit us. Are the spices ready?"

"MOTHER!" LEILA CALLED from the drawing room and was at once annoyed when her mother failed to hear her. "She must be gossiping with the servants again," she told Bobo, who smiled indulgently and said, "Why not, if it makes her happy?"

"I know," said Leila, "but it is hardly dignified."

Bobo was looking at some Rajput miniatures. "Lovely," he murmured with sensuousness, trying to enjoy them like a taste.

"Mother is often not dignified," Leila said. "For instance, with Krishna. It is very awkward for me when she is so soft with Krishna."

"Lovely," said Bobo, "but probably fake." He looked up and asked, "Why awkward?"

"It might make Krishna think— You see," she said with emphasis, "I want it to be *quite* clear that everything is finished and there can be no reconciliation."

"But isn't that obvious? When you and Munni are living here?"

"But Mother keeps calling him!" Leila cried in exasperation. "When none of us are at home, she goes quietly to the telephone and says, 'Krishna, come and eat a meal with us.'"

"Poor fellow," murmured Bobo, who had inherited some part of his mother's sympathy.

"Yes, but what about me?" Leila demanded. "Because you and Mother feel sorry for him, do you want me always to be tied to an incompatible husband?"

Bobo yawned (how he hated argument, and his sister was very argumentative), but politely tried to cover it up.

"It is very difficult for me," sighed Leila, and then she said, "I am going to telephone."

Her mother, emerging from the kitchen, was glad to see her telephoning. She knew that Leila's mood always improved at the telephone. Already her daughter's voice was quite cheerful. "We shall just have to call an extraordinary meeting, that is all," she was saying. Her telephone conversations were always full of references to meetings, subcommittees, resolutions, agendas. She was an enthusiastic committee woman and had many committee friends, to whom she telephoned and with whom she exchanged, several times a day, important notes and papers, which were carried to and fro by a scared young clerk specially hired for the purpose.

"Leila was complaining that you gossip too much with the servants," Bobo told the old lady. He said it with good humor, but nevertheless in the patronizing tone that all her children used toward her. The old lady did not mind. On the contrary, she rather liked being patronized by her children. They were so much cleverer than she had ever been.

"Yes," she said, smiling radiantly, "I talk too much. Shall I bring your milk?" And then she said, "Oh, Son, why won't you get married?" She did so want him to. But Bobo only smiled, showing his pointed, wide-spaced little teeth and his gums. She sat down and said dreamily, "I wish one of you two boys would get married. I could arrange so nicely for you." She could talk like this to Bobo, but not to her other son. If she diffidently mentioned marriage to Satish, he only clicked his tongue and made a movement of irritation.

"And you would be happy," she told Bobo, looking at him with appealing eyes. "With a wife and children you would be so happy!" And maybe with a wife and children he would become more active, and would no longer lie all day on a sofa, reading and looking at objets d'art. Of course, she realized that that was his work, and she was always proud when an article he had written appeared in one of the art magazines or in the Sunday edition of the *Statesman*. But still she did wish he would *move* a little more, if only to stop him from getting too fat.

"Why not talk to Satish?" Bobo teased her.

She shrugged. "He is so busy, poor boy," she murmured.

"So busy making money and a name," Bobo said, a trifle acidly. The two brothers did not get on well together. Satish had taken very much after his father; like his father, he had gone in for law, and he had already established a very remunerative practice for himself. He was hard-working and ambitious, which Bobo decidedly was not.

KRISHNA TURNED UP punctually at lunchtime. He was nervous and therefore was giggling in that rather silly way he had. The old lady glanced apprehensively at Leila and saw, as she had feared and expected, that Leila was already looking irritated. Krishna must also have noticed, for he giggled harder, and then, feeling obliged to make some remark, said, "Hot again today, no?"

"Yes!" cried the old lady, so eager that her voice trembled. "Yes, hot!" Now Leila was frowning at her mother, too. Bobo, still lying on the sofa with a big, glossy art magazine, said, "Are we going to discuss the weather?" Krishna laughed out loud. Munni came in and said, "Oh, look, Daddy has come." Her grandmother would have liked to see her greet him more warmly, but Munni made no further move toward him. Krishna looked over his daughter's head, pretending, in his shyness, not to see her.

They were already seated round the huge, heavy-legged dining table when Satish came in, saying briskly, "Sorry I am late." This briskness and his hasty entrance, combined with a frowning air of preoccupation, were enough to make them all feel ashamed of their idleness, which had allowed them to sit down, spaciously and in good time, for their lunch. The old lady got up, flustered and hurried; she seized the tray from the bearer who was serving them, and began herself to fill her son's plate. Satish let her serve him but said "Why do you fuss so, Mother?" in a calm, patronizing voice.

"Allow me, Son," she said, her hands shaking a little as she piled food onto his plate. "It is my pleasure." Satish was so much like his father that she even felt toward him as she used to feel toward her husband—inadequate, and as if she had neglected some part of her duty. Then, in her youth and middle age, this feeling had penetrated her completely, so that she had felt dissatisfied and unhappy, but now it was only a kind of surface disturbance, which left her great depths of calm unrippled. Perhaps she was even glad of this disturbance and tended to exaggerate it slightly, because it made her feel that she was still sufficiently in touch with her children and had not yet given herself over to her own happiness alone.

After a while, Satish said, "Well, if you want to file your divorce papers, you had better make up your minds."

"How long have I been telling you that my mind *is* made up?" Leila said at once. So then they all looked at Krishna, who became so confused that he giggled; that confused him further, and with flushed face he bent close over his plate and ate. The old lady called quite sharply to the bearer, "Give Krishna Sahib water! Don't you see his glass is empty?"

"It is better to get these things over and done with," said Satish, in his brisk, busy voice.

Bobo drawled, in deliberate contrast, "Don't hurry them into something they might not wish to do."

"There is no question of *not* wishing," said Leila.

Bobo shrugged and waved his hand to the bearer to bring the rice around again.

"What are divorce papers?" Munni whispered to her grandmother.

"Mother," Leila said in a loud voice, "please don't encourage Munni to speak before everything on her plate is finished."

"Eat, child, eat," the old lady obediently murmured. She remembered so many meals in this room, around this table—her husband stern and domineering, like Satish, and her children tense with conflict. And she herself full of unhappiness, because she did not know what to do or what to say. She still did not know what to do or what to say, but now she was only gently sad because she could not show her children the way to her own peace.

"Anywhere else," said Leila fiercely, "everything would have been settled and finished long ago."

"Now we shall hear about poor, oppressed Indian womanhood," Bobo said, with a smile.

"For you, everything is a joke," Leila said. "But it is true. In Europe and America—"

"Why don't we remain to the point?" said Satish shortly.

"It *is* the point!" Leila said. "Our attitude of mind is wrong. We don't understand that divorce is a natural thing in any enlightened society."

Krishna was as shy and embarrassed as a young girl, picking at his food with the point of his fork, his eyes lowered.

"Yes, yes," said Satish. "But what is it you want to *do*?"

Munni looked up from her plate. She was a little afraid of her Uncle Satish, but she found him interesting. For instance, she found it interesting that he should suggest doing something. She liked to hear such talk; it offered possibilities. Nothing of what the others said ever offered possibilities, which was why she usually did not bother to listen to them.

"But I have told you," Leila said.

"Oh, no. Not again," said Bobo, peering into the bowl of dessert the bearer was offering to him, and then casting an accusing look at his mother.

"Tomorrow I will make carrot *halwa*," she promised him.

"And you, Krishna?" Satish said, now looking directly at his brother-in-law, who, thus forced to commit himself, glanced helplessly around the table. His mother-in-law smiled at him encouragingly, but he was too nervous to smile back.

"Yes," he said, at last. "Of course."

There was a silence. The old lady tried hard to think of

something suitable to interpose, but it was Leila who spoke first. "Really!" she said, in an exasperated tone. She also sounded half triumphant, for, after all, her point was being proved.

"Of course," said Krishna, with a heroic effort, "if Leila wants—" He looked distressed. "Of course," he said again, "if she wants—" And then he giggled and quickly resumed eating. The old lady felt she loved him terribly. Leila put both her hands to her forehead and said, "This is frightful for my nerves."

AFTERWARD, SATISH PACED up and down the drawing room, looking at his watch and saying, "I have just half an hour." Bobo, replete and drowsy, was again lying on the sofa and leafing through a magazine with a dreamy smile on his lips. A note had just come for Leila, and she sat on the edge of a chair and opened it; she frowned and pursed her lips and looked busy, while the young clerk who had brought it stood in front of her with his head bent. Everybody seemed to be waiting for something.

The old lady got up and hurried to her room. Only for one minute, she promised herself. She sat in front of the little table with the image of Vishnu and the photograph of her guru, and—God forgive her—at once forgot all about her children sitting so puzzled in the drawing room. Everything now was clear and serene. Her guru looked at her out of his silver frame; he had large, burning eyes and an ugly mouth, with thick, unshaped lips. The very first time she had seen him, nine years ago, she had known that he was the man who would guide her. Not much had been said. She had gone to see him with a friend. He sat in a bare little room over a sweetmeat shop. There were several other people in the room, sitting around, not doing anything much. Out on the veranda, which overlooked the street, his wife sat tending a brazier, and a fat, naked little boy sat beside her and watched.

Her friend had asked the guru several questions, but he had only smiled instead of replying. Then, suddenly, he had turned, not to her friend but to her, and his eyes had burned as he gazed at her and said, "If you look for it, peace is not hard to find." So now she sat cross-legged before her little table, surrounded by vast fields of peace, in which her spirit frisked like a lamb. While downstairs in the drawing room Bobo yawned and said, "Where is Mother?" lazily patting his hand against his open mouth.

"Why does she always disappear like that?" Leila asked. She licked the flap of an envelope in an efficient way and handed it to the clerk, who still stood humbly before her. "Now, see that you deliver this at once, but at *once*," she said sharply.

"Perhaps she is resting?" Krishna suggested diffidently.

"Poor Mother," Bobo said. They often said "Poor Mother," for they felt she ought to be in need of pity. Their father had always been the strong force in the family, and it was only to be expected that after his death she should be lost and broken. That was why they said "Poor Mother" and, when they remembered, were kind and considerate to her.

"Yes, but since we are here to *discuss*," Leila said, and Krishna again looked embarrassed. Satish flicked out his wrist to look at his watch; he frowned and managed to look pressed for time. Bobo, observing him, put on a deliberate gentleman-of-leisure act, crossing his plump legs as he lay on the sofa.

Munni quietly crept up the stairs and into her grandmother's room. She came up behind the old lady and put her arms round her neck and whispered into her ear, "They are all waiting for you." But Grandmother did not move. Maybe she was dead. Munni peered round into her face. Grandmother's eyes were wide open, and her mouth, too, was slightly open, with the tip of the tongue showing. She looked very strange. What if she really was dead? They would put a red cloth over her and carry her on a board down to the Jumna, and there they would burn her till there was nothing left of her but ashes. "Grandmother!" Munni suddenly cried. The old lady said, "Yes, Munni," in a quiet voice.

After a while, Munni said, "When people get very, very, *very* old, do they die?"

"Yes," said the old lady cheerfully, "they die."

There was another pause, and then Munni asked, "Grandmother, are you very, very, *very* old?"

"Oh, yes," said the old lady, even more cheerfully.

"No!" Munni cried angrily. "The cook's mother is much older than you are! I know!"

The old lady smiled and began to stroke Munni's hair. They sat like that together, and the guru looked at them out of the photograph.

"When people die," the old lady said, "they become happy."

"But they are burnt; how can they be happy?"

"Their spirit is happy," the old lady explained, and she smiled, her eyes looking far into the distance, as if she saw there vast flowering plains for spirits to be happy in.

WHEN MUNNI AND the old lady got downstairs, Satish said, with an air of finality, "Well, I have to be going," and slapped his pocket to see if his car key was in it. "Already?" said the old lady, in a somewhat dazed manner. She was blinking her eyes as if she had just woken up, which made Leila say, "Really, Mother, you could have postponed your nap for *one* afternoon." Her mother at once looked contrite and blamed herself for selfishness.

"Nothing settled, as usual," Satish said. "If only you people would let me know what you want."

"But I have told you!" Leila cried. Krishna bent his head and pretended to be engrossed in the back page of a folded newspaper.

The old lady ventured to say, "Perhaps it would be better to wait." Her voice was cracked and nervous, and after she had spoken there was a silence, so that she wished she had not spoken.

"Mother doesn't understand," Leila said, at last. "She still thinks the marriage bond is sacred." She made a schoolgirl face of distaste to show how completely she dissociated herself from such an attitude.

"You can't expect Mother to give up the ideas of her generation so easily," Bobo said.

"No," said Leila, "but that is no reason why she should criticize *our* ideas."

The old lady sat humbly, with her hands folded in her lap, and listened to them talking about her. She thought that they were right, and that she was old-fashioned, with no conception of the modern ideas and principles that guided their lives. She admired her children for being so much more advanced and intelligent than she was, but that did not prevent her from feeling sorry for them. If only she could have shown them—opened the way for them, as it had been opened for her that day in the shabby little room where people sat around casually and the smell of cooking came from the veranda.

"You can give me a lift in your car," Leila told Satish. "I have a meeting."

Krishna got up at once and said, "Let me." His eyes and voice begged, quite without shame. But Leila turned away from him and followed Satish. Krishna sat down again, looking unhappy.

Perhaps she could show Krishna, the old lady thought. She looked at him tenderly and thought that maybe she loved him best of all. Bobo had gone to sleep on the sofa. His heavy head had dropped sidewise, and his mouth was slightly open, to allow big, regular breaths to escape. The old lady put out one finger and laid it on Krishna's wrist. What she had to communicate could not be said in words. But she felt him to be ready for it; he was unhappy and tender and lost. She could feel him seeking for something, straining for something, without his knowing it himself. She wanted to pray to be able to help him. Slowly, she stroked his wrist with her finger. Come with me, she wanted to say.

"Grandmother," Munni said sternly, watching the old lady stroke Krishna's wrist, "you know very well Mummy says we mustn't be too kind to Daddy."

(1958)

The Elected

THE DAY THE ELECTION WAS TO BE HELD WAS A HOLIday. Sudha was vague about what kind of holiday it was—whether it was to commemorate the martyrdom of some Sikh leader, or the death anniversary of a Hindu saint—but the point, as far as she was concerned, was that her husband would not have to go to the office. He lay in bed, sleeping with abandon, his shirt crumpled, his arms and legs sprawled, on his face a tender smile of contentment. She glanced at him once or twice, with distaste. His smile of contentment annoyed her even more than his air of sloth; he had, she thought, so very little right to it.

Her eldest son had gone off early in the morning—she did not know where. This not knowing was irritating, but even worse was the fact that she suspected he had not gone to places she could approve of. Neither of her sons ever went to places or did things or thought thoughts she could approve of. So when she saw her second son also making ready to leave, she shouted at once, "Where are you going?"

He hardly turned around from the door. "Out," he said, shrugging one broad, handsome shoulder.

She came running after him. "What out? Where out?" He was already sitting on his bicycle. She stood in the doorway. "Have you no studies to do?" she asked. "Why must you roam about in the city like a no-good?" Again he shrugged, and then he began to cycle off at a leisured pace. She went out onto the little square of grass in front of the house and stood there with her arms akimbo, shouting after him, "And your examinations? How will you pass in them without studying?" He never turned his head. She noticed that her neighbors on the right had come out onto their little square of grass to listen to her. She did not look in their direction at all but walked back into the house with a swagger that showed her contempt for them. She had not been on speaking terms with them for nearly five years.

She squatted in the kitchen and measured out the day's ration of lentils and flour. Her trained eye and sure hand gave her a precision that her small servant boy, standing in front of her and watching, could not but regret; every morning he hoped she would make a mistake and take out a little more, which would mean more for him, but she never did. Afterward, she got up, dusted her hands, and said, in the threatening tone she always used toward him, "Now, see that you clean the lentils properly." All the time, she was thinking of the elections.

She was thinking that of course they would elect her treasurer again. She had been treasurer of the Kalam Nagar Association of Lady Residents ever since it had been formed, three years earlier. In fact, she had been one of the original organizers and had worked hard to get together her fellow housewives in the Kalam Nagar housing colony. Though the activities of the Association—the socials at which they drank tea and the meetings at which they talked about doing things for the poor—had not come up to her expectations, she still valued her post as treasurer very highly. Of course, she thought, they would have to elect her again; they would not dare not to. But she was not quite easy about it. She knew that some of the members did not like her. Because she held her head high and her shoulders squared, and did not condescend to speak to everybody, they said she was proud and undemocratic. When she thought of this, she inflated her nostrils and gave a short, contemptuous laugh, which frightened the servant boy.

Her husband had got up from his bed. He was stretching himself and smiling with pleasure. "Today is a holiday," he said happily. He was always happy when it was a holiday; though he went to the Ministry uncomplainingly enough day after day, he had no interest in the work he was made to do there. Now he sat on the porch, smiling and drinking tea and basking in his freedom. He waved gaily to the neighbor on the right, with whom, in spite of Sudha, he was on the same cordial speaking terms as he was with everyone else. "Well, Mr. Tirath Ram," he said, "how does it feel not to have to go to office!"

Sudha, who no longer cared when he spoke to her enemies, said, "I have filled a bucket for your bath." This was a pointed reminder, for she hated to see him sitting there unbathed, unkempt, and sunk in indolence and unambition.

"Perhaps I will sleep a little more," he said to her. "I did not come home till four this morning." He smiled, thinking of the concert he had attended, at which the audience had sat enthralled until the early hours of the morning. "Ah, how he played!" he said, swaying his head as if he could still hear the music.

Sudha suffered that spasm of annoyance her husband's enthusiasms always evoked in her. But she knew it was useless to make any comment, so she returned to the kitchen and shouted at the servant boy, "Get off with you to sweep the bedroom! Must we live like pigs because you are a lazy good-for-nothing?" She squatted on the floor and cut up vegetables for the midday meal. Her hands worked quickly, but her large, beautiful eyes brooded and were full of thought. It was not right for them to say she was proud and undemocratic. Was it her fault that she had been born to stand out from other women? They would have to vote for her again as treasurer; they must recognize that she was a leader, a personality—someone to look up to and obey.

She knew she had a great capacity for power. She was a large, strong, handsome woman, and her ambitions were as powerful as her body. She had always had the feeling that, given the opportunity, she could do anything. But there was no opportunity; she had been born wrong, married wrong. So she had to sit there and cut up vegetables, smoldering with fires that had never been called on to burn. She felt like that all the time. Sometimes she could not bear it, and then she broke out, and there were terrible scenes in the house with her husband and sons—scenes in which she raged and screamed, and they ignored her. They had got used to her. She would scratch her face and tear her hair and screech like a madwoman. Afterward, she would lie across her bed and sob for hours. And then, when it was all over, she was sorry. She wanted to ask forgiveness, but did not know how to, or of whom. Sometimes she tried to pray, but God would not come near her. For days, she walked round the house like a penitent, silent, shuffling in slippers, her eyes downcast.

She finished cutting the vegetables and placed them on a tray, ready for cooking. Her movements were deft but impatient, because the work came too easily to her and she wanted to be finished with it and to get on to other things, though there were no other things waiting for her. She heard voices outside, and laughter. Her husband's friends had arrived. She made a wry face, though of course she had known they were coming; they always came when it was a holiday. They were laughing with pleasure and embracing one another, even though they had all met at the concert the night before. Sudha's husband stretched himself luxuriously and said, "Today I am a king." That was what he said every time he had a holiday. How she despised him for it! A man should be a king in his work, not in his leisure. He should be constantly striving to do great things and reach high places. But neither her husband nor his friends ever strove to reach anything.

She stood in the doorway of the tiny living room and looked

at them. Her hands were on her hips, and she did not try to disguise the supercilious expression on her face. But her husband did not so much as glance at her, and the others followed his lead. They were all sitting on the floor, on grass mats, though there were a few chairs in the room; they had pushed these out of the way. They were discussing yesterday's concert, in tones of rapture. "Such music should be drunk like wine," they said. "As the flower opens to rain, so my heart opens to this music." Talk, Sudha thought. That is all they can do—talk. She despised the lot of them. There was Ramchander—like her husband, a clerk in the Ministry of Mines and Fuel—who wrote Urdu poetry in his spare time; Mohan Das, who played the sitar and lived on his father-in-law; Meher Chand, an insurance agent, who was said to be in love with a dancer, a common prostitute; and one or two others of the same kind. They all wore wide white pajama trousers, with thin muslin shirts embroidered at the shoulders. Their hair was heavily oiled and scented, and curled at the nape of their necks. That was the sort of company her husband kept. She stood there in the doorway trying to force him to turn around and look at her and take note of her contempt. But he never did. It was strange that he, who was so weak in everything else, should be so strong in regard to her.

THERE WAS NOTHING left to do in the house, so she combed her hair—hastily, even impatiently, though it was beautiful hair and worth a lot of trouble—pulled a sari over her head and went out into the sun. She walked past the long, long row of government quarters for Grade 3 government servants. She had been living here for fifteen years, and during those fifteen years the quarters had become more and more dilapidated, in spite of the coat of whitewash that was given to them by the Public Works Department every October. They were tiny, thin, stable-like houses, put up in a hurry and meant to be pulled down in a hurry. But they never were pulled down, and Sudha had to go on living there. Every year, in April, she hoped her husband would be promoted, so that they would be eligible for a better type of house. But this never happened.

She crossed the hot, dusty children's park, turned the corner by the Family Planning Clinic, and came to the row housing higher-grade officers. This was the area to which she had aspired for all these fifteen years. Here there were somewhat larger and more solidly built houses, with bigger plots of grass in front; each house had a real bathroom, with sanitation. She knocked on the door of No. 12-A, and Pushpa Devi came waddling out. "It is good you have come," she said. "There is still much to discuss."

Sudha followed her into the sitting room, where Pushpa Devi's husband sat at the table with a lot of files before him and a preoccupied, ill-humored expression on his face. He did not even look up at them, he was so busy. "We had better go into the bedroom," sighed Pushpa Devi. They sat on the flowered counterpane, and Pushpa Devi said, "Even on holidays, he brings home his files. Work, work, work, all the time."

Sudha composed her face. "In my house it is the same," she said. "These men . . ." She looked at Pushpa Devi with burning eyes, as if challenging her to contradict the lie.

But Pushpa Devi was too phlegmatic and too well satisfied with her own position to discuss these personal subtleties. She said, "Now, about the election."

Grateful for the other's restraint, Sudha said, "Of course you will be elected president again."

This was received without comment. Pushpa Devi knew that unopposed reelection was her due, and that there was no one else well placed enough to be considered for president of the Kalam Nagar Association of Lady Residents. She scratched under her bun of hair, and said, "Kaushalya is also being returned unopposed as secretary."

There was a pause. Sudha knew that another name had been put forward, in addition to her own, for her post of treasurer of the Association. She gave a quick, probing glance from under lowered lids at Pushpa Devi. But Pushpa Devi only said, in a calm, matter-of-fact tone, "You and Nilima have been proposed for treasurer," as if it made no difference to her which of them was elected.

Pushpa Devi's daughter looked in at the door. "I am going to Auntie's house," she announced.

"Go, child," said Pushpa Devi, in her somewhat whining voice, which suggested she was resigned to everything. She turned to Sudha and said, in the same voice, "Young girls nowadays have a lot of freedom."

"Of course, we women must struggle for the freedom and emancipation of our daughters," Sudha said. But she said it without feeling. She had no daughters, and would have preferred to have had the freedom and emancipation for herself.

"All day she is studying in the college," whined Pushpa Devi, in a self-satisfied way, and Sudha felt the familiar bitterness, which came to her every time she heard of young girls going to college. How she had longed, in her own youth, to go to college and learn and be something! But her father had not believed in educating his daughters.

"How different from our own times," said Pushpa Devi.

"Who will take charge of the ballot boxes and count the votes?" Sudha asked. She did not care to hear any more about Pushpa Devi's daughter.

"I think it has all been arranged." Pushpa Devi never took much interest in detailed arrangements. She confined her duties as president to presiding over meetings—sitting, fat and passive and dignified, in a special chair in a prominent place.

"Whom has Kaushalya appointed to do the counting?" Sudha asked. She wanted to talk about the election. She wanted to draw some expression of opinion out of Pushpa Devi about the fact that someone else had also been proposed as treasurer.

"I think it has all been arranged," Pushpa Devi repeated vaguely.

Her indifference made Sudha angry. She got up and said proudly, "I must go."

Pushpa Devi's husband still sat working in the sitting room. Sudha's glance swept haughtily over the sunburned bald patch in the middle of his head as he bent industriously over his files.

"We will meet again this evening," said Pushpa Devi.

Sudha did not reply. She walked home briskly. She felt angry and humiliated and in a mood to quarrel with her husband. He was just seeing his friends off. He stood beaming in the doorway and called after them, "At four o'clock, then!" When he turned back into the house, he was still smiling with pleasure. She wanted to shout at him, "How dare you smile? What is there to smile at?" But she knew he would ignore her, merely shrugging his shoulders, as if he were shrugging away the antics of a madwoman.

She followed him into their living room. He sat cross-legged on the floor and glanced through the newspaper. She looked at him intensely, willing him to look back at her, but he continued idly and easily to turn the pages of the newspaper. At last she said, in as controlled a voice as she could, "They say Pushpa Devi's husband will be promoted again soon." She spoke like that, controlled and polite, because she knew it was the only way to make him take any notice of her.

"Maybe," he said, turning a page. Evidently, the subject was not of the remotest interest to him.

"And you?" she said suddenly, and her eyes burned.

"I?" He laughed. "In my next birth, perhaps."

She wanted to shout, "And I?" What infuriated her most was the way he took it for granted that because he was satisfied and had no ambition, she must submit forever to being the wife of an ordinary clerk, living, with little money and no position, in a ramshackle government quarter. He never realized her vast ambitions, her longings for achievement! She looked at him almost with hate as he tossed aside his newspaper and calmly yawned. On the end of the yawn, he said, "You could bring me food now, if it is ready."

He ate neatly and gracefully, his slender fingers darting with precision from one bowl to the other. His head was bent over the tray, and she looked down at his hair, which was as thick and black as it had ever been, though he was nearly forty years old now. And then she thought of the head of Pushpa Devi's husband, bent industriously over the files, and the bald patch, burned black by the sun, and she thought of the pinched, ill-humored expression on the face of Pushpa Devi's husband.

"Your friends are coming again this afternoon?" she asked, in a sneering voice. She did not want to feel proud of her husband. What was it, after all, to be smiling and handsome? It was the man inside that counted, the strength and ambition in him. But he had neither strength nor ambition.

"Mohan Das is bringing his sitar," he said. "We shall have music, and Ramchander will recite his poetry. Ah!" He sighed in happy anticipation.

She turned contemptuously and went into the bedroom. She brooded into the oval mirror hung up on the wall. She always looked into a mirror when she wanted to brood about her unhappy life. Even as a girl, she had done it. She had sat and scowled at her own beauty. What good was it to her? She had never wanted to be admired for that; she had wanted to be admired for her achievements, and to do something, be something extraordinary—a doctor, a woman bandit, the wife of the

Prime Minister. But nobody had ever encouraged her ambitions. On the contrary, she had often been beaten because she was not satisfied, like the other girls in the house, with sitting in the women's quarter and learning household duties from her mother and aunts. So she had been glad when they had arranged her marriage; she had hoped for everything from that.

She swung from the mirror and went back to where her husband had just contentedly finished his meal. She shouted at him, "And I suppose I am to serve tea to all your loafer friends!"

He did not even look surprised. "The servant can do it," he replied casually.

She wanted to sob, but instead she tossed at him, with clenched teeth, "You and your friends!"

He stretched himself. "I think I will go and sleep a little," he said.

Like Ram and Sita, people had said when they were first married; like Krishna and Radha, for they had both been beautiful. And she had glowed and been happy, looking forward to her boundless future. He was only nineteen, but, through an uncle's influence, he had already obtained a post with the government as a Grade 3 officer. That was twenty years ago.

"Yes, go and sleep!" she shouted. "Go and sleep your life away!"

He made only a small sound of annoyance. "Today your black devil is in you again."

"You are my black devil!"

"Ah, leave me alone," he said, and went into the bedroom.

She ran after him. "And your sons, too! Where are they? Loafing about in the town all day!"

"Go away."

"You and your sons! All of you the same!" She stood before him, challenging him, her eyes flashing, her fists balled. Her hair had jumped out of its pins.

Suddenly he shouted, "Go away!" Now he was angry, too. This did not happen often, and she knew she would have to go. Otherwise, he would not hesitate to hit her. She was afraid not of the blow itself but of its aftereffects. It would make her feel ashamed and humiliated for weeks, but he would forget within the hour and behave as if nothing had happened.

"God, God," she murmured to herself—not in real prayer but only because she felt in need of help. She rolled up the mat on which he had been sitting and called to the servant boy to take away the tray. Swiftly, deftly, she tidied the room. Her heart was beating fast. She wanted to do something strong and brave and violent. But there was only the election.

THE ELECTION WAS held that evening, in the garden of the kindergarten school. Everybody drank tea and ate sweetmeats from little saucers. There were fairy lights in the trees, left over from the children's Diwali celebrations, and a standard lamp had been brought out. Fifty-four of the seventy-eight members of the Association were present. Pushpa Devi sat under a tree, in the only armchair there was, drinking tea and listening, without any appearance of interest, to what the members standing around her were telling her. Kaushalya, the secretary, who was also the teacher of the kindergarten, was moving from group to group; she was sharp and lively, and talked a lot. She was better educated than the other members, and was, in fact, a BA, and so usually had the last word on how things should be done. Every now and again, she and Sudha went into important consultation. Nilima, Sudha's rival for the post of treasurer, sat on one of the tiny benches with her friends. One friend held her hand, and all of them often looked toward Sudha. But Sudha did not look back at them. She consulted with Kaushalya, had a few words with Pushpa Devi, and talked here and there with her chosen friends. She held her head high and knew herself to be a person of importance in the Association.

Kaushalya raised her hands in the air and clapped them for attention, just as she did when she called in her kindergarten children from the playground. It was time to start the meeting. "Come along now, everybody!" cried Kaushalya. She and Sudha sat on either side of the president, the three of them facing the rows of chairs and benches.

Kaushalya said, "We all know what we are here for today." Most of the members looked shy and ill at ease. They were all housewives, with low-salaried husbands and many children, and they had never moved much outside their kitchens and courtyards. "We are all free and equal here! It is like the elections for Parliament that are held in this great India of ours, when everybody—men and women, young and old—can vote for whom they like! And that is just what we want you to do now!" Kaushalya rather liked to speak. There was some disturbance—papers for the voting were being distributed, and since many members did not know what they were for, there was a lot of whispered explanation and argument.

Sudha looked over the rows of members. She saw plain, squat, puzzled women staring suspiciously at the blank pieces of paper that had been given to them. She thought, if they don't elect me, I shall have to sit there with them and be one of them. She would have to see Nilima simpering in her place as treasurer, and Pushpa Devi sitting there stolidly, with her knees apart, as if nothing had changed.

"Now, has everybody brought her pencil, as you were told?" Kaushalya said, in her bright kindergarten voice. Many of them had not, and the available pencils were passed from hand to hand, and everybody tried to see what her neighbor had written. Sudha knew that if they did not elect her, she would never come to the Association again. Even that would be finished for her.

They did elect her, however. It took some time for the result to be announced, for the three members selected to count the votes kept getting the count wrong, and had to start all over again several times. Sudha sat tensely, with a haughty look on her face. This did not change when she heard Pushpa Devi make the announcement, in her usual flat, querulous voice. She had won by eight votes. Her heart leaped, but it was not until the meeting was officially dissolved that she relaxed her stern expression. She began to talk with her friends, and then she could not hide the fact that she was happy. She talked rapidly, teased and joked, and laughed frequently, throwing back her head and showing her full, strong throat and her perfect teeth.

She came home glowing like a young wife. Her husband and his friends were sitting out on the little patch of grass in front of the house. Ramchander was reciting his poetry, in a low and feeling voice: "And soft, like a bird in its nest, my heart stirs with love for you." His audience breathed sounds of ecstasy. Their white clothes glimmered in the dark. Mohan Das rested against his sitar. From time to time, his fingers moved lazily over the strings, plucking sensuous notes that throbbed into the darkness. Sudha swept past them into the house. Her eldest son had come home and was lying in the bedroom on the bed. Sudha turned on the light, and he put up a hand to shield his eyes. "Why are you lying like this?" she asked. He did not move. She glanced into the oval of mirror on the wall, saw her eyes shining in deep black pools of satisfaction, and could not help smiling to herself.

"Get up, Son," she said. "A boy like you—where will you get by only lying on a bed?" Still he did not move. "You must strive and work and *be* something. Are you asleep?"

"Yes," he muttered.

"God has given you so much. He has made you a man, and healthy and strong . . ." She sat on the bed and stroked his hair and his cheek and his shoulder. Both her sons were strong and handsome, with smooth skin the color of wheat. "You must go out into the world and fight and work till you are a great man and everybody looks up to you," she said.

He yawned and slowly rose from the bed.

"I have been elected again for treasurer," she said, with a shy, proud quiver in her voice.

He dawdled out, and after a while she came running after him. "At least one of us in the family is trying to be something!" she called.

He joined his father and his father's friends on the grass outside. The poet's voice oozed into the night: "Like the doe caught by the hunter, I lie in the snare of your eyes." Sudha stood in the doorway and looked out at the dim white shapes on the grass. She leaned her head against the doorpost and felt tears behind her eyes. Rich, honeyed sounds came trickling from the sitar. It did not seem such a great thing to have been reelected treasurer. She thought of the plain, squat women puzzling over the voting papers, and knew that she was as far as they were from being a doctor or a woman bandit or the wife of the Prime Minister. "At the jingle of your ankle bell, my ear turns into a flower," the poet said. She felt tired, and slightly old, and wished her husband would leave his friends and come to her.

(1960)

A Birthday in London

MR. LUMBIK WAS THE FIRST GUEST TO ARRIVE, RATHER too early. He had a big bunch of flowers in tissue paper, and wore a tweed jacket with leather buttons, which gave him a jaunty air. "A happy birthday, and so many of them," he said to Sonia, bending over her hand to kiss it with that special tender air he had adopted toward her.

Sonia was flustered by his early arrival, by the flowers, by the tender air, which she never knew how to deal with. She blushed, and this made her seem like a lovely young girl receiving her first suitor. "Mr. Lumbik," she said, "you shouldn't. An old woman like me has no birthdays."

"Ow, ow!" he cried, clutching his ears, which stood away from his head so that the light shone through them. "They are hurting, hearing you speak such things!"

She laughed, all young and gay. "You and your jokes. You should be ashamed, Mr. Lumbik."

"One little birthday favor," he begged, holding up one modest finger. "Just one little little favor from the birthday child."

She again became somewhat agitated and turned away to look out of the window and down into the street, where a line of double-decker buses were swaying their way up to the West End. She hoped Mr. Lumbik wasn't going to ask for a kiss, though that was what she rather expected. She didn't want to kiss him at all—not even to bend down and peck at his cheek, which was never shaved well enough for her liking.

"Not 'Mr. Lumbik,'" he begged. "Not ever again 'Mr. Lumbik.' 'Karl.'" He put his head to one side and looked up at her pleadingly out of pale, aging small eyes. "All right? 'Karl'? Such a nice name."

She didn't reply. Instead, she went out across the hall and into the kitchen to fetch the *Apfelstrudel*. Mr. Lumbik followed her on his soft crepe soles. He didn't press for an answer. He prided himself on his knowledge of women, and Sonia was the type one had to proceed with gently and tactfully, for she was of very good family and had had a romantic upbringing.

"Now I have a surprise for you," he said, following her back into her room and watching her as she lovingly placed the *Apfelstrudel* on the table laid for the birthday party. "You will be pleased to learn from me that now they have granted me my British citizenship."

"How nice," said Sonia, concentrating on the last-minute touches to her table. She had been a British citizen for ten years, and the thrill had worn off.

"Yes, a special telephone call from Scotland Yard." He dialed an imaginary telephone and held an imaginary receiver to his ear. "'Hallo, Karl Lumbik? You are now a very small member of the very big British Commonwealth. God save the Queen, Karl Lumbik!' 'God save the Queen, Mr. Scotland Yard!'" The imaginary receiver was replaced and Mr. Lumbik stood at attention.

Sonia laughed. "How funny you are!" Everything was a joke to him. If only Otto had been a bit more like that. But Otto had always taken everything very tragically. When they became British citizens, he had taken that tragically, too. "Yes, our passports they have given us," he had said, "but what else have we got?" "Ottolein," she had cried, "be happy!" But no need to tell Karl Lumbik to be happy.

He was using his tender voice again. "So now I am a very eligible cavalier, I think." But it was the wrong note, he saw at once;

she had turned away from him and was adjusting Otto's framed photograph on the table by her sleeping couch. "I think again I have opened my big mouth too wide," he said ruefully, so that the defensive expression went from her face and she couldn't help laughing. She never could help laughing with him—he said such comic things. She tried to be remote and dignified, but, after all, she was the same Sonia Wolff, née Rothenstein, she had always been. The big laughing girl, they had called her. She always had been big, though graceful—large bosom, large hips, a fine full-blown flower on slender stalk legs—and she had been forever laughing, or on the brink of laughter, her short, curved upper lip trembling over her healthy teeth.

There was a ring at the doorbell, and Mr. Lumbik glided out into the hall like an expert butler. "Come in, come in," he said, bowing deeply at the entrance door. "The *Apfelstrudel* has come out very well."

"Where is the birthday child," cried Mrs. Gottlob in her hoarse, uninhibited voice. It was a voice Sonia knew only too well, for she had heard it often enough, screaming up the stairs about lights that had been left burning and baths that had not been cleaned after use; Otto, on hearing it, used to grow pale and very quiet, so that Sonia had to go downstairs and be as charming as she could be, accepting and admitting everything to stop Mrs. Gottlob from shouting and upsetting Otto. But, of course, all that was over now, and Mrs. Gottlob was no longer the landlady but a friend.

She came in now and gave Sonia a big smack of a kiss and a box of chocolates. "The kiss is for love and the chocolates for eating," she said.

The box was very large and ornate, tied with a blue satin ribbon. It was just like the ones Otto had so often brought for her in Berlin. He used to come tiptoeing into what they called the morning room, where she would be sitting at her escritoire writing letters or answering invitations, and, smiling and pleased, the box held roguishly behind his back, he would say, "Let us see now what nice surprise there is for us today." And she would jump up, all large and graceful and girlish: "Oh, Otto!"

"So," said Mrs. Gottlob, sitting down with a creak and a groan, "how does it feel like to be twenty-five?"

"Already twenty-five!" cried Mr. Lumbik, clasping his hands together in wonder.

"Even my baby, my Werner, is nearly twenty-six," said Sonia, shining and proud as she always was when she spoke of either of her children.

"And where is he today, on Mutti's birthday?" demanded Mrs. Gottlob. "Again out with the girlfriends, I think?" She shook an extremely fat forefinger. "I know your Werner—a very bad boy."

"If you are not a bad boy at twenty-six, then when can you be a bad boy?" said Mr. Lumbik. He gave a reminiscent smile. "Ask them in Vienna about one Karl Lumbik at twenty-six—la, la, la!" He tilted his head, thinking of the girls and the cafés and Karl Lumbik in a tilted hat and camel coat.

"Ask them in London about one Karl Lumbik at fifty-six," Mrs. Gottlob said. "The story will not be different, only it is an old good-for-nothing where once there was a young good-for-nothing."

"You are giving me a bad reputation," said Mr. Lumbik, not ill-pleased, running his hands down the lapels of his coat and swaying back and forth on his heels.

"I had a letter from my Lilo today," Sonia said. "My birthday letter. Just think, all the way from Israel, and it arrives exactly on the right day. And there are nice photos, too." She took down the letter from where she had propped it proudly on the mantelpiece and showed Mrs. Gottlob the photos of Lilo and her husband—sunburned, stocky farmworkers with open collars and rolled-up sleeves—and their blond, naked baby.

"*Ach*, the lovely baby," crooned Mrs. Gottlob lovingly into the photo. "He is like your Werner, I think. I remember just like this your Werner's hair went when he was four years and first came to live in my house."

Mr. Lumbik peered over one of Mrs. Gottlob's shoulders and Sonia over the other. "There is also something of my dear late Papa in him," Sonia said, sighing for her father, a large, healthy, handsome man who had loved good living and had died at Auschwitz. "And also, I think—you don't think so?—of my dear late Otto. The eyes, you see, and the forehead. Otto had always such a wonderful forehead."

Mr. Lumbik glanced toward Otto's photo, by the sleeping couch. The wonderful forehead, he thought, was mainly created by the absence of any hair on the head. He remembered Otto Wolff as a small, bald, shrinking man, very tired, very sick, very old, in an expensive German dressing gown that had grown too big for him. Mr. Lumbik had always thought what a pity it was that a fine woman like Sonia couldn't have married something better. Though, of course, Otto Wolff had been a very wealthy factory owner in Berlin, and it wasn't quite fair to judge him as he had known him—only a poor refugee who couldn't speak English, had no work, and lodged in Mrs. Gottlob's house.

"Yes, perhaps also our good Mr. Wolff," said Mrs. Gottlob, considering the grandchild. "What a fine gentleman he was. Lumbik, I always say, never have I had a fine gentleman like Mr. Wolff in my house."

A little tear came into Sonia's eye, but she was smiling with pleasure. How good Mrs. Gottlob was! Sonia had always told Otto that she was a good woman, in spite of her loud voice and crude manners. But Otto was so sensitive, and, of course, he had always been used to refined people and it was difficult for him to adjust. The tear ran down her cheek, and she wiped it away with her monogrammed handkerchief. "Yes, Mrs. Gottlob," she said, "we will none of us see a fine gentleman like my dear late Otto again. Oh, if you had known him in Germany, when he had the factory and the villa in Charlottenburg, what a respect you would have had for him then!" She could see him as she spoke—always dapper and neat, in his well-cut suit made of the best English cloth, wearing spats over his handmade shoes, and smelling of gentleman's eau de cologne. All those years in Germany—from the time when she first met him at Marienbad, when she was seventeen and he thirty-six, right until 1938, when they had to leave—he had always looked the same: small, bald, rosy-cheeked, fresh, elegant. Only in England had he suddenly become old and mostly worn his dressing gown.

Mrs. Gottlob gave a big sigh, which heaved her overfed body. "Yes, there we were all different people." She thought of Gottlob's butcher shop, where you got the finest liver sausage in the whole of Gelsenkirchen, and sighed again. "Still, here we all are, no bones broken, eh, Lumbik?"

The doorbell rang again. "That must be Else," Mrs. Gottlob said.

TINY ELSE, AS plump as she was short, came in, all breathless, her coat flying open, her gray bun half drooping out of its pins, an enormous old leather handbag tucked under her arm. "See, again I am late!" she cried. "What can I do? Always work, work, rush, rush, Else this, Else that. Every day at five o'clock I feel like giving my notice." She put down the handbag and fumbled at her hair, while Mr. Lumbik stood behind her and gallantly helped her out of her coat.

She gave him a suspicious look. "Are you making a joke of me again, you there, Lumbik?" she asked, but then she continued immediately, "Just think, today at half past four she comes to me: 'Else, one little work; this skirt to be shortened for a very special customer.' 'Mrs. Davis,' I say to her, 'it is half past four.

I am today invited to a birthday party in Swiss Cottage at five-thirty sharp—'"

"Enough of your blah-blah-blah," Mrs. Gottlob interrupted her, "and at least wish something for the birthday child."

Else raised both her hands to her forehead and flung them out. "You see, even that has completely gone out of my— Wait, I have brought a present!" She began to grabble in the vast interior of her handbag and brought up wrong things like keys, a bunch of safety pins, and a bottle of aspirin. Then she held up a letter and cried, "Oh, I must tell you—what news!"

The letter had a German stamp. Sonia, who always got excited when she saw letters with foreign stamps, cried, "I hope good news?"

"And what good news—my compensation! Ten thousand marks!"

"Else, how nice!"

Mrs. Gottlob snatched the letter. "You should have asked for twenty thousand," she commented when she had finished reading it. She was quite an expert in compensation. All her friends, all her lodgers, had had compensation from Germany for their losses; she herself had collected handsomely for the butcher shop. Of course, Sonia had had the most of all, for she and her family had lost the most. Sonia was a rich woman again now, which was as it should be.

"Ten thousand is also a nice little bit," Else said, all red with pleasure. "Now, what shall I do with my ten thousand? I think perhaps first a nice holiday in Switzerland in a good hotel."

"Oh, Else, let's go to St. Moritz!" Sonia cried. She clapped her hands together, her eyes shone, her big body swayed on the slender, elegant legs. "I was there with Papa and Mama in— When was it? Years and years ago, when I was fifteen. Oh, it was so beautiful!"

Mrs. Gottlob now said to Sonia, "*Na*, and the birthday coffee?"

Sonia went out into the kitchen, and soon she came back with the coffeepot and they all sat round the table.

"So today is a good day for us all," Mr. Lumbik said. "First, there is Someone's birthday." And he leaned across the table, languishing, so that Sonia became shy and peered down into her coffee cup, and Mrs. Gottlob gave him a sharp push and said, "Keep your eyes to yourself, Lumbik." He shut his eyes immediately and sat up, prim and sheeplike, so that Sonia and Else burst out laughing, like two schoolgirls. "Always a success with the ladies," he said. "So first this birthday. Then Miss Else gets her compensation and goes skiing in St. Moritz."

"Yes," cried Else, "I will break my legs also for my ten thousand! We only live once, tra-la!"

"And Karl Lumbik is made a British citizen, Class Four," Mr. Lumbik went on.

"So," said Mrs. Gottlob, her mouth full of *Apfelstrudel*, "you are also one of us now."

"That is just what she said to me when I got mine—that Mrs. Davis," Else said. "'So you are one of us now, Else.' 'Yes,' I said, 'Mrs. Davis, I am one of you.'" She gave a snort of contempt. "I would rather tear out my arms and legs—'one of us'! If she opens her mouth, at once you know what class of people she comes from." Else herself came from a very respectable family and never forgot what was due to her. Her father, Emil Levy, had been a high school teacher and a leading citizen of Schweinfurt; he had also been a very patriotic German until the Nazis came, and there had always been a picture of the Kaiser and his family in the Levy drawing room.

Sonia said, "English Jews are all so uncultured; they are not like we were in Germany."

"Uncultured!" Else cried. "If you say to her 'Beethoven,' she will think you have said a bad word."

"Do you know about Moyshe Rotblatt from Pinsk, who was taken to *Tristan und Isolde*?" Mr. Lumbik asked.

"None of your kind of stories now, Lumbik," Mrs. Gottlob said. "You are in good company."

"The best company," Mr. Lumbik said. "Twenty years ago if you had said to me 'Karl Lumbik, in twenty years' time you will be drinking coffee with three very fine ladies in a luxury flat with central heating and a lift—'"

"Well, thank God, we are all a bit better off than we were twenty years ago," Else said.

"If only he had waited," Sonia said. "He never believed things could be well again one day. I would say to him, 'Otto, it is dark now, but the sun will come again.' 'No,' he said, 'it is all finished.' He didn't want to live anymore, you see."

"There were many days I also didn't want to live anymore," Else said. "After I had sat for ten hours at the back of the shop, sewing my eyes out for Mrs. Davis, and then come home to the furnished room where the bed wasn't made and I couldn't find a shilling for the gas meter to heat up a tin, I would say to myself, 'Else, what are you doing here? Father, mother, sisters all gone—why are you still here? Finish off, now.'"

"Who hasn't had such days," Mr. Lumbik said. "But then you go to the café, you play a game of chess, you hear a new joke, and everything is well again." He smiled, and a gold tooth twinkled so merrily, so bravely, that Sonia's heart quite leaped and she thought, He is a good man.

THE FRONT DOOR opened, and Werner, Sonia's son, came in. "Oh, nice," he said. "A coffee party."

"What coffee party?" Mrs. Gottlob said indignantly. "It is a birthday party."

"Oh, my God!" Werner said. He clapped his hand over his mouth and looked at his mother with large, guilty eyes.

"So he has forgotten the mother's birthday!" Mrs. Gottlob cried.

"I thought only husbands forget birthdays," Mr. Lumbik said.

"What can I say?" Werner said to his mother.

"No, no, what does it matter?" she said quickly.

"Of course it matters. It matters terribly." He took both her hands and kissed her cheek with a slightly condescending affection. He was the same height as she was—a handsome boy with thick brown hair and an elegant air.

"No kissing, now!" cried Mrs. Gottlob. "You are a bad boy and should be smacked."

"For one kiss from Werner I also would forgive him everything," Else said.

Werner stooped down to kiss her cheek, saying, "How are you, Tante Else?"

She shut her eyes in rapture. "Sonia, why do you have such a son?" Sonia looked on, smiling and proud.

"Sit down next to the old Gottlob now," Mrs. Gottlob said, patting the seat beside her, "and tell her all about your girlfriends."

"Which one would you like to hear about?" said Werner, sitting down. He hitched up his well-creased trousers and crossed one leg over the other to display his elegant socks. "There's the blond one, then there's the brunette, and my favorite, the redhead."

"Mine come in only one color," said Mr. Lumbik. "Gray." But now that Werner was there, nobody listened to him.

Mrs. Gottlob shook her finger at Werner. "You can't impress me. For me you will only be little Werner Wolff who comes running down the stairs to his Tante Gottlob's kitchen and says, 'Tante Gottlob, bake a nice cheesecake for me!' Yes, yes, now you pretend you have forgotten!" She pinched his cheek, a bit harder than he liked.

"Of course not; how can we ever forget?" Sonia said. She spoke in a hearty, grateful voice, though she would have preferred to forget the years in Mrs. Gottlob's house, and the bed-sitting room where Otto shivered over the gas fire, and the noise of the other refugee lodgers quarreling over whose turn it was to use the bathroom.

"Werner," Else cried now, "only think where we are going! To St. Moritz!"

"St. Moritz?" He lifted an eyebrow, smiled, looked charming. "But Mutti must have been there, long ago, with Mama and Papa."

"He is laughing at me!" Sonia wailed, stretching out a hand as if to defend herself.

He caught her hand, kissed it, and continued, "That must have been the year after Karlsruhe—or was it the year after Bad Ems, when she had that lovely white lace dress with a flower at her waist and played the piano by moonlight?"

"Well, laugh, then," Sonia said, "but they were beautiful times. Mama's health was delicate—"

"Of course," Werner put in with mock solemnity.

"Shush, now! And just think, Else, twice a year we would go for holidays, once in summer, once in winter, always to some very beautiful place where we lived in big hotels—"

"With red plush carpets and a winter garden and five-o'clock tea à l'anglaise," Werner said.

"All right!" Sonia cried, tossing her head in girlish defiance. "So you laugh, but if we hadn't gone to Marienbad that year, where would you be now?" She looked round triumphantly, having made her point.

Werner clasped his hands and swayed his head like a coy

little girl. "And whom did pretty Sonia Rothenstein, on holiday in Marienbad with Papa and Mama, whom did this well-bred well-brought-up young lady meet in Marienbad?"

"Werner, today you are terrible," said Sonia, all glowing and happy.

"Yes, yes, it is always like that," Mrs. Gottlob said. "They make fun of the parents." She tried to pinch his cheek again, but he got it away in time.

"It is strange," said Mr. Lumbik, still a few paces behind. "I have stayed in so many hotels in my life, but none has ever had a red plush carpet."

"Tell more, Werner!" Else said. "I want to hear the whole romance!" Her round cheeks were glowing; she had loved romance all her life, and now, a spinster of fifty, was as eager for it as ever.

"Else, why do you encourage him?" Sonia protested.

"But I must hear what it is like when a young lady goes on holiday to Marienbad. Perhaps shall we go to Marienbad instead of St. Moritz, Sonia? Who knows what will happen to us—you with your looks and me with my ten thousand? We have a fine chance!" She nudged Sonia's arm and screwed her apple-round face into an expression of bliss.

"I will tell you something else strange," Mr. Lumbik said. "You know, I have never been away on holiday."

This time he was taken notice of. "Never away on holiday!" cried Sonia and Else, and Mrs. Gottlob said, "Is there another of your jokes coming, Lumbik?"

"Really, it is quite true. In Vienna, why should I go away on a holiday? My whole life was a holiday."

"Yes, yes, we know what kind of a holiday," Mrs. Gottlob said.

"I had my friends there, my chess, my girlfriends, the café houses, the opera—what should I want with a holiday?"

"How silly," said Else. "Everyone wants a summer holiday. Every year, when the schools were closed, my father took all six of us to the mountains, and we stayed there in a pension. It was called Pension Katz. I remember it so well."

"And then, afterward..." He spread his hands and hunched his shoulders. "A poor refugee tries to make a living, he doesn't make holidays. But all the same, I'm a much traveled man—Budapest, Prague, Shanghai, Bombay, London. Is that bad for one lifetime?"

"What sort of traveling is that?" said Mrs. Gottlob. "That is only tramping."

"It is true," Mr. Lumbik admitted. "Some people travel for pleasure, for—how does one say?"

"For kicks," Werner said.

"'For kicks.' Thank you. And some travel because—yes, because they are kicked. Is this a bad pun, Mr. Werner? I am being very English now, for I am making puns so that I can apologize for them."

"There is no need to boast, you there, Lumbik," Else said. "We have already heard how you are a British citizen now."

"Yes, now I am a British citizen, and no one can say to me anymore, 'Pack your bags, Lumbik! Time to move on.' It is so restful, it is quite bad for my nerves."

"Well," Werner said, lazily stretching his legs, "it's time for me now to do a bit of bag packing."

Sonia looked up with large, anxious eyes. "Werner, what for?"

"I'm off to Rome soon," he said, and, seeing his mother's face, added, "Oh, come on, darling, I told you I might be going."

She lowered her eyes and clenched one white hand in her lap. Mr. Lumbik looked at her with tenderness. The others were looking at Werner.

"How exciting, Werner!" Else said. "Why are you going?"

"There are things doing there, and I'm tired of London. So 'Pack your bags, Werner! Time to move on.'" He smiled his handsome smile at Mr. Lumbik, who did not respond.

"So it's not good enough for you with the mother anymore,"

Mrs. Gottlob scolded. "This lovely flat, the beautiful meals she cooks for you—you leave it all and say goodbye."

"What will you do there, Werner?" Sonia asked in a small voice.

"I told you, there's lots doing there—films and—oh, lots. Don't worry, darling," he said, trying to sound light and gay, but with an edge of exasperation all the same.

"Of course I don't worry," she said quickly. There wasn't any need to worry. There was enough money now and he could do in Rome what he did in London—a little film work here, a bit of art photography there, a lot of parties, a lot of girlfriends.

He looked at his watch. "Heavens, I must fly! I've got a date at seven!" He disappeared into his own room, which adjoined his mother's. The moment he had gone, Sonia began to cry.

"Sonia, *Liebchen!*" Else cried. Mrs. Gottlob clicked her tongue and said in her rough way, "*Na*, what is this?"

"How silly I am," Sonia sobbed. Mr. Lumbik tactfully looked at a picture on the wall that showed Sonia's parents honeymooning in Biarritz. "You see, I keep thinking how different it would have been," Sonia said, wiping at her eyes with her little handkerchief. "Otto would have retired by now and Werner would be running the factory. He would be Werner Wolff, Director of SIGBO; everybody would know and respect him—"

"So who respects me here?" Else cried. "For Mrs. Davis I am only her alteration hand, but I know I am still Else Levy, daughter of *Oberlehrer* Levy, of Schweinfurt, so what does it matter to me what Mrs. Davis thinks?"

"But the children," Sonia said. "We know who we are, but what does my Werner know, and my Lilo?" At the thought of Lilo, new tears came and she clasped the handkerchief to her eyes. "My poor Lilo. I had such a lovely girlhood—such lovely dresses, and always parties and dancing classes and the *Konservatorium* in Berlin for my piano playing. And she has had only hard work

A Birthday in London

in the kibbutz, hard work with her hands, and those horrible white blouses and shorts—" Her voice broke and she said, "My handkerchief is quite wet."

"The birthday present!" cried Else, snatching her large leather bag. She fumbled inside, and this time came up with three lace-trimmed handkerchiefs. "Happy birthday, Sonia. It is very good lace."

"Oh, Else, how beautiful!" Sonia said gratefully and immediately used one to wipe her eyes.

"You see, it is a very useful present," Else said. "But next time it is only for blowing the nose. No more tears, understand?"

"And I would like to know what cause for tears you have," Mrs. Gottlob said. "You are alive, you are healthy, the children are alive and healthy. What else matters?"

"You know," Mr. Lumbik said, "sometimes I say to myself, 'Lumbik, what have you achieved in your life?' And then I answer myself, 'I have survived, I am still alive, and this is already a success story.'"

"For once, this Lumbik has also something sensible to say!" Mrs. Gottlob said. "Be grateful to God for still letting you be here, Mrs. Wolff, and leave your Werner and Lilo to look after themselves."

"One thing I have been asking and asking myself," Mr. Lumbik said. "For me it is a very serious question: Shall I be offered some more *Apfelstrudel* or no?"

"Look what a bad hostess I am!" Sonia laughed, giving a last wipe at her eyes before taking up the silver cake lift.

"Always thinking of the stomach, Lumbik," Mrs. Gottlob said. "*Na*, perhaps another cup of coffee will also do us good."

"We will start celebrating the birthday all over again!" Else cried. "Birthday parties are so nice, and today we'll have two!"

"For such a special birthday child," Mr. Lumbik said in his tender voice, "even two isn't enough."

"*Ach*, Mr. Lumbik," Sonia said reproachfully, blushing.

He held up one entreating little finger. "Remember my birthday wish from you!"

"Karl," she said dutifully, pouring coffee, with a smiling face.

"This is something new now," said Mrs. Gottlob.

Else gave Mr. Lumbik's arm a pinch and said, "You have been making sheep's eyes at Sonia long enough; now it is my turn. I am also a nice young lady."

"You are all three nice young ladies," said Mr. Lumbik, and this compliment made Mrs. Gottlob laugh so much that she went quite red and got a cramp in her throat.

When Werner came out of his room, dressed for his date, he found them having a very merry party. "Well, I'm off," he said, but no one heard him. Mr. Lumbik was telling a story about his experiences in Shanghai. "Bye!" called Werner. Only Sonia glanced up at him. "Are you going, Werner?" she said in an absent-minded way as she poured another cup of coffee for Mr. Lumbik. Werner smiled at their preoccupation; he was glad to see them having a good time.

(1960)

Wedding Preparations

FROM EARLY MORNING, THINKING OF DENIS'S ARrival, Mrs. George was cross. She followed Kathleen around, saying: "I'll speak right out, Kath, don't think I won't." Kathleen, frying the lodgers' breakfast, remained serene. She refused to, or simply couldn't, envisage a quarrel between her mother and Denis. So all she said was, "You'll give baby his bottle at 10:00, won't you, Mum, and don't forget to burp him."

"Goodness gracious me," Mrs. George replied in irritation, "who are you telling, you think I never seen a baby before." Kathleen served breakfast to the silent, respectful lodgers and Mrs. George sat with them, sideways on a chair and sighing over a cup of tea. "Going down to the station to meet him," she complained to the lodgers. "Don't see anyone meeting *me* at the station," she said, discounting the fact that there was never such occasion. The lodgers noncommittally chewed their breakfast bacon, but they were listening avidly; it was all very interesting, and they didn't often have interesting things happen in their lives. "Coming here, *lording* it, how dare he," said Mrs. George, blowing on her tea. But the lodgers had to go off to work, and then there was only Rosie, who wasn't a sympathetic listener. She was in a hurry for, as usual, she was late for the shop.

She flung on her coat and dashed on her lipstick: "Now, Mum," she said on her way out, "don't go wasting your energies—keep it all for when he's here."

Mrs. George followed her to the doorstep and shouted after her: "Don't you worry, I won't be sparing of anyone's feelings!"

When the train came in, Kathleen at once saw Denis at the window and she smiled and waved, but he wouldn't look her way. Even when he got off, he didn't greet her, only said: "I had a terrible journey." She was all concern and picked up his bag. "Leave that now," he snapped, when he realized. He had been irritated with her even before he saw her, but it was worse now. He had forgotten quite how plain she was; and having the baby certainly hadn't improved her. He wished she were dead.

"I wanted to bring baby," she chattered happily, "but it's a bit cold out this time of the morning for the poor little mite." What did she mean by poor little mite, he thought suspiciously; was this a reproach, was she starting already? "Wait till you see him, Denis," she said, "oh, he's such a love."

"All babies look the same to me," he replied firmly; he wasn't to be got that way.

Mrs. George hadn't bothered to change out of her stained housedress which, indeterminate in cut and color, sagged about her sagging figure; she had also neglected to comb her hair or wash herself with any degree of thoroughness, and so was ready to receive Denis with a triumphant take-me-or-leave-me defiance. His self-possession, which, with Kathleen, was always enormous, wavered somewhat before Mrs. George, and he didn't quite know how to answer the challenge of her "So you've come, have you." "He'll want to see baby first," Kathleen said, and he didn't now have the nerve to contradict her. The most he could do was to be as unresponsive as possible; so, while Kathleen bent over the baby with love and rapture and then glanced smiling back at Denis to draw him too into this warm scene, he kept his face deadpan and passive. Even if he had felt anything tender at this first sight of his son—which he didn't—he wouldn't have admitted it; the whole thing was just a ghastly mistake, Kathleen's mistake, and Denis couldn't afford to get involved. So he just looked coldly at Kathleen, instead of at the baby, at her thin neck and glasses and at her smile which seemed fatuous to him; and he said, "You've let yourself go rather, haven't you," though as soon as he said it he realized it wasn't quite right, because it suggested that there had in the first place been anything to let go.

"Denis, he's *you*," she said, gazing down into the baby's face. It was kicking its legs, which were red and mottled with baggy nappies slipped down to the knee.

"You needn't rub it in," he replied. "I haven't denied anything." But she didn't get the intended nastiness; she had always been slow to see when she was being offered offense.

Mrs. George joined them in the bedroom, and she too looked down at the baby and said: "Makes you think, don't it." Denis stiffened to the defensive, and not a moment too soon. "I'm sure he's glad to see there's a father somewhere around, after all," Mrs. George continued. "Though what sort of a father—"

"Now Mum," said Kathleen calmly.

"It's time someone spoke out," Mrs. George defied her, "and if you won't, well I'll have my say."

"Kathleen and I have talked things over, Mrs. George," Denis said severely, "and she quite understands my position."

"Be blowed if I do! Disgusting, I call it, getting a girl into trouble and then not doing the rightful—"

"This is intolerable!" cried Denis, looking at Kathleen for help.

"Come down, you must be famished for a cup of tea," she said. He followed her as quickly as dignity would allow. Mrs. George shouted after him from the top of the tiny dark stairs: "Run, rabbit, run!" The baby began to scream, Mrs. George picked it up and rocked it with a fervor which made it scream more: "That's right, love, you tell him," Mrs. George shouted, loud enough to drown his cries and be heard throughout the house, "you tell your father what we think of him!"

Down in the little parlor Denis ran his hand through his thin fair hair. He paced up and down and said: "I shall catch the next train back."

"You mustn't mind," Kathleen said.

"If I'd known that you were going to expose me to such a vulgar attack, I would certainly never have consented to come in the first place."

"You tell him, love!" screamed Mrs. George to the screaming baby.

"I rather flatter myself," said Denis, "that it isn't everybody who would have come the way I have."

"I do appreciate it, Denis," Kathleen said, without irony. "Only Mum is upset—she doesn't understand, you see—"

"I should have thought you had had plenty of time to make her understand!"

"I know, dear."

"Don't call me dear!" He swung round at her, stung by this approach to the domestically intimate.

"Do sit down now, Denis," she said, with some authority, and he sank down on the hard old sofa, which creaked as he did so.

"The cheek of it," Mrs. George was shouting to herself or the baby upstairs, "the nerve."

He leaned his elbows on his knees and his head between his hands: "If you knew all I've been through." She sat beside him and laid her hand on his bowed head. He let it remain there, for he knew she really felt for him and it was good to have someone feeling for him. "What can I do?" he appealed. "You know I'm not ready for marriage yet. I've explained—"

"Yes, you have. It's all right, I don't want you to do anything, I'll be all right, Denis."

"Leaving a girl in the lurch like that!" shouted Mrs. George.

Denis lifted his head and said: "For God's sake, make her shut up."

"She doesn't mean any harm," Kathleen said. "Try not to listen." She herself felt at peace, happy. She had felt like that all through the last months of her pregnancy and ever since the birth of the baby; and, now that Denis had come to visit her, she seemed to have everything.

"I've seen it too often," Denis said. "Men getting married too early and tied up with babies, and not enough money coming in—"

"It is hard," Kathleen agreed.

"I made up my mind long ago: not before I'm thirty and not before I've got a job in a better school with a better scale."

"You're right," Kathleen said, listening with sympathy though she had heard it all often enough.

"What's the use of just mucking along? You want to have a properly ordered life." He was as aware as she was that he had often told her this before, but it made him feel better to say it again, he was explaining himself. Besides, he rather enjoyed talking to her; it recalled those cozy evenings round the gas fire in his bed-sitting room, before all this happened, when she had sat with him and he had felt that at last he was getting the love and understanding he needed, even if it wasn't from a very exciting source.

Mrs. George, the baby dramatically in her arms, came in and said: "A fine sort of schoolteacher you make."

"Come to Mother, dear," said Kathleen, holding out loving arms for the baby.

"What do you teach them poor children? How to get girls into—"

"Mrs. George," said Denis, with dignity, "I have not come here to listen to your cheap taunts."

"My cheap what?"

"I'm taking baby back upstairs," Kathleen said. "Sleepy-time!"

"Cheap what? What did he say?"

Denis desperately followed Kathleen upstairs.

"And my girl?" Mrs. George shouted after him. "What have you made of her schoolteaching?" She began to climb the stairs after him, clutching a rheumatic knee. "That proud we were of our Kathleen—a real lady-teacher—"

"We could just go down to the shops, there's one or two things I ought to get," Kathleen said.

"Come on then," Denis said, "hurry up."

"And now what's to become of her and that mite?"

"I'll wait for you down in the street." He went running down the stairs again, brushing rudely past Mrs. George who had just arrived at the top. "Off again?" she shouted. Denis paced up and down in front of the little brown house. Kathleen appeared, maneuvering a pram down the front step. "What are you doing with that?" he cried.

"Baby likes a bit of fresh air."

"You don't suggest we both— Oh, my God."

Mrs. George had got down the stairs again and stood stern in the doorway: "I suppose some people is born without a sense of shame."

"Come on then," Denis muttered through clenched teeth. Kathleen pushed the pram, and he walked beside it. He was sure that all down the street limp lace curtains stirred and sharp-nosed women whispered and pointed: "There he goes— see, there he is, the father." He marched grimly beside Kathleen. If she thought she could trap him like this, by parading him through the town, she had better think again. He would take the next train back to Birmingham, back to the school, back to the bed-sitting room, back to his independent life, which was his to do what he liked with. The end of his pink-tipped nose quivered, and he felt close to tears. Kathleen was smiling down into the pram, her glasses were slightly askew, her hair draggled over her ears, there was a faint flush on her sallow cheek, and she looked almost drunk with peace and happiness.

Rosie came home from the shop in the evening, and when she saw Denis she put one hand on her hip and rocked her knee: "Well well," she said, "Daddy's come." She kept on looking at him, and he smoothed his hair and fumbled at his tie. It was not only the way she looked and smiled at him that put him out, it was Rosie herself. She was quite unexpected. She was so dark she might have been Spanish, with Spanish eyes and hair and all. Flashy, Denis called her to himself, to get his balance back; she wore a red dress and a lot of lipstick that clashed with it—tarty he added to flashy, but he was still a bit bowled over. She was so very far from what he had expected of Kathleen's sister. Mrs. George stood eagerly behind her, as if she were poking Rosie to go on and say things. But Rosie only looked and rocked her knee, making Denis feel all his physical inadequacies.

Kathleen came to his rescue: "Don't make Denis shy, Rosie," she said, smiling.

Rosie flung back her head in a roar of unladylike laughter: "Shy, is he? I know one occasion he wasn't shy"; and she winked a dirty wink at Denis. He was indignant—but more with Kathleen, for exposing him to this.

When the lodgers came back from work, everyone sat round a table in the tiny parlor for the evening meal. The baby's pram, with the baby sleeping inside, stood by the fire.

"I'm starving," said Rosie, falling to. Denis pecked at his food; he felt very refined in this company. The three lodgers, sturdy silent workingmen in dark clothes, were on their best behavior, sitting with their elbows drawn in and their eyes lowered and imposing a clumsy control on their enormous hands and feet. "You behave yourselves, lads," Rosie told them, "we got a schoolteacher here with us, he'll rap you one over the knuckles soon as look at you."

"Fine sort of a schoolteacher," grumbled Mrs. George.

"What's that you say, Mum?" Rosie inquired in a loud voice. "You got anything to say, then speak up."

"Oh, I'll speak up all right, never fear," her mother retorted in a foreboding voice. The three lodgers chewed their food and tried to make as little noise as possible with their knives and forks.

"We're all friends here," said Rosie. "Nothing hidden, everything clear and aboveboard." The baby gave a wail in its sleep. "See what I mean?" said Rosie. "For all the world to see and hear." Kathleen had jumped up and was solicitously rocking the pram to and fro. "Don't she make a lovely mother?" Rosie said in a terribly warm voice to Denis.

"Only one thing missing," Mrs. George rumbled.

"Third finger left hand," Rosie said.

Denis patted his tie. "Come and sit down, Kathleen," he said in a sharp voice. "Your food'll get cold."

"Isn't he thoughtful?" Rosie asked the lodgers. "Oh, he'll be a good husband for our Kath, won't he, lads?" The lodgers cleared their throats and looked up at the ceiling. "When is it to be?" Rosie turned suddenly on Denis.

He shifted his eyes away from her and said in a precise thin schoolmaster voice: "I was under the impression when I came down here that Kathleen and I would be allowed to discuss things in private."

"Oooh," said Rosie, rounding her mouth and sticking an awed forefinger into it, "don't we talk refined."

"Wish she could have had the baby in private," said Mrs. George bitterly. "But it's difficult to keep a thing like that"—and she rounded her hands in front of her stomach—"private from your neighbors, isn't it."

"Private part's finished now, love," Rosie told him. "We've

come to the public part." She nudged the unresponsive arm of the lodger nearest to her: "You heard that?" she said and gave a roar of laughter.

"That proud we were of her," said Mrs. George. "'Our Kathleen is teaching school up in Birmingham,' I'd tell people, 'she's a proper teacher, been at the Teachers Training College and all.'"

Denis pushed back his chair and got up. "There's pudding to come!" cried Rosie.

"I'll speak to you outside," Denis told Kathleen. She followed him to the door. "When's the next train back to Birmingham?" he said.

"Don't mind them," Kathleen said gently. "They don't mean harm."

"No whisperings out there!" cried Rosie from inside.

"I should never have come," he accused her.

"Oh, Denis, it's been so happy for me having you here." And she said this with such feeling, her eyes behind the glasses shone with such love and happiness, that he felt fortified against her two angry relatives and the three silent lodgers. He was justified, and more than justified, by the mere fact that he was here and making her so happy. She had always had this effect on him: she made him feel significant and wanted and since, without her, it was difficult for him always, or even often, to feel that way, he carried on with her even though she was, in appearance and personality, so far from anything he would have liked.

Rosie came out and said: "Spooning in the dark, eh?" He turned away in indignation, but Kathleen giggled, silly as a child: "Rosie, the things you say."

"Kathleen, the things you do," Rosie retorted. "Or have done to you." She nudged Denis's arm with what he considered offensive familiarity: "You like my turn of humor?"

Mrs. George came out: "He going to sleep here?"

"I'll be making his bed on the sofa," Kathleen said.

"When is there a train back to Birmingham?" Denis asked her.

"Not so fast," said Rosie. "There's one or two things to be settled first."

The lodgers coughed within the door. Rosie opened it and ushered her mother and sister inside and pulled Denis unceremoniously by the sleeve. "Sit down, boys," she told the lodgers, who stood shuffling their feet. "We got no secrets from you."

Denis ostentatiously brushed at the arm of the sleeve by which Rosie had pulled him in. "I wish to catch the next train," he told Kathleen haughtily.

"You'll be wishing to take your family with you, no doubt," said Rosie.

"Wishing to? He'll be having to," Mrs. George put in grimly.

Denis suddenly cried: "I'll not be forced into anything!" He was trembling and running his hands through his thin hair. He got like that at school sometimes, when he found the boys too much for him; then he paced up and down on his dais in front of the blackboard, running his hands through his hair and scolding in a quivering and unnaturally high-pitched voice. He tried to pace up and down the room now, but stumbled over one of the lodgers' large black boots.

"Oh, Denis," said Kathleen in a voice full of calm compassion, "why do you get upset."

"Let him do the needful," said Rosie, "then there'll be no need to get upset." Denis looked at her with hate but had to note again that, tarty she might be, flashy she might be, but she was still uncommonly good-looking. In face of this, he did his best to restore himself to his dignity and replied in a precise voice which deliberately stressed his own refined accent in contrast to her very unrefined one: "I hope I may be allowed to judge my own right course of action."

"Blimey," said Rosie, "what's that mean now."

"Coming here," said Mrs. George, "talking big . . ."

"It means," explained Denis, feeling a bit more pleased with himself, "that I hope I know my duty as well as anybody else."

"And that means you're going to marry her?" said Rosie with narrowed eyes.

"Certainly," replied Denis without hesitation, "if that's what Kathleen wishes." He jerked his cuffs from out of his coat sleeves and felt master of the situation. He didn't care what he was committing himself to—all that could be sorted out later—he only cared about redeeming his personality before Rosie and the lodgers and the ill-disposed Mrs. George.

"Come on, boys," Rosie said to the lodgers, "this calls for a drink."

"Why do you make Denis say things he doesn't want to say," Kathleen said in a tone of gentle reproach. This tone had always been very effective with erring schoolchildren who, seeing her so sad, had burst into tears and cried "Oh, Miss!"

But it made Denis angry. He turned on her and snapped: "Leave it to me to decide what I want to say and what I don't."

Rosie came to back him up: "Don't you start confusing the issue now, Kathleen." He liked being backed up by Rosie, it gave him a feeling of security and of being on the right side.

"As long as we know where we stand," Mrs. George said suspiciously.

"I think I am a man of my word, Mrs. George," Denis said with proud dignity.

"We'll talk about it in the morning," Kathleen said in a soothing way, as if everybody were drunk.

"We'll go to the Registry Office in the morning," Rosie challenged Denis.

He spread his arms as if to say, I am ready. He was pleased with the effect he had made: he had coolly taken the wind out of their sails, so now there they were, a bit foolish and not quite knowing what attitude to take up toward him. He paced up and down the room, as much at ease as if he were in his own classroom; and, when he again stumbled over one of the lodgers' boots, he gave an ironic little bow of apology which made the lodger blush beetroot.

"It's a bargain then," said Rosie.

"A bargain," Denis agreed playfully. He looked at her with pleasure, almost congratulating himself on her good looks, as if it were she he was going to marry.

"I suppose we'll have to say better late than never," Mrs. George conceded grudgingly.

"We'll talk about it in the morning," Kathleen said again, but no one listened to her. They all, including Denis, went to bed in a highly satisfied state of mind. The lodgers too were pleased, they had been invited to the Registry Office and a drink to celebrate afterward and were looking forward to it; it would make a really nice change for them.

Denis woke up in the middle of the night and realized that he had committed himself to get married in the morning. He thought how it would be if he took his little suitcase in hand and sneaked off to the station. Only he didn't know what time there was a train to Birmingham, and Rosie might follow him to the station to find him sitting there waiting, and then he would have to come back with her, led home like a dog. He couldn't face Rosie again except the way he had faced her in the evening: as a man resolute in purpose and prepared for marriage. He groaned and jumped up from the hard sofa on which they had bedded him. He couldn't bear the loneliness of his dilemma and wanted to find Kathleen. He groped his way up the narrow stairs in darkness, but when he had got to the top he didn't know where Kathleen was. Heavy snores came in threesome chorus from the lodgers' room; once, the stream of sound stopped, caught up in a startled snort, and Denis only dared breathe again when it continued.

He was terribly afraid of waking up the lodgers and having them find him on the stairs; they would raise the alarm and haul him up before Rosie and Mrs. George. Mrs. George would be even more horrible at night than she was by day; Denis pictured her toothless and—from literary memory rather than from any actual experience—in a nightcap. And Rosie? He thought experimentally of a flamingo nightdress; he also imagined curlers in her hair, but even they became her. Standing on the tiny landing, his heart beating to the snores of the lodgers, he wondered where not Kathleen but Rosie was. She would be lying in bed, all large and warm, and maybe her eyes were open, glittering in the dark; he couldn't imagine her sleeping, only sharp and awake. What would she say to him if he blundered by mistake into her room? Perhaps she was waiting for him: she looked the kind of girl who waited for men to come to her at night. He imagined himself caught up in her warm bed, devoured by her arms and thighs, and stood there in his striped pajamas with his mouth open and a great desire on him. But then the baby started up, and after a while he heard Kathleen making comforting noises at it. He remembered what he had come for and called to her cautiously through the door. She appeared at once, holding the baby. "Come down," he said to her without further explanation.

She put the baby back to sleep and joined him down on the sofa in the parlor. He was lying inside the blankets, but he didn't invite her in, so she sat at one end and hugged herself with both arms to keep warm. He said grimly: "Fine mess you've got me into."

"Oh Denis, you don't really have to—"

"Then what?" he turned on her. "A nice fool I'll look, after the way I promised."

"It's all right. I'll explain."

"Explain," he repeated contemptuously.

"Honestly, Denis," she said, convinced and convincing, "I

don't want you to marry me. You don't have to worry about me. I'll be all right."

"What will you do?" he asked grudgingly.

"Oh, I'll get some job teaching—you know I love teaching and there's always a demand. Mum can look after baby while I'm at school." She sounded so cheerful and it all seemed quite easy and practical, so that he really didn't see why she shouldn't.

"You feeling cold?"

"I'm all right," she said, rubbing the tops of her arms.

"Want to come in?" and he slightly lifted his blankets.

She crept in gratefully and stayed right up till it was almost dawn.

In the morning Mrs. George, Rosie, and the lodgers all came down dressed in their best. "Ready?" Rosie said to Denis with a challenge to which he at once rose. He met her look with one equally bold and said "Certainly" in a haughty voice; not for anything, not with full realization of all the consequences, would he have budged from this position. But everyone was shocked when Kathleen came dressed in her usual dingy housedress with an apron round her. "Not very bridal, are you," Rosie said. Kathleen smiled and said: "It was all only a joke."

"A joke!" cried Rosie and Mrs. George, and the lodgers clicked their tongues, they were that shocked.

"*We* wasn't joking," Rosie said grimly at Denis.

"Now don't be silly, Rosie," Kathleen said in a sensible voice and knelt down to clean the grate.

"He's been talking to her!" cried Mrs. George, shooting an accusing forefinger at Denis.

"Shame," murmured the lodgers.

"What you been telling her?" Rosie asked with narrowed eyes.

"Telling her?" said Denis, righteous and innocent.

"Then what's she carrying on like that for?"

"He's been bullying her!" cried Mrs. George.

Denis looked furiously at Kathleen's back crouched over the fireplace. "Go and change," he told her. "You can't come like this."

"Come where?" said Kathleen.

"Oh, my God," Rosie said, "do we have to start all over again?"

"Go on!" Denis shouted at Kathleen. She turned round and saw him so angry that, with a resigned sigh, she got to her feet and went upstairs at once.

When she came down again, she was wearing her Sunday suit, which was a bit old-fashioned but still in good condition. "That's better," Rosie commented. "Now we can be proud of our bride."

"It's not right," Kathleen said miserably.

"You leave it to me to say what's right and what's not," Denis told her in a state of high exasperation.

"I'll get the pram out," Kathleen said.

They went down the street in what was almost a procession. Denis walked in front, hemmed in by the three lodgers square and sturdy in their navy blue suits; he marched between them with a firm tread, ignoring them, determined to look free and willing. Behind them came Rosie and Mrs. George. Rosie waved and smiled right and left at the people down the street who stood watching them from behind their curtains or openly from their doorsteps. Kathleen, pushing the baby in its pram, made up the rear; she had her head down and looked a most reluctant bride.

(1961)

In Love with a Beautiful Girl

ALTHOUGH AFTER A FEW MONTHS THERE THE IDEA OF India was still exciting to Richard, the place itself and especially his daily life in it had become dull. He had rented an expensive, up-to-date flat in an area full of other such flats and of people (mostly non-Indians) very much like himself in status, income, and way of living. Even when he went visiting away from his part of the town, it was only to go to similar places with similar flats and similar parties and similar people giving them. Life for Western man, it seemed, ran very much to a pattern in India, and so did Western man himself. Richard, however, did not think of himself as being identical with other people, and he certainly did not find much point of contact with his colleagues at the High Commission, or with those others who made up the circles in which he was expected to move. They all seemed to him very much in the tradition of the white man in the colonies, and the fact that the tradition had been broken did not make any difference in their personalities. Nowadays, they were expected to pay tribute to Indian culture in art, architecture, dance, and so forth, to have some carefully selected Indian friends, and occasionally to serve Indian curries at their parties, but once these requirements were fulfilled they were free to follow their natural inclinations and speak negatively of the weather, the servants, and (after the Indian friends had gone home) of the Indian character.

The only apparent alternative to this, Richard discovered,

was to go eccentric. One avoided the social round and concentrated, Indian style, on developing the soul, or the self, or whatever it was that clamored for deliverance. This was the way taken mostly by unattached lady secretaries at the High Commission or librarians of the British Council, who took to wearing a sari and traveling round the country in third-class railway carriages. Most of them went very eccentric indeed and were not a pleasure to know, but there were exceptions, and one such was Mary, with whom Richard became friendly. She was not the sort of girl he would have chosen if the range had been wider. Himself slender, lively, and good-looking, he had a leaning toward very decorative girls, and decorative Mary decidedly was not. She was heavily built, with big hips and legs, and the clothes she wore did not minimize this defect. She had nice eyes, though—clear and of an honest blue—and an easy manner that won her many Indian friends. She was good-humored about letting eager Indian youths get into conversation with her in public places, and she would invite them home to her flat. They brought their friends, and she played the gramophone and mixed drinks for them and let them read T. S. Eliot aloud to her.

    She and Richard had a pleasant friendship. They had the same sort of liberal mind and agreed on basic attitudes, which made them automatically allies in the colonial-style English society in which they found themselves. They spent much of their free time together, and they always found something amusing to talk about, even if it was only the antics of their fellow Britons. They also liked to talk about India and swap their impressions of the country. It was an agreeable relationship, though in many ways dissatisfying to Richard, especially when he stopped to think how many hours he spent having amusing conversation with Mary at her place or in his own smart flat, with the up-to-date decor and the air conditioner going, when outside lay what he had grown up to think of as the most passionate, beautiful, and mysterious country in the world.

When he met Ruchira, he was more than ready for her. She was beautiful, mysterious to him, and, he was sure—it could not be otherwise—passionate. He courted her assiduously and was well received. Fortunately, she came from a family that prided itself on being modern and forward-looking, so that no difficulties were put in the way of his seeing her. On the contrary, he was encouraged to visit the house frequently, and whenever he did he was first held in conversation by Ruchira's father, who had been at Oxford and liked to talk about those halcyon days. The house was large and beautifully kept by many unobtrusive servants—full of flowers and chandeliers and, here and there, tiny glittering golden gods that were kept apparently for decoration rather than devotion. The family was an exceptionally good-looking one, with several handsome brothers running up and down the stairs with tennis rackets or driving away at top speed in sports cars. The mother was elegant and faded, with an air of melancholy because she was an aging beauty and an air of distinction because she came from a royal house and was called Princess. These graceful people and the graceful house in which they lived were, for Richard, a most pleasing setting for the jewel that was the object of his attentions. Here Ruchira's charms were seen to their full advantage. What better place for her laughter to echo in than these tall airy rooms, her slender young figure to move in than that garden of velvet green lawns and old trees? It was all an ideal he might have dreamed of in his undergraduate days, or before that, when he was a schoolboy and wrote poetry.

Ruchira, however, thought her home dull and old-fashioned, and longed for those worlds of Western sophistication to which she hoped Richard would introduce her. He did, in fact, introduce her quite soon to Mary, and this was a great success with Ruchira. She loved Mary's flat and all those books; she sat on the floor and had a gimlet and a cigarette and said how much at home she felt. Actually, though, she did not look very much at home; she was too glamorous for the place. In silver earrings and a very soft silk sari of white and silver, her long wide eyes brilliant with excitement, she sparkled like a crystal chandelier fit for some raja's palace but not for Mary's modern-intellectual apartment. The gimlet took quick effect, and she talked rather more and more freely than she might have done without it. She spoke of her love for literature and her longing for—she couldn't quite express it, but something different from what she had hitherto experienced: for a life of books, thought, emotion, and, above all, of interesting people. She wanted to meet many interesting people—artists and writers and such, famous tennis players, film directors, anyone, indeed, who had ever done anything memorable. She asked eager questions about Paris, which had always been her ideal (the painters, the sidewalk cafés) and to which her father had promised to send her as soon as the foreign-exchange situation eased a little. She would study something there, she wasn't yet quite sure what. Of course, painting would be the most logical choice, but art had never been her best subject. What else was there? Literature? Leatherwork? Perhaps Richard and Mary could suggest something? She looked up at them eagerly, radiant, and Richard was grateful to Mary for being charmed by her and for answering her quite seriously, weighing possibilities with her.

Afterward, when Richard drove her home, they were both of them intoxicated—he with her, and she with three gimlets and the exciting evening she had spent. She said she liked and admired Mary very, very much. She asked a lot of questions about her. She said she had always wanted to meet someone like that—intellectual, well-read; there were not many such people in the world Ruchira's family inhabited. Her brothers and their friends, she said, didn't care for the intellectual life at all; only sports and dancing and a good time, that was all they wanted. And her mother—well, he knew what Mummy was like: never opened a book in her life, and when she saw Ruchira reading would tell her she was spoiling her eyes. So to meet someone like Mary was a revelation, and such a nice person, too, and she wasn't really bad-looking. Her eyes were good, and perhaps if she dressed a bit better . . . But of course a person like Mary could never be bothered to think about clothes; that was too silly and frivolous. Ruchira, too, had no time to spare for people who thought of nothing but what to wear. Richard, driving his car, glanced sideways at her and said, "That's a marvelous sari you've got on," and she looked down at it and smoothed it over her lap with an involuntary little smile. He stopped the car and regarded her with the frankest admiration.

"Are we home?" she said, peering out of the window.

"Nearly," he said. He got out of the car and went round to the other side and opened the door for her. "Would you care for a walk?"

She was first astonished, then delighted. "*Cra-zy!*" she exclaimed as she got out of the car. They were outside a park that was locked, but it was easy to climb over the barrier. He leaped over first, then turned to help her get across more carefully, so as not to rip her sari. Her hand lay lightly in his, but she hardly noticed; she was busy looking down at herself to make sure nothing happened to her sari. When she had got safely over, she exclaimed, "*Cra-zy!*" again and, with a laugh, ran ahead of him down the path in a spirit of adventure.

The deserted park had a sixteenth-century mausoleum in it and was flooded with moonlight. Ruchira, a slim shape glittering in white and silver, ran swiftly over the grass and up the steps of the mausoleum, but she didn't go in. It was dark inside, and the stone tombs could just be made out as three long, eerie shapes by the moonlight that filtered in through the latticed walls. She stood in the entrance and gave a little shudder. He said, "Awful to be dead, isn't it?" Bats squeaked high up in the vaulted dome.

"There is an Urdu couplet," she said. "It goes, '*Jin ke mahalon men hazaron rang ke*' something, something . . . Very beautiful. I'm so fond of poetry, but I have a terrible memory. These are very old tombs. Hundreds of years. How old is Mary?"

"Hundreds of years."

"Stupid." She gave him a chaste little push. "Doesn't she want to get married? Will she always stay single, you think?" And before he had time to say anything, she added, "Does she believe in free love?" She looked at him eagerly.

He wasn't very old—about twenty-five—but it was many years since anybody had seriously asked him anything like this. He looked back at her in loving amusement and countered her question with "Do you?"

He saw her expression change. A moment's doubt or fright, mixed with excitement, flitted across it. Then she laughed and ran away from him down the steps of the mausoleum. He followed and sat down on the lowest step. "Well, do you?" he said.

She stood in front of him, and, looking up at her, he saw her head flung back, her throat in a curve of defiance. "I hate our system of arranged marriage," she said. "I don't want that. I want to be free like Mary, and I want to love also and to be loved."

"Sit down," he said, and she recklessly did. Now they were so close together that he could feel her warm body breathing. She was very excited, but brave, too. She looked straight into his face and dared him to do his worst.

He kissed her. Her body was tense and her lips dry, but she kept quite still. She had a superb smell, which was not only perfume but something else, more mysterious and feminine than anything he had before encountered. Her soft, dusky skin also felt different. Perhaps it was because she was Indian, perhaps because she was more beautiful than anyone else he had ever kissed. He took his lips from hers and buried his face in her hair. But she had had enough. She pushed him away, which was easy, he was so weak with love, and got up. "Mummy'll wonder what's happened. She always waits up for me. I've told her hundreds of times don't, but she's so— Be careful, there is a ditch here. That would be funny if you fell in, wouldn't it?" All the way home, she was in a much better mood than he was. In fact, she seemed distinctly pleased with herself, and excited and full of wonder and admiration at what she had allowed him to do.

RICHARD LIKED TO think of himself as a cool sort of person, and he was. True, he had always been fond of girls and had a flair for affairs—he was rarely uninvolved in one—but he had always known how to measure himself out, how much to give and how much to keep back, so that these liaisons, although never short on emotion, did not consume a larger slice of his life than he meant them to. With Ruchira, for the first time, he lost control. His response to her was more abundant than anything he had known before, and flowed, moreover, beyond the girl herself, into the country that was hers. He no longer knew where it was Ruchira he loved and where India. Suddenly, after months of lying quiet, his feeling for the place took fire. He listened to Indian music, not evaluating it coolly, as he had done before, but with a leap of the heart, feeling Ruchira herself or his rich feelings for her in each strange, throbbing note. He visited museums and looked at frescoes and sculptures, and although Ruchira herself was slim, even willowy, he identified her with those heavy-breasted, wide-hipped Hindu beauties, and reveled in their sensuousness because he thought it was hers. But it wasn't only in art and museums that he sought and found her;

it was everywhere—in the streets, the sky, the air, in flowers and water and trees. Sometimes, mad with longing, he would get up in the middle of the night and go out into the streets to savor the silence, and the sky and moon overhead, and a ruined mosque with a jasmine bush growing in its compound. He read Indian legends and became acquainted with many gods and tried to understand about the silver and the shell, the serpent and the rope. The smell of incense filled him with desires.

Mary, however, talked about Ruchira just as if she were any other girl. She even compared her to all those youths who came and read poetry in her flat and listened to records. "Not," said Mary, "because they're all that keen on literature and music but because they think these things stand for a glamorous, cosmopolitan life." Like Ruchira, she said, what they really enjoyed were the gimlets and the cigarettes and the doing something different from everybody else. Richard argued that that wasn't unlike adolescents everywhere, but Mary said that what made it strange was the certainty of what they would go back to when this phase was over for them. "Religion, caste, joint family—the lot. They'll be as staunch supporters as everybody else."

"And Ruchira?" he asked. He loved talking about her and hearing her talked about, no matter what was said.

"Oh, that's easy," said Mary. "She'll marry someone rich and buy a lot of beautiful saris."

Richard laughed. He could not claim that this was unfair or that it left out of account Ruchira's spiritual riches. He didn't believe in those spiritual riches—didn't, in fact, want them for her; she was enough as she was. And he liked the idea of her buying a lot of beautiful saris. He could see her doing it, in some expensive shop, surrounded by silks and obsequious salesmen, with a deep look of satisfaction in her eyes.

He always enjoyed visiting Ruchira in her house. The whole atmosphere of the house pleased him—that sense of leisure, money, and unquestioned status which had disappeared in England before Richard was born but which Ruchira's family still enjoyed as an unshakable birthright. Ruchira's father poured Scotch whiskey for Richard and talked to him of the Oxford he had known in the thirties, of his wine merchant there and his tailor and his dear old bedmaker, Mr. Norris. And Ruchira's mother, the Princess, who was to be found at any hour of the day in her drawing room drinking cups of tea from a dainty tray and wearing long diamond earrings, would invite him to join her. Conversation with her was strange but not disagreeable. She would ask him his views on compulsory birth control or some such topic of current interest, and in between her questions there would be long silences while she stirred her tea and sighed and looked out of the window. What Richard liked best was to sit with Ruchira on one of the verandas overlooking the garden, on a swinging sofa, heaped with cushions, that was large and broad enough to sleep on. They would drink iced lime water and look at the huge leather-bound family albums—at photographs of Ruchira's paternal grandfather in a high stiff collar and a pince-nez, or her maternal grandfather smothered in gold brocade and a turban that came down almost over his eyes, sitting cross-legged under a canopy and having a fly whisk waved over him.

But Ruchira quickly grew tired of staying home doing nothing and demanded to be taken out. At first, she was satisfied for the two of them to go on solitary strolls in romantic ruins. She picked flowers and wound them in her hair and urged him to recite English poetry to her. But after about half a dozen such strolls—during each of which she allowed one kiss, none of them ever leading to anything further and each one of exactly the same quality and duration as the first—she asked for something more exciting. What she wanted most was to be introduced to interesting people. She was forever questioning him not only about Mary but about all his colleagues and their wives and anyone else he might know from other embassies. But he did not want to introduce her to any of these. They were too dull, pompous, conventional, and not worthy of her, and he steadfastly refused to let her accompany him to any of the dreary cocktail parties and receptions that he had to attend. The only party that he ever took her to was an "unconventional," nondiplomatic one given by Mary, and this did not turn out to be enjoyable for Ruchira.

What had she expected? Certainly, it appeared, something very different from what she found. The party was to have been very informal—gay, impossible—and with this end in view cushions were strewn on the floor and the latest hit records played on the record player. Nevertheless, the atmosphere remained formal, and the guests seemed unable to relax. They were mostly the young men who so often came to visit Mary—students, clerks, airmen, who normally made themselves very much at home in the place. But today they felt constrained because it was a party. They knew that at a party one had to behave in a certain manner, and they hoped to pick up the knack as they went along. None of them seemed to have realized how informal the affair was meant to be, and had come in what were rather obviously their best suits; this made it difficult for them to relax on the floor as they usually did, and though they tried their best to look easy against the casual cushions strewn all over, the creases in their trousers kept them stiff as cardboard. All of Mary's social tact and easy manners failed to get the party going. Every now and again her determined efforts induced a little spurt of animation, but it always died down very quickly and left the guests eyeing each other suspiciously or staring into space with a constipated expression. Even those who were usually very friendly together were today like people who didn't want to trust each other and didn't want to be caught out—wary tourists trapped in unfamiliar territory.

Ruchira did not sit on the floor but remained stiffly in a chair. Like the other guests, she was dressed too elaborately for the occasion, in a pale-rose brocade sari and rather a lot of expensive jewelry. Her eyes were lowered, and she did not make any attempts at conversation. When Richard tried to talk to her, she would only answer in monosyllables. He was no more successful with the other guests, among whom he tried to mingle, and when his eyes occasionally met Mary's they both shrugged and looked at each other in amused consternation. At one stage, Ruchira disappeared from the room and Richard found her in Mary's bedroom. She was sitting on the edge of Mary's bed, her hands in her lap, staring sulkily at the wall. She didn't stir when he came in. "What's the matter?" he said.

She gave, so lightly as to be almost imperceptible, that upward toss of the head and downward twist of the mouth with which Indian women express displeasure and contempt.

"You want a drink or something?"

"When you have finished enjoying your friend's party," she said, "I'm ready to go home."

"Now, what's this?" he said, and sat down beside her and laid his arm round her shoulders. At once, she jerked forward, saying fiercely, "Don't touch me!"

"You're being absolutely silly." He succeeded in sounding English and cool, but he didn't feel that way. Her perfume pervaded Mary's bookish bedroom; her gold necklace, set with rubies and pearls, sparkled round her neck. He had to check a desire to get down on the floor and bury his face in her pale-rose lap.

"All right, so I'm silly, but please take me home."

He looked at her quizzically, one eyebrow raised, the way he had looked at other, earlier girlfriends when he had been displeased with them. This made her drop her haughty manner and say, "It's such a horrible party. Why did you bring me here? I'm bored, there's no one to speak with—"

"I'm here. Mary's here."

"Mary!"

"You said you liked her."

"Why should I like her? She's only an old maid. And all those awful people she has asked to her party—no one like that would ever be invited to our house, and if Mummy knew you made me meet such people—" He took her hands, but she snatched them away and cried, "I suppose she thinks I'm not good enough for her English friends!"

He was appalled. There was such a large-scale misunderstanding here that he didn't know where to start clearing it up. He tried not only that evening but for several days afterward, but never with the slightest success. Ruchira was not interested in listening to explanations; she didn't want to be reasoned with. She would listen only to the promptings of her own heart, and these were too strong to be affected by anything he might have to say. She was immensely proud, immensely intolerant, utterly unfair. And he loved her all the more for it, for being so strong and unreasonable, like some force of nature—a monsoon storm or a tiger in a jungle. How insipid by comparison were the pleasures to be derived from talking with Mary, even though they did agree on so many things and had the same sense of humor. Ruchira had no sense of humor at all—or, rather, a very simple one; she thought it funny when people fell down or bumped their heads—but it didn't matter to him. When they were together, he laughed differently, not with her but always at her, out of a deep delight with the way she was.

HE SAW LESS and less of Mary—indeed, of everyone he had known hitherto—and was not as meticulous in the performance of his duties as he ought to have been. All he wanted was to be with Ruchira, and when he couldn't be with her, he preferred to be alone to think about her, to read, study, listen to Indian music on records. He became quite knowledgeable about certain aspects of India—could, for instance, talk intelligently on the various exponents of Bharata Natyam or the differences between Shankaracharya's and Ramanuja's commentaries on the Vedanta Sutras—and he liked to spread all this new information before Ruchira, who seemed impressed and nodded at everything he said and contributed, "Yes, we have a very ancient culture. Many foreigners like Max Müller have come to study our philosophy." Then he laughed and tried to kiss her, whereupon she pushed him away and jumped up. The time for being serious was over, and she cried, "Come on, let's go!" and ran to sit in his car. Often, nowadays, she made him take her out dancing; she had been taught by her brothers and danced supremely well, but he couldn't do much more than walk her stiffly round the floor. She had a lot of fun laughing at him and trying to teach him, and she loved being there with him in a crowded restaurant. He liked it, too, although the food was dreadful, and so was the interior decoration, and the band was very loud and not always in tune. But the floor was packed with gay young Indians, all of them superb dancers, their supple bodies twisting and shaking, and the girls all kicked off their shoes and were lightly dancing on slim brown feet.

Sometimes, when they were at her house for too long and he didn't take her out anywhere, Ruchira became very melancholy. She would sit on the swinging sofa, holding on to one of its ropes and leaning her head against her arm and pushing herself with her feet into gentle, lazy motion. She would look out into the garden, at the prize chrysanthemums, the rose creepers, the pigeons, and the butterflies, but without taking pleasure in anything she saw. At such times, she didn't care for him to share the swing with her, so he would sit on the top step of the veranda, looking up at her and waiting for her to become more responsive. From time to time, Ruchira's mother would call some question out of the drawing room, where she was drinking her unending cups of tea, and sometimes her face, framed in long swinging diamond earrings, would peer out at them through the French windows, looking worried, and Ruchira would say irritably, "We're all *right*." The Princess would withdraw, and Ruchira's feet would give an angry push to the swing, which made it go to and fro in irritable jerks.

On one such occasion, when her mother had disappeared, Ruchira burst out, "I'm so tired of it, why can't she leave me *alone!*" and hid her face against the arm holding the rope of the swing. Richard didn't say anything but continued sitting on the step of the veranda in a sympathetic attitude.

"I thought when I left college everything would be different. I'd been so looking forward to this time, and now it's the same, the same, the same every day!" She was wearing a garland of jasmine blossoms in her hair, and, impatient to be fiddling with something, she took it off and tried to tie it round her wrist instead. "I thought I was going to do such a lot," she said as she tied. "I was going to visit so many places, different countries, and meet people—"

"Ruchi?" called the Princess from inside.

"Yes, yes, yes!"

"All right," the Princess said mildly, and probably poured herself another cup of tea.

Richard said, "Why don't you marry me, and then you can go to all sorts of places with me."

After a short pause, she said, "You're only saying it because you feel sorry for me."

"No," he said. "As a matter of fact, I've been thinking of it for ages."

This was not strictly true. He had not thought of himself as getting married. He enjoyed being by himself and had intended to stay single for some years to come. His feelings for Ruchira were, he thought, too *different* to be mixed up with thoughts of marriage, and although he had sometimes wondered how he would be able to part from her when the time came for him to be posted to some other country, to think of taking her away with him seemed no more realistic than to think of taking away India itself. She belonged here. Nowhere else was good enough for her—no other country, indeed, no other city but this one of ruins and gardens and fantastic moonlit nights. He would not have dared remove her from her setting.

He ought to have known there was nothing she wanted more. Although she did not commit herself on that first day when he asked her, nor on subsequent occasions when they returned to the subject—and she often returned to it—she was certainly very interested in all he might have to offer her. The idea of being a foreign diplomat's wife pleased her, and she had many questions to ask, such as where he might expect to be posted next, and whether one had to give and go to very many parties, and how long it would be before he expected to be a full ambassador. Her questions made him laugh, and she herself made him laugh, too—the way she did not in the least pretend to care for him but only for what he could offer her. He teased her about it, became mock plaintive, and asked, "And me?"

"Oh, you," she said, and tossed her head. "Who cares about you?" But then she put her hands on his shoulders and looked into his face with deep, promising eyes, so that he felt that afterward—after he had satisfied all her conditions, and she had allowed him to marry her—she would love him. The thought of that excited him so much that he felt he must do everything she wanted, for now he had forgotten about not intending to get married and was only afraid that he would lose her. And for fear of that he dared not admit to her what had been becoming more and more clear to him for the past year—that he was not cut out to be a diplomat and would never do well. Before he and Ruchira had started talking about the future together, he had, in fact, already half-decided to leave the service and had toyed with all sorts of other delightful possibilities. He would return to Cambridge and study anthropology, or take a teaching job in America, or live cheaply in Spain. Now he could no longer think about these things but, for her sake, had to pretend to himself that he liked it where he was and that one day he would become an ambassador and she—how distinguished a figure she would make!—an ambassadress.

He began to take her to those cocktail parties and receptions that were to him an unpleasant duty but to her a promised land. And at once, from the very first one he took her to, he realized that she had been right and he wrong. This was all the more strange because the first party was what, left to himself, he would have regarded as a particularly dreary one. It was given by one of the trade commissioners, a red-faced man with a red-faced wife, both of whom Richard and Mary had always considered exceptionally dull and colonial. Their house was furnished in conventional English style, but with those few Indian touches (carved Kashmiri tables, and papier-mâché cigarette boxes decorated with Mogul horsemen in turbans) that were nowadays obligatory as part of the new policy of cultural contact. The guests were most of them very much like the hosts, which was not surprising, since they did the same kind of job, lived in the same way, had had the same education, and talked with the same accent about the same things (transfers and postings, house-rent allowance, children's schooling). Everyone looked rather alike—even the women, who all wore ill-fitting dresses made of shimmering Indian silks that had been meant for better things.

Ruchira, however, was enchanted—by the place, the people, the party, everything. She wore a brocade sari, and its myriad-colored threads were caught in the light now as pink and now as gold. Her eyes sparkled, and she smiled so expectantly that her fellow guests, who were not usually attentive to strangers, smiled back at her, showing their bad English teeth, and talked to her about the weather and the merits of various hill stations. She met them more than halfway, holding conversation on any subject presented to her and exchanging platitude for platitude, but her face was so full of vivacity and happiness that while her lips moved and spoke one thing, what she was actually saying was something quite different: *"O brave new world that has such people in it!"* And so impressed was she by the manner in which everyone spoke that her voice began to change, and to the best of her ability she, too, spoke flat phrases in flat English accents. She mentioned to several people how much her father had enjoyed his years at Oxford. She ate salami, olives, dainty canapés; she drank sherry. Once, when no one was looking, she squeezed Richard's hand and then burst out laughing, while her eyes roved impatiently round the room to see who next would come up and make conversation with her.

THE ONLY PARTIES she refused to go to were farewells for Mary, who was posted back to England just about this time. Nor did she want Richard to go to them, which meant that he saw nothing of Mary until about two days before her departure, when he managed to get to her flat. Most of her furniture had already gone, and she was in the process of packing up the rest of her belongings, helped by several of her young men, who were eagerly scrabbling among packing cases and little heaps of discarded goods. Mary was busy—she seemed to be the only one seriously packing—but she found time to sit with Richard for a moment in a corner of the room. Out of habit, he looked round to see whether there were any interesting new books he could borrow from her, but of course there weren't; everything had gone, the shelves were empty.

She didn't reproach him, not even jokingly, for having dropped her so abruptly, but she did ask him quite soon why she had never been allowed to see Ruchira again. Richard looked a bit embarrassed, and she said, "It was that awful party, wasn't it?" and without waiting for him to confirm this went on, "I never seem to be able to do anything right here, you know? There's always some misunderstanding."

One of the young men showed her a corkscrew, broken but with a decorative wooden head to it, and, eyes modestly lowered, asked her what to do with it.

"Oh, just chuck it away," she said absently, and turned back to Richard. "In some ways, I'm actually glad I'm going."

"It is to be thrown away?" the young man asked her. Suddenly he lifted his bashfully lowered eyes, radiant with hope as they looked at her. "Can I take it away?"

"But it's *broken*, Rajee." Nevertheless, he bore it off, gazing at it in love and triumph, and for the rest of Richard's visit young men came up bearing useless objects that they asked for permission to take away.

"It isn't that I didn't like it here," Mary said. "But it's been so ridiculous. I mean, here was I doing my absolute utmost not to be the English lady from the High Commission, only to find that that's precisely why I'm made friends with—not because I'm Mary, with lots of liberal ideas and unconventional attitudes, but because I've got duty-free liquor and the latest records."

"So what?" Richard said.

"So nothing, but it's humiliating to be loved only for what one values least—one's broken corkscrews."

"What's it matter what you're loved for, as long as you *are*?" Richard said. And, intercepting a surprised look from Mary, he went on, quite harshly, "Why the hell should anyone love us for ourselves? We're not all that bloody marvelous, are we?"

She didn't answer. In fact, she suddenly remembered that she was in the middle of her packing. She got up and attempted to close a suitcase, and all the young men sat on it to help her. They laughed and kicked their legs in the air and had a lot of fun and jokes.

AFTER HE LEFT Mary, Richard drove straight to Ruchira's house. They were due to go to the Flag Day celebration at the Swedish Embassy. Ruchira wasn't quite ready yet—it always took her hours to get ready for these parties—so he sat in the garden to wait for her. It was very still in the garden, and warm and full of scents; the moon was bright silver. Once, Ruchira leaned out of her lighted upstairs window and called down to him, "Won't be a sec!" She was brushing her hair and wearing her white-and-silver sari, which he thought of as her moonlight sari. He wished they didn't have to go but could sit here in white wicker armchairs and play cards and perhaps listen to music. Some of the trees in the garden were squat and round, others tall and pointed, but all were black and absolutely still, as if they weren't trees at all but something painted or cut out against the sky, which shone like silver paper. Richard thought of a miniature he had once seen—a lady and her lover reclining on cushions; it was night, but fountains sparkled, flowers bloomed, girl musicians played on viols, and far and shadowy in the distance a city slept, amid dark hills and trees. The lady's breasts were uncovered and hung about with pearls that gleamed in the moonlight. Richard shut his eyes and didn't know whether the too sweet scent of night flowers that assailed him came from the garden or from his memory of the miniature.

Ruchira, shimmering in her white and silver, moved lightly across the lawn, full of energy and impatient to be off. He held out his hand to her and, when she failed to take it, touched her wrist. "Don't you know you're supposed to stand up for a lady?" she said. "Anyway, stop lounging, it's late."

"Sit with me for a minute," he pleaded in a lazy voice.

"It's late," she repeated, but she sat down—not so much, it turned out, to oblige him as to be able to readjust the bracelet on her wrist. "I hate to be late," she said as she did this. "I mean, half an hour is all right, you're supposed to be late by half an hour, but not more. That's rude, *and* you miss all the fun— There's something wrong with the catch." She imperiously held out her arm to him, and he began to fiddle with the bracelet. "Carol Bennett is going to be there. I have to see her and fix up about Thursday morning at the pool. I like Carol, she's nice— Oh, I suppose you think only your Mary is nice, with her fat legs and all those books she has. Everybody likes reading and books and all that, but, good heavens, what's the use of making a fetish out of it the way she does? I mean, first you have to live. How can you know about anything unless you've actually lived? Haven't you finished with that yet? You *are* slow."

"I think there's a screw missing."

"I think you have a screw missing." She laughed at her joke, throwing back her head; her teeth gleamed, her laughter was high, girlish, and clear. "Oh, leave it. Never mind." She took the bracelet off and stuffed it into his pocket. "And don't forget to give it back," she said, and slapped him playfully on the cheek. "Ready? Well, you look *almost* all right. Mummy, we're going!" When there was no answer, she said, "I suppose she's in her bath. When she is not drinking tea, then she is having a bath—that's my poor mother. Give me the keys, I'll drive. No, I want to, you drive so slowly. Let's get some zip into her. I can't understand why you have that car, anyway. Why don't you have one of those snappy sports models like that Italian's, what's-his-name? By the way, did I tell you he has asked me to play tennis with him? Shall I?" She looked at him teasingly. "Shall I, Richard? Well, what am I to do, when you can't play tennis properly or dance or anything? Naturally, I have to find other people who can do these things, when you're such an awful dud."

In spite of these derogatory words, she put out her hand and tousled his hair. Encouraged, he tried to hold her, but she slipped away from him and ran to the car and started it before he could catch up with her. In fact, she drove it off for a little way down the road and then stopped and watched him running after her. She leaned out of the window and laughed at him in her high-spirited way.

(1966)

An Indian Citizen

NEAT IN HIS PERSON, AND JUST AS NEAT THE ROOM HE left behind him, Dr. Ernst fastened the padlock on his door and dropped the key into his top pocket. The padlock—supplied by the authorities—was huge, and if someone happened to be passing while he was locking up, he often pretended that he had got his finger caught in it. "Ooh," he would say, and wave his fingers painfully in the air and purse his mouth for a soundless whistle. But it was not a joke he ever made in the mornings. In the mornings, he knew, everyone was far too busy to take any notice of him, let alone his jokes.

The apartment block in which he had been fortunate enough to get a room was one occupied mainly by assistant editors in the Publications Division or section officers in the Ministry of Education, all of them civil servants in the medium-income groups, whose energies in the morning were concentrated on reaching the office in time. Since bicycles were beneath their dignity and none of them were rich enough to possess a car, getting to the office meant getting on a bus, and it was this task ahead that accounted for the grim, determined expressions on their faces. The ladies strode along purposefully in their saris, all of them intellectuals, graduates, wage earners, emancipated, and on an equal footing with men—the pride of modern India. Some of them grasped short umbrellas, with an air that made it clear that, if necessity demanded, they would use them to sharp effect in the bus queue.

Dr. Ernst had no office to go to, but he got up and went out at the same time as everyone else in the mornings. He felt better that way—not left out of anything but part of a busy world. Once, for a short, glorious time, he, too, had been an office worker. He had helped to put out bulletins in the Ministry of Information and Broadcasting and had compiled a weekly newssheet on the eradication of household pests. He had been very happy, though of course he had not expected to be kept long; he had known that sooner or later the job would have to be handed over to a genuine Indian subject, not an "ersatz" one, as he liked in fun to call himself. But it had been good while it lasted—not only the working in an office on regular hours like everyone else but also the knowledge that on the first week of every month a sufficient salary would infallibly turn up.

He walked among the crowd of officegoers toward the main gate of the apartment block, here and there raising his panama hat in a greeting that was courtly but at the same time unobtrusive, so that those who were in too much of a hurry could, with a good conscience, pretend they hadn't noticed. One or two of the hurrying figures he looked at with pleasure. Miss Jaya, from Room No. 146-A, for instance—a valued employee in the Ministry of Scientific Research and Cultural Affairs, walking slim and neat and upright in a green patterned sari, with her hair balanced on her head in a shining coil. Youth! thought Dr. Ernst with a smile. Youth and energy and confidence—the future. And he smiled again and thrust out his chest, looking after pretty Miss Jaya, and felt as if he had been fired with an ideal, a confirmation that life could be beautiful and good.

"Ernst!"

It was Lily. She was looking out of the window of her room with a woebegone air. All the windows in the block were crossed with iron bars, to keep the burglars out, and Lily peering through the bars, with her head to one side and her hair drooping sadly over her eyes, reminded him of a symbolical painting he had once been much moved by, entitled *Humanity*. However, he was not moved by Lily; he had seen her too often, looking just like this.

"Come in and talk to me," said Lily in a voice as woebegone as her face.

Suppressing a sigh, lingering a last fond look on the disappearing figure of brisk Miss Jaya, he turned aside and entered Lily's room.

"Right in," she commanded as he stood hesitating at the door.

He never liked to go into Lily's room. It was strange how different it was from his own, even though the rooms were absolutely identical in construction and in their basic furnishings, which were supplied by the authorities and consisted of a file cupboard for wardrobe, a serviceable wooden bed, and a dressing table that was really only an office desk with a mirror attached. Lily had a vivid taste, and she had smothered these bare necessities in curtains, cushions, rugs, hangings, masks, prints—all Oriental, all folk art, and all very dirty. Dr. Ernst, on the other hand, had added almost nothing to the room he had been given; he really didn't have anything except two wooden bears from Switzerland, which were meant to serve as bookends, a photograph of his parents in an oval frame, and a thirty-year-old alarm clock that still kept excellent time. But he was scrupulous about maintaining everything absolutely neat and clean and scrubbed. He did this himself every morning, with a bucket and soapsuds and a brush and a lot of vigor, his sleeves rolled up over his thin arms. In summer, when there were dust storms and everything in the city was covered with thick layers of dust and one could even taste it between one's teeth and smell it up one's nostrils, he would carefully wipe his yellow duster over everything in his room as many as five or six times a day. Anything out of place, any disorder or grime anywhere in his room was like a giving in to that chaos which had seemed perpetually to lie in wait for him ever since he started on his enforced travels, almost thirty years ago.

"I feel so awful," Lily wailed. She was squatting under the window on a little couch she had made out of old boxes covered with a thick hand-spun cloth featuring block-printed horses and riders. "There's something terribly wrong with me."

Dr. Ernst managed to look sympathetic, though secretly he was thinking that what was wrong with Lily was that she needed a good scrub and bath. How trim Miss Jaya had looked, how neat and smart and ready for her work! Lily sagged on her couch in a crumpled flowered wrap, her face too white and a bit puffy, and her hair a tangled, clotted nest.

"No office today?" asked Dr. Ernst.

She looked at him as if he had done her an injury. "In my state?" she said in a robust enough voice.

In his heart, he condemned her. She never appreciated how lucky she was to have a job here, even though she was English. She worked as a monitor in All India Radio—in the Chinese Section, strangely enough—and, instead of being grateful, she carried on as if she were being exploited. She frequently skipped days and was always grumbling about her salary.

"Oh, do sit *down*. You're making me nervous."

Dr. Ernst fidgeted. "I have to get going."

"What for? You're no wage slave like the rest of us. You lucky sod. Go *on!*" she said, pointing an impatient foot at a disintegrating cane hassock, on which he then had to lower himself gingerly.

He sat, uncomfortable and ill at ease, his thin knees pressed together, while she talked. She had a rather whining sort of voice, which rose and fell; it was loud while she was in the middle of her subject, then sank into a mumble as her interest in it diminished and rose again as she started on something new. As always, she had plenty to say, and as she went on, her servant appeared and served them cups of coffee. He was a crafty old man in a pair of tattered striped pajamas, who did rather well by means of little commissions he paid himself out of the bazaar money. Dr. Ernst, always ready for refreshments, would have drunk his with pleasure, but at the last moment noticed there was a smudge of lipstick on the cup, so he put it aside; he was still, in spite of his hardships, fastidious in these matters.

And now Lily had got onto her best subject of all, the one that always formed the climax of her conversations: her latest love affair. She had been in India for some three years now, and in that period of time had already been in love several times. Hers was a passionate nature, and indeed it was passion that had got her out to India in the first place, in pursuit of a handsome young Indian, who, whatever promises he might have made her in London, did not feel up to them once he had safely reached home ground. She had hardly got over that disappointment when she was in love again, and from there she never looked back, passing from passion to passion, each one more burning and more hopeless than the last.

"He was so beastly to me," she was complaining. "Wouldn't speak to me properly, made me pay for the dinner—he's such a brute." But when she said "brute," her eyes lit up and she leaned forward, smiling, eager, to add, "But so handsome! Isn't he the handsomest, handsomest creature you've ever seen?" She pushed Dr. Ernst's knee quite hard in her anxiety for his assent and confirmation.

He couldn't quite remember this latest young man and might be confusing him with one or two of his predecessors. But he said, "Terribly, terribly handsome," and smiled at her with his perfect, pearly plate of teeth. At that moment, he forgave her the smudge of lipstick on the coffee cup and much else besides. He admired her perseverance, her refusal to compromise: all her young men had been excessively handsome and desirable, and not one of them had even remotely returned her feelings. They made her suffer, and yet she chose only them, only these paragons, and never stooped to measure her affections to a lesser man more within her range. Only the best was good enough for her, and she would go on desiring it, though doomed forever to consume herself in her own flame.

"You should see him with his clothes off," she told him indelicately. "Like a god. *Such* shoulders, so broad, and hips you don't know how slender, like a boy's. Even to think of it—ooh, I can't bear it!" She moaned with joy and hugged herself tight, and her wrap fell apart, revealing her legs, which were pale and plump, with the flesh shaking like a dewlap from the underside of the thighs.

How old was she now? Thirty? Thirty-two? Still young by his standards, but he knew that she would never marry, just as he never had. For he, too, had been like her—had loved and desired only what was infinitely beyond him. He had always wanted to marry and had the most superbly imaginative vision of the bliss that would he waiting for him in that state, but his one condition was that his partner should be a paragon. He would settle for nothing less. This trend of his had started long ago, at school, where he had loved little Lise Freuhlingslied, pert in frilly apron and kid boots, who never looked at him without a scornful toss of her blond mane (topped by a blue satin ribbon), while Sophie Mann, who truly loved him and was ever eager to share her ham roll with him in the lunch break, could not get as much as a look or a thought from him. Yes, he could have married many times over, later in Amsterdam, in Beirut, in Bombay, but always to the Sophie Manns, for whom he had no time to spare because he was too busy being in love with the Lise Freuhlingslieds. So here he was, now, sixty and single, though not sorry for it, because he had kept his ideal uncompromised and still, however improbably, within his reach.

Lily crooned softly, "I think he's got a terribly cruel streak in his nature." Then she added, "They all have. All these Indian men. I think they like to humiliate us." She sounded very easy and even rather pleased about it, as if she liked being humiliated.

"No psychoanalysis, please," said Dr. Ernst. "I hear it's out of fashion."

"And, you know, they always pretend to like our white skins and admire us, but really I think—yes, I'm sure, I'm sure, they *despise* us."

"What are you saying?" cried Dr. Ernst.

"Hate and despise us," she said with relish.

He got up from the cane hassock. He would not hear such things spoken. Indians had always been so kind to him and he owed them so much. A place to live, a nationality, friendship, respect—all this they had given him. He said, very primly and in rebuke, "Most of my friends are Indians."

Lily made a rude sound. "Like hell they are. You hardly know any, for all you've been here donkey's years." When she saw him about to protest, she cried, "All right, name them, name them!"

Without hesitation, and proudly, he stood and ticked off his finger. "Sri Manohar, Minister of Moral Reformation. Her Highness of Palangkot. Dr. Lall, M.P.—"

"You call those friends? Why, you're just their"—she shrugged and said in her careless, rude, English way—"their hanger-on."

Dr. Ernst was insulted. He compressed his lips, and his face took on a vicious expression. He had always been a mild and friendly person, but if he felt himself insulted by people whom he did not consider his superiors he wanted revenge. When he was a student of philology at the university, there had been a group of students—crude, unmannerly fellows—who had not been very nice to him, so that when he caught one of them cheating in the examinations, he had not hesitated to report him to the authorities. This had ultimately led to the young man's expulsion, but Dr. Ernst had not been sorry; quite on the contrary, the memory of this act filled him even today with a sense of righteousness and justice done.

He looked at her and felt prompted to home truths. "There is nothing wrong with you that you can't go to your office, only you need to wash, that is all, and tidy up this room, which is not fit for a human being to live in."

She wasn't the least bit offended, but laughed in a genuine, frank way. "A real pigsty, don't I know it. Oh, don't be cross. Sit down, I want to talk."

But he was offended, and as a mark of disrespect he put on his panama hat right there in the room and walked out of the door, ignoring the plaintive shouts she let out after him through the iron bars.

HE WAS STILL upset when he reached the road, but once he started walking his mood changed. How lucky we are, he thought—always a blue sky. And he looked at it with an almost proprietary smile. It really was an undeniable, unflecked, irreproachable blue, and the sun was shining not too hotly yet, and the air was high and clear. The morning office rush was over, and only a few slim young college girls in freshly laundered saris stood at the bus stop. The streets here were broad and unpaved and lined thickly with very tall, very stately trees in different shades of green. Set back far from the road, each one in its own beautifully kept garden, were white houses with pillars and verandas. Their gates were ornamental, and at some of them hovered little groups of servants (the bearer, the gardener, the watchman). An elderly lady went by, slow and stately under her parasol, and a servant in white uniform was walking a beautifully groomed Alsatian on a red leather lead. Everything was leisured and green that morning, with many kinds of birds singing and twittering in the trees. Under such conditions, who would brood over personal feelings, over a slight received? Certainly not Dr. Ernst; he had passed too long a life, and one too full of setbacks, not to be able to shake off passing moods and take full advantage of whatever moments of happiness were offered to him. He breathed the fragrant air, listened to the birds, and looked at the college girls. And who was Lily, anyway? He hummed to himself—some gay tune that rose from goodness knows what depths of past contentment.

But he had not yet decided where to go. Other people went out to work every morning; he went out to put himself in the way of work. Keeping up his contacts, he called it. Certainly one had to make people realize that one was still there and still ready to oblige, so that when friends heard of someone who wanted German lessons or French lessons or Latin (he was willing to teach anything, even Viennese, he often joked), then the first person they would think of would be Dr. Ernst, especially if they had recently seen him. Especially as he was always so grateful; he would thank people effusively, over and over, in his most gallant Continental way, for recommending him, so that they felt pleased and began to have as high an opinion of themselves as he obviously did.

He wondered, as he walked, who he should go and see this morning. He felt inclined not only to keep up contacts but also to spend a pleasant morning chatting with friends. The nicest place to go, of course, was Maiska's, and already his thoughts and footsteps were turned in that direction. It was always cozy at Maiska's. She was a middle-aged European woman, plain, dowdy, yet with a charm born of good nature and sympathy, which made her the center of a whole group of friends. No one ever called her by her first name, whatever that may have been, or by her married name, which was a Bengali one, for at one stage she had had a Bengali husband. Everyone always called her by her maiden surname, Maiska. She had a job in the university teaching various European languages—she knew a great number of them, and it was said she had even learned Bengali during her brief married life—and she lived in a flat near the university, in a house rather shabby and crowded, with dirty stairs and choked drains. But once inside Maiska's flat, everything was quite different. True, in her furnishings she had largely made use of cheap Indian hand-loomed materials, yet somehow the total effect was completely, cozily European. There were many ashtrays, usually well filled with stubs, and comfortable armchairs to sit in and good pictures on the walls and good books in the bookcases.

Dr. Ernst had spent some of his best hours there. Maiska really knew how to make one feel at home, and there were usually one or two other friends with her—members of that band of displaced, lonely Europeans, like Lily and Dr. Ernst himself, who constantly gravitated round her flat. Only the week before, they had had a lovely party there. The Linskys had brought potato salad, and Anna Shukla had baked one of her cheesecakes, and Herman had showed them a whole range of new card tricks (he was so clever, they had all agreed—a real magician). Evenings at Maiska's were the best, but even during the day it was a very pleasant place to visit. He was already looking forward to the cup of coffee she would serve him—good strong European coffee, not like Lily's weak English brew. Hopefully, he wondered if he would meet any other of their friends there—Anna Shukla perhaps, or Herman, or Charlene, who was a Buddhist and lived in a Buddhist ashrama. They would talk and play the gramophone, and perhaps they would all cook up some sort of tasty lunch together on Maiska's little electric ring. But in the middle of these pleasant speculations, he suddenly remembered Lily and how she had said, "Name them, name them!" and then it became a matter of pride not to go to Maiska's today. She was, he told himself, only one of many possibilities, and today it so happened he felt more like visiting one of his Indian friends. He remembered the names he had mentioned to Lily—Sri Manohar and Her Highness of Palangkot—all his good friends who would welcome him, though of course they were all busy, important people, and it was necessary to make an appointment first and pass through several secretaries. But, good heavens, there were others—many, many other good friends, whose doors were always open to him and who would be delighted to see him anytime he cared to call.

MRS. CHAWLA WAS not in a very good mood. She was to have had her singing lesson that morning, but her singing master had not turned up. Unfortunately, this happened quite frequently, and every time it did she contemplated dispensing with his services. But when he came again the next time, she always forgave him very readily, for he had a charming smile and was altogether so young and debonair that it seemed no more than his due to have to work only when he felt like it. Still, it was dull and disappointing not to have one's singing lesson when one had been looking forward to it, and today, after having scolded her servants on various points of disorder, she retired in a huff to her bedroom, where she lay down on the floor and began to do her yoga exercises. She was in the middle of the Sarvangasana and had got her legs laboriously into the air and was bending now one and now the other when her servant knocked timidly on the door. "No!" she called at once. "I'm busy!"

When she heard, however, that a sahib had come and was waiting downstairs in the drawing room, she became a little better pleased and got up and began to brush her hair before the mirror.

She entered the drawing room with a smile. Dr. Ernst struggled instantly to his feet (not very easy, for Mrs. Chawla's decor was in true Indian style, with seats at floor level). He noticed at once that the smile with which she entered grew stiff and uncordial when she saw that it was he. His heart sank—he had often been an unwelcome visitor—but it was too late to retreat. In an attempt to put her in a better mood with him, he arched himself reverently over her hand and brushed it with his lips; he knew that Indian ladies, though they pretended not to like it, were always flattered by this form of greeting. But today she was ungracious and withdrew her hand too quickly, and afterward he saw her wipe it on the end of her sari.

He had long since learned that the trouble with dropping in on people without any specific purpose but only for the sake of good fellowship was that the atmosphere tended to be strained. Today he did his best, yet Mrs. Chawla took no trouble in return—only sat there and made no attempt to look anything but sulky and bored. He admired her so much, both for her appearance and for her personality. She was a tall, proud woman with a fine bosom and a fine pair of fiery eyes. She was very artistically inclined, a founder member of the Intimate Theatre Club and one of the principal organizers of the Indian Music Circle. One glimpse into her drawing room revealed at once that she was a deeply cultured person, for it was full of wonderful artistic pieces, such as a huge carved chest (once a village dowry chest, but nowadays very fashionable as a sideboard), a heavy brass tray from Kashmir that was used as a coffee table, a delightful old-fashioned urn and bowl made of copper, and a silver rose-water sprinkler. Sticks of incense smoldering from incense holders gave a richly Indian smell and atmosphere to the room.

He had often complimented her on the indigenous quality

of her interior decoration, but when he did so today—as usual, contrasting it favorably with the fashion of yesteryear, when everyone had prided themselves on their imported sofa suites and Axminster carpets—his compliments were not received as graciously as they usually were. On the contrary, she was even quite snappish. "At last, we are allowed to enjoy our own cultural heritage. Now that we are no longer under the heel of foreign imperialists," she said, and then she glared at him for a moment as if he, too, poor Dr. Ernst, had ambitions to be a foreign imperialist.

He blushed and began to talk fast. He agreed with her heartily about the baneful influence that resulted from the forcible grafting of one culture onto another, and then he proceeded to eulogize all aspects of Indian art—architecture, music, dance, drama, food, dress, customs, and ceremonies. He went on and on, though she wasn't listening, and he knew it. He felt compelled to make it clear how completely he was on her side, on India's side. He longed to hear her say something encouraging in reply, to give him some assurance that she accepted his allegiance, and the fact that she didn't made him go on desperately talking. As he talked, he looked at Mrs. Chawla with eyes that were soft and hurt and shamelessly appealing as a child's, and when she yawned, opening her mouth wide and half closing her beautiful, passionate eyes, he longed to cry out, "If only you knew how I love, how I admire you!" She lounged on her silk-covered, floor-level seat, and though it was a little difficult for him to make himself comfortable and he had to shift his legs from one side to the other, she seemed perfectly at her ease, leaning with her elbow on the bolster behind her, with one hip pushed out and her large legs under the sari folded effortlessly beneath her. While his eyes never left her, she hardly glanced at him, but lay back inert and passive, now yawning, now putting her hand inside her low-cut blouse to scratch lazily.

But suddenly she changed. She sat up, and all that inert mass throbbed with animation, and her sleepy eyes opened wide. She cried, "So late!" and Dr. Ernst turned to where she was looking and saw a young man with curly hair and a fine pair of shoulders. The young man was smiling in a relaxed way and said, "Better late than never, I think."

No one glanced at Dr. Ernst. Mrs. Chawla and the young man sat on the carpet, the young man with a small harmonium. She began to sing scales. "*Sa-ray-ga-ma-pa-da-ni-sa,*" she sang, and the young man nodded. She glanced at him, and he said, "Go on, go on," and made her do it over, while he kept on nodding. Finally, she said, "Oh, I am tired of your scales," and he said, "You must obey your master." Then she began to plead with him charmingly, putting on appealing little airs, pursing her mouth, lowering her eyes, plucking at the hem of her sari, but all in such a way that one knew she wasn't really pleading and that it was only a game. He answered, too, as if it were a game and he only playing at being the severe singing master, and they both wasted quite a lot of time chatting back and forth. Dr. Ernst smilingly put in a word, pleading playfully for Mrs. Chawla to be allowed a song, but he was not heard.

At last, when she had begged enough, the singing master gave way and allowed her to sing. It was one of those ambiguous devotional songs, where no one can be sure who is crying out to whom—the soul to God or the lover to the beloved. She tried to sing with feeling, but it was obvious that she did not have much talent. She sang slowly and stolidly, and the young man as stolidly accompanied her on the harmonium, making a resigned face. Dr. Ernst enjoyed the performance. He leaned forward eagerly, and there was a smile of delight on his face. Of course, he realized that she did not sing well, but it was not her singing that moved him so much as the picture she made. She and the young man together. They sat in the middle of the carpet, which was floral in pattern and as fresh and delicate as a meadow of flowers in a Mogul miniature. But the two figures—though they were grouped like lovers, close together, he with his instrument, she giving song—were not in the least delicate but, on the contrary, solid and strong, he with his broad chest and his coarse, handsome face, and she with her large, rounded limbs hidden but suggestively delineated by the folds of her sari; her full throat was flung back and emitted loud, lusty sounds. Their heads were close together, both richly covered with healthy, shining, blue-black hair.

When the song was finished, Dr. Ernst clapped in applause. "Bravo!" he cried in his enthusiasm, and after that, "Encore!" just as if he were at the opera in Vienna. Mrs. Chawla for the first time turned her face and gave him a short, absent smile before turning back to the young man and telling him something in a low voice. He shrugged in resigned agreement and began to play the harmonium again while she embarked on a second song. But she had not got very far when he broke off and made some criticism. He did this in an ungracious, almost contemptuous way, so that she stopped singing and her expression became sulky. They looked at each other in dislike. Dr. Ernst, hoping to make things better, said, "To a layman's ear, it sounded very nice," but this did not have the desired effect. Instead, Mrs. Chawla turned her look of dislike on him; her eyes blazed, and she said, not to him but into the air, "It is very difficult for me to concentrate on my singing when others are here to create a disturbance."

Dr. Ernst saw it was time to go. He picked up his hat, got up, and made his farewell bow, holding his hat against his navel. Once outside, he forced himself to be cheerful and walked briskly along. It was foolish, he told himself, to feel hurt or slighted; she had not meant anything personal. It was only that she was having her lesson, and of course no one wishes to be disturbed during a lesson. It was kind enough of her to have let him stay as long as she did. She was his good friend and esteemed and liked him as much as he did her. You silly old Ernst, he chided himself, always so touchy. That was his trouble—looking for offense where none was meant. It was a very bad trait in him.

SOMETIMES DURING HIS morning peregrinations he was lucky and was offered lunch, but today was not such a day. He entered a coffee bar and carefully studied the menu. Actually, he didn't have to do this, for he frequented the place, and every other one like it, often enough to know that there was nothing to tempt his palate beyond hamburgers, hot dogs, and vegetable cutlets. Yet every time he came, he insisted on reading the menu—which had managed to get very dirty in spite of its cellophane covering—before giving his order. Perhaps there was the hope that some new dish had been added (he was always dreaming of new dishes; his appetite was really much too good for his slender resources). Or perhaps it was because studying the menu was part of restaurant-going, recalling days when one entered such places not solely for eating but for other, less tangible reasons, the way his parents had gone to restaurants, and he, too, long ago. They had gone not because they had to but because they liked to once in a while, leaving their comfortable home and dressing up in going-out clothes, all of them on special behavior, ready for an evening of elegance and entertainment.

The coffee bar was a somewhat shabby one, with peeling crimson-and-gold moldings. The patrons, however, were not in the least shabby but very well and even flashily dressed in the latest California-style clothes. Most of them were students or recent graduates who had not yet taken up any burdens but were still comfortably looked after by rich and indulgent parents. They none of them seemed short of cash, casually ordering a succession of drinks and dishes that made Dr. Ernst, who was usually hungry, even hungrier, and there was certainly no shortage of twenty-five-paisa coins to put into the jukebox, which played last year's American hit tunes interspersed sometimes with the latest wailing, weepy Bombay film song. At one time the jukebox had been a trial to Dr. Ernst, for it was loud and very shrill in a mechanical, tinny way, but now he had got used to it and even liked it and would have missed it if it had stopped. He had begun to recognize many of the tunes and had learned to tap his feet to them the way the young men did—only he did it more decorously, with his feet hidden under the table.

He liked the place. He sat alone in a corner, eating his hamburger and shaking the bottle to get out more of the congealed ketchup. When he had finished eating, he enjoyed simply sitting there and watching the other customers. He watched them with the same pleasure he watched Miss Jaya going off trimly to work in the morning, or Mrs. Chawla and her music teacher—admiring them for their youth, their vitality, the future that lay before them. None of the people in the restaurant spoke to him or took any notice of him, but he didn't expect them to. They were as infinitely above him, he felt, with a not unhappy inward smile, as Lise Freuhlingslied, or as Lily's handsome young men were above Lily herself. They even looked, in comparison with Lily and himself, a higher kind of being, with their healthy, brown, glowing skins, and their brilliant dark eyes and strong teeth and hair. How well they fitted in with everything—and here he thought not only of the coffee bar, with the loud jukebox and the crimson-and-gold moldings, but of everything that lay outside: the intensely blue skies, the birds and beasts that lived in jungles, the rivers, the vast mountain ranges. It all belonged to them and they to it, man and nature made to each other, while he and Lily and Maiska and Herman and the rest of them would always remain only pale, stray strangers.

Much as he liked being there, with the jukebox and the young men, he always found after a while that a great oppression took hold of him, as if something too heavy had been laid on top of him. A ridiculous sensation, due only to the noise and the smoke, he knew that, but all the same it was strong enough to make it necessary for him to leave. He paid his bill, leaving a tiny tip, and got up. Just as he reached the door, a new party of youths came surging in—a pride of bearded young Sikhs in flaming turbans and tartan shirts and expensive leather boots. Smiling, banging the jukebox, anticipating pleasure, they moved forward in a solid unseeing phalanx, so that Dr. Ernst, though he lifted his hat and said "Excuse me, excuse me, please" was pushed back and could not reach the door. No one noticed him, and it wasn't till they had all found chairs for themselves and were banging on the tables and shouting for the bearers that Dr. Ernst managed to regain the door and slip out into the street.

It was no longer pleasant outside. The day's heat had got into its stride and was white and electric sharp. Pariah dogs lay panting in little patches of shade, and from time to time a motorcar passed by, very swiftly, all its chromium burning and flashing white fire. Otherwise, the streets were deserted, for the heat was a tyrant that strode the pavements and forced people to scuttle away to the nearest place of refuge.

MAISKA'S WAS NOT quite the nearest, but it was near. Unfortunately, Lily had got there before him, but for the time being he didn't even mind that, he was so glad to have arrived. He sat in one of the comfortable armchairs and shut his eyes for a moment, allowing heat and exhaustion to drain out of him while Maiska ministered with something cool to drink. There was a kind of ache around his chest and stomach, but that would pass off, he knew; it always did. All he needed was rest. The curtains were drawn in the room, so that everything was shrouded in a soothing dusk. Maiska and Lily were both lounging with their feet up on the settee, and it looked as if they had been there for a nice long comfortable time. They were both smoking Maiska's Egyptian cigarettes and drinking coffee out of thick pottery mugs painted in running colors. Records were scattered about on the floor near the record player, which was open and still humming, though the last record had finished playing.

Although he meant to keep his eyes shut for only a moment, he found himself slipping more and more into a pleasant haze, in which he was vaguely aware of Maiska's and Lily's voices talking together and the fan turning overhead and a hawker in the street calling digestive powders for sale and someone shouting on the stairs and someone else clattering up them with a bucket.

When he woke, suddenly opening his eyes, he found Maiska looking at him. She smiled at him, and he smiled weakly back and wanted more than anything to shut his eyes and go to sleep again. But he made an effort and sat up in the chair in which he had been drooping. A moment's uneasy thought—had his mouth fallen open? Had he snored? He hated to be seen too privately, off guard. He took out his handkerchief and passed it over his wet, perspiring face and neck and head. "Must have dropped off," he mumbled and smiled again at Maiska apologetically.

She said, "Go on, sleep a bit more," and looked at him with sympathy, as if she knew just how tired he was and how he didn't want to wake up. But he had to. Of course, a nap in the afternoon was nothing to reproach oneself for (at his age and in this climate!), but one also had to know when to cut it short. Otherwise, there was the danger of sinking too deep and giving way to the desire to sleep forever and not have to get up at all anymore and walk around and meet people. He put away his handkerchief and patted and jerked and brushed at his crumpled clothes to get them dapper again.

While he was doing this, he said, casually, not looking at Lily, "I spent a very nice morning with Mrs. Chawla."

"I can't stand her," Lily said at once. "A conceited, stupid cow."

"She asked me to come again very soon." Then he shouted at Lily, "Be careful how you speak of my friends!"

He was very angry, and it did him good. He shouted some more, and what a relief it was not to have to curb one's feelings for once but to be able to indulge them, to relish a sense of one's own injury. No one tried to stop him, and only when he had finished did Lily say, quite mildly, "I didn't know she was your friend."

"You didn't know," he repeated in exasperation. "I told you: I have many, many Indian friends."

He waited for this challenge to be taken up and was partly mollified when it wasn't. Maiska cleared a space on the table and placed a mug of coffee in front of him, into which she spooned sugar, murmuring to herself, "Two and a half," for she always knew exactly how much sugar each of her friends took and didn't have to ask.

Dr. Ernst was not very angry anymore, but he felt Lily shouldn't be let off too easily. He said, "Put your leg down," for she was sitting in an easy but not decorous position. "Aren't you ashamed? No wonder all your young men don't want to look at you."

"Don't rub it in," said Lily plaintively, at which Maiska laughed, but, to cover up any tactlessness, she quickly added, "Never mind, one day she'll meet the right one."

"But I have!" wailed Lily. "They've all been the right ones! It's always me who's wrong."

Dr. Ernst inwardly agreed. She *was* wrong. He looked at her, not so much in distaste now as in pity, feeling sorry for her because her body was clumsy and her skin too flabby and white. She couldn't help this, poor thing, but why had she come here, why had she stayed here, in a country where man and nature were colorful and lush and without pity? He thought of Mrs. Chawla, of the young Sikhs in their boots and tartan shirts, and he leaned toward Lily quite tenderly and gave a little tug at her skirt to make it cover her knees, and then he said, in a smiling, paternal voice, "That's better."

Maiska was putting another record on her record player. She did not have many records, and those she had were old and none too clear, but they were all only the highest classics. There was Brahms and Beethoven and Bach, and often her friends gathered for an informal musical evening. They had all spent last New Year's Eve like that. Maiska and Lily and Dr. Ernst and Charlene and the Linskys and Herman and Anna Shukla. Maiska had served beer and sandwiches, and they had put on record after record, and though at first they had had some conversation, as the night wore on they grew silent and listened only to the music and each thought his own thoughts. At midnight, they were playing the choral part of Beethoven's Ninth Symphony and they all got up and wished each other a happy new year. "*Freude, schöner Götterfunken*" had sounded, loud if a little blurred, from the record player, filling the room and their hearts, and some of them (including Dr. Ernst) had had tears in their eyes.

He could not identify the record she had put on now, but it was some sort of flute concerto—graceful and happy. Mozart, he suspected, though he didn't like to ask, in case he was wrong. His foot tapped and his head nodded in time. It was much, much nicer than Mrs. Chawla's singing. Suddenly he felt proud and European and full of affection for Maiska and Lily, co-heirs with him of a wondrous heritage—Mozart! Versailles! Goethe's Weimar! Lily was smoking a cigarette, making the end of it red and wet with lipstick, and puffing out too much smoke, and Maiska brought more coffee in a saucepan and refilled their mugs brimful. Dr. Ernst began to sing with the music, and, not content with that—so gay did it make him feel—he got up and put his hands beside his face and crossed his feet at the ankles, and thus played an imaginary flute, swaying this way and that and, at particularly piercing moments, getting up on his toes as if to reach with the music up to Heaven.

(1967)

Foreign Wives

MRS. CLARA PANIWALA, TRIM, BLOND, FIFTY-FIVE IF A day, and wearing a skintight, poison-green silk dress, stood in the doorway, one hand on her hip: "Dreadful," she pronounced.

"I know, oh I know," admitted Fay, the owner of this indeed dreadfully disorderly room.

"*And* you've been crying."

"No, I haven't," said Fay, wiping away some new tears from her already pink-rimmed eyes.

"I suppose it's the children again," said Clara as she picked her way fastidiously into the room.

Fay responded with a new gush of tears. The handkerchief which she clutched in her hand and now brought ineffectually to her eyes was already very wet. Clara gave several impatient clicks of the tongue.

"Raju had a boil on his knee," Fay sobbed. "And all Matron said was, it won't kill him, will it. So heartless." She buried her face in the wet handkerchief.

"They're perfectly well looked after in that school, and you know it."

"But I want them with *me!*"

"What, here?" and Clara looked eloquently round the dreadful room.

"Yes, I know," Fay said, sobering quite suddenly. "It wouldn't do. I'm an impossible mother."

Clara said, "I don't suppose you're thinking of offering me a cup of coffee, are you?" She clapped her hands and called "Mithan Lal!" but there was no answer from the servant.

"He must have gone to the bazaar," Fay murmured guiltily. "I'll make it, wait."

"Stay where you are. I've drunk your coffee once, thank you, that was enough. Pfui," and Clara pulled a face with a very central European expression of disgust on it. Wobbling slightly on her too high heels, she tripped out into the kitchen and started bustling around in there amid indignant shouts of "The dirt! Fantastic! Just let me get hold once of that precious Mithan Lal of yours!" Fay had followed her and was apologizing profusely. Clara took no notice of her but went on bustling and in a remarkably short time had produced some remarkably good coffee which she then, with the verve of a trained maid, carried on a tray into the sitting room.

"Just let him come," she said as they drank. "I'll give him something. I'd like to see my Bipin behave like that—but he's a treasure! A jewel! Yesterday, just think, Fay, all morning serving coffee and snacks to the bridge party—"

"Oh was it yesterday?"

"Of course, Thursday, morning, what a memory you've got. Charlene came too, in a new trouser suit she'd sewn herself—horrible. Eight of them stayed to lunch, and then in the evening Her Highness dropped in, so of course the poor fellow had to start making French toast, Her Highness loves my French toast. 'Just for five minutes, Clara,' she said, but she stayed talking for three hours, all her troubles, poor soul." Clara sighed.

"About His Highness?"

"I've told her, I keep telling her, 'Kuku, men are like that, all of them, from the highest to the lowest,' but will she listen, no she cries and cries here on my shoulder"—Clara clapped that part—"and tells me I'm her only friend—oh, good heavens, now what's the matter?" for Fay too had begun to cry again.

"I'm thinking of Naraian."

"*No*," said Clara as one who has had enough and too much.

"Now he won't even speak to me on the phone. The day before yesterday, after I'd been to see the boys, I rang him up to talk about things and *she* comes on the phone and says he's not in—but I know he was, I know it, Clara."

"If you don't pull yourself together," Clara said, "I'll walk straight out of that door—" she pointed at it warningly.

"I can't help it. I love him."

"You love him," Clara repeated jeeringly.

"I think she's expecting a baby."

"Naturally, a man marries a new young wife, soon she is expecting a baby, that's not quite unnatural."

Fay began fumbling about her person, then around the room, finally had to admit—"I think I've run out again."

With a snap Clara opened her smart bag, with another snap her gold cigarette case, which was inscribed

> Claralein
> > Küsse
> > > Amour
> > > > For Ever
> > > > > Eugen

Paris
6 Mai, 1932

Next—snap!—her lighter: "I know you have no matches, don't tell me," and then snap, snap, snap, lighter, case, bag, all closed back again.

Squatting on the floor, her long slim legs tucked sideways, thirty-two years old and, though unkempt, not at all bad looking,

Fay smoked and looked contemplative. "It was all my fault," she said. "And it wasn't as if I even liked Ranjit, I mean not that much, not like Naraian—"

"Please!" said Clara, holding up one hand, full of rings. "No old histories, if you don't mind. I've had one rule always: no looking back, what's happened has happened and tomorrow will also be a fine day."

"Once when I was in the fifth our class teacher Miss Wilberforce wrote on my report *Has a weak character and is easily led*. I've never forgotten that. I adored Miss Wilberforce, she was a terrific teacher and a mountaineer too, she was the first woman to climb some peak or other—"

"I've noticed with all my English friends: what's happened to them at school is always the most important, what comes after—nothing. And the rest of us don't even remember we ever went to a school! I'm sure I didn't, not in this world." She laughed harshly: "What you need, all of you, is a good dose of the school of life the way we've had."

Fay bowed her head in acknowledgment of the superior quality of Clara's sufferings. Although no one was quite sure exactly in what countries Clara had lived or what she had undergone there before finding her haven with the late Mr. Paniwala, it was generally known that hers had been a checkered career: and since it had run its course across several continents and against a background of international upheavals, it had acquired a depth and grandeur which were outside the scope of Fay's purely private mishaps.

However, true to her policy not to dwell on the past, Clara now said briskly, "Better than to spend your time thinking of what your old schoolteacher said, why not have this place turned out and given a good scrubbing? Disgraceful."

"I really must get rid of Mithan Lal one of these days," Fay began vaguely but Clara cut her short by waving a finger with a big turquoise on it in the air:

"Absolutely no point in it! The next one will be just the same and God forbid he might have a bad character on top of it all and you won't be safe in your own bed. No, all your Mithan Lal needs is a bit of discipline, like the rest of them. You think my Bipin is any different? The moment I let go even this little bit, he'll be sitting out on the stairs with the other servants playing cards and smoking filthy bidis. But he knows how far he can go with me—oh, we understand each other very well, my Bipin and I." She made a grimly satisfied mouth like a person who has after a struggle succeeded in triumphing over a situation.

"Of course," she added after a while, "it works both ways—I'm not like some of those Indian families, you know how they treat their servants. Once I was staying at Begum Sharifa's house in Palangkot, such a rich family living in such style, but their servants! In rags and treated like animals, worse than animals, I tell you I couldn't bear to stay in that house for more than three days. And when I gave the servants a little tip, the Begum was annoyed, she said I was spoiling them. What do you pay your Mithan?"

"Mithan? Oh—forty, I think, and food."

"Make it forty-five and you wouldn't do any harm. A rupee or two more, they'll be happy and what is it to you."

Fay sat up and looked at Clara with wide-open eyes: "Oh but you don't know! I'm so broke, I can't afford another *penny*."

"Nonsense."

"I'm telling you—the situation here is desperate. Honestly, Clara, I don't know what to do, I simply can't manage any more on what he gives me—"

"Then he must give you more."

Fay relapsed into her slouching position and made a resigned gesture with the hand holding the cigarette.

"But *de*-finitely," asserted Clara and sat up straighter. "What do you mean—the man brings you here, straight *pst* like that two children, and then when he's had enough goodbye? No, that would be a little too easy." She raised her buttocks a fraction off the chair, smoothed the tight green silk over them, and settled back again with an indignant little laugh. "A man has to pay for his pleasures, nothing in this life is free. That's what I used to tell old Paniwala, poor old man, not that he needed telling, rest his soul; *he* knew his obligations."

"Naraian does pay for the boys' schooling and that's quite a bit—and now with her expecting a—"

"Whose fault is that? Is it yours? Did you make the baby? Did you have a good time with a new young wife? No. He's earning enough, let him pay. Big house, big car, two wives—I'll tell him if you don't want to. Leave it to me. *I'm* not shy." And again she wore that grim look of triumph, remembrance of battles past and won: "You can ask the Paniwala family and their lawyers, they'll tell you."

Fay suddenly said, "I've been trying to get a job"; and then, looking shamefacedly at Clara, "Yes, I know, it's ridiculous when I can't even—my mother used to say, how will you ever make your way when you can't even keep your own stockings mended? And of course she was right . . . I hate to be a sponger, Clara, and as soon as Mithan comes I'll send him out for some—"

Clara brought out her cigarette case again and this time she didn't put it back but left it out near Fay.

"Need I say, my job-hunting has been to the highest degree unsuccessful. It's amazing the number of people who don't want to employ me. All India Radio—the Handicrafts Board—the Films Division—the National Small-Scale Industries Corporation—"

"You're a fool. Don't you know, don't you know even that much, that none of these places will ever employ a foreigner? India for the Indians . . . Why didn't you tell me? I could introduce you to people."

"Lots of people have been introducing me to lots of people, but nothing ever seems to work out."

"Yes, I know the sort of people who have been introducing you. Rubbish! Nothing! Who are they? What can they do? I don't know how you ever got mixed up with these sort of people in the first place—psha—sitting around with them in these dirty coffeehouses—" She narrowed her eyes: "What about that musician boy? I hope that's finished at least."

"Yes," said Fay, not without regret.

"Ten years younger than you—"

"Eight."

"You have no sense. You're not a bad-looking girl, Fay; in fact if you only took a little bit more care of yourself, went to Madame Alice sometimes for a good shampoo and set—perhaps bought a pumice stone to get the nicotine off your fingers . . . I can introduce you to so many people, you know that. Important people who could help you."

Fay said, "Sometimes I think I'm beyond help or redemption."

"Don't talk like that," Clara took her up very sharply. "Once you start thinking about yourself like that, in no time you're *here*," and she pressed her thumb flat down on the side of her chair to demonstrate a squashed object. "Like poor Bridget after Ram left her, she was always saying let me die, I'm no use—terrible—and of course if she could have pulled herself together a bit, it need never have come to what it did." She shook her head and curled her upper lip in pity.

"I've been thinking a lot about Bridget lately."

"Be quiet. You think about your boys, that's more sensible, and all right, think about getting a job, a little bit of work never did anyone any harm. I'm going to introduce you to Sri Ram Bhola Ram, you know who he is? B. R. Electricals and Hindustan Enterprise and Jai Hind Industries—a millionaire. *Multi*."

"Oh gosh," said Fay and nervously pushed at her hair.

"He's always dropping in at my place. Bholi I call him. He enjoys a drink, a bit of fun, music—going to you, Clara, is like going to Paris, he tells me. Not that he's ever been to Paris. But he speaks English quite nicely and when he's with me he's very relaxed. At home he's a strict vegetarian of course but—well," she shut an indulgent eye, "he's rather fond of an omelet or a cutlet, especially if I cook it for him myself. You'll like him. He's a gentleman. And for him what would it be to give you a job of six, seven hundred? He could fit you in anywhere in one of his firms. Ten like you, if he wanted to."

"But would he want to?" Fay wondered. She helped herself to another of Clara's cigarettes and said gratefully as she did so, "You've saved my life."

Clara bridled: "Certainly he would want to. If *I* introduced you, and if you troubled to make yourself a little bit pleasant."

Fay kept her head lowered and said in her throwaway English manner, "How pleasant?"

Clara was angry. When she was angry, all her tight, disciplined little body drew itself together, her sharp jawbone with its edge of loosening flesh was thrust upward; her light blue eyes opened wide and stared at Fay. "I told you Bholi was a gentleman," she said and tapped a tiny foot in high-heeled, ankle-strap shoe.

Fay hastened to withdraw. She was profuse in declarations of how she hadn't meant anything, that it had been just a silly remark, she talked fast and breathlessly with self-deprecating little laughs in between and stared anxiously at Clara till she saw her relax and the angry look disappear out of those light-colored eyes. It was part of Fay's character to be terrified of offending anyone, but she was especially terrified with Clara. She knew Clara to be a wonderful friend but also, when once roused that way, an implacable enemy.

"Of course I'd love to meet Mr. Bhola Ram," Fay said, still talking fast. "It's awfully nice of you to suggest it and it'd be marvelous if he could find me a job—"

"Slowly, slowly," said soothed Clara. "One thing at a time. First we'll have a little evening together—"

"That'd be lovely," Fay said ingratiatingly.

"Get to know him, let him get to know you."

"Quite."

"Then afterward we'll see, who knows how things will develop. If he likes you—well, we'll see. Don't count your chickens before," she hesitated, and Fay quickly helped her out: "They're hatched."

"Charlene of course," Clara continued, "has been trying for ages to get me to introduce her, but I don't think he'd have much to say to her. You should have seen her in that trouser suit! But he might take a little fancy to you, you never can tell. To be friends with someone like Bholi," she said weightily, "it's not something to be sneezed at."

"No."

"Do you remember that Czech girl, Nina, who came out here to marry one of the Mallik boys? And then the family wouldn't allow it and she was left high and dry, do you remember? Not even the fare home." Clara gave a snort of indignation, which next moment however was transformed into one of triumph: "She certainly didn't have to sit and cry after him for long. She met one of those Bombay businessmen, some Gujarati name, in textiles I think, went away to Bombay with him and he helped her with a little shop. Now she's doing very, very well, only the smartest people—she can certainly snap her fingers at those Malliks now," and Clara snapped her own and gave a pert laugh as if it were her own victory she was celebrating, certainly that of her own side. But then suddenly, her fingers still in midair, the laugh just off her lips, she stopped short and stared at Fay in amazement: for Fay had her head down and tears were rolling out of her eyes and her mouth was puckered like a child's.

"I know, I'm mad," Fay said, wiping at her cheeks with the heels of her hands. "I keep thinking," she said and more tears came. "When I was first married and came out here—"

"O-la, wonderful!" cried Clara. "Now we'll hear old stories! Old romances!"

Fay smiled through her tears. "It was so nice, I can't tell you. Naraian used to take me for tonga rides, hours and hours, you know how slowly they trot, and he'd point out all the interesting sights on the way—this is Humayun's tomb and this is Safdarjang's—only he always got them mixed up, he told me all wrong I found out afterward—" she smiled again and finally wiped away her tears and blew her nose like a brave girl.

"Beautiful memories," said Clara, "who hasn't got them?" Her hands folded in her lap, her head to one side, she looked into the distance, remembering who knew what people and what places. But a split second later she had leaned forward toward Fay—"How much will you get for them when you need it? Hm? Who'll give you anything for them? Hm? How much?" She thrust out her chin in a pugnacious manner at Fay and rubbed thumb and middle finger together at her as if she were demanding payment there and then.

"You're right," Fay said.

"Tcha," said Clara with a disgusted downward movement of her hands, throwing everything away, letting it all go. She helped herself to a cigarette out of her gold case: "After this I've got to rush," she said as she lit it with her little gold lighter. "I'm having lunch with Mrs. Mrichandani, there's a small party and she wants me to make zabaglione for dessert. And I promised I'd look in on Her Highness later in the afternoon, perhaps read to her a little bit if she hasn't got a headache. She's very fond of historical books, novels about the Mutiny are her favorite. What are you doing today? Not sitting in one of your dirty coffeehouses, I hope?"

Fay looked embarrassed. "I've got someone coming to see me, a bit later, not now—" She gazed round her vaguely, as if searching for a clock to tell her the time.

"Who is it? Some man?"

"He's just a boy really . . . He's from Calcutta," she said in a rush. "He's lonely here, no friends, no money—"

Clara looked up to the ceiling and struck her forehead in a dramatic manner. Her bracelets jingled loudly.

"What else can I do, you tell me, Clara—just sit here by myself day in, day out? Thinking of the boys, and Naraian—and London . . ." Murmuring apologetically, she helped herself to another of Clara's cigarettes. Her hands were shaking with emotion.

"A little bit of *courage*, that's all that's needed," said Clara, pronouncing "courage" as a French word.

"I keep having such a stupid vision—of Hampstead Heath, of all places—that pond where children sail boats, and the pub opposite—"

"*Courage*," said Clara again in French.

"If it weren't for the boys, I'd go back like a shot. What's there to keep me here? Why should I be here? The heat gets me down, I don't think I can stand another summer . . . And everybody taking advantage of you all the time . . ."

Clara opened her handbag and took out her compact. She peered into it carefully and began, with concentration, to repair her face.

"Not only the beggars and the people who sell you things, but everyone you meet practically," Fay was saying.

Clara was determined not to listen. During her years in India she had heard plenty of outbursts of this nature—had had quite a few of them herself—and she knew that, once people got started on them, it was difficult for them to stop and they invariably said more than they meant; and then afterward they would feel ashamed and the people who had listened felt ashamed too.

"You know I gave my watch for repairs?" Fay said. "They took out all the jewels—and this is a shop I've been going to for years. There are hundreds of things like that all the time. It makes me so miserable I could"—she let out her breath and ended in despair—"I don't know."

Clara lowered the lipstick with which she was about to outline her lips: "All right, if you want to be miserable, *be* miserable: but please, I have enough of my own here"—and she tapped the hand holding the lipstick against her heart—"without having to take on yours too."

Fay, an easy blusher, blushed. She got up off the floor and, in her embarrassment, began to tidy around the room. She put the coffee cups together and emptied the ashtray into them. Clara was intent on painting her lips and so could not speak for a while, but as soon as she had finished and was rolling back her lipstick, she said, "Now, no backing out, I'll fix up an evening with Bholi; perhaps supper next week? Just the three of us."

"Thanks awfully, Clara."

"We'll see what he can do for you. And don't forget about that appointment for shampoo and set. I liked the navy and white you were wearing for New Year's—"

"I gave it to Mithan to iron and he made a big scorch right in the front."

"Your fault. I don't allow my Bipin to touch anything except hankies and panties, all the good things I do myself." She wriggled her hips and passed her hands down them to smooth the wrinkles out of her tight dress. Then she put compact and lipstick inside her handbag, but before replacing her cigarette case, she took out all the cigarettes and left them on the table for Fay. "Look at that, your Mithan still hasn't come back—he'll have something to hear from me next time I meet him. Be a good girl," and in spite of her very high heels, she had to stretch up in order to kiss Fay's cheek.

The moment she was alone, Fay dashed into her bedroom and began frantically to open and shut drawers in an attempt to find something clean and pretty to wear. There was no time for a bath, so instead she liberally poured scent over herself. Her young man would be coming any minute. He was a good-looking young man, very dark with huge eyes and long, curly black hair, and thinking of him she began to hum a little song to herself. The tune that rose instinctively to her lips was that of "As I was going to Strawberry Fair," and with it she had a vision of a tall blond gentleman farmer in a tweed coat casually tapping a riding crop against his leg. This vision had always for some unknown reason come to her whenever they had sung this song: and now she saw them all singing it, in the music room, Miss Wilberforce at the piano nodding at them and sometimes raising one hand off the keys in order to beat time with it; and all the girls stood very straight in their tunics and black stockings and their heads were raised and their voices high and their cheeks were rosy and their eyes were clear, and Fay had always wondered whether any of the others thought of gentlemen farmers as they sang.

"Oh Christ," she said aloud to herself, struggling into her clothes, half smiling half tearful, and inconsequentially added under her breath, "Give us this day our daily"; but then there was a rap at the outside door and, hastily zipping up her skirt, she called out, "Just a *min*-ute!" in a trilling voice to her visitor.

(1968)

Day of Decision

THERE WAS NO ONE ELSE, SO DILIP TALKED TO HIMself. "I must do it, I must," he said. He sounded forceful, though he didn't know himself about what. When the old servant brought him his tea, he told him: "Yes, Chotu Ram, it's time for a change, I've made up my mind. Things can't go on like this." Chotu Ram took the opportunity to air his own views of life—dwelling mainly on the superiority of the old days over the present deplorable state of affairs—and went on at such length that Dilip, feeling his train of thought disturbed, got irritated and sent him away.

Later he complained to his mother that Chotu Ram was getting too old and garrulous. And the mother laughed ruefully and said "Old, old—yes, we're all getting old." So then Dilip was sorry that he had brought up the subject and wished he hadn't; but by then it was too late, for his mother had begun on her own complaints which were mainly to do with being old and not many people caring for you anymore and perhaps one was even a nuisance to one's own children. "Mama!" Dilip disclaimed dutifully, but she said no, it was true and perhaps it was only natural for why should anyone care for the old, they were all too often only a nuisance and younger people had their own lives to lead. Then she said she had this pain again, and Dilip, fighting down his desire to run away, asked "Which one?"

"The old one."

"In your knee?"

"No here." She pressed her hand to her side and looked at him with piteous eyes.

"You want me to call the doctor?"

She made a frail gesture: Why put people to trouble? Why bother about an old person? So he went to the telephone and the doctor said he would look in about eleven. His mother was so grateful to him for doing this and became at once so cheerful and affectionate—"Have you had your breakfast, son? Did they make scrambled eggs for you?"—that he was glad he had indulged her.

But his sister Savira was annoyed when he told her what he had done. "There's nothing wrong with her," she said. "It's only a whim."

"I know," Dilip said, "but—"

"Last week she called him four times. And there was nothing. Absolutely nothing."

She frowned over her task. She was sorting old sheets, to see which could still be mended and which had to be used up for rags and bandages. She was always busy with some such task. It was she who was responsible for the high gloss and polish on everything in the house, the obedient servants, the punctual, delicious meals. She was a widow, nearing forty, and getting much too fat.

"There's a letter from Vinod."

She said it in such a way that he knew it contained something special, probably something unpleasant to himself. He waited.

"They are coming next month," she said, turning over sheets, exaggeratedly casual.

"What, *all* of them?"

"Then what." She was still very calm. She even spoke with satisfaction, showing him that she, at any rate, was actuated by right feelings and was glad when a visit from their brother and his family was in the offing. But Dilip knew that she was not all that glad either. She had got used to a quiet life and did not care to have her hushed, polished house overrun by a lot of visitors.

And because she knew that he knew her real feelings, she revenged herself a little bit: "Are you going to the office today?" she asked, looking not at him but only at her sheets and shaking her head over them.

"I may look in," he answered coolly. He left her and went into the room they called the library because it contained all the books in the house. There were some leather-bound legal tomes dating from the time when their father had studied law, an almost complete Dickens, the *Life of Sri Ramakrishna*, *Princes of India*, and a complete set of Proust which Dilip had once ordered from London and had not yet got round to reading. He put his feet up on the sofa and opened the day's newspapers. He yawned. It was so early in the morning, but he was tired already. No, he would not go to the office today. He did not go most days. No one there wanted or needed him. His brother Virender and a trusted old accountant were in charge. They told Dilip nothing. At one time, many years ago, he had tried to take a closer interest in the family business but all he had succeeded in doing was to get on Virender's nerves. Once Virender had come to the house and had shouted and made a big row; he had shouted at their mother and Savira too, telling them to keep Dilip out of his way and not let him come to the office. Since then, Dilip had hardly gone there; when he did, he shuffled around uneasily in the outer offices and felt like a stranger and was treated as one.

His eyes roved over the newspaper, but he was not taking much in. He said to himself, between yawns, "I must do it, I must." He meant he must change his whole life. It could not go on like this. He was not getting anywhere and also he was bored and tired. This was not the way he had imagined things would turn out for him.

Should he get married? When people were married they

seemed automatically to get a lot more respect. Look at Virender, look at Vinod. They were always being held up as examples to him. Yet what had they achieved more than he had? Only that they had households of their own, and wives and children; whereas he was still at home with Mother and Savira and all the old servants and all the old furniture and had not yet struck out on his own. Just because of that everyone thought he was less than they were.

But he didn't really want a household of his own. What for? There were already enough households and enough householders, all leading the same kind of lives and wanting the same kind of things like a new electric ice-cream mixer or a holiday in Kashmir. He had nothing against these things, but he did not think he would want to limit his vision to them alone. And he liked children—he was very fond of his nephews and nieces—and perhaps he would have liked to have some of his own, but finally, well, children were children and then they grew up and then they too would become householders and so it went on. And he wondered: Was it enough? Was this what one's life should finally lead to?

So far, he had to admit, his own life led to nothing. Yet there was still possibility: ways were still open to him. It was true, he was over forty, and had lost his figure and a lot of his hair. But inside him nothing had changed. He still loved poetry and music; he was still far too excitable; he was still in love. He folded the newspaper and tossed it aside with the gesture of a man of action. He decided to telephone Amita. Today he would again ask her to marry him. He had often asked her and she usually said yes, but then it never came to anything. Getting a divorce for her meant a lot of trouble, and neither he nor she knew how to set about it; so they just carried on the way they always had done. Usually he was fairly content with that arrangement but not always, and especially not when, as today, he was in a mood of decision.

But on the telephone they told him she was having a bath. He knew that this meant he would not be able to talk to her for hours, because after her bathing she spent a lot of time powdering herself all over with an enormous puff, very slowly and smiling into the mirror as she dabbed. Then she rubbed cream into what looked like wrinkles beginning to form round her eyes, and fondled and oiled the soles of her feet to make them soft, and what was left of the oil she rubbed into her thighs. She did everything in slow motion, lingering over it because she enjoyed it so much. Sometimes she sighed with contentment, and it was all so pleasant and soothing that she became quite drowsy and perhaps even sank down on her bed and shut her eyes, and suddenly she was fast asleep with the little smile of pleasure still on her lips and her oiled thighs spread wide and her hair wet from her bath spread out glistening black on the pillow.

Dilip enjoyed thinking of her like that, but he found it frustrating not to be able to talk to her. He had wanted to so much, not only to settle their future but also to hear her voice purring at him warmly over the receiver and calling him sweetheart, darling, and her own lovely pet. When he thought of her, Dilip felt strong, and hope surged in him that everything could turn out well and life would begin for him in earnest. Only they must be together—without her he was nothing, with her he could become everything. He would be very determined now and force the issue on her. Yes, divorce would be difficult, it would be an obstacle, but what were obstacles for except to be overcome by human strength and resolution?

Savira passed him, carrying a bowl full of roses from the garden. She carried them into the drawing room and began to arrange them—rather gracelessly, for though she was tidy, she was not really artistic. Dilip had followed her into the room. He was longing to talk to someone and, failing Amita, it would have to be Savira. He said, "A lot of things will have to be changed."

Savira didn't say anything, but she appeared to be listening. This encouraged him, for she didn't always have time to listen to him. Often she simply brushed past him, intent on some household task. He went on quickly: "I must get married."

"Who to?" Savira said—irritating him, spoiling his mood. As if she didn't know! Everyone in the house, in the family, perhaps in the whole town knew about him and Amita. They had been the way they were for ten years now and had never made a secret of it. For ten years also he had made resolutions to marry her and had often enough told Savira and his mother and everyone else he thought might be interested. And now she said "Who to."

He was about to make a sharp retort when she said "There's the doctor." Dilip too could hear sounds of arrival, a brisk voice, and then brisk footsteps going to the mother's room. Savira said, "I don't know why you had to call him." She added: "Forty rupees every time he comes," and clicked her tongue in reproach.

Dilip said, with dignity, "Surely Mama's peace of mind is worth forty rupees," but Savira had already walked away, following the doctor into their mother's room to see what he did for his forty rupees.

Dilip rearranged the roses in a better way and sniffed them, and then he too went to the mother's room and paced up and down outside the closed door. When the door opened and the doctor came out, followed by Savira, he stepped forward with a correct look of concern. Behind Savira, through the half-open door, he could see the mother sitting up in bed, doing up her last button with a rather smug invalid expression on her face. Dilip walked the doctor out of the house. He paced beside him, his hands behind his back. The doctor was a good deal taller than Dilip, and he also had a finer, more upright figure. He had studied in America and was a respected and fashionable practitioner with many patients who felt proud of and reassured by his American know-how and his calm, confident manner. It was in this calm, confident manner that he now told Dilip, as they walked out of the house side by side in manly fashion, that there was nothing wrong with his mother except nerves and certain inevitable debilities of old age for both of which conditions fortunately modern science had its remedies. The confidence of his tone was enhanced by a certain lightness—a suggestion that nothing need be taken too seriously, everything was under the control of the doctor and modern science, and one could even (so he made clear by an occasional short, rich laugh) afford to be a little bit flippant about these old-fashioned human anxieties. Dilip liked the doctor's tone, and when the doctor laughed he laughed with him to show how he got the point and was entirely on the same side. It so happened that Dilip did not need reassurance—he knew there was nothing wrong with his mother—but if he had done, he recognized how perfectly the doctor's manner was calculated to give it. He admired him for this. Suddenly he was sure that the doctor was married and had children and lived in a nice house. He admired him for that too. As he watched him drive off in his car, Dilip was fully determined that he too would get married.

But Amita was still having a bath. At least that was what the servant said, though Dilip was sure she had fallen asleep and would now only wake up when she felt hungry. This would not be before quite some time, because before her bath she had no doubt partaken of a very substantial breakfast—she never sat down to a meal that wasn't substantial, it simply would not have been worth her while. He saw that there was no other way but to go to her house and wake her up. He sighed—he would have preferred not to go out but sit around and finish reading the newspaper till Savira would say it was time for lunch. But this was a day of decision, so he had to make some sacrifice. He went to his mother's bedroom to tell her he was going out. He always told her when he was going out, and where he was going, and when he was coming back. Savira also had to be told.

His mother was still lying in bed; she said she didn't feel like getting up. Dilip said, "But the doctor said you were all right." She shut her eyes. "Aren't you all right?" She made a weary gesture with her hand. "Chotu Ram has gone to get the medicine," Dilip said in the same cheerful voice as the doctor's. But his mother only moved her hand in the way she had done before. How old her hand was, and frail, and the skin loose as if it no longer belonged to the bones. Dilip looked down at his own hand and was relieved to find it plump and firm.

Savira came in with a tray which she put down on the mother's bedside table. "She hasn't eaten anything," she said. She stirred around in a cup and held it out to the mother, saying "Come along now." The mother turned away her face. "Do you want me to get angry," Savira said.

"You must eat," Dilip said gently.

"I *can't*," said the mother in a despairing voice.

"Can't, can't," said Savira, "what does that mean? You heard what the doctor said: nothing wrong at all. Just nerves, imagination. I could have told you that without forty rupees. Come along now." And she stirred the spoon relentlessly around in the cup.

The mother's face was turned toward Dilip. To his amazement he saw a tear drop from her eye: just one tear from one eye. Like the skin of her hand, this tear too seemed to be a separate entity, having no connection with the old suffering body that brought it forth.

"Let it be now," he said. He couldn't bear to look at his mother in case he should witness another tear fall. Instead he looked at Savira; their eyes met, she sighed and put down the cup.

"Vinod is coming," Dilip told his mother to cheer her up. "Has she told you?"

"I told her but she wasn't a bit happy," Savira said. "I don't know what's the matter with her today."

"They will make a lot of noise," the mother complained.

"Is that the way to speak," Savira said, truly scandalized. The fact that her mother was voicing her own deepest feelings only heightened her sense of outrage. But Dilip was not ill-pleased.

"Well I'm going along to see Amita," he told his mother. "Can I get anything for you?"

"What should I want?"

"A nice bar of chocolate?" Dilip said temptingly, but she gave what was almost a cry of pain: "I can't *eat.*"

Savira said, "This is a new piece of nonsense now."

"She'll feel better after her pills," Dilip said. "Today I'm going to settle things with Amita. We shall definitely get married as soon as she can get her divorce."

"I don't want any pills," the mother said.

"They'll be very good for you. You'll see how well you feel. Will you like it when I marry Amita?"

The mother again made that weary gesture with her hand.

"It takes years to get a divorce," Savira said.

"Not if you have a good lawyer," Dilip said and got up to go. "Mama, you're sure you don't want anything? What about a little bottle of eau de cologne? To rub on your head for headache? Nice nice," he said, rubbing his own forehead to demonstrate.

"She still hasn't opened that bottle Virender brought from abroad," Savira said. "Will you be home for lunch?"

Dilip hesitated, but only for a moment: "Yes," he said. He turned to go without looking at Savira. He knew there would be a tiny expression of triumph on her face: again he had given her proof that the food prepared in her kitchen was better than in Amita's. But there could be no two opinions about that.

IT WAS AS he had suspected, and he found Amita asleep in her bedroom. She was even in the same position as he had imagined her—stark naked with her legs apart and her hair spread like a great damp black fan over the pillow. At first she didn't want to wake up, but when finally she opened her eyes, she was happy to see him and smiled and tousled his hair. One thing about Amita, he had never known her not to be happy to see him—the moment she caught sight of him, even when he woke her out of a deep sleep, her face lit up, she smiled so that dimples appeared in her cheeks, and then she made some tender gesture toward him.

He sat down on the bed beside her and played with her hair. He unfolded his plan of marriage to her, and she said, as usual, "All right, darling." Then a child's voice called her, and she started up on the bed and said, "Quick, cover me." He looked round and, snatching her silk kimono that lay crumpled on a chair, he threw it over her naked figure, and between them they tugged at it here and there to cover her as decently as possible. Not a moment too soon, for the door had already opened and her little boy came in and asked, "Now what shall I do?"

"Why is he at home?" Dilip asked.

"He has mumps. Did you cut out all those pictures, darling?"

"Come and see."

"Just let Mummy get dressed." She winked at Dilip. "You go with him," she said and smiled down at herself lying naked under the precariously arranged kimono.

Dilip went with the boy into the sitting room. Amita's husband was a government servant, and their house was a government quarter allotted to him according to his status. It was to a standardized design but was quite roomy and could have been made attractive if Amita had been less careless and untidy. The room was a mess. Besides the snippets of paper lying around like a snowfall from the boy's activities, there were some other things scattered about that had no place in a sitting room (such as a tangled ball of string and a broken umbrella). The breakfast things had not yet been cleared away, and there were toast crumbs all over the table and an open pot of yellow jam with a spoon stuck in it.

Dilip admired the pictures the boy had cut out, but at the same time he also looked apprehensively at the boy himself. His jaws were swollen, and Dilip wondered whether mumps was catching. He felt his own glands and asked the boy apprehensively, "Does it hurt?"

"Not now," the boy said. "Look at this one."

"Is it a reindeer?"

"A gnu," the boy said.

Dilip kept on tapping his glands, first one side, then the other. Was it his imagination, or were they not swollen already? He didn't mind an occasional cold to keep him in bed and coddled by Savira with tasty hot drinks, but he dreaded any real illness, especially one entailing discomfort and pain. As soon as Amita came in, he asked her, "Is mumps catching?"

"Very catching," she said. "Haven't you had it?"

"I don't remember."

Now he was really worried. But Amita didn't seem to think it was anything important. She was admiring the boy's cut-out pictures and advising him what to do with them. Her hair was still loose, and she had a comb in one hand which she occasionally ran through it, attempting to get the knots out. She hadn't worn her sari yet but was in her waist-petticoat and short blouse so that her midriff was bare, and the soft, pale-brown flesh bulged in a fold over the string of the petticoat.

"What about the other children?" Dilip asked.

"They're at school."

"Have they had it?"

"No, but I'm sure they will all get it now, one by one. I'll buy you a big scrapbook," she told the boy, "and on one side you can stick all the mammals and on the other all the—what do you call them—you know, birds and insects."

"What about fishes?"

"Have you had it?" Dilip asked.

"I've been trying to remember. Probably. I think I had everything."

"Can you get it twice?"

Amita laughed: "Why are you so worried? You'll look nice with mumps. Plump and nice." She made a sound as if she were eating something delicious and tenderly pinched his cheek.

The boy asked, "Are fishes mammals?"

"I'm not worried for myself," Dilip said. "But my brother Vinod is coming to stay from Bombay. What if his children catch it from me? That would be very bad."

Amita stretched up and ran her comb through what was left of Dilip's hair, murmuring as she did so, "What a pretty boy."

"Why can't you be serious!" Dilip cried. "You're not serious about anything. Not about that other thing either."

"What other thing?"

Dilip groaned and turned away from her. The boy asked again, "Are fishes mammals?"

"Are fishes mammals?" Amita asked Dilip.

"Some are. For instance, whales. Have you got a picture of a whale?" The boy shook his head. "I'll get you one. It's a great big fat animal . . . I've come here to talk to you," he told Amita in exasperation. "It's so important but you won't listen." He thought she was opening her mouth to say something so he shouted, "Don't ask what about!"

"No, I know what about," she said. "Why are you getting angry? Don't you see how much there is on my head? This poor boy sick, and the servant hasn't come back from bazaar yet and there's so much to do." She dusted a few toast crumbs from the table by way of making a start.

He felt sorry. She didn't usually refer to her domestic troubles but allowed him to disregard them. When he thought of their relationship, it was only of himself and her he thought, ignoring all the things that went with her—such as her children, this house, the unpunctual servant, the uncleared breakfast table, her husband, and other troubles of whose existence he was not even aware. He felt sorry for her, also ashamed of his own insensitiveness and the way she so readily forgave it. A wave of tenderness for her passed over him and he murmured, "Let's go in the other room."

Without another word she turned and walked ahead of him into the bedroom. Her habitual swing of the hips was more than ever evident now that she was not wearing her sari and the great curves could be seen swaying—tic-toc, regularly, with slow enjoyment—within the petticoat. As soon as they got to the bedroom, he embraced her and ran his hands down her sides and hid his face against her neck, tasting the soft skin which she had rubbed with oil and washed with soap and dusted with talcum powder but which still retained its own rich, womanly smell. "Please marry me," he said.

"All right, darling," she said, her eyes shut in pleasure at his embrace.

But he let her go and left her and sat on the bed. "No," he said, "it's not possible for you." She came and sat next to him with her arms round him, holding him; he looked so sad. She comforted him and he said, "Why can't we be like other people?"

"We *are* like other people."

"No—I mean married—always together."

He thought about his life at home, his loneliness, and his lack of status. He said, "Till my personal life is settled, I can't get started on anything." She kissed his cheek with hot lips; her breath enveloped him. But he kept on with his thoughts, and in these he imagined that she was asking him, "Get started on what?" and he became irritated with her.

"We've talked about it so often. Do you think I'm not serious? There is a lot of scope in the interior decorating business. People are becoming very conscious about interiors."

"It's a good idea."

"I intend to read up on it quite a bit. And I told you about the man in the garage who has invented something to do with gears? Of course he's just an ordinary mechanic and needs someone with business know-how to exploit the idea. There's a fortune to be made out of a thing like that." There were so many possibilities. How often they had talked about it, he and Amita, about all the opportunities that were waiting to be seized! If only he could just settle himself and get his personal life moving on a more dynamic course. It was being with his mother and Savira that kept him back.

"Every day people are getting divorced," he said. "It's very common nowadays and not at all difficult."

Amita was looking at herself in the full-length mirror, exercising her hips by swinging them to and fro. "I suppose it's too late now to start again with my dancing," she said wistfully.

"And he'll give. He won't mind."

"No."

There was a pause during which Amita undulated her hips.

"How has he been?" Dilip said.

She answered with a light movement of the head to indicate all right.

"He hasn't . . . ?"

"No, he's been fine."

Amita's husband was unfortunate. He drank a lot and liked other women, usually of a lower class; he also beat Amita when he was in a bad mood. Sometimes Dilip found her with bruises on her body. How sad he was then! He kissed those bruises and his eyes filled with tears. But Amita didn't make much of it; she even managed to laugh, especially when she saw that he was crying. She tousled his hair and said it was all right. Then she laughed some more and described how she had to comfort her husband in exactly the same way because he too had cried and had felt very sorry for what he had done to her.

"I want to take you away," Dilip said. He said it with the same anguish and passion with which he had said it for the past ten years. He longed indeed to take her away; also to have her always near him, always for himself. And not only that: "I have to get married!" he cried. "Without marriage, what are you? Nothing."

Amita, still standing before the mirror, now had her hands on her hips. She stamped her feet up and down in the ta-*ta*-ta, ta-*ta*-ta rhythm of the Kathak dance she used to learn. While she was doing this, Dilip suddenly sounded off on the institution of marriage:

"What is it, after all? Merely a hollow social form. And because of this our lives have to be ruined and wasted."

"It's terrible," Amita said sympathetically. She attempted some intricate footwork, chanting the rhythm out loud as an accompaniment; from time to time she said in the middle, "Oh! I've forgotten everything," disappointed with herself.

"I don't care for convention," Dilip said. "I would take you away tomorrow and we would live together and not care one jot for what anyone says. But there are others." He frowned. "My sister Savira is a very conventional person. Her first thought is always, 'What will people say?' That is her only consideration." Now that he had started getting angry with Savira, he could not stop, and all her shortcomings, all the ways in which he felt she hindered him, came into his mind: "The only thing she thinks about is how to keep the house clean and tidy. That is what she lives for. How frightened she is that something might be dropped on her carpets, or someone might by some accident scratch the sideboard. If it weren't for her, we could be so comfortable in that house, you and I. There's such a lot of space. I would move out of my room and we would take the big bedroom upstairs."

"And then the children could have your room."

"Yes," Dilip said, attempting to suppress his dismay. He loved to indulge himself in visions of Amita coming to live with him, but he always managed to evade all thought of the children who were attached to her. And indeed it was impossible to think of them living in his house with his mother and Savira, making a noise, stamping up and down the stairs, disarranging the furniture—and that not just for a week or two, as when Vinod brought his family, but for years, forever—no, it could not be thought of.

"Mother was so strange this morning," he said. "You know what she said when she heard Vinod was coming? 'They will make a noise.' Can you imagine! Her own son and grandchildren!"

"Old people get like that."

"And Savira pretended to be very shocked. But you know in her heart of hearts she feels the same. I can tell—yes, even though she pretends to be happy and smiles on her face, really she is also thinking of the noise they will make and how they will disturb everything and be a lot of trouble. She is such a hypocrite."

Amita had given up her dance steps before the mirror. She began to put on her sari. She sighed sadly: "If only I hadn't been so lazy . . . I wanted to practice—I liked it—but . . ." she sighed again.

"You are lazy. Look at the way you go to sleep after your bath."

"Yes—I sleep, I eat, I listen to the radio—and in the meantime what happens? I get fat—and old—"

"No no."

"Yes! And you too! Look at you!"

At that, Dilip really looked down at himself. There was no doubt that he too was getting fat. It was all those heavy meals of Savira's; and he never seemed to get time to do any exercise. Perhaps he ought to take up tennis again. He and Amita both: they could go to the club in the evenings and have a game or two.

"Do you still have your tennis racket?" he asked.

"What are you talking about? Here I'm thinking about our life, everything we have become, and you—Go home! I'm tired of you. I don't want you."

He tugged at her sari to make her sit down with him on the edge of the bed. He kissed a tear from her cheek. "Why do you think I've come today?" he said in a voice breaking with tenderness. "Why am I here? Only to tell you that now everything is going to change."

She did not return his caresses nor did she react in any way to what he said, as if these words had no meaning for her. The boy came in and said, "There is a telephone for Uncle."

"For me?" Dilip said, looking at Amita in surprise.

"Come here baby," Amita said to the boy, and as he approached her, she reached out for him, grabbing him, and drew him close to her. She held him tight and kissed his face all over, murmuring "Mummy's pet, my angel."

"You shouldn't do that," Dilip said. "Not if you're not sure if you've had it or not."

"Oh go away. Go and take your telephone."

"It will only be Savira. I suppose she wants me to bring something from the bazaar. As if I'm her servant," he grumbled.

It was Savira. But a strange, shaking, incoherent Savira: "Mama's not well," she said. "Come quickly."

At the sound of this familiar voice cracked so strangely under the strain of something unfamiliar, Dilip felt as if his heart dropped plumb through him and with such force that his legs began to shake. His voice became like Savira's, and they spoke to each other like two ghosts: "Have you called the doctor?"

"He's here. Come quickly. Quickly."

Amita came out of the bedroom. She looked at his face, and her hand was already poised over her heart ready to clutch it.

"Mother's not well," he said.

"Is she very bad?"

"I don't know." But he did know, that was why his legs were trembling.

Amita uttered an appeal to God. Then she straightened Dilip's shirt and smoothed his hair and kissed him goodbye. He remained quite passive and went away; it was only when he was walking down the street that he remembered she should not have kissed him because of the infection.

THE FIRST PERSON Dilip met at home was Chotu Ram who was standing by the stairs with tears running down his cheeks. When he saw Dilip, he began to cry out loud and to wail and clutch his head in agony. Dilip went past him straight into the mother's bedroom. The doctor was there, and Virender; they were conferring together, both looking grave and important. Savira was on the other side of the bed, holding the end of her sari in front of her mouth. Dilip went and stood next to her. The doctor and Virender did not seem to have noticed his entrance—at any rate, they went on conferring together without looking up.

The mother looked the same but also terribly different. She had always been small and in old age had shrunk pitifully, but now she looked so entirely wasted that it was impossible to think that this body, as insubstantial as a withered leaf, could ever have sustained any life. And how still she was, what a dreadful lack of movement. Only this morning he had noticed how her flesh had hung from her bones and he had felt sad at this stigma of old age. But that flesh had moved—it had had life in it—and the tear too that had fallen from her eye and had wrung his heart—that too had been warm and had dropped from a human being who had suffered and cried "No, no, I can't eat!"

"Mama!" Dilip exclaimed and sank to his knees and buried his face in the bed. He cried and sobbed—in great grief and anguish, but also with a strange feeling of relief, almost triumph, that he could do so, that he was alive and had that inside him which could make him feel these terrible human emotions and give expression to them. And through his cries he became aware that Savira too had begun to shout out loud and now she too had sunk onto the floor and was next to him. They turned to one another, and it was good to feel her in his arms and to feel her tears falling on his neck and her bosom squashed against him and heaving with the same pain that was tearing him apart.

Virender was asking for Vinod's telephone number. Savira said she had it written down, she got to her feet and went out with him to put in a long-distance call. The doctor, left alone with Dilip, began to explain to him about the cause of death. He was as calm and confident as ever, just as if he had predicted this all along. The pills he had prescribed for the patient were lying on the bedside table; Chotu Ram had fetched them from the chemist, but she had never taken them. Dilip saw the doctor pick them up and look at them with brief professional interest and then put them down again. When he had finished his technical explanation, he ended up, "Very sad"; but it was not possible for him to look sad because he remained so well-groomed and unruffled and in complete command of any situation that might present itself.

And Virender, now returning from the telephone, gave exactly the same impression, even though his eyes had become a little red. He began to discuss practical matters with the doctor, such as arrangements for the funeral and would blocks of ice be needed to preserve the body till that time. The doctor gave his opinion, and they talked to and fro in calm, manly voices, without taking any notice of Dilip and Savira: not so much ignoring as *sparing* them because they were still weeping copiously and did not look capable of practical thought. Dilip noticed how they left him out, but he did not care. Let them talk, he thought; at that moment he did not esteem or envy them. On the contrary, their preoccupation with practical matters seemed childish to him. At such moments, he thought, it was nobler to be like Savira who was swollen and soggy with tears, gave out short pushing cries like an animal, and beat now her breast and now her head with her fists. The doctor and Virender went on talking about what time the electric crematorium should be booked and the hearse ordered. Dilip's eyes were again on the terribly still figure on the bed. A fly was now buzzing impudently around the face. Dilip waved his hand at the fly without succeeding in chasing it away, and then he too cried out like Savira and began to beat himself about the head.

Chotu Ram came to call him to the telephone. Dilip knew it would be Amita and he didn't want to talk to her. He wanted to stay here with his mother's dead body and grieve over it with Savira. He accompanied Chotu Ram reluctantly. The moment they were outside the door, the servant—quick as lightning in spite of his old bones—went down to the floor to touch Dilip's feet.

"What are you doing!" Dilip cried out.

"Your Honor," Chotu Ram said, "Baba Sahib, I'm your child."

"Get up."

"I look only to you. You're now my mother and my father." And Chotu Ram joined his hands and looked up at his master in humble submission.

Dilip understood that Chotu Ram was afraid there would be changes in the house and that he would be dismissed. At that moment he also understood that he, Dilip, was now master, and that it was up to him to decide whether there would be changes or not, whether the house would be sold or kept on, whether he and Savira would continue to live here or go their separate ways. All this was now up to him.

"Get up," he said again. He proceeded to the telephone. He picked up the receiver but, before speaking into it, he told Chotu Ram, "Why do you worry? I'm here to look after you."

Amita's voice came anxiously over the telephone.

"It is all finished," Dilip told her with dignity and without tears. "Mother's gone."

Amita emitted a cry of shock. Then she began to commiserate with him. Her voice was saturated in love and grief. She told him she knew how terrible it was for him, what it was to lose a mother and such a mother, who had loved him so much; and he had loved her too, he had been a good son and had made her last days happy and that was now his only comfort, if one could speak of comfort in such a loss. Everything she said, and the deep feeling with which she said it, touched him to the depths of his being. He responded to her words with a new gush of tears and with broken words of thanks to her, not only for what she was saying but also for being there to envelop him with her love in this hour of darkness.

Savira came to join him by the telephone. She stood very close to him. She could hear Amita's voice talking, talking, caressing him over the telephone. Savira did not take her eyes away from his face.

He realized that Savira was looking at him in the same way Chotu Ram had done. She too was afraid there would be changes in the house. And then Dilip himself began to be afraid that things would change—that others would come to live in the house—that their quiet routine would be disturbed—that Savira would no longer be able to cook and care for him. He returned her frightened look and they gazed wildly at each other, seeking reassurance.

"Darling, my pet," Amita was saying, "please speak to me. Say you can bear it." Savira let out a wail. "Who's that?" Amita asked.

"She's gone!" cried Savira. "She's left us!" She clung to Dilip and, calling out to their dead mother, reproached her for going away and leaving them alone like this, two helpless orphans. When she said that, Dilip's grief knew no bounds and, still clutching the telephone, he clung to Savira as she clung to him and they hugged each other's stout bodies and wept together and promised never to leave each other.

"Shall I come?" Amita said. "Do you want to see me?" And when he didn't answer, she went on, "It's all right—if you don't want me now, I'll come tomorrow. Whenever you say. Whenever you need me."

Savira was still weeping copiously, but Dilip noticed that, beneath its grief, her face had taken on the same expression it had worn earlier in the day when he had told her he would be eating lunch at home and not in Amita's house.

(1972)

An Intellectual Girl and an Eminent Artiste

GABY WAS NOT INTERESTED IN INDIAN MUSIC (NOR IN India) so she did not go to the concert. She nearly did not go to the party either and when she did she wished she hadn't. She would have gone away again, but she had been alone in her apartment all day—in fact, for several days—and felt reluctant to go back there.

She did not care for Baqir Khan any more than for the others at the party; if anything, less. She at once saw that he was a great show-off. This did not surprise her, for although her experience of Indians was limited, she had found all of them to be great show-offs. Of course she had only met them at New York parties where, if one did not show off, one would not be noticed. But Indians seemed to do it more than anyone else: or perhaps they just had more to do it with. At this party there was one Indian student, handsome as from *The Arabian Nights*, who never spoke a word but sat at people's feet and looked up at them; and an Indian girl in chiffon veils and gold-painted eyelids who chirped and fluttered around the room. But neither of them had a chance against Baqir Khan. Actually, he was not as good-looking as he might have been (the student outdid him there a hundred times)—nor, for that matter, all that young. But he appeared to have a wonderful personality. He sat in the same place all evening and people formed an admiring group around him. He also appeared to be something of a raconteur, for Gaby could hear his voice rising on a series of anecdotes that were received with gusts of laughter. He cried, "No, wait wait wait!" and then he would say more and they would laugh more. But their laughter was not so much of amusement—evidently what he was telling them was not as funny as he thought and they pretended—but admiration and appreciation of his personality. They were paying homage to him in his double role of Indian and eminent artiste.

Gaby did not form part of this admiring circle, and she might have spent the entire evening without meeting him if the hostess had not insisted on introducing her. Gaby, though not exactly somebody, was also not entirely nobody: she had published some critical articles in papers of good standing and had the reputation, confirmed by her looks, of being a New York intellectual. The hostess, in effecting the introduction, made the most of these credentials (there weren't many people at the party who had even that much—their hostess, though ambitious and quite skillful, was not yet very successful). Gaby, who realized that her claim to fame did not go far enough to impress Baqir Khan, was surprised at the amount of notice he nevertheless took of her. He gave her a look that was penetrating, and estimating, and went, it seemed to her, a long long way. She wondered why he bothered: unless of course he bothered like that with everyone, just in case they might one day be useful to him.

Was it because of that look, or again because he remembered everyone, that he recognized her at once when they met again a few days later? It was a chance encounter in the elevator of her apartment building. When it turned out that he lived in the same building, she did nothing more than exclaim politely over the coincidence; but he felt it necessary to assure her that he was quite comfortable in this apartment, which had been rented for him by his sponsors. He also told her that he was here for six months at the invitation of a wealthy foundation to teach and give recitals of Indian music. Although she showed only the minimum of interest in this information, he went into detail like a person who is convinced that everything connected with himself must be of interest. They parted in the street. Probably there would be more such encounters, but Gaby gave no thought to them. It did not occur to her that their meetings would ever be anything other than routine.

But their next meeting, though it was again in the elevator, was not in the least routine. At first there were only the two of them. They had met in the lobby, had acknowledged their acquaintance and with it the necessity of making conversation till they could be released from each other's company. At the sixth floor another passenger joined them. It was about two in the morning, a noiseless lonely time. The elevator, lit by a shadowless light, shot upward like a capsule released into space. The new passenger was a woman with white-blond hair straggling around her shoulders: she wore a white suit and white knee-length boots. She said, "Could you give me five dollars, please." She reinforced this demand by showing them a razor blade. The purpose of this razor blade was not clear: Was she going to use it on them or on herself? She looked like a woman who might slash her own wrists or had already done so—unsuccessfully but perhaps more than once—in the past. Baqir Khan fumbled at his pockets but he was trembling so much that he had difficulty getting his money out: when he did, the note shook in his hand. She said "Thanks" and zipped it into her pocket; she got off at the next floor without another look at them.

Baqir Khan got off with Gaby at her floor as if afraid to travel any further on his own. He accompanied her into her apartment. He sank down on her sofa. The first word he spoke was "Terrible." He wiped perspiration from his face.

Gaby, herself far less affected by the incident, offered him a drink. He refused it. He said, "Her *face*," with horror.

It had not made such a great impression on Gaby; she had seen so many like it. Although at first sight young, it had been middle-aged with a dead skin overlaid with bright suntan makeup. The expression was that of a failed middle-aged life: nothing unusual at all.

"Terrible," he said again. But he was beginning to recover. The first sign of this was that he took note of his surroundings. His eyes took in her apartment in the same way he had taken her in when they were first introduced at the party. Having done so—having estimated it—he looked at her. Again she had the feeling that he was looking far. She became self-conscious—knew herself too tall, too lean, too flat-chested. She had devised a costume for herself that she wore almost all the time: a long gown that left her long neck bare. A long bead necklace was her only ornament.

But he too was suddenly self-conscious. He sat up straight, put away the handkerchief with which he had wiped away his perspiration of fear. He felt he had to assure her: "I was not afraid."

"Of course not," she said (thinking to herself—"not much!").

It seemed he could read thoughts. He said, "You thought I was afraid." He laughed: "Ha, ha!" He began to tell her a long story of how once he had been attacked in Calcutta by a gang of bad characters and had routed them single-handed. As he told this tale, he became again the boastful, lively character she had met at the party. His eyes danced with delight at his own fine qualities. He was wearing Indian dress, a loose raw-silk shirt and an embroidered shawl over one shoulder.

"No, I was not afraid," he said again when he had finished. But then he took on a puzzled look; he said, "I felt—" and could not go on to say what. This was what was puzzling him. Obviously he was not used to discussing complicated feelings.

But she was. It was in a way her forte, she had done it all her life. She explained to him that it was not for himself that he had been afraid but for this woman and the horrors that beset her, what she represented: that life could take such forms and be such hell.

"Yes," he said. He was relieved to have it all explained to him; so relieved that he said, "Now where is this drink?"

He didn't wait for ice or soda. She had hardly poured hers when he was already holding out an empty glass. She refilled it for him. "Do you know where I have come from?" he said.

"A party," she said.

"Of course! Of course! There are always parties. But *afterward*."

The way he said that and looked at her mischievously with his head on one side, she said, "I can guess."

He put his head back to laugh uproariously. Then she had to fill up his glass again. He became serious and said, "It always happens." Then he asked her "Why?" with full trust that she would be able to explain this to him too as she had explained his feelings.

"Maybe because you're a very attractive man."

"Oh, of course!" Again he roared with laughter. But there was something modest in that: as if he didn't pride himself at all but knew there was some other cause.

"Often I think," he said, serious over his fourth drink, "I think: poor women. To be so—"

"Hungry?"

"Very good! Very good! It is like people with food. They eat and eat and still they are not satisfied. This lady who took me to her home tonight: such a fine apartment—costly, beautiful— she should be so happy. But when I wanted to leave, she wept.

She begged, 'Again! Again!' I said, 'Madam, excuse me.' I don't get tired easily, but tonight with her it was too much. I didn't want to any more. I wanted to go away. I'm not tired now," he invited Gaby.

She explained, "I don't sleep with people unless I'm in love with them."

He was amused. He asked, "Are you in love very often?" The expression "in love" was obviously a joke to him.

She said, ruefully: "Often enough."

He laughed; she did amuse him. He said, "Then why not with me?" He added, "Is it because I am Indian?"

"Oh, really," she said. She was quite outraged. But that too he had said as a joke. He didn't for a moment believe it, he was much too proud of himself.

Again he looked around the room. "Books books books," he said. "Have you read all of them? I think you are an intellectual."

"You think I'm sexless, don't you?"

She could have bitten off her tongue. What had made her say it? To a man like him! And at three o'clock in the morning.

He asked her for another drink but did not take up her stupid remark. Instead he said, "Do you live here all alone?"

"Yes, I like it. What's the matter? I *do* like it. You don't believe me?"

"Perhaps. I know some girls like very much to be . . ." Coming upon yet another missing word, he filled it up by finishing his drink and held out the empty glass to her. When she hesitated, he said—how good he was at reading thoughts!—"Don't be afraid. This is nothing for me. Look at me: Is there any change? Do I look like a drunken man?" He certainly did not. He was bright and alert. His eyes were rather small and with a Tartar slant, but they lit up his whole face and made it—though there were plenty of lines (he was certainly in his forties)—young, quick, volatile, amused. She did not look back into those eyes but she did refill his glass. She felt she was in the presence of a very powerful man.

ALTHOUGH, AS SHE had admitted to him, she fell in love quite frequently, she had never before done so with a powerful man. Coming to think of it, she had never really met one. Everyone she knew was like herself. They were intellectually sensitive and analytical and were tormented by modern problems. Such was her type. Baqir Khan was diametrically its opposite. Was that why she kept him secret? She had never done that with any of her lovers. But now she liked to do it. She especially liked to keep him secret from her mother, although it always amused her to think of him while she was in her mother's apartment. His presence there (even though only in her thoughts) made her laugh.

All through her adolescence, the person who had irritated her the most was her mother. To her at that time Sophie was a caricature of everything that Gaby herself had wanted to be and then, seeing it distorted, had dreaded to become. Like other Central Europeans of her education and background, Sophie loved good books, good music, good paintings: in that field, only the highest and best, *das Hoechste und Beste, das Klassische*. She had a pretty though rather simple face, and whenever she spoke of cultural matters, she took on a very special expression. This irritated Gaby more than anything. She would try and share her feelings with her father who lived separated from her mother, but all he said was, "So what if you don't like her face when she talks about Beethoven?" Gaby had answered, bitterly, "It's all right if you're not there to *look*"; but in fact later she too outgrew, or at least learned to overcome, her childish irritation.

Nowadays, and especially since her father's death, Gaby went to visit her mother quite frequently. It was home for her. Sophie's apartment was a very expensive one but it had a poor view; in fact, no view at all, it was completely closed in, Gaby hated that but it seemed to suit Sophie. She always liked, she said, to create her own atmosphere, and she did so by means of swathed and looped white silk curtains under heavy velvet drapes, a chandelier, a grand piano, and a lot of books in glass cases. Here Sophie sat drinking coffee and nibbling at *Bäckerei* with Uncle Rudolph (whom she had lately married after many years of cohabitation). The room was so dark that most of the time the chandelier had to be on. But there was a good deal of atmosphere and Sophie and Uncle Rudolph were happy. They both enjoyed Gaby's visits although both were somewhat nervous of her. Uncle Rudolph was also culturally inclined—he and Sophie read, visited museums, went to all the good concerts—and was very interested to hear Gaby's opinions on modern trends. He listened to her with the most flattering attention, inclining his head in her direction, and when he missed something. he said *"Pardon"* (in French) and cupped his ear.

But in fact Gaby never spoke of anything that was important to her during these visits. It was a hangover from those stormy earlier years when Sophie had desperately wanted to know and felt it her right to know. Gaby had resisted violently and they had had terrible scenes. Now all that had died away—Sophie was resigned and Gaby indifferent—and they were free to talk of nothing, or almost nothing. But beneath that nothing Sophie was listening all the time, Gaby knew, and not only listening but *hearing*. No one else in the world—no, not one of her friends with whom she discussed everything—knew Gaby's state as well as Sophie with whom she discussed nothing.

ONE MORNING, COMING down to her own apartment after having spent the night upstairs in Baqir's, Gaby could hear her phone ring and ring. She did not hurry very much to answer it.

She glanced through her mail, hoping the phone would stop. But it didn't and at last she picked it up.

"My God," Sophie said. "Where have you been?"

"I was washing my hair."

"And last night? And all day yesterday? And at two o'clock in the morning?" Sophie sounded hysterical, really beside herself—which was perhaps why she dared do something she hadn't dared in years: she *shouted* at Gaby. "I'm your mother! I have a right to know!"

"But know what?" Gaby said—laughing, and thereby conceding (also for the first time in years) her mother's right.

"Don't treat me like I'm an idiot. Do you hear me? Are you there? My God, she's hung up."

"I'm here."

"Darling," Sophie said, "please don't hang up—I know I'm an idiot and I'm stupid and foolish and anyone would lose their temper with me—but I couldn't sleep all night. Every half hour I rang you. And Rudolph is out of his mind, too. We were just going down to take a cab and come straight over. Yes, yes, yes, I know—you're right—I'm ridiculous, but one reads such things in the papers."

"Of course if you're going to read the *papers*."

"Only yesterday a girl was found in her apartment, just round the block to you. And the other day an elderly woman, sixty-five years old—sixty-five, Gaby!—with nothing on except her panties."

"Oh, please don't tell me these stories. As if one doesn't hear enough."

"They're not stories, they're facts facts facts. Go and look in the morgues—just go and see—all right, I'm stupid, but then to hear the phone ring and ring and ring and thinking of you alone in that apartment and no one answering—"

"There's someone at the door."

"Gaby! Will you come and see us today? Will you?"

"I must go. All right, all right, I'll try."

She went to the door and opened it without thought. There was a man she didn't know out there. He was very tall, very broad, and had red hair. He wore a brown suit with a silver pinstripe. He said he was the building inspector and had come to inspect a complaint she had made regarding her kitchen ceiling. She stepped aside, he came in and shut the door behind him. They were trapped together in the tiny vestibule. He was truly enormous. She realized that if she screamed now no one would hear her. Her heart beat. Unable to speak, she pointed to the kitchen. He went in there; she went into her bedroom and locked the door. She snatched up the phone. "Come down quickly," she told Baqir. "Hurry." She put down the receiver and listened to sounds from the kitchen. There wasn't anything. She remained sitting on her bed, waiting.

The red-haired man called to her from outside: "Miss!" She looked at the locked door, she didn't answer or move. "Miss?" He didn't move either. She didn't know what he was doing out there or what he was waiting for. She was waiting for the doorbell. When it buzzed, she jumped up and unlocked the bedroom door and went out. The man had already opened the entrance door and he and Baqir stood staring at each other. Then the man stepped aside and said, "Excuse me." Gaby realized that he really was the building inspector.

"We'll have it fixed," he told her. "I'll be sending the men up."

"Would you, please? Thank you very much." She was laughing breathlessly. "Come in," she told Baqir. "They'll be coming soon?" she said to the man, who was already outside the door. "I'd like to have it fixed, it's been a nuisance. Thanks." She called again after him down the hallway: "Thank you very much!" She shut the door and went on laughing. Baqir was astonished.

"He was the building inspector," she said. "He came to look

at the kitchen ceiling. Bits of plaster fall in the food, probably poisoning me . . ." Now she was laughing at the expression on Baqir's face. "I just panicked," she said. "It was talking to my mother—"

"What did Mother say?"

"Oh, she was telling me horror stories about what happens to girls who live alone."

"Right!" he shouted. "Mother is right!"

He ran into her bedroom and began frantically opening her closet and chest of drawers and pulling out her clothes. He stood there with his arms full of nighties and panties and holding a pair of her walking shoes in his hand.

"You are coming with me," he said. "Upstairs."

SHE DID GO with him that time, but not to stay. She stayed one or two days sometimes and quite often she stayed the night, but sooner or later she always wanted to get back to her own apartment. She needed to be alone and quiet, and that was impossible in his apartment. She never knew quite how many people were living there or who they all were. There was not much furniture and at night they tended to curl up wherever they found a convenient place. Many of these people seemed to have come with him from India. There were his accompanists, some of whom played drums and some twangy one-stringed instruments, and then there were unspecified attendants who were sent on errands and did a great deal of Indian cooking in the kitchen (a smell of spicy curries had seeped not only into everything in the apartment but down the hallway as well). There were a number of pale young American disciples who wore sandals and Indian shirts and strove to be as humble as an Indian disciple and to obliterate their personalities in the presence of the guru. Gaby found it very irritating to be surrounded by so many people all the time, but Baqir took their presence entirely for granted. It even seemed to be a condition of life for him. They moved and sat and lay all around him—sometimes he had to step over them—but he found it quite easy to ignore them. This was utterly impossible for Gaby. Every one of those people was a personality that impinged on her and sometimes to such an extent that she felt like screaming. Of course she repressed it, and instead ran away downstairs to her own apartment. Baqir, on the other hand, never felt the necessity to run away but he screamed quite often. Suddenly—apparently for no cause at all or only the most trivial—he would rage and stamp around. Then everyone was very quiet and sat with lowered eyes, waiting for him to finish. Sometimes he slapped people and once he chased an offender all around the apartment, brandishing his slipper. But he always calmed down again quite soon and then everyone, including the people who had been slapped, resumed their activities, and he too carried on as if nothing had happened.

THERE WAS ONE room with a bed in it, and whenever he wanted to be alone with her, he took her in there and shut the door. Suddenly there was complete silence in the apartment; it was as if when he was not there everyone else ceased to exist. Then he and Gaby could be very private together. Besides everything else, he liked having conversation with her. It seemed to be something new to him—to be with a woman and when their business together was finished not to get up and go away but to continue lying there and talk to her. For Gaby of course it was not new at all. In her experience that had always been the best time for talking; but whereas with others it was usually she who did most of it—volubly, subtly, intelligently (she was at her best then)—with him she just lay there and listened. Sometimes he talked so much that she nodded off and when she woke up he was still talking. He himself tended to be the main topic, and when he touched on others, it was usually in reference to the role they played for him. The person who played the smallest role seemed to be his wife. She was hardly ever mentioned, and when Gaby asked about her, he shrugged and said, "She is a simple lady." He had been married to her when he was seventeen and she fourteen. They had six children.

But he had several great passions in his life: for his guru, his mother who was dead, and a younger brother. These he loved above everything—even, it seemed to Gaby, above his own six children. Perhaps because they were his alone whereas the children he had to share with his wife and his wife's family. He rated one's own blood relationships as the highest, and when he questioned Gaby about her life, it was never about her career, lovers, friends—those aspects that for her came first—but always about her family. He felt very sorry for her that she had no brother or sister, and very, very sorry that her father was dead. He exclaimed, "But then, how you must love Mother! How you must cling to her!"

Gaby laughed, imagining herself clinging to Sophie. But after a time she admitted, "Well—really—we don't get on too badly nowadays."

"Tell me about her."

He seemed really eager to hear, like a person asking another to show him his most precious treasure. But Gaby did not think of Sophie as her most precious treasure and could only speak about her in those half-exasperated, half-tolerant and amused terms in which she thought of her. This shocked him deeply.

"I can't help it," she defended herself. "We're so—unlike."

"But Mother! *Mother!*"

"So what?"

He was rendered speechless. He even shrank from her a little—they were lying naked on his bed together—as if she disgusted him. Then Gaby was hurt and even somewhat desperate, feeling barriers rising between them. She moved up closer to him and overwhelmed him in her embrace. At first he was cold but she persisted, holding his scented, hairy body against herself until he yielded.

He tried to remonstrate with her; he said, "A mother is—" As so often happened with him, his feelings were stronger than any words he knew of; usually she helped him out but this time she couldn't.

"Who cares for us the way she does?" he said. "She is everything for us. She is the earth that gives us nourishment. Her love guards and protects at every step. Oh Ma!" he cried and shut his eyes. When he opened them again, she saw that there were tears in them. She was amazed and deeply shaken, but he did not seem to be all that much put out. He said, "Whenever I think of her, my heart—" He made an upward surging movement with his hand. "As long as she was living, there was always a place for me. One sacred spot on this earth."

"But what about your wife?"

"Wife is not mother."

Gaby said, "She should be more."

"How is it possible? It cannot be. Wife's heart is with her own family—with mother and father and the home where she lived in happy days of childhood. But for the mother we are her all."

"It so happens," Gaby said, "my mother is remarried."

"That doesn't matter. You will always be first for her. The child is always first."

Gaby could not honestly contradict this. She knew Sophie to be very fond of Uncle Rudolph but at the same time recognized that her feelings for Gaby herself were of a different quality.

"Oh," he cried suddenly, "how I long to meet her!"

"Who?"

"Mother."

"Mine?" Gaby laughed the way she always did when she thought of the two of them meeting. Then she said, "Well, why not? You can if you want."

He was so astonished that he held her away from himself for a moment, the better to scrutinize her face. It did not seem to him that she could be serious.

That made Gaby laugh again: "She likes meeting my boyfriends," she said.

"Oh, you Americans! You Americans!"

AT FIRST SOPHIE and Rudolph were very nervous with Baqir: they were always nervous with Gaby's friends and afraid they might not live up to their standards. But Baqir soon put them at their ease. He took everything on himself, talking ceaselessly and with large gestures. Gaby had not seen him this way since the first time she met him when she had thought of him as a show-off. Now she realized that he was not showing off but putting himself out to entertain and make everyone happy. Soon Sophie and Rudolph were quite relaxed, and although they had read up something of Indian music and were ready with questions about raga and *talam*, they now forgot all about them and simply enjoyed their unusual guest.

And what cook would not have been gratified to see the way he fell on the food and ate it with loud noises and relish? Sophie tripped on her high heels between kitchen and dining room, humming glad snatches of Mozart, and she kept refilling his plate till he held his stomach and cried for mercy. By this time she had laid aside her more sophisticated personality and became for him just a housewife, a mother whose one concern it was that he should enjoy her cooking. He complimented her on everything—not only her cooking but her flowers, her table arrangement, her furniture, her beautiful home. At one point he leaned over and admired her dress, respectfully touching the coffee-colored lace that cascaded from her neckline. Sophie—who did have a lot of chic—became quite simple and shy. Then Baqir invited her to gang up with him against Gaby and her invariable costume of long woolen gown and bead necklace. They also commiserated with each other on Gaby's skinniness due to insufficient feeding, and those cigarettes! Terrible! Also her beautiful hair which she had inherited from Sophie's side of the family—"And just see what she does with it!" Sophie cried, running her hand over Gaby's rough-cut hair. Gaby jerked away but not before her mother had managed to steal a quick kiss at her temple. Baqir watched them with a tender expression on his face, and Uncle Rudolph also looked happy though he delicately turned aside to sniff the flower in his buttonhole as if not wishing to intrude.

FROM THAT TIME on Sophie and Rudolph attended every recital that Baqir gave in New York. They found the atmosphere very moving and beautiful. The audience was quite different from other concert audiences. They were mostly young and had pale, fine-drawn faces that spoke of spiritual experiences. All of them participated in the music—some gave exquisite little cries, some sat in trancelike concentration. The stage was decorated with banana leaves and a backdrop featuring an abstract Indian motif. Baqir and his accompanists, dressed in Indian clothes, sat on a carpet ringed around by their American disciples who were also dressed in Indian clothes and who strained forward with their mouths open like plucked and hungry birds.

For Sophie, Baqir's playing was an emotional experience that left her shaking from head to foot. She could not understand how Gaby could keep so cool about it. But Gaby never did get excited about Baqir's music. She realized that one could learn to like it very much but she would not do so. She felt that it played on too many soft feelings and allowed, indeed invited, one to sink into luxurious soul-sensations. She saw it happening all the time to the disciples who filled the apartment, those intense young people, many of whom had once been on drugs but now didn't need them anymore because they had found Baqir and his music. Middle-aged ladies also seemed to be susceptible to it.

Sophie complained to Baqir that Gaby was a cold, unemotional, overly intellectual girl and she did not know how an inspired artiste like himself could bear to put up with her.

"Yes, she is terrible," he agreed. But he was smiling. It did not in the least offend him that Gaby resisted his music. On the contrary, it even amused him—the way he was sometimes amused when she held out against him physically and then surrendered to him after all.

"You will learn to love," he often said calmly, with regard to her attitude toward Indian music.

WHENEVER GABY SPENT the night with Baqir, she woke up to the sound of prayer. She lay on the bed, stark naked and leaning on her elbow to watch him. He was prostrate on his prayer carpet, his head covered with a knotted handkerchief, and repeatedly knocking his forehead on the floor while murmuring the names of God and his prophet. When he had finished, he got up, took off his handkerchief, and went out to shout at people for not having his tea ready. He had told her that really he ought to be saying his prayers five times a day but being a very busy man and a sinner he usually managed it only once. But he never missed that: he told her that it would be impossible for him to live through his day if he did not speak to God first thing in the morning. He could not understand how she was able to live without prayer, without religion. He did not think it was possible for any human being.

"That's what my father came to feel," she told him. "But only toward the end."

"And before?"

"Oh, he was quite an old-fashioned Middle European reared on Hegel, Marx, and Bergson." The expression on his face made her kiss him with ardor: she loved being with someone who was unfamiliar with these names.

But then she grew serious again. She rarely spoke about her father and then only to those to whom she felt very close. Terrible sad feelings stirred in her heart. She had always had more in common with her father than her mother, and during her college vacations she had often gone to visit him in his large, empty Riverside Drive apartment. He spent his time reading and going for walks. But he grew sadder and sadder, Gaby did not know why. Each vacation she found him a bit worse. He—so rational, Western-educated—began to talk about religion. It was then he said what Baqir said. "It is needed," he said. "Like water, air." She found him reading strange books of Jewish mystical writers with whom he had nothing in common. He had had a completely secular upbringing, his father (a banker) had been an ardent German patriot, and all had forgotten they were Jews till the thirties came. Even then it did not mean much to them beyond a historical accident. But now he began talking about the *Devekut*, the mystical intent, the yearning of the soul for God.

"Ah," said Baqir, moved to ecstasy by these words.

"Yes, but it didn't do him any good," Gaby said. Baqir held her against him; she could feel his heart beating against her as if it were in her own body. "He killed himself," she said.

Baqir cried out in horror and grief. His reaction was so immediate that the event became immediate too and she was overwhelmed by the feelings of those days.

"I didn't see him the last few weeks. I was away at college. I thought he was all right when I left him. Oh, he was melancholy but I thought it was more in a philosophical way. I couldn't understand that anyone could actually be living all those things. I was so used to discussing them . . ."

"You were very young."

"He *jumped*," she said. "So many were doing it in those days—it was like an epidemic and the papers didn't even bother to report them anymore," She shut her eyes against his chest and derived strong comfort from his heartbeats, which were as regular and powerful as hammer strokes.

BAQIR WANTED HER to move in with her mother. "Who has ever heard," he said. "A girl lives alone without food—"

"I do eat."

"Yes, I have seen: raw herring and cigarettes. And there is the mother longing for the daughter and to cook and care for her—"

"Are you really suggesting I move in with Sophie and Uncle Rudolph? Can you be serious?"

"It is very very serious. Anything can happen. You saw that man—if he had attacked you . . . I have heard many cases."

"But you're here."

"And when I have gone?"

But in fact neither of them ever thought much about his departure. His contract still had several months to go and they did not care to look beyond that time. Both of them tended to live in the present, though for different reasons: indeed, for opposite reasons. Baqir looked upon the future as a necessity over which one had no control. "Who knows what will be tomorrow," he said, and "It is not in our hands." Gaby on the other hand felt that it *was*. One could control—one could manipulate—and it was one of the privileges of independence to do so or not as one wished. And it was often more enjoyable not to. She had been through many love affairs and enjoyed letting them develop in their own way, to take their own time, to let them ride even though they usually rode to their end. That too was part of one's freedom.

He hated to hear her use that word. "Yes, freedom to become mad," he said. "Like that one." He pretended to be holding something sharp in his hand: "Give me five dollars," he said in a falsetto voice.

Gaby laughed; she said, "I think you want us all behind the veil."

"My wife is not in purdah," he said proudly. "She is quite free to go here and there wherever she wishes. Only she does not wish."

As always when his wife was mentioned, Gaby had an uneasy feeling. She did not like to think of his wife's life. She spent all her time in the house—on that side of it in which the women lived. Baqir had described this house as having many little rooms curtained off from each other and from the passages and stairways that wound around them. It was a very old house in the heart of the city. The men and children spent a lot of time on the roof to catch some cool air, but his wife did not like to go up there because of people looking. She was a very shy lady. That was why she wore the veil when she went out—not because he asked her to (he didn't care at all) but because she was so simple and shy. Anyway, she hardly ever did go out. Only once a year regularly she went away on a pilgrimage to a holy shrine where she made offerings and said prayers for one week. Then she came home and stayed there quiet and refreshed, having prayed for all of them.

"UNNATURAL" WAS ONE of Baqir's worst terms of derogation. He was beginning to apply it more and more frequently to all things American. The weather had changed and that made him very gloomy. He hated wearing an overcoat and shoes on his feet, and indeed these things did not suit him. They muffled up his silk and embroideries, they impeded his large gestures, they dragged him down, made him look ordinary. He mostly stayed indoors now, together with his accompanists and attendants who also could not bear the cold outside. They did a lot of Indian cooking because they could no longer eat American food. The dry overheated air of their apartment was saturated with curry, oil, and incense. Everyone was terribly homesick. Baqir often spoke to Gaby about India now, and when he did so his face took on a soft, loving, melancholy expression. When she did not respond, he became irritated with her. He contrasted her unfavorably with her mother who, he said, had a warm, loving nature whereas Gaby herself... He shrugged.

"What's wrong with me?" she asked. "Tell me."

"You hate India."

"How can I? I've never been there."

"And your mother? She also has never seen. But already she loves it with all her heart."

"My mother has a very romantic heart."

He thought perhaps Sophie had been Indian in her previous birth. But Gaby had always been American. That was why she was so unfeeling and critical about India.

"But I haven't said a word!"

"It's true," he said in reply, "we are a very poor country. We don't have the gadgets and other conveniences; in this respect we are very backward. But it is not like here. Look at it," he said, indicating the window. It was early afternoon, dull, cold and sunless. Already the lights had come on in many windows: these provided the only points of brightness—though colorless and electric—to gleam through the shrouded winter day.

"How can human beings live like that? Weeks, months without sun. No trees, nothing green. It is unnatural."

Actually, though she did not tell him so, Gaby loved winter days. She hardly turned on the heating in her apartment; her mind was cool and active and she always managed to do some interesting work during these months. When she looked up from her books and out of her window, it was with satisfaction at the spare, concrete buildings set off like an architect's drawing against the frosty sky.

One day, when Baqir and Gaby were in his bed together, a commotion started up outside the door. This was most unusual at such a private time. And even more unusual—indeed unprecedented—there was an urgent knock on the door and people called out to Baqir to come quickly. He grabbed a towel to wrap around his waist. Gaby threw on a robe and followed him. Everyone was shouting and gesticulating. They were clustered around one of the American disciples, a meek pale little girl who always wore a peasant blouse and a long skirt that was muddy from trailing on the ground. Now these clothes were torn and her face was bruised and bloodied.

It appeared she had been attacked in the street by a young man who had demanded money from her. She did not have any to give him and told him so, and when he did not believe her she had invited him to search her and the shabby little cloth bag she carried. He accepted this invitation, and when he found there was really nothing, he hurled the bag away and struck her about the head and face. Then he had walked away and she had come upstairs. In contrast with everyone else, she was really quite calm. She said that at first he had accosted her politely and it was only afterward, through disappointment, that he had become rough. As Baqir and all the others became more and more worked up, she became more and more apologetic, as if it had been her fault.

"I should have had some money on me," she said to Gaby who was the only one calm enough to listen to her; also the only one sufficiently collected to help her wash the blood off her face. "One always should. Ouch."

"I'm sorry. It's the disinfectant."

"It's okay. It didn't hurt . . . I think he needed it very badly. He looked kind of desperate. He really had to have it."

"He must have gotten it from someone else," Gaby said. "The next person he asked. So he's all right now."

"I guess," she said miserably. Gaby continued to sponge her face. They both listened to the shouting in the other room. It was all Baqir Khan now: everyone else had fallen silent out of respect for him.

The girl said, "He didn't look like a bad boy. He wasn't any older than me. He wasn't very big either; I guess I *could* have hit back."

"Please keep still."

Obediently the girl raised her face. She had a sweet pale little flower face. She said, "I don't like to do anything violent because of my music and meditation. Hurting yourself is worse than anything that can happen to you from outside. I used to be with a boy who was always hitting me for no reason at all. He really suffered. Oh gee, listen to him," she said as Baqir shouted outside. She swallowed in fear: "Do you think he's mad at me?"

"No, I think it's just in general," Gaby said.

Yes, Baqir was angry in general (with America), but also in particular with the girl—and with Gaby. He said this was the result of girls living alone and unprotected. It could very easily happen to Gaby too, any day, he said. It would be her own fault, and the only person he felt pity for was her poor mother who was being driven out of her mind with fear.

"But it's just a risk," Gaby argued. "Everyone has to live with risks. You can get knocked down by a truck, drown in the river, a brick can fall on your head. Anything."

"Such violence! Such evil!"

"That's everywhere too."

He shook his head in disagreement, so she said, "That famine you had last year—there were such things in the papers, one couldn't bear to look. And when it's not famine, then it's epidemics or floods—and always those pictures of the corpses and those that survive, and who can tell the difference? I can't. And then you think if it's like that, anywhere in the world, if that's how it can be for people, then what's the use? For any of us."

Because she was so upset he was very gentle with her. He told her, "It is quite different. Not at all as you think. All right—famine, flood—all these things: but, Gaby, they are *natural*. They come from above. They are not like what you have here."

WHEN THERE WERE still two months left of his contracted stay, something happened to cut it short. She didn't know quite what—he never did make himself clear—but she gathered that he had been *betrayed*. This was the word she heard over and over again, and when he said it, his Tartar eyes became very narrow. He muttered a lot, mostly in his language but sometimes in English and she could hear phrases like "they would soon learn"; "they would see who they were dealing with, what sort of a person." Hitherto he had been on excellent terms with his sponsors—on first name, embracing, joke-telling terms—and he had spoken with high praise of their fine qualities. Now their true characters had been revealed to him.

"But what happened?" Gaby kept asking. "What did they do?"

Apparently it was something too terrible to tell her. Or perhaps he considered it beyond her understanding. Only the other Indians understood. They all drew together and glowered and muttered. There was a dark, vengeful atmosphere in the apartment. It shut out both Gaby and the American disciples—not only because they could not understand the language that was being spoken but also the emotions generated were so incomprehensible to them. The Indians had all become like conspirators. Somewhere it seemed an enemy lurked and they were all preparing against him. Treachery was going to be met by treachery. Baqir's eyes glinted. "Let them look out," he said again and again. He did a lot of telephoning; there were even long-distance calls to India.

One day he was shouting so loud on the telephone that Gaby thought he was talking to India again. But it was only to the local office of Air India: "I don't care!" he was shouting. "Just see we get on! It is your duty! Do you know who I am?" On this last he threw down the receiver. He rushed into his bedroom and drew a trunk from under his bed. He flung clothes into it. He was still muttering. Gaby followed him but he did not appear to see her. "How can you go?" she said at last. "You can't just walk out on your contract."

That drew him up. He stared at her, but she felt it wasn't her he was staring at but someone else and it was a person he hated. "No?" he said. "I can't? I can't?" He thrust his face into hers. "Listen," he said. "Once I was invited to play in Afghanistan. The fee was very high, there were many special invitees. Kings and prime ministers. It was a very great occasion in celebration of the birth of a prince after many daughters. But just before my recital was to begin—already all the eminent guests were assembled—there was one underling, a little courtier: he showed discourtesy not to me (let him dare!) but to one of my party. I did not wait one moment. 'Pack up!' I cried. 'We are leaving! There will be no music today!' We went straight from the palace to the airport, leaving the guests sitting on carpets in the audience hall. And they were kings and prime ministers! Then what do you think I care for these people here? For these *Americans!*"

"And I?" she asked.

He had too many things on his mind to answer her. From

now on he was busy all the time. She saw that his thoughts were already in India. He went on shopping expeditions to buy shiny, gilded gifts to take back with him. He was no longer interested in anything in New York except what he could carry back home. He even forgot to say goodbye to Sophie and Rudolph. When at the airport Gaby reminded him—she was one of a large, large party who had come to see him off—he said, "Get them on the telephone."

She went to a public phone and when Sophie answered, Gaby said at once, "Baqir wants to say goodbye to you."

But when she tried to attract his attention to call him to the phone, she could not do so because he was surrounded by too many people. There was joking and embracing and many messages. The airline officials were struggling with a mountain of luggage, bags and tins and musical instruments.

"He says to tell you goodbye," Gaby said to her mother. She made her way through the crowd surrounding Baqir. By this time he was hung about with garlands made of marigold and rose petals and silver tinsel. He was laughing and embracing continuously. He also laughed while he embraced Gaby. "You will come?" he said. He didn't listen for an answer. His eyes were dancing with excitement. Although for a moment they gazed deeply into hers, they seemed to be gazing into distances beyond her. He pressed her against his chest so that some of his flower petals came off on her coat.

The smell of them remained with her all the way back in the cab: that, and some other scent he always wore, dabbing it into the hair on his chest. She told the driver her mother's address. Sophie and Rudolph were very tactful, but after a time she did not want to remain in the room with anyone. She went out on the balcony. It was a freezing night. She felt cold and very alone as if stranded on a mountain ledge. Buildings surrounded her like icy cliffs and canyons. They blocked out all but a small rectangle of night sky, but in any case she didn't look up, only deep down below where the traffic flowed and churned. If she jumped now, she would be splintered and shattered by this city she loved. It did not seem in the least difficult or inappropriate.

Sophie came out on the balcony, carrying Gaby's coat which she put around her shoulders. She led her in. Gaby was freezing and Sophie took one hand and rubbed it back into life and Rudolph, murmuring *Pardon*, took the other. Gaby let them do this for her. She also let Sophie pick the few remaining petals off her coat. His scent had already frozen in the winter air. Sophie murmured to her in baby German, and they didn't let go her hands till they had rubbed them warm again.

(1973)

A Very Special Fate

NO ONE NOW REMEMBERS SYNTHESIS UNLIMITED OR its founder, Dr. Mohanty, though in his time he had been quite a famous guru. Hardly anyone remembers Nancy Tennyson, either. She has one sister left in England—who is, like Nancy, in her seventies now—but they correspond only at Christmas. Nancy has never gone back to England; she has been living in Cooch-Nahin, in India, ever since Dr. Mohanty passed away nearly thirty years ago. He had sent her there to start a new center for Synthesis Unlimited. It was the fourteenth center he had established in India, besides several in Europe and one in California. But while she was getting the house ready in Cooch-Nahin, news reached her that he had died while on one of his voyages to Europe. Some said it was a heart attack, others that he had simply lain down and not got up again. This latter sounded right to her; he would have done it like that—just decided to go away, and gone. He was buried at sea, and that was right, too, for he had often spoken of the Ocean of the Absolute into which all men must be absorbed.

After his death, the various centers of his Movement closed down one by one, until Synthesis Unlimited remained only in Cooch-Nahin, with Nancy as its sole representative. She just went on living by herself in the house she had rented for the Movement. She did not often leave her room, and then only to provide herself with bare necessities from the stalls in Cooch-Nahin's impoverished bazaar. She was a strange sight there, with her bobbed white hair, her short skirt, her wrinkled stockings over her frail legs. But the people of the town seemed to have gotten used to her, and even the children no longer ran after her. I suppose in a way she had synthesized with the place, being as worn out and worn down as all the rotting houses and rubbled tombs of Cooch-Nahin.

I heard rumors of her lonely existence out there on my travels around India. I had come on a quest of my own, and one or two people told me about this old Englishwoman who had come on another quest some fifty years earlier and had never gone away again. They said she was half starving, half crazed. No one I spoke to had ever met her; they had just vaguely heard about her. I began to be curious, and I manipulated my wanderings in the direction of Cooch-Nahin.

North India has many towns like Cooch-Nahin, which have grown for no particular reason out of the surrounding desert plain and seem on the point of crumbling back into it. They are like overnight shantytowns, except that they are very old, with fragments of fortified walls and unidentified tombs and dried-up wells. The inhabited parts of town—the houses, shops, and temples—look as old as the ruins, but they can't have stood for more than fifty years and they will not last much longer, because nothing lasts very long in India. Things are always reclaimed soon.

Like most towns, Cooch-Nahin has a main bazaar fronting the motor road and a tangle of alleys forming a hinterland behind it. The alleys are dense, narrow, and crowded. Nancy lived at the heart of them, and on the day when I looked her up at last I had to wind my way along some very dirty gutters to reach her house. Groping up a staircase, I found myself on an open gallery facing into a courtyard, and there, hanging up her underwear on a clothesline, I saw a very old, very white woman in a blouse and skirt.

She was neither starving nor crazed, though she was no doubt very lonely. I was the first English person she had met in a long time, and she seemed to enjoy talking to me. We had both been at Cambridge, it turned out, so we had something in common. She still spoke in a Girton accent. It was at Cambridge that she had met Dr. Mohanty, in the late 1920s, and had become interested in him and his ideas. He seems to have been a man of striking personality who fascinated many people. He fascinated Nancy so much that, after her graduation, she resolved to dedicate her life to him, and followed him to India. She was twenty-two years old.

I stayed with her for a while in Cooch-Nahin. She let me sleep on the sofa in her room—a room as unexpected there in the middle of Cooch-Nahin as Nancy herself. It had some quite comfortable pieces of European furniture, which had belonged to Dr. Mohanty—a desk, a sofa, a little round table with a tasseled cloth, on which stood his photograph. She had bookshelves reaching up to the ceiling, and stacks and stacks of dusty papers on the floor. These papers, which she was editing for posterity, were about Dr. Mohanty's lifework. As far as I could gather, he had attempted a synthesis of all that was highest and best in the Hindu, Buddhist, Judeo-Christian, and Muhammadan religions.

On most nights, I found it too hot to sleep inside her room, so I borrowed an old string bed and carried it up to the roof. The sky at night was very different from the heavy, dust-laden weight that smoldered over the town all day. I slept well, dreamlessly, and woke up refreshed. The days were hot and heavy. Nancy and I sat inside her room, making the most of her rattling black old table fan, which often stopped, whenever the electricity went off. It was hot in there! Nancy and I wound wet towels around our heads and kept our feet in a basin of water—in the same basin, for she had only one. It was during these hours that she told me about her life with Dr. Mohanty.

WHEN NANCY HAD first come out to India, she lived in a house that Dr. Mohanty rented in a suburb of Bombay. Or, rather, someone had rented it for him; there were always people to do these small practical things for him. A sign had been put up in the little patch of garden in front, reading "Synthesis Unlimited." Passersby had thought it was some kind of business, and once a municipal inspector had been sent to investigate, because the suburb was a residential area where no business activity was permitted. Dr. Mohanty had been much amused. He told the inspector, "Certainly it is a business, but on a cosmic scale, my friend." The inspector recognized Dr. Mohanty at once as a spiritual person and bowed down and touched his feet with the respect due such a person.

Nancy had always seen him surrounded by many people. In Cambridge, it had been students and dons' wives; in London, society people and intellectuals. Some of them had followed him to India, and now all were living together in the house in Bombay. He always needed helpers—not just part-time ones but people to be at his beck and call by day and sometimes by night. He had arranged for Nancy to have a little room of her own, next to his, with a bed in it and some shelves where she could keep her things. Not that she had very much. She had brought the minimum of clothes with her, and soon she cast them aside and bought herself a few saris to wear—quite cheap and ordinary ones. She also bought a pair of sandals, which she left outside on the threshold, along with everyone else's, and padded around the house on naked feet.

Her parents, dismayed by her departure to India, had appealed to some English people who lived in Bombay to look after her. But when Nancy received their invitations, she ignored them. That was not what she had come to India for! She was repelled by the very idea of this official colonial society—this was the end of the twenties, two decades before Indian independence—and she wanted no dealings with what she thought of as the alien oppressor. She considered herself entirely on the other side—on India's side, on Dr. Mohanty's.

"But what is my side?" he asked her once, when she stated her case to him in these words. "I thought that is what I am here for. Synthesis Unlimited," he reminded her.

"Not them," she assured him. "You can't synthesize them. No, not even you."

He laughed, but the fact was he rather wanted her to accept these invitations to the homes of British officials. "No stone must be left unturned," he told her. For it was as he said: he didn't belong to any side but wanted to embrace them all. He always said that he wasn't in the least political, in the ordinary sense of the word, and didn't care a tinker's curse—as he sometimes put it— who ruled India. Who ruled *here*, he said, tapping his heart, that was what mattered. She understood, and admired his point, but was still unwilling to accept the invitations. He didn't insist. He never insisted on anything, with her or with anyone. Each person had to be absolutely free in his or her choices. "My rule," he said, "is to have no rule, except from within."

That was all very well for his Indian followers, who were by nature meek and mild. But his Western followers tended to have strong, unruly temperaments that seemed to cry out for some sort of outer direction. Among them there was a divorced Italian countess—a woman in her forties, tall and still handsome, who looked elegant even in the simple saris she affected. She was an insomniac and spent her nights walking around the house looking for someone to talk to. Whenever she found Nancy awake, she would tell her how she had first met Dr. Mohanty in Paris and had recognized him at once as the person she had been looking for all her life. She had not hesitated to give up everything and follow him. In him she had at last found what she craved with all her being—someone to whom she could submit herself completely, who would, as she put it, take her in hand and master her. Here she would throw a longing look toward his door, which he liked to keep closed at night—closed against her and some of the others who were apt to come in and engage him in their problems.

Several of the followers were on bad terms with each other. The Countess, for instance, was at daggers drawn with a lady from Holland. But their quarrels didn't disturb Nancy any more than the heat, or her attacks of dysentery, or the cramped conditions under which they were all living. At that time, she was far too caught up in the greatness of her adventure—what she thought of as her very special fate—which had taken her so far away from everything she had been born to and had immersed her in a movement with the highest ideals known to mankind and brought her to live in constant proximity to a man such as he, Dr. Mohanty.

I often studied the photograph of him in Nancy's room in Cooch-Nahin. I don't know how old he was when it was taken, and Nancy couldn't tell me. She said that he was always the same, that he never aged or changed in any way from the first day she knew him till the last. In the photograph, he was wearing a suit and tie and gold-rimmed spectacles. Behind these spectacles his eyes were somewhat slanting, giving him the tribal look peculiar to people from his native province of Orissa. His high forehead was slanting, too—it slanted back into his hair, which was long and black and very straight: more Chinese than Indian. He had the look of a wise Oriental, but at the same time—perhaps because of the gold-rimmed spectacles—he gave the impression of a Western intellectual, someone sharp and analytical. I could not really make out what he had been like—neither from the photograph nor from what she told me, though she told me so much. Sometimes he seemed one thing, sometimes another. When I told her that, she said, "That's the way he was." Apparently, he could not be described or pinned down with particular attributes.

After Nancy had been there about a year, they had left the house in Bombay and begun to travel all over India. They had rented other houses in other places and put up the sign of Synthesis Unlimited. There were many followers with them, but they were not always the same people. Some went away, some were sent away, and some were left behind in each new house to look after the progress of the Movement in that place. But he kept Nancy with him all the time. She was happy. She loved the long, long journeys across India, with nothing to see for miles except desert and ruins—sometimes a dried-up river looking like a dead animal, and sometimes real dead animals and dead stumps of trees. When they arrived at railway stations, there were people waiting with garlands, and they would all be piled into open horse carriages and driven, garlanded, through towns that were always the same—dusty, intricate, and rubbled. Only up in the Himalayas was it different. Then there was cool air like ambrosia, and grand vistas opening up of snow-clad mountains. But Dr. Mohanty would never let them stay there long. He said it was not yet time to come up here, that their work lay down below in the walled-in little towns simmering in the summer heat.

It was his habit suddenly to tell his followers that he had planned a journey, usually some hundreds of miles away, and that they must be ready to leave with him at four the next morning. For years Nancy was cheerfully ready, but then one day when he did that—she had been in India about ten years by then and was no longer so very young—she burst into tears. He was amazed. He sent everyone out of the room and questioned her. "Are you ill?" he asked. "What is it? No, Nancy, you must tell me." She kept shaking her head. He persisted. Was she mentally upset in any way? Had anyone been unkind to her—perhaps he himself unwittingly? She kept saying no. But then at last she said that she was tired, and when she said that, she wept more. She hadn't realized till that moment how exhausted she was—fatigued right into her bones and marrow. It was inconceivable that he could understand—he who was forever charged with new energy, so that his brown skin shone and glowed. But he seemed to understand perfectly. He nodded. He blamed himself. He had been inconsiderate, and for this he begged her pardon. He said, "Of course you will not travel with us tomorrow. You will stay here and take perfect rest. I insist," he said. "Perfect and absolute rest."

But when she appeared next morning at four, packed and ready along with everyone else, he said nothing. Perhaps he had forgotten their conversation—though this was unlikely, because he did not usually forget anything.

IT WAS SHORTLY after this incident that he planned another trip to Europe and told Nancy he would take her with him. She was excited. To be going back after all these years and to see the places she had known—all probably unchanged, though she herself had changed so much and was really more Indian than English now! She intended to wear only saris there; everyone should understand where she stood. She bought a few new ones and packed them in her little trunk. But two days before they were to go to Bombay to board the P&O she fell ill. She woke up vomiting, with a headache and a high fever. The next day she was worse. Dr. Mohanty came into her room and stood over her bed (really a pallet spread on the floor) and called her name. She tried to answer but was unable to make the effort.

He went away, and later a local doctor came. A bed was brought, and she was lifted onto it from her pallet. Then Dr. Mohanty was there again; he was dressed for traveling, in a canvas suit, with a leather flask slung across his chest and a solar topee. He gently pressed down her aching head as she tried to raise it. He said, "Poor Nancy." He told everyone standing around in the room, "I want the best possible care taken." He did not come again, and when she asked after him they said he had gone. The Italian countess, who had been deputed to look after her, applied ice packs to Nancy's head when the fever rose. At first she did it with great care, but then she became slapdash, and after a time she, too, was not there anymore. When Nancy asked, they said she had gone away to Sikkim. More people went away, and now Nancy was mostly alone, except for the Goan cook and a few Indian followers who sometimes looked in on her.

When the fever abated—it had been typhoid—she was too weak to do more than just lie in her little dark room. She watched the patch of sky through a barred opening in the wall that served as a window. When there was moonlight, the sky shimmered like water. It was a good time; Nancy felt that she was recovering from the fatigue that had eaten so deeply into her. The house was silent and peaceful except for the cook clattering in the kitchen, and very early in the mornings an old man living in the house sang devotional songs. There were also temple bells several times a day (the house was in the holy city of Benares). Nancy thought she would just lie there and get better, and by the time he returned from Europe she would be fully recovered. Her looks would have improved, too, by that time. The fever had left her cheeks sunken and with a dreadful pallor, and her hair had been cut off, as was the custom in cases of typhoid. (The Countess had done it with her nail scissors, very jaggedly.) Nancy hoped it would have grown again by the time Dr. Mohanty came back. It did grow, but still he did not come back. As she became stronger, she also became rather impatient. The rains had begun, and everything in the house molded. Then she got another infection, and though it did not last very long her cheeks became sunken again.

When at last he came back, he looked wonderful after his stay in Europe and the sea voyage home. As always, he was full of energy and health. He had brought a new disciple back with him, an American girl called Mary-Ellen. She too was full of energy and health. She bought herself some cotton saris, and from then on she always wore those, and sandals. Mary-Ellen loved everything, and she went to see all the temples and took boat rides on the river and walked through all the streets—even the street where people had come to die. The sight of the dying lying in the dirt along the sidewalk did not seem to disturb her any more than the dead burning on their pyres on the bank of the river. Her eyes never ceased to shine with wonder and delight.

Now that Dr. Mohanty had returned, the house began to fill up again, and soon all the little rooms and passages were crowded with disciples, who settled down wherever they could find a corner for themselves. Dr. Mohanty moved Mary-Ellen into Nancy's room. It was the first time he had allowed anyone to share this room, which was next to his. Of course Nancy did not say anything—how could she, since it was his wish? But he must have known her feelings, because he said that Mary-Ellen would be useful to her, and that he wanted someone to take proper care of her after her serious illness. He even made a joke and said that this was the sole purpose for which Mary-Ellen had been brought from England. And Mary-Ellen said sure, she'd be glad to, and gladly she rolled up their two pallets every morning and scrubbed the room out with water and a broom. She even offered to wash Nancy's clothes—not only because Nancy was weak from her illness but also, she said in her earnest way, because she considered it a real privilege to serve someone who had herself so long served Dr. Mohanty.

The Italian countess also came back. She did not like Mary-Ellen. She said to Nancy, "Why is she here? What has she come for? She is quite the wrong type." The Countess considered every woman follower of Dr. Mohanty the wrong type. They were too young, too unintellectual or too overintellectual, or attracted to him for the wrong reasons. The Countess sincerely believed that only a mature woman with deep experience of life such as herself—"and you, Nancy," she added generously—could be considered a suitable follower. Nancy had to agree that Mary-Ellen was terribly young. She threw herself into everything with such tremendous energy and did all the wrong things, like going out in the hottest part of the day and eating food from the bazaar, with no ill effects at all. She also sat up at night to do meditation, or joined the old man in his hymn-singing at dawn, and she was even learning Indian dance. This last took a tremendous amount of energy; she stamped up and down in ankle bells and contorted her limbs and leaped into the air. When Dr. Mohanty saw her dancing, he smiled and said, "Goodness gracious, Mary-Ellen," and then looked at the Countess and Nancy, inviting them to smile, too.

The Countess became more and more critical of Mary-Ellen. She would come into the little room Nancy shared with the girl and sniff the air and ask distastefully, "Has she been burning incense?"

"Yes, for her *puja* prayers," Nancy replied.

The Countess wrinkled her nose, both at the incense and at the Hindu prayers. Nancy really did not like either. Sometimes she woke up at night and saw Mary-Ellen sitting cross-legged on the floor before some little Hindu gods she had bought, with her lips moving, her eyes shut. Incense smoldered thickly.

"Doesn't she understand?" the Countess asked. "She must be made to understand. She's subverting the whole Movement." She closed her eyes and murmured, "Synthesis, Synthesis, Synthesis Unlimited," like a prayer.

The Countess also complained to Dr. Mohanty. "Master," she said—this was what she always called him—"isn't it true that if a person goes too far along one Way, it is a threat to the Synthesis of all the Ways?" She looked at him pleadingly. "Guide me," she said.

He did so without a moment's hesitation. "The farther you go," he said, "even if it is only along one Way, the sooner will you reach the crossing point where all the Ways meet." He regarded her testingly through his spectacles, and she was careful to look meek and say, "Thank you, Master." Whatever disharmony there may have been among his followers was always in his absence. In his presence, harmony prevailed—he saw to that.

Although Nancy woke up very early in the mornings, Mary-Ellen was always up and out before her. She had explained to Nancy that she was too excited to sleep much. Once, Nancy went to look for her. The house was on the river, and steps led down to the water. Dawn was just breaking. Ascetics in saffron robes and some destitute widows lay curled up on the steps along the waterfront and on the stone platforms intersecting them. The only moving thing as far as the eye could see was Mary-Ellen. She was on a platform some distance away from the house, outlined against the gray dawn sky, with her arms raised. She was dancing. From this distance her solitary figure looked beautiful and religious. Nancy came nearer. Mary-Ellen was doing not strictly an Indian dance but some variations of her own invention. She had tucked her sari closely around herself, so that it looked more like a toga. Her feet—long, slim, and very white—flashed as she danced. Her thin arms were like branches waving against the sky and the water. An ascetic slept face upward behind her, with his beads and begging bowl beside him, and his saffron robe trailing along the steps.

When she had finished her dance, Mary-Ellen came and sat beside Nancy on the steps. She was out of breath. Her cheeks glowed and she was smiling. "I have to dance," she said. "To express myself. Otherwise, I don't know what would happen. I might just . . . go off with a bang!" She tucked a strand of short blond hair behind her ear, but it came loose again quite soon and lay against her cheek.

"I hope to be calm one day when I've been here as long as you and done all that discipline and meditation," she went on. "I love discipline and meditation. But just now, just yet, it's all too much. Too much." Her chest heaved as if it were all inside her and really was too much.

"Did you like my dance?" she said. "I made it up myself. It's different every day and I never know what it's going to be. But I always say the same words to myself." She clasped her hands and raised her face to heaven. "'O thou lotus-eyed One, do not delay. Don't you see, my blue-throated lover, how I pine and fret,'" she intoned. "It's to Krishna—he's always called blue-throated, I don't know why." Nancy tried to explain, but Mary-Ellen was not too interested. "Oh, is that it?" she said. "Well, anyhow, even though it is Krishna, that's not who I think of." She paused and wrapped her arms around her knees and looked across the water. It was very gently rippled by a breeze, which also played through her hair.

"Sometimes I tell myself he's an incarnation," she said to Nancy. "It could be, couldn't it? Krishna is supposed to have incarnations, the same as Jesus Christ, and people see Him and recognize Him even when he looks"—she laughed—"well, sort of everyday, with those specs and all. You must think I'm just a silly billy. And if he heard me, I guess he'd be mad at me, except he never does get mad. He's terribly kind and patient with me.

All of you are. You and the Countess and everyone. I love being here with you all."

She went on talking. Nancy could see her lips moving, but her words were drowned out by the bells that suddenly began to sound from many temples. Mary-Ellen raised her voice, but Nancy still couldn't hear her, because cymbals began to clash along with the bells. Now everyone was waking up. The ascetic behind them had sat up—his face was rather coarse, not ascetic at all—and he was yawning and scratching. Mary-Ellen unclasped her arms from her knees and put them around Nancy instead. "I never felt this way all my life long," she said. "I never knew people could feel like this." She spoke into Nancy's ear to make sure she was heard, and Nancy felt her sweet warm breath along with her words.

DR. MOHANTY WAS planning another extended tour of the various centers in India. Everyone was packing up, the house was in upheaval. Although Nancy did not particularly like the house, or her dark little room—or, for that matter, the holy city of Benares—she felt reluctant to leave. She had got used to being here, and she was tired. Also she could not bear the thought of the coming journey. But there was no choice; she packed her few things along with everyone else, and was ready.

But when Dr. Mohanty saw her, he said at once, "You are not well, Nancy." In the midst of all his preoccupations, he never missed a thing.

That evening, he asked her to go for a walk with him. No one else was allowed to accompany them. He liked to stroll along the riverbank at this time of day, when the steps leading down to the water were crowded with worshippers. He had many friends among the priests and holy men and often stopped to chat. He looked very different from everyone else in his suit and collar and tie. He made Nancy lean on his arm.

"I would like you to stay here," he said. "No, Nancy, listen to me. It is best for you." He caught her arm closer to prevent her from withdrawing it. "Don't worry. I shall leave plenty of work for you. There are certain publications to be prepared, and I can trust no one else. No one but you. Your work is here now. Nancy, Nancy, listen to me!"

"Don't leave me behind," she said.

He made an impatient gesture. "'Leave behind,'" he said. "What does it mean? This is not at all worthy of you, Nancy. Or of our work together." He looked at her with tenderness. "Come," he said, "sit here. You are tired."

They had reached the platform on which Mary-Ellen had danced. He dusted a place with his handkerchief and spread it for Nancy to sit on; he held out his hand to help her. She did not take it.

She said, "I suppose you're taking Mary-Ellen."

He remained with his hand out. He gave her one of his searching looks, then laughed. "Ah, Mary-Ellen," he said in a tone of appreciation. "Nancy, my hankie will blow away if you don't sit on it." So she did as he wanted, and he sat next to her, with his knees drawn up and his arms clasped around them in the same way as Mary-Ellen.

"I like her very much," he said, smiling at the thought of her. "She is so—how to say—"

"Young."

"Yes, young, and also— Shall I tell you something, Nancy? She reminds me of yourself in the beginning. How you were once upon a time. Perhaps it is why I like her so very much. Do you also like her?"

He paused, she said nothing. He waved to friends passing in a boat.

She said, "You're tired of me."

The smile with which he had greeted his friends faded. She continued stubbornly, "That's why you don't want to take me with you. You want someone . . . younger now."

"Unworthy," he murmured. "How unworthy."

"Now you know what I really am," she said. "What I really want."

She reproached him for the years that had passed. She had not known until that moment how bitter they had made her. To do his work, to be always near him, close to him—she thought it had been enough. Now she felt it had been nothing. There was something quite different, an intimacy far more ordinary, that she desired. "I am ordinary," she said. "Like the Countess, like Mary-Ellen. We're all ordinary. What you call unworthy. It's only you who are . . . worthy."

He got up and held out his hand to help her up. He did not want to hear any more. He walked by her side with his face averted, no longer waving to friends. He was shaken and wounded.

But by next morning, at the hour of departure, he had quite recovered. He instructed her about the work to be done during his absence. Her main task was to see some pamphlets of his through the press. She went up on the roof to watch everyone leave. Three horse carriages had been ordered to take them to the station. One was piled with luggage, another with various followers, and the third was for Dr. Mohanty and Mary-Ellen. He climbed in first, she jumped in after him. Both looked up to wave to Nancy. Their faces were radiant, his glasses dazzled. Then he gave the order to start, and the three carriages moved away. Mary-Ellen waved to Nancy for as long as she could see her and blew a kiss before they turned a corner.

Mary-Ellen never came back. Later Nancy heard how she had fallen sick in a remote up-country town near Bhopal. After some days she had to be removed to a hospital. Unfortunately, the hospital services were very inadequate; there were not enough doctors or nurses or medicines or anything except patients, of whom there were too many. Dr. Mohanty had been worried about her, especially because he had had to continue his tour program. He had even considered canceling some of his lecture engagements so as to be able to stay near Mary-Ellen till she was better. But she said on no account must anyone be disappointed of his presence just because of her stupid illness, and anyhow, she told him, she was better already. So he went, though reluctantly. Mary-Ellen was not better; in fact, she got worse and worse, and the doctors did not know where to find Dr. Mohanty or anyone else belonging to Mary-Ellen. So when she died there were only strangers with her, and they couldn't wait to communicate with anyone she had known but had to arrange her cremation very quickly because it was the hot season.

When Dr. Mohanty returned to Benares, he was more fit and energetic than ever. He at once examined the work he had commissioned Nancy to do—he read with great speed, and when he spotted a mistake pointed to it as infallibly as a water diviner. But when he had finished examining everything, he said, "Very good," and praised Nancy for what she had done in his absence. He wondered how he could exist without her. Never, he said—he and she were as one now, their bond was indissoluble. He had not yet mentioned Mary-Ellen.

When he at last did, a day after his arrival, it was not at all in sorrow but with the same glad smile with which he had spoken of her when she was alive. He explained to Nancy that thinking about Mary-Ellen did sincerely make him glad. Had Nancy ever seen her dance? Well, then, he said with another smile, she must know what he meant. This dancer would never stop dancing. *She* would have no falling off, would never grow old or tired or embittered. Oh, and by the way, he said, they would not be seeing the Countess again; she had left them. She had written him rather a bad letter, but he didn't hold it against her—not at all, on the contrary, poor woman, he hoped she would find fulfillment in her new life, which was in the communal settlement of a Russian spiritualist at Lake Geneva. Unfortunately, he was used to receiving such letters from followers who for reasons of their own (which he always respected) had decided not to follow him any longer. And their accusations were always the same, always personal and bitter, so that he had long since realized that these were directed not against him but against themselves. Thank goodness, he said, that such a thing could never happen to Mary-Ellen. She would remain forever fresh—fresh as dew, he said with pleasure. And also, he said, one had to be grateful that she had not survived, because her disease had affected her eyesight. He had been told that during her last two days she had been totally blind, and she would have remained so had she lived.

Both the Countess and Mary-Ellen were soon replaced. So many followers came, from Europe and America, that Nancy lost track of them. She also found it difficult to distinguish one from another. There seemed to be always at least one or two young girls—very bright-eyed, very eager—who were not only interested in the Movement but also learned Indian dancing or to play the sitar. They always wore saris and moved freely around the streets, loving everything. Nancy no longer wore saris. She gave them away to the new followers, and from the bottom of her trunk she retrieved the blouses and skirts she had brought with her when she had first come to India. They were in the style of that time; the skirts were too short, but she wore them anyway and darned her old lisle stockings. She rarely left her dark little room now, and when she had to, she wore blue glasses to protect her eyes from the sun.

For the first time, she became homesick for England, and

when Dr. Mohanty again prepared to go on a foreign tour, she looked forward to accompanying him. She looked forward to so many things and remembered so much she thought she had forgotten. But he said, "No, Nancy, I would not like you to come." He gave no reason for his decision. He seldom did, because everyone knew that whatever he decided was for the best. Nancy also knew it, but for the first time she found it hard to accept this without question. She lay awake at night, listening to the regular breathing of the pretty Swedish girl who shared the room with her at that time. This girl would be sailing with him; he always needed a secretary-companion. Nancy buried her face in her pillow. She had done this often enough in recent years, but now it was not only because she could not go with *him*—he had got her used to that, over the years—but because of everything she had not seen for so long.

A few days before his departure, she went to him and said she wanted to go. "I have to," she said. The Swedish girl, who was taking dictation from him, looked up in surprise at the willful tone of her voice. He finished dictating, then sent the girl away.

"I have to," Nancy said again when they were alone.

He nodded. Of course—she might have known it—he was fully aware of how she was feeling. He was silent for a while, collecting his thoughts. But already she felt strangely soothed, just to sit with him like this in silence. She shut her eyes and thought that whatever he decided would be all right.

She could not go, he told her at last. He meticulously explained the reasons on which he had based his decision. It was best not only for her but for himself, too; he emphasized that. "Yes, Nancy," he said, "it is pure and simple selfishness on my part. Why should I hide this from you?" He took off his glasses; whenever he did that, he looked strangely weak, vulnerable. His eyes were dreamy and terribly shortsighted. He smiled apologetically. "I need you so very badly," he said. "Without you, it is—nothing is—" He made a helpless gesture, unable even to find the word that could define how it was without her.

"If you go away now, you will never come back," he said. When she began to protest, he shook his head, knowing better. "It is so," he said. "You will want to stay there."

"I shall want to be where you are."

"You will be in England. It is spring, the flowers are in bloom. What are they called—the little yellow ones? There is a nice breeze, sometimes rain. You will see all the places you used to know—also people. You will say, 'Ah, yes, it is home.' And then one day I shall say, 'Now, Nancy, it is time to return to India.' What will you do then? No, wait, wait. Think of all this. Yes, this house, the river, the smells—you know the smells—and the heat, Nancy. All this. And when it will be time to come back, you *will* think of it, and then you will say, 'I can't, I can't.'"

He paused, to let his words sink in. And she knew they were true, because already she felt like saying it: "I can't, I can't."

Then he continued in quite a different tone, brisk and resolute. "If I allowed this to happen to you, Nancy, I would be at fault. Indeed, I would be much to blame if I exposed you to any test beyond your strength. Your place is here," he concluded, and although he still had his glasses off, he looked no longer weak and vulnerable but so strong that she knew all she had to do was lean on him and let him guide her, and it would be for the best.

(1976)

Commensurate Happiness

MARIE AND HUGHIE WERE COUSINS. ON ONE SIDE OF their family—the side they had in common—they were of German Jewish origin; the members of that family were mostly small and stocky, but they tended to marry tall, fair, fine-boned Anglo-Saxons. Marie and Hughie both sprang from such a combination, and they both took after the Anglo-Saxon side and were slim and blond and had difficulty getting shoes narrow enough to fit them.

Since their parents had a lot of divorces and personal crises, Marie and Hughie were mostly with their grandmother, Jeannette. They grew up in Jeannette's apartment, among all the heavy German furniture she had brought from the house she sold after her husband died. When Marie and Hughie sat playing together on the carpet, with all that furniture rearing and looming above them, they looked like two sprites, two changelings, fairy children in a forest; while Jeannette, who was short and squat with a long nose, watched over them like a benign witch. The apartment was so dark—it was on the Upper West Side, in a huge, ornate, turn-of-the-century block hemmed in by similar blocks—that often the chandeliers had to be kept on even during the day.

Jeannette, two generations earlier, had married her cousin. Unlike Marie and Hughie, they hadn't known each other as children because Otto had grown up in Germany. He had come to New York to join the branch of the family firm there and was soon expanding and reorganizing it on an unprecedented scale. They had been a staid, dull firm, but Otto changed all that. He was able, energetic, and passionate. He didn't get married till he was nearly forty, and then, unlike everyone else, he didn't marry an Anglo-Saxon but Jeannette. Maybe because she loved him so terribly and was so constant and also fierce; fiercely possessive. After they were married, he continued to have affairs but, until Wanda, they were nothing much; anyway, their marriage lasted longer than the other, mixed ones, and they also had more children, and lived in a Greek Revival house on Eleventh Street that could take all the furniture and other possessions that he inherited from his side of the family as well as what she brought from hers.

Jeannette wanted and expected Hughie and Marie to get married; Marie wanted and expected it too; and Hughie just expected it. The only one of the three who was in a hurry was Jeannette. Marie knew that there were a whole lot of things Hughie still had to achieve before settling down, so she was glad to wait. She graduated from college, and then she took her master's, and then—since Hughie still wasn't ready—she got a very interesting cultural job with the Asia Society. Hughie meanwhile began to be an architect but got impatient with the math and physics part of it and switched to graphic art; and he traveled in Europe and in the Middle East and farther east and Mexico; he tried many places. He also had many different kinds of friends whom he introduced neither to one another nor to Jeannette and Marie. Marie liked to think of him leading this very exciting life and coming home and telling her about it. She loved and admired him, for himself and everything he did.

Jeannette, his grandmother, tended to be more critical; sometimes very critical. When he changed courses again—from graphic art to art history—she asked for unreasonable explanations; and when he left in the middle of that to go on a trip to

Spain with a friend, she quarreled with him. Hughie was upset, and Marie, driving him to the airport, had to soothe him all the way and make excuses for Jeannette. And when she got home—stifling the feeling of sadness that overcame her whenever he left on one of his trips—she had to soothe Jeannette and make excuses for Hughie. But then Jeannette turned on Marie; she said she was spoiling Hughie by always giving in to his whims and even applauding them. Marie, a gentle girl with a lot of patience, couldn't help looking a bit superior (how little Jeannette understood her own grandson!); so that Jeannette, not at all gentle and still very short of patience in spite of her seventy years, became quite angry with her.

Next day Jeannette complained to Wanda. It was their day for having lunch together, and they met in their usual place, in the Palm Court at the Plaza. Although Wanda took an interest in Hughie and Marie—naturally, since she was almost family—she was not the best listener in the world, for her attention span was short and she tended to go off rather quickly on to some preoccupation of her own. This was very irritating to Jeannette. There were many, many things about Wanda that irritated Jeannette, but of course the wonder was that they could be this way together at all, having lunch. In this hotel too—the very place where Jeannette had first seen Wanda, over forty years ago.

When she looked up from where she now sat in the Palm Court over her lunch, Jeannette could see the staircase she had been descending on that occasion. She had just come from a committee meeting of the Lovers of the Opera and was walking down the stairs with other committee members—matrons like herself, in sober hats with veils—when she had caught sight of Wanda and Otto emerging from the cocktail lounge. Wanda, walking in front, drew many eyes beside Jeannette's: she was born to walk through hotel lobbies, balancing herself on heels like stilts, her small head with its crest of red hair held so high she couldn't possibly be aware of all the people looking at her. Otto was frowning rather anxiously as he followed her; he kept his eyes fixed on her round, high, little backside bobbing in front of him in electric blue silk, so he never looked up and was unaware he had been seen. He was balancing a little pile of flowered packages.

"He's got too much of his grandfather's money," Wanda said, when Jeannette complained to her about Hughie. "And no discipline. The young people in this country don't know what discipline means." Wanda had lived in America since the thirties, but she still spoke with a German accent and her opinions were often very German too. "It's ridiculous, taking all these courses. Art school, what's that? The school he should be attending is the school of life."

But what was the use of getting irritated with Wanda? Jeannette told herself. At least she was a person one could talk to about one's grandchildren and who listened, in between spearing bits of crabmeat on her fork. Sometimes she extended this fork to Jeannette to let her taste; and Jeannette reciprocated by letting Wanda taste her chicken.

WHEN HE RETURNED from Spain—as always when he returned from a trip—Hughie gave a carefully edited, though lively and amusing, account to Jeannette and Marie; and the next day he went to see Wanda to tell her about it too. Only when he got there she had just fired her maid and was very upset at being left without one. She and the maid had had their argument in the middle of the latter's cleaning, and the furniture was still upside down just the way she had left it when she had stormed out. "Using such dirty words, I had no idea she was such a dirty person," Wanda complained to Hughie. She was sitting in the middle of all that upheaval, smoking furiously and trying to calm herself by laying out cards for solitaire.

Hughie began to tidy the apartment. He even completed some of the cleaning. It wasn't difficult to clean Wanda's apartment. It was the same place Otto had taken for her in the thirties and had the same pieces of furniture—the glass and steel tubes—that had been considered smart at that time. Wanda had never bothered to replace them; she had no interest in possessions other than clothes and personal ornaments.

"Darling, how sweet of you," she said absently, when she noticed what Hughie was doing.

"Have you had anything to eat?"

"To eat? Don't make me laugh. Not even a Nescafé—she went like that, shouting her dirty word, not worrying if I'm dying of hunger and thirst. And this a woman I've pampered for six months. Thank you, darling," she said, as Hughie gave her some coffee he had made in her kitchen along with some fancy but rather stale cookies he found out there. "Listen to me, sit here, close to Wanda: Jeannette's angry with you." And she made angry round eyes at Hughie to show him how angry his grandmother was. "She told me about it at lunch. I had quite a big job to calm her down, I can tell you. But I spoke up for you, you should have heard me."

"What was it about?" Hughie asked, though making a show of being more interested in her game of solitaire than in what she was saying.

"What is it ever about, with your grandmother? She is just an angry woman by nature. I'm the one and only person in this world who knows how to manage her. With tact and psychology," she said, frowning at her cards, though when Hughie tried to place one for her, she slapped his wrist.

Wanda had always prided herself on her tact and psychology

in dealing with Jeannette. Shortly after Jeannette had had her unexpected glimpse of Wanda in the Plaza, she had a phone call from her. Wanda spoke just the way Jeannette had expected—in a German accent that came from deep down a throat husky with cigarettes. Wanda said how fortunate it was that they were all grown-up people who could sit down and talk sensibly; and she invited Jeannette so to sit and talk any morning except Thursday which was the day for Wanda's masseuse. Jeannette got herself ready to go the next morning (a Tuesday) as though for a guilty assignment. She even changed her clothes several times—to little effect as they were all the same sort of clothes and she the same person (with a bad little figure and a face that could never be called anything but interesting). But when she got to Wanda's, it appeared that the masseuse's day had been changed. Jeannette waited perched on the geometric furniture, hearing the sound of blows ringing from the bedroom and Wanda's shouts of pain. But when Wanda came out, she had her arm around the masseuse and made jokes with her in German and kissed her goodbye. She also kissed Jeannette and was glad she had come and now they would have an adult talk together. Unfortunately there were annoyances—like the maid bringing coffee in the wrong set—that had an irritating effect on Wanda; and although she continued cordial with Jeannette, the frank talk they were to have had together degenerated into Wanda complaining about Otto, how selfish he was, and really not as generous as a man of his means could afford to be. Still, at the end of it, Wanda was pleased with the way it had gone, and that evening she told Otto how he wouldn't have to worry any more about his wife and family because Wanda has just managed all that beautifully, with tact and psychology.

She continued in that belief and never had any conception of the terrible scenes between Otto and Jeannette, or the upheavals within their family. But everyone else knew—and as they grew up, Marie and Hughie knew about it too, though it had all happened at a time when their own parents were still children. Both their parents—Marie's mother and Hughie's father—remembered thumping the piano as loudly as possible to drown out the noise of battle from the master bedroom. Also, they remembered when their father had moved out of the house and, sobbing loudly, had dragged his pigskin luggage down the stairs; and his visits to the house laden with presents for them which their mother afterward didn't like to see them play with. If they were sick, he would come to the house and sit by their bedside reading aloud—till it was time for Wanda to be chaperoned to a cocktail party or tea dance, when he would jump up and hurry away, even if he was in the middle of a chapter. The youngest child, Walter, was only four when all that started and used to creep into his mother's bed at night; and when he woke in the morning, he found his hair drenched in Jeannette's tears. In later life, it was Walter who had had the most difficulties of all the children; but none of them really could be said to have done anything very much beyond marrying and divorcing and remarrying and spending a lot of money on themselves.

MARIE DIDN'T HAVE much contact with her mother, any more than Hughie with his father. When they spoke of them to each other, it was usually in the third person. "She phoned again today, from Mexico," Marie would say to Hughie who turned his eyes up in sympathetic despair; or "He wants me to come out to the Island to meet his new girlfriend"—and then it was Marie's turn to say "Oh poor Hughie." As far as they were concerned, their family was each other, and Jeannette. They felt a responsibility to Jeannette, and that it was up to them to compensate her for everyone else's failings.

But now they had begun to fail her themselves; and she

began to nag them, so that they sometimes took pains to avoid her. This was easy for Hughie who had a lot of places to go and people to see. But Marie didn't have many friends—she had never bothered to make any, having always had Hughie. When her day at the Asia Society was over, all she could do was come home. As soon as she let herself in, there was Jeannette calling, "Is that you, Marie? Is Hughie with you? Where is he?" She followed Marie around and grumbled: "We don't know where he goes, who he goes with—or who he talks to all those hours on the phone." And then: "Who's the friend he went to Spain with? You don't know? He didn't tell you? But he used to tell you everything."

To escape her grandmother, Marie often pretended to be tired and went to bed early. She lay awake in the dark, listening for Hughie to come home, but all she heard was Jeannette bumping about in the apartment. The place was so crammed that it was impossible not to bump into some massive piece of German furniture at every step. But each piece held memories, and Jeannette stumbled about among them, sighing and talking to herself like the old woman she was. Then, late late into the night, Marie heard Hughie come in. Jeannette turned on him at once, so that the next thing Marie heard was his impatient reply and then his bedroom door shutting and the key turning. Jeannette rattled the handle for a while and tried to talk to him through the door; but getting no answer, she gave up and went to bed. Marie waited for her to stop groaning and tossing and knew Hughie was waiting too. When at last there was silence from their grandmother's bedroom, Hughie opened his door and stood there very still, making sure everyone was asleep; and then very, very softly he lifted the receiver of the phone in the living room and talked into it very, very softly.

But one night he made a mistake and thought Jeannette was asleep when she wasn't; or maybe she fooled him, pretending to be. So that night what Marie heard was Hughie quickly replacing the receiver and then Jeannette—"Who were you talking to?"

"No one," Hughie said. "A friend."

"What friend?" After a silence, she demanded: "And Marie?"

"What about Marie? She's got nothing to do with it. I told you, I was talking to a friend." His voice rose in the half-hysterical way Marie knew and dreaded: "Why Marie, who's Marie?" He said, "I'm sick of all this," and went back and locked his door again and Jeannette rattled it again and Marie put her pillow over her head.

After that, Hughie spent more time with Wanda than he did at home. He even received mail at her apartment and made some of his long phone calls from there. She wandered in and out of her bedroom where he lay on her bed, whispering into her pale blue telephone. Sometimes she said "Still talking?" but, intent on business of her own, had no time to listen for an answer.

MARIE CAME TO see Wanda—of her own accord, which didn't happen often. Wanda was pleased and said they would have a wonderful tête-à-tête together. She loved having tête-à-têtes with Marie, and afterward she always reported to Jeannette how Marie had completely opened her heart to her. Actually, though, it was Wanda's heart that was opened. She talked to Marie about all sorts of intimate matters—even about Otto and how terribly passionate he had been. Wanda confided to Marie that she had never really liked that part but had submitted to it with patience, so that Otto was generally in a good mood and bought her things she needed.

Marie listened in what appeared to be complete absorption, with her hands folded in her lap and her feet in terribly good shoes placed side by side. But that day she suddenly said in the middle—"Has Hughie been here?"

"Hughie?" Wanda was taken aback by this unexpected interruption.

"Has he been to see you?"

"Darling, of course he's been to see me. He's here every day. If I were a few years younger, I'd begin to have thoughts. I'm no longer used to having young men lying on my bed crying, though once upon a time, I can tell you—"

"Hughie *cries*?"

"You should have seen him yesterday after he had this big loud row on the telephone with someone."

Marie was holding a teaspoon, and it made a tiny clinking sound against her cup; she put it down and said in her usual steady little voice: "What was it about?"

"I wish I knew, darling—I was trying to listen but I had this idiot man here who had been sent to repair my air conditioner. And by the time he was through, my nerves were so bad, I had to take something. It happens every time I have to have one of these people here—the working men in this country, that's a chapter in itself."

"And you don't know who he was talking to?"

"It was someone called Chuck. Hughie kept saying 'Chuck, listen to me, Chuck!' Is it the friend he went to Spain with? I asked your grandmother at lunch yesterday, but she started shouting and getting excited. Really, sometimes I think Jeannette is not a normal person. She said it was none of my business, none of her business, none of anyone's business who are Hughie's friends. This she says to me."

Marie had noticed that Jeannette no longer waited up for Hughie. By the time he came in, she was always fast asleep—at least, judging by the utter silence in her bedroom. Hughie began to be less cautious, and one night, shortly after her visit to Wanda, Marie heard sounds from his bedroom that made her bolder than usual. She got out of bed and into her negligee and matching slippers; she went to Hughie's door and breathed through the keyhole: "Let me in, Hughie."

"Go away, Marie," he replied.

But she stood there in silence, till he opened. She slipped in and turned on the light. "Don't!" Hughie cried out in a low voice, and hid his eyes behind his arm.

She turned it off again at once.

"Don't dare ask anything," he said.

"I'm not."

They spoke in whispers. They were used to that from childhood, for their grandmother had always been alert and would call out to them, "Children, what's wrong?" Something had been wrong quite often. With Hughie, that is, and then Marie had had to come in to comfort him. That had happened every time he had any contact with either of his parents; or some boy he liked very much at school liked another boy better; or he had quarreled with his best friend, or he didn't have any friends—Hughie had a lot of upsets and disappointments in his life. He didn't actually seek comfort from Marie on these occasions—he was secretive and didn't want her to know and was angry if she found out by herself; but he always submitted to the comfort she offered, and they ended up in his bed together, with him peacefully asleep and she holding him or just looking at him by the light shining from the windows of the building opposite.

That's how she saw him now; and by this light his face didn't look all that changed from when he was ten years old. The only difference was that, perhaps with repeated disappointments (after all, Hughie was nearly thirty), his mouth drooped somewhat at the corners; and his eyes, though the same beautiful glass-green, were no longer as clear as they had been, as though washed too frequently by tears.

"Is Jeannette asleep?" he asked.

They stood in the middle of his bedroom and listened. It was quite eerie not to hear her call out to them: "Children?" As if she were no longer there; or no longer cared; or didn't want to know. She had been that way ever since the night she had caught him on the telephone.

"Is she all right?"

"Of course," Marie replied. "She's asleep. Let's get in bed. Just to hold you," she pleaded.

He wanted it as much as she did: to be held in someone's arms and be comforted. It was years since he had allowed her to sleep with him, though how she had longed to repeat that ecstasy of her childhood. Only it was not repeated now—on the contrary, there was even a sort of pain in her that she didn't want to acknowledge: but there it was, though he lay in her arms just the same sweet way he had done in their childhood.

THEN IT WAS Wanda's birthday, and that was a day of traditional celebration for all of them. It had come about in this way: Wanda had always set great store by her birthday, and during the years Otto lived with her, it had been celebrated with the panache he knew to bring to such an occasion. Then had come his terminal illness, and after he left the hospital, he couldn't move back to Wanda's but had to be brought home to Jeannette. Wanda's birthday had come around just a few weeks before he died, and Jeannette could not refuse his request that they should celebrate it in the house on Eleventh Street. So it happened that the first time Wanda was allowed to enter their home was in honor of her own birthday. She arrived full of expectation as to what treats had been prepared for her. Her genuine excitement and pleasure, her complete unconsciousness, turned the afternoon into an enjoyable birthday party. Otto had been propped up in a chair, and the two other guests present— Hughie and Marie, aged six and three—ran around as excited as Wanda, stuffing their mouths with birthday cake and chasing balloons around their dying grandfather.

After that, though Otto was no longer with them, the rest of them never missed a year. Sometimes Hughie was off on one of his trips, but wherever he was (one year it was as far away as Afghanistan), he managed to get through to them on the telephone. The year of his return from Spain he was there, and it was he who opened the door to Wanda and was the first to congratulate her. She advanced into the apartment with caution, almost on tiptoe, as though at every step she was expecting to stumble over some surprise that she was not yet to know about. She had done herself over from top to toe: her hair was an orange flame, her eyelids matched her new emerald silk dress, and she was hung about with every kind of valuable trinket. And she smiled and smiled, with brilliant capped teeth slightly askew within her scarlet lips, and wobbled over the carpet on legs as long as a stork's and now also as skinny.

The afternoon tea of the first celebration had by now been replaced by an elaborate evening meal. This was cooked by Jeannette, who was a magnificent cook (her father, and then her husband too, had been a gourmet), and took days of preparation. It was good for her to be engrossed in this activity: the last birthday party always recalled the first, giving rise to feelings she thought to have transcended years ago. So she exhausted herself in the kitchen, mumbling over her cooking pots, and when Wanda arrived, she only had time to dash out of the kitchen, peck Wanda's cheek, and return at once before anything got burned.

Wanda sat enthroned on the high, floral sofa, waiting to be made a fuss of. Hughie brought her drink—he knew what she liked: very sweet sherries or liqueurs, she drank the way other people eat chocolates; and Marie brought the stool with the needlepoint spaniel on it for her feet. "So much fuss just because it's someone's birthday," smiled Wanda. As always on this day, she was in a fabulously good mood: but this year there lurked something extra in her smile, as if she looked forward not only to the surprises prepared for her but had one of her own. Soon she began to throw out hints, for there was this about Wanda—she loved secrets but could never keep one.

She said, "This year the birthday child is going to ask for a very special something."

"A present?" Marie and Hughie asked—looking at each other, for of course all her presents were already bought and wrapped.

She laughed, adoring it that she could mystify them. "You'll see," she said. "You'll hear. I've thought it all out. All up here in my own mind."

"I can't wait," Hughie said, shutting his eyes in an absolute passion. "You'll have to tell me."

"A secret," she said, laying one finger on her lips. But it was too much for her that Jeannette should be kept out of it, and she went to join her in the kitchen.

Marie and Hughie looked at each other again: "What could it be?" Marie wondered. But Hughie shrugged; Wanda and her secret had already gone from his mind and something else had taken its place that made his mouth droop. But when he caught Marie's sympathetic gaze on him, he said "Let's get our show on the road" and swung away from her with his graceful swinging step. He went into the dining room to get the table ready, and she followed him to act as his assistant. She was never allowed to do anything more than fetch and carry, but she liked doing that, admiring his tremendous gift for arrangement and decoration. But today he ordered her about with a rather cold imperiousness, bustling around as if to make it clear to her that nothing beyond folding table napkins and arranging silverware to its best advantage was on his mind.

JEANNETTE WAS NOT pleased to have Wanda come into the kitchen: puffy, red, and streaked with dough, she felt at an even greater disadvantage with her than usual. But of course Wanda didn't give a thought to any sort of comparison between herself and Jeannette—she never did, any more than a bird of plumage would have done, stepping on dainty claws among dun sparrows.

She launched straight into her secret: "Jeannette, what do you want more than anything in the world? . . . Imagine, Jeannette; shut your eyes and imagine—Wanda is the fairy godmother, she holds a wand, she says 'Make a wish!'"

She shut her own eyes in blissful wishing—at the same time extending a hand as though it held a wand. But Jeannette pushed past her with a heavy casserole dish to be put in the oven.

Wanda opened her eyes again: "You're no fun . . . It's something to do with your family," she prompted. "What do you wish for most in your family? Like, for instance, for Hughie? Jeannette? What do you wish for Hughie? If you could wish for him?"

Jeannette gave her a quick look. But Wanda went on smiling in the blandest way, so that it was clear she meant only the blandest, nicest thing.

At that moment Hughie himself came in, warbling "Time for presents!" He put one arm around Wanda and the other around Jeannette and led them both into the living room. Here Wanda uttered her annual cries of complete surprise at her presents laid out on top of the grand piano. But she very quickly undid all the pretty packaging, and putting on her glasses, placed those things that would be useful to her on one side and those that had to be taken back and exchanged on the other.

Then they all crowded into the dining room for the meal Jeannette had prepared. They had to sit wedged against the walls, for the dining room was too small for the enormous suite of table, chairs, and sideboard that had belonged in the Eleventh Street house. As the rich meal progressed, their physical discomfort increased, till they felt as heavy as the furniture that wedged them in. It was also hot and dark in the room, for Hughie had drawn the curtains and lit festive candles in the candelabras.

He sat at the head of the table in what had once been, long ago and in another house, his grandfather's place. He tried to make things go, was amusing and attentive. Marie did her best to back him up, but, unlike Hughie, she wasn't sociable by nature. And this year it was particularly difficult because of being so worried about him and having to struggle not to show it. But he was aware of it, and it made him devote himself very hard to Wanda without ever turning to the side where Marie sat. As it got hotter and hotter in the room, he became exceedingly thirsty and drank more wine than he should. He was laughing a lot and on a high note like an overexcited girl. He kept refilling Wanda's glass too, so that she became quite high-spirited. She was certainly enjoying her party, the only unshadowed person there.

Then it was time for dessert and champagne. Jeannette, after placing the crystal bowl of lemon cream and macaroons on the table, tried to return to the kitchen, but Hughie summoned her back. He opened the first bottle—the cork flew up, the champagne gushed out and streamed over the edge of the glass into which he quickly poured it. That made him laugh and he sucked it up and poured again and drank again. "Wait, Hughie," said Marie, so he drank more, and more, before any toasts had been made at all.

Now Wanda's hour had come. She ordered everyone to sit down; she waited for their silence. She raised her glass: "All right," she cried, "the first toast is for me, the birthday child!"

and she obligingly waited for them to drink to her. Then she stood up and continued, "But today the second toast is even more important than the first—"

"Impossible!" cried Hughie.

"Oh yes, it's very possible: because the second toast is to you—and to Marie!"

"Sit *down*, Wanda," Jeannette said, even tugging at Wanda who fought her off and continued:

"*To what we hope you will be telling us today!*

"*Hughie and Marie!*

"*Hooray, Hooray!*"

Hughie was the first to drink, but before he could get very far, Marie said, "Why don't you have some water"; she offered him the glass she had filled for herself. He pushed her hand aside, so that the water spilled out and over the tablecloth and dripped down the sides onto Wanda's lap, causing her to scream. Marie was already running around for dry cloths to soak up the water before it could get to the table and ruin the polish.

Wanda was so wet, she had to go and take off her dress. She did so in Jeannette's bedroom, and afterward she had to be wrapped in one of Otto's brocade dressing gowns. She was cross now—her party mood spoiled: because of her dress, and also her surprise toast had not met with the applause and gratitude she had expected. Jeannette hadn't yet said a word.

"Aren't you pleased? Isn't it what you wanted? What's the matter with you?" Wanda said.

"My God, not like that," Jeannette said.

"Then like what? That's the way it has to be done: if young people don't know where they're going, the family has to take over."

AS A MATTER of fact that's how it had been done with Jeannette and Otto. She had adored him for four years and he had been kind to her. Then their aunts got together and one of them—the one Otto had got along with the best: a theatrical designer, with cropped black hair, short skirt, and tons of makeup—had had a serious talk with him. The following weekend Otto had driven Jeannette out to the house of another aunt on Long Island. That aunt was musical and had a string quartet playing in her garden on Saturday nights. Otto and Jeannette had sat side by side on chairs under a magnolia tree. A tiny breeze had sprung up, and Otto, pretending to think that was why Jeannette was trembling, went inside to get her shawl. And with the same movement with which he placed this shawl over her shoulders, he also made her rise and led her—the music still playing—down to the seashore. The words he spoke to her there were a continuation of the music, and also of the sound of the ocean that had moonlight split up in it and rolling in its waves. That night, while Jeannette lay awake on her bed by the open window, the musical aunt in the Hamptons telephoned the theatrical aunt in New York, and after that for several days everyone in the family was on the telephone to each other.

It did not take Jeannette long to find out that the expectations she had had that night had been excessive. She did have happiness, but it was of a different order from what she had anticipated. For instance, on that day of Wanda's first birthday party, when Otto was still there: after Wanda had gone home with her presents, he had lain in bed, completely exhausted from having sat up in a chair for an hour. His hand dangled over the edge of the bed. Jeannette had taken it and held it in her own, and though he had no strength in it at all, he had attempted to press hers: attempting, she knew, to express his gratitude for having had Wanda in the house and providing her birthday treat for her. But then—and especially in comparison with the great effort he was making just to press her hand—that had seemed a very small thing to have done; and she had brought his hand up to her lips, to make him understand that it was she who was glad and grateful.

HUGHIE WAS DIFFERENT from his grandfather in every way. Otto hadn't much liked drinking, but when he had to, he could hold it. Hughie liked it, but couldn't hold it. After Wanda's toast, he had to lock himself in the bathroom, and when he came out, he was chalk-white and suffused with perspiration. Marie knew what to do. She bedded him on the sofa in the living room and wiped his brow to which his hair was sticking. In one way, she was sorry to see him so ill, but in another she was not: Hughie's mother had been an alcoholic and so were several of his uncles on that side of his family. But Hughie always threw up.

She busied herself with folding the wrapping papers Wanda had left scattered around the room. She glanced frequently at Hughie, lying there with his eyes shut in exhaustion. When he opened them, the first thing he said was: "Wanda is a fool. She's worse than a fool. She's an imbecile: literally. I mean it."

"Jeannette says Wanda's brain is the size of a pea. That's why she's got this terribly small head. Like a peahen."

"I feel awful. It happens every time. Every *time*," he said, in a fury with himself.

"I'll get the cologne," Marie said.

The cologne he liked was in Jeannette's bedroom. Marie found Jeannette crouching on a stool at the foot of the bed, fierce and brooding like a little old witch. Wanda was laid out on the bed, her head with its flaming hair raised on a pillow, her eyes shut: wrapped in Otto's scarlet, emerald, and gold dressing gown, she might have been dead and embalmed for thousands of years.

"Is she sleeping?" Marie whispered.

"No, she's not," Wanda answered for herself. "She's lying here thinking how can people be so selfish and ungrateful."

"Don't worry about her," Jeannette told her granddaughter. Then she said: "What did Hughie say?"

Marie was usually so controlled that she could even stop herself blushing; but when she did blush—as now—the blood could be seen to flood very quickly under her light skin right up into her light hair.

It wasn't that Jeannette didn't feel for her, but she had to press on: "He does care for you. He loves you. As far as he can, he does. What more do you want?" she added—rather impatiently, for it seemed to her that Marie was being unreasonable in her expectations. She too would have to learn that one lived on earth and not in heaven.

"Marie!" he called from the living room.

"You see," Jeannette pointed out. "He can't be five minutes without you."

"He's *ill*," Marie said. "He wants the cologne." She went out with it quickly; there were tears in her eyes that she didn't want anyone to see. She didn't realize that there were tears in Jeannette's eyes too, rising as though from the same source in Marie's heart.

Before rejoining Hughie, Marie dashed cold water on her face, but of course he knew what was going on. That's what so often made him mad at her—that he always knew about her, and knew that she did about him, without either having to say one word. It was like being one person with her instead of two, and he resented it—to be so commingled with a girl.

She sat massaging his temples on the sofa where he lay, fair and dreamy, amid the floral bouquets of the upholstery. The fragrance of lemony lime cologne enveloped them. After a long while, he said—or rather, whispered (they knew they were being listened for): "We could, you know. If you want to."

"You don't have to take any notice of what *she* says: Wanda."

"But we could."

"Children?" Jeannette called to them from the bedroom.

Hughie put his hand over Marie's mouth.

"Children?"

All of them—even Wanda lying mummified on the bed—listened intently. But nothing was heard except clocks ticking—all those useless old clocks from Eleventh Street that Jeannette couldn't bring herself to part with.

As soon as Hughie took his hand away, Marie whispered: "We don't have to; just because *they* want to."

"*I* want to," Hughie said—irritably, for he always disliked it when Marie didn't at once fall in with his wishes.

"Is it my birthday or isn't it my birthday!" Wanda trumpeted from the bedroom.

Her party wasn't even finished yet; the dessert hadn't been eaten nor the champagne drunk. They wedged themselves back into the dining room. The table was wrecked of course, and the candles were beginning to gutter. But Hughie opened another bottle. Wanda repeated her toast. They drank to Hughie and Marie. Wanda looked triumphantly at Jeannette and challenged her: "Say 'thank you, Wanda darling.'" When Jeannette wouldn't, she called her a stubborn old woman—but smilingly, for she was very pleased with herself and what she had achieved.

(1980)

Grandmother

NOWADAYS, WHEN SHE LOOKED IN THE MIRROR MINnie found herself looking very much the way she remembered her grandmother. Her grandmother had spent her days in a steamy kitchen, cooking and washing for her large and very poor immigrant family, but she had been of a joyful disposition. Under her ugly black clothes, her body had been plump and volatile, and she had Polish Jewish eyes that sparkled and danced. Minnie looked like her now, because she was of the same type—small, plump, and (thanks to M. Jean, her hairdresser) blackhaired. She was also happy, and it showed.

Sometimes it showed too much, and she had to disguise it and pull a longer face than she really felt like. This happened especially when she was with her daughter, Sandra, for Sandra, being miserable herself, often resented her mother's good moods. Everything had turned out wrong. What had been planned for had been Sandra's happiness, not Minnie's. Sandra had had everything her parents had longed for most in life, but it had not been the blessing that was expected. Sandra was heavy and blond and beautiful; she took after her father's Galician family, and, God knows through what intermingling of blood, could have been any Polish peasant girl. Her parents, Minnie and Sam, had sent her to private schools and bought her expensive clothes and everything else anyone could possibly want. All this had enabled Sandra to mix with very good people and to marry Tim, whose family, of combined Dutch and Scottish ancestry, had three hundred years of American history behind it—as Sandra often pointed out. At the wedding, Sam had been as gleeful as when he purchased some piece of antique furniture or a picture that he had been told was valuable.

When Sam died, Minnie very quickly sold off everything that Sandra didn't want and went to live in a hotel on Central Park South. It was to be just a temporary measure, till she found someplace suitable to live. Sandra, who was bored and alone most of the time now, occupied herself with selecting apartments for her mother to buy or rent. Sometimes she found houses for her in the country, too, and Minnie, to oblige her daughter, would tramp around with her all day or make long auto trips looking at places she didn't want. These days usually ended badly, with Sandra in tears of rage and frustration because Minnie wouldn't commit herself to anything, and Minnie, dead tired, could hardly wait to get back to the hotel, where she could take her shoes off and phone Ralph to come around quickly and give her a head massage.

"Why do you *do* it?" Ralph remonstrated with her when she was in a state of exhaustion from one of these excursions. "Wearing yourself out for nothing—I don't like to see it."

"I have to have a place," Minnie said. She was lying with her eyes shut on one of the brocade sofas in the living room of her hotel suite while Ralph rubbed her temples with his slim, flat fingers. He did a wonderful massage—he had learned it from his mother, who had learned it from her mother, who had been a midwife in Baghdad.

"Well, okay, then let Sandra look for it," Ralph said. "Or Mickey and I will. What's the use of your running around ruining your feet?" And he picked one of them up in his hand—a round little stockinged foot, which he held as if it were something precious.

"I know a place," Mickey said from across the room, where he was fiddling with the TV.

"What do *you* know? Where is it?" Ralph asked him, and when Mickey told him he began to scold him, saying how did he expect Minnie to live in such a crummy neighborhood. Mickey defended himself, and they quarreled the way they always did—a nice way that showed that they really loved each other—and Minnie smiled to herself as she lay on her sofa, deliciously relaxed and with her eyes shut, hearing their two voices raised like children's in argument.

After that, Ralph and Mickey spent a lot of their time apartment hunting for Minnie. They even took her car out of the garage and went all over Westchester and Fairfield Counties, to look at places for her. When they saw something they liked, which was often, they called her up and described it to her in great excitement. But, at the same time, Ralph wouldn't let her come and see till they found something that was 100 percent all right; he said this was their job, not hers. They gave a great deal of their time to the search and probably lost opportunities for work by missing possible auditions (both were in show business and both were looking for work). Sandra, meanwhile, also continued to search out places for her mother, so that Minnie began to feel very much under pressure.

The fact was, she loved living in the hotel; it suited her very well. She had moved in here once before, six years ago, when Sam was still alive. Soon after Sandra's marriage, Sam had taken up with a very young girl who said she was a fashion model. Well, anyone could see at a glance what kind of model she was. But Sam had been so infatuated that he had to have her near him day and night, so he moved her right into the apartment, into what had been Sandra's room. Minnie had packed up her clothes and jewelry right away and had gone to live in the hotel. Then Sam moved the girl out fast enough, and he called Sandra and complained to her about how her mother had left him, he didn't know why. He told Sandra to go to the hotel and make

Minnie come home again, which Sandra did. "How does it look," Sandra had accused her, "with Tim's family, and all?"

Minnie didn't answer how does it look what your father is doing, but she did say, "Tim's mother is separated, too."

"Yes, but she lives in the country," Sandra said. At that time she still liked and admired her mother-in-law, a very upright woman who tended an herb garden in her house at Red Hook and hunted for bargains in New York State Dutch furniture. "And if you must live in a hotel," Sandra said, "why this one? I just met your friend Marjorie coming up in the elevator with some terrible-looking boy with green hair. I'm sure she keeps him. It's disgusting."

The reason Minnie had chosen the hotel was that Marjorie had installed herself there after the dispute over her late husband's estate was settled, and another friend of theirs also lived there, on very good alimony. Minnie had had a good time with them, but it turned out that she could only stay a month, because Sam wouldn't give her an allowance. In fact, he was only prepared to pay the bill on condition that she return home to him when the month was up.

But now she had all the money she wanted, and she could afford to live wherever she liked. Ralph and Mickey had their own place a few blocks away—a nice little studio and not too expensive, although Minnie, who paid their rent, wouldn't have minded if it cost more (she was ready to spend; it was Ralph who was careful for her). They took many meals in the hotel, in one of the restaurants, or they called room service. Minnie's suite usually had trays standing around in it, for one or the other of the boys was always hungry and had to call for something. If there was a good cabaret on in the hotel, the three of them might drop in on that for an hour or two, or else Ralph brought his guitar along and played and sang for them after dinner in Minnie's suite. And they always had plenty to talk about, making plans for their future. Ralph and Mickey had a lot of plans, and these always included Minnie. She was their family; they didn't really have anyone except her and each other. Mickey's mother was in a state mental asylum, and Ralph had lost his mother a few years before he met Minnie. So they really depended on and needed her.

Sandra hated seeing their trays standing around in the living room. "Whose is this? Who's been here?" she would say, as if she didn't know perfectly well. She would ring for someone to come and clear up, and then she'd walk around with a severe face, straightening the cushions on which the boys had lounged and picking up the scattered copies of *Interview* and *People*. If her father's photograph had got behind too many boxes of tissues and bottles of moisturizer on Minnie's dressing table, she moved things around and made it stand out front again. But sooner or later she would drop that and give way to her own troubles. These were all to do with her husband. She sank heavily onto a sofa and stared ahead of her with unhappy eyes. She looked like someone who didn't know what had hit her; she had never heard of people having to be unhappy. Minnie certainly hadn't told her. She had never let on to her about Sam, and whenever there had been a bad fight in the house while Sandra was there—when roused, Sam got mean and cruel—Minnie saw to it that it happened inside their bedroom and with no sound coming out.

Minnie talked about Sandra with Ralph. She had got in the habit of talking everything over with him, and of course that meant with him and Mickey both, for they were rarely apart. But Ralph was the understanding one; he was all softness and sympathy, whereas Mickey sometimes sounded quite callous. It was Mickey who said about Tim, Sandra's husband, "What's she expect, with a character like that?"

They had met Tim. He had dropped in unexpectedly on his

mother-in-law one afternoon while they were there, having their usual relaxed time together. Tim was glad to join them; his was a sociable nature, and he was always ready to spend a pleasant hour if things were slow at the office, as they often were. On this day, he was soon mixing drinks all around, and since everyone else was tongue-tied, he took over the entertainment himself. While Ralph and Mickey looked at him with blank, too attentive stares, he told them about a ball game he had been to the night before at Yankee Stadium, and then he began telling risqué jokes, for he had somehow got it into his head that Minnie loved them. ("At least, the old girl's got a sense of humor," he often told Sandra—who had none.) So he sat there in the biggest armchair, telling a story about a Pole and a nun, and laughing so much himself that he didn't notice how it shamed everyone else—especially Ralph, who was very refined and squeamish. Minnie was relieved when at last Tim got down to business. He told her that he was waiting for a bank draft to clear and then leaned over her shoulder while she wrote out the check he needed. "That's really good of you, really generous," he said, deftly picking it up the moment she had finished signing it. He was always genuinely grateful for her loans and the way she handed over the check without a murmur. He embraced her warmly as he said goodbye, and he shook hands with the two boys and said how pleased he was to have met them, as formal and courteous as if they were his equals, except that the way he looked at them, his frosty blue eyes glinting with amusement, was not the way one looks at equals.

ONE DAY, RALPH and Mickey came in very excited with news of an apartment they had found, a penthouse duplex with an enormous dropped living room and a great view looking east.

They began to describe it to Minnie, but she said, "It's no use, boys." She began to weep very quietly into a little handkerchief.

"Now, what's this? What's up?" Ralph said, kneeling by the sofa on which she lay wrapped in her robe. She was soft and fragrant after a long hot bath with salts. She always took long baths when she was upset—it was a sure sign with her, and Ralph blamed himself for not having noticed it as soon as he came in.

She said, "It's Sandra."

"What's she done now?" Mickey cried. "I'll fix her!" When Ralph turned around to give him a furious look, he winked to show that this was just to make Minnie laugh.

"She wants to leave Tim. She wants to move in with me."

After a moment's silence, Ralph said, "I'm glad. I don't like to see her living with him. Making her unhappy like that—it shows in her face. Awful."

But Mickey said, "What about us?"

"What *about* us?" Ralph said and glared at him again. Minnie raised her head. It was almost exasperating to see Mickey sprawled in his usual place by the TV, eating a cheeseburger, but it was also touching and beautiful, for Mickey looked just the same as always, with his fresh complexion and his straw-colored hair. He wore faded jeans and no shoes.

"She won't like us coming to see you, Minnie," Mickey explained.

"You'll have to excuse him," Ralph said angrily to Minnie. "He can't think of anyone except himself. It's the way he grew up."

Ralph himself had grown up in a different way, and Minnie was reaping the benefit of that. Ralph knew how unhappy women could be. His mother had had a very hard time of it, struggling to support them both (first as a cocktail hostess and then selling stockings in one of the big stores). Her boyfriends had never stayed long, and the only person she had had to comfort her was Ralph, so he was very quick to sense other people's unhappiness. He was subtle, too—he knew, perhaps better than she did herself, how Minnie was affected on different levels, was torn in different ways.

"I guess it's for the best," Minnie said at last. "You're right—she ought to leave him. I shouldn't say it, but sometimes I want to kill him. I wouldn't say it to anyone except you two."

Ralph said, "It's a wicked world, Minnie. We *have* to hate sometimes. Whenever I came home crying, Mama would go right out after the boys in the street with an umbrella or kitchen knife, anything she could lay her hands on. We were alone in a pretty rough neighborhood. I don't suppose any of you will believe me, but whenever anything happens to me she's still there. She always knows. Last week—when they nixed me for that dinner-theater gig in New Jersey? After promising me for weeks—"

"It's a shame," said Minnie.

"Sadists," Mickey said.

"Well, when I put down the phone Mama was standing right there next to me at that booth at the corner of Fifth and Fifty-Third. I swear it. In her hat and blue coat she had. I know you don't believe me."

"I've had a ghost sitting next to me," Mickey said. "It was in Cleveland, at the Trailways bus station. There was this fat old black lady with a hearing aid, and I asked her, 'Excuse me, would you know where the eight-ten from Chicago is coming in?' She didn't say anything, and I thought it was on account of her bad ears. So I turned around to look it up on the board, and when I turned back she was gone. There was no one there. Just a chair with no one sitting on it. Later, I heard there was an old lady died of a heart attack the night before, right there in that station. I guess I'm psychic."

"I guess you're a fool," Ralph said.

Minnie said, "Sandra says she's found an apartment for the two of us. She wants me to move out of here by the end of the month."

They were silent. They were sitting almost in the dark, for although the suite had several fancy brass lamps, they cast only a very discreet light in the corners. The brightest light came from the TV screen (a car chase was in progress). The velvet curtains were drawn, shutting out the view of dusk breaking over Central Park and shutting Minnie in with her two boys. How could she bear to lose all this? She didn't know what to do. Ralph pressed her hand, because he knew all these things she was feeling.

But it was Mickey who said, "Hey, listen, I've got an idea." It was very simple. He suggested that they should *all* live together—he and Ralph and Minnie and Sandra, all four of them. Hadn't he and Ralph seen the perfect apartment for it that very day? He began to describe it—the penthouse duplex, the dropped living room—and also to apportion the space. They could have a piano in the living room so Ralph could work on his audition material, and a little upstairs place where Mickey could practice his tap steps, and there were terrific closets for all Minnie's clothes and shoes, and a nice little bedroom for Sandra, and, best of all, the terrace where people could sit. "Like for Sunday brunch?" he said. "Under an umbrella? With stripes and a little white fringe on it?"

Ralph said, "I wish you'd shut up. Just shut up—okay?" But out of the corner of his eye he was looking at Minnie to see how she was taking all this, and she was looking at him in the same way, for the same purpose. There was such deep understanding between them, they each knew at once about the other. It wasn't him that Minnie had to wonder about now, it was Sandra, and wasn't that strange, for Sandra was her own child, whereas she had only met Ralph less than two years ago, in a dance studio where he had been partnering her friend Marjorie.

SANDRA HAD ALWAYS been closer to her father than she had to Minnie. The two of them looked alike and they had always been proud to be seen together. Both were tall and well built, and as fair as gentiles. They had also shared some interests; Sandra had been more appreciative than Minnie of the turn-of-the-century gold-leaf and inlaid furniture Sam had collected. She also esteemed his position in the plate-glass business and the fortune he made there. Like Sam, Sandra had always had respect for money and knew that no one was anything without it.

Minnie didn't share this feeling. She and her friends had often said to each other, "Money isn't everything"—it had been a sort of theme song with them, over their lunches at Trader Vic's, or under the dryers at M. Jean's. All of them had rich husbands, and all of them were unhappy with them, for various reasons. However, once the husbands had gone (they all seemed to go sooner or later, either dying or running off with someone younger), it turned out that money was everything after all, or at least a great deal. With Marjorie, for instance, the older she got the more she clung to it, and she begrudged spending on anyone but herself. At one time, Ralph had unstintingly given his time and company to Marjorie, but she had always paid him as little as she could get away with. It was the same with all the escorts she had, not to speak of her maid and the chauffeurs of the cars she hired and the girl who came in to do her nails.

Minnie was just the opposite; she really appreciated her money, because of the nice things it allowed her to do for Ralph and Mickey. She wished she could do more. She would have spent anything, she often said, to help Ralph forge ahead in his career. His work was not developing in the way he had a right to expect. He was so talented. Besides being a pretty good actor, he was a fabulous ballroom dancer, and as for his voice, "Well, if you shut your eyes," Minnie told her friends, "you wouldn't know it wasn't Mel Tormé." But his agent had recently got rid of most of his freelance clients, so Ralph wasn't even being sent up for auditions anymore. In a way, this was just as well, because he was really too sensitive and suffered terribly every time he wasn't called back.

Mickey explained to him, "You have to wait until Saturn and progressed moon rise before things will happen for you."

"How long will that take?" Minnie asked, but Mickey couldn't tell her. He couldn't tell for himself, either, for Mickey was also in an unfavorable conjunction and hadn't had a break in more than two years. His unemployment had run out, and he had to find some sort of job, like working in a parking lot, before he could qualify for it again. But, unlike Ralph, he wasn't in the least cast down, perhaps because he knew about the stars and how impossible it was to get away from the iron laws of their necessity. Or maybe it was only because he was younger. Mickey was only twenty-one, whereas Ralph was getting on for twenty-eight, though you wouldn't think it unless you looked very close.

Ralph was looking at himself very close now, in the gilt mirror that hung over the fake fireplace in Minnie's suite. He saw some very fine lines that were beginning to form at the corners of his eyes—also the slight downward droop of his lips—and he made a better, younger face at himself at once.

Minnie said, "You'll see, it's like Mickey says. You have to wait. It's not as if anyone can keep talent down. That doesn't happen."

"Not in a hundred years," Mickey said, backing her up. "I've never seen anyone who can do a Garland song the way you do it, making people laugh and cry at the same time. That's real talent. You don't get that every day."

Ralph looked from one to the other. "You think so?" he said.

He was shy, hesitant, self-doubting, so that they talked faster, saying every nice thing they could think of. Then slowly a smile came over his rather melancholy features and transformed them. He began to hum one of his songs. Minnie took it up, and so did Mickey. When Ralph broke off, they both cried out in protest. Ralph smiled more—taking pleasure in giving pleasure—and then he took his guitar and sat down with it to play and sing.

Minnie had to hold her hand over her heart, it was all so beautiful—to hear him and see him, slim and olive-skinned, in a white shirt open almost to his waist. How Oriental he looked as he sang, half closing his lids over his mystical eyes. He was the son she had never had, the beautiful Jewish boy of her dreams (actually, he was of a Muslim sect converted to Christianity), and he was singing for the two people he loved best in the world—for her and for his friend Mickey, from Colorado Springs.

His song was an old love ballad that his mother used to sing. It was about a young girl at a window watering her plants, now with her little watering can, now with her tears. It was so deeply sorrowful that it seemed to be not only about this girl but about everyone else, too, who suffered, everyone who had ever lost what was most dear to them. But then the song changed. Just when everyone was about ready to cry their eyes out, suddenly the verse rose up in joy: "But there has been love! Love was mine! Was mine! Yes, mine!" Minnie and Mickey laughed out loud. They had heard it a hundred times, but it was new every time, unexpected. Ralph smiled at them and encouraged them to join in, and they did. "Yes, mine!" they sang, and all three laughed and sang again.

"I COULD HEAR you from the elevator," Sandra said. No one had seen her come in. They stopped smiling and singing. Ralph got up to put away his guitar, and he nudged Mickey to get up, too, in honor of Sandra. Ralph had lovely manners.

But Sandra said, "Sing it again."

Ralph looked at Minnie and, having got her approval, he sat down with his guitar and sang the refrain all over again. The two others didn't join in this time, although Mickey flexed his knees and snapped the fingers of both hands in the air and, for the finale, gave a little spin around on one heel. Even Sandra was smiling, and, with a dreamy look in her eyes, she twisted a loose strand of hair around her finger. But the next moment she tucked the hair back where it belonged and said to Minnie, "I have to talk to you."

As soon as they were in the bedroom, with the door shut, Sandra said, "He's left his job."

Minnie tried to remember which job this might be. Tim had had many, usually found for him by his relatives or family friends. He had been with an investment firm, in real estate, with a bank and a travel agency, and once he had been the public relations director of a small airline. He always started off with a lot of dash and spirit and made a very good impression, but after a while he got tired and stopped going to the office.

"Not that it was anywhere near good enough for him," Sandra said. "Only, when he doesn't have a job he gets restless. What are those two doing? Are they listening at the door?"

"Oh, they wouldn't," Minnie said, truly shocked.

"He doesn't get up till three in the afternoon, and then of course he can't sleep at night. God knows where he goes all night or who with— What's that noise, if they're not listening?"

She strode to the door and opened it, as if expecting to catch someone at the keyhole. She stood there, amazed at what she saw. Minnie came to see, and cried out, "Boys! Not now!" For Ralph and Mickey had got into one of their fights. They stood glaring at each other, their faces close together, clenching and unclenching their fists. Both were under medium height, and slight in build, so they might have been two children.

"Excuse me, dear," Minnie said, hastily brushing past Sandra as Mickey swung at Ralph and missed. Minnie danced around them; she wrung her hands and implored them to stop, but they took no notice of her. It was a scene that had been played out among the three of them before and was new only to Sandra.

"What's going on here anyway?" Sandra said.

At the sound of her voice, they stopped fighting immediately. No one would have thought that anything had taken place, they were friends again so perfectly. In cheerful unison, they got ready for departure, Ralph picking up his guitar and Mickey putting on the fedora he had found at a thrift shop to wear on his straw-colored hair.

FROM THAT DAY on, Sandra stayed in the hotel most of the time. Perhaps it was to keep her mother's two friends away, perhaps to escape from Tim, but if it was the latter her move was not successful, for Tim kept turning up as regularly as the boys used to. He lounged around and ordered trays in the same way they did. For Minnie, it was odd to see his heavy form stretched out on the brocade sofa in place of lithe Ralph or skinny Mickey. She would have liked to make him leave and she waited for Sandra to do it. But Sandra said nothing, and he ensconced himself deeper and behaved as though he had every right—was, indeed, expected—to come there. And it seemed he was, for when he turned up late one day Sandra challenged him at once: "Where have you been?"

"With a terrific blond, of course," he said. He picked up Minnie's gilded antique telephone and pretended to dial, with a very solemn face. "I promised I'd give her a call."

Stupid as an ox, Sandra rose to his teasing. "What are you

doing!" she cried. "Who are you calling?" She tried to wrest the receiver away from him, but when she saw the amused look in his eyes she let go. She said, "You ought to be calling your uncle—that's who you ought to be calling. He wants you to meet with those people." Tim was mixing himself a gin and tonic, merrily stirring and twirling and clinking ice cubes, so she addressed herself to Minnie. "They really want him—Colfax and Wilbur," she said. "Didn't Daddy have some investments with them? They're a top firm. Tim could get any job he wanted, if only he'd pull himself together. They thought the world of him at Transfer Travels. They said they'd never had anyone like him. If only you'd pull yourself together," she said, talking to Tim now. She watched him finish his drink, and then he stretched out the empty glass to her. Automatically, she took it; she even went over to the cocktail cabinet and already had the gin bottle opened when she recollected herself. "I must be going crazy," she said and banged down the glass. He refilled it himself, pretending to grumble at her for being so disobliging.

Sandra didn't talk about moving anymore but now seemed content to stay with Minnie in the hotel suite. She had brought a few of her clothes there, though most of them were at home with Tim. This made it necessary for her to go back there frequently, and sometimes she didn't return to the hotel for several days. When she did return, it was always in a rage and vowing she would never, never see her husband again. But if he didn't show up in the hotel by evening, she became very restless and in the end she tried to phone him at home, always finding some compelling reason that she had to do so. If he wasn't home, she would try a few other places where he might be—even out in the country with his mother, which meant she had to force herself to speak to her cordially—and if she couldn't find him she would be frantic. Minnie didn't know what to do or even think. Minnie had never been that way with Sam. When he was away, she was glad, and when he returned it was like being put back into irons.

Ralph and Mickey took her to the apartment they had found. It was a West Side duplex, high up in a very fancy building overlooking the Park. They took her from room to room, and it was fantastic. The apartment had belonged to a fur dealer who had had to sell it on account of financial difficulties. There were Corinthian pillars of blue plaster, and walls and ceilings covered in flower-printed damascene. The principal bathroom had mirrors set into the ceiling and a statue of a classical nude. Mickey climbed into the circular sunken bath and lay there with his fedora on. His eyes were closed, and he moaned in ecstasy.

Ralph took Minnie's hand in his; he looked into her eyes and said, "Do you like it? I knew you would."

They stood holding hands. When Minnie looked up, she saw all three of them reflected in the mirror set in the ceiling. This mirror had clouds, stars, and angels painted on it to simulate a vision of heaven.

"We'll have parties," Mickey said from out of the bath.

"As long as we don't ask too many people," Ralph said. "I don't like too many people coming in. Trampling in. This is going to be a real home, just for three people—four—who love each other. For a real family."

But when Minnie took Sandra there Sandra looked very dubious. She tapped a plaster pillar and said, "I can just see Tim's mother coming in here."

"She's not going to come in here," Minnie said.

"You should hear her. Even about Daddy. All those things I took from the house—Daddy's gold cabinets and stuff? She said to her sister right in front of me, 'Doesn't it make you weep, the way these people spend money?' Of course *they* never spend any. They use tea bags three times over."

"I'm going to buy it," Minnie said. "We're going to move in here."

"Tim thinks it'll work out about that job. They're very lucky to get him, and they know it."

Minnie walked away. She went into the kitchen, which was a serious workplace, geared to the production of elaborate meals. She and the boys had already decided that they were going to have a housekeeper. Mickey knew this girl who was really an actress but was an absolutely fabulous cook and could do anything—buttermilk doughnuts, prawn curry, chicken gumbo, you name it.

Sandra followed her. She said, "He wants me to come back to live with him."

"The boys really love you, Sandra."

"Let me stay with you in the hotel," Sandra said. "Just till he gets himself straightened out. It's not having a job that's so demoralizing for him. Not going to an office and all of that. It would be for anyone, wouldn't it? You don't know what happened last night."

Again Minnie escaped her—this time to the bathroom with the classical statue.

"He *knew* I was coming there," Sandra said, following her. "I told him I had to come home to get my black skirt to take to the cleaner's—he having kindly spilled all that mayonnaise on it when he was too blind drunk to see what he was doing. I even told him the time I'd be there, so he'd know, but when I let myself in first thing I saw lying on the floor was this pair of—"

"But why do you go!" Minnie shouted. "Why do you go there!"

"My skirt!" Sandra shouted back. "I told you! My black skirt!"

She began to sob. Minnie held her, both of them standing under the mirrored heaven of the bathroom ceiling. Sandra had never cried much, not even as a child, so now it was difficult for her, and her sobs came out dry and hard, as if stones were being shaken out of her by someone bigger and stronger.

CRYING CAME MUCH easier to Minnie, and it was even pleasant to cry when Ralph and Mickey were there to comfort her. They said it didn't matter about the apartment; there would be others, and meanwhile what was wrong with this one? They meant their own studio, where Minnie now spent a lot of her time, because the hotel suite seemed increasingly to be occupied by Tim and Sandra. Both the boys said that the other place would have been much too big and a headache to keep up, whereas their own little studio had everything anyone could want.

It was very cozy. The sweet mild smell of pot was mixed in with the smell of Mickey's favorite pork chops fried in their own fat. Ralph kept the atmosphere very warm and slightly moist, for the plants he tended and cherished. As a result, they flourished and put out juicy leaves that spread themselves over the many photographs of Ralph's mother at various stages of her life. In the earliest, she was a big-breasted girl sitting among many sisters, all with the same eyes, on an overstuffed sofa, before a carved screen; in the last, she was on a beach chair, grossly overweight, looking sick and old. Yet when she died she was younger than Minnie was now.

"I love you in that chair," said Mickey, looking at Minnie in her own special rocker they kept for her. "Just like I've seen ladies sitting on their porch with little children, reading them stories."

"Where have you seen that?" Ralph asked and answered himself: "In the movies."

It was true, Mickey's vision of family life was not based on firsthand experience. But it was very strong. It was he who had found the sampler of "Our Home Is Our Sweet Heaven" that now hung, rather brown and moldering, on the wall, which was papered with jungle foliage. Ralph had supplied the cotton prayer mat—with a design that featured a mosque—that hung on the opposite wall. It had come from the same antique shop as Mickey's sampler. Ralph had liked it because it reminded him of something he vaguely remembered seeing in his grandmother's prayer room.

Minnie said, "You know that first time I went to live in the hotel?" She had told them about that, as she told them about most things. "There was a woman used to come and see Marjorie. She said she was Russian, from the czar's family. Marjorie said she was from Pittsburgh, but what's it matter? She was really gifted. She could tell you anything, past or future. We'd have long sessions with her—Marjorie and me and this other friend we had living in the hotel, June. She told June she would have to be in the hospital, and that came completely true within six months. Poor June, I've never seen anyone go down so fast." She rocked and sighed.

"And you? What did she tell you?"

If this was designed to allay Minnie's sighs, it was absolutely successful. Minnie began to giggle—so much that she had to cup one hand before her face.

"Go on, tell us," they said, and when she wouldn't they began to guess. "A big part in a movie? . . . A handsome stranger?"

"Not one but two," she said when she could speak for laughing. "*Two* handsome strangers. I swear to God she said that. 'You'll have two lovely little boys to look after,' she said. 'I can see them—one fair, one dark. Very dark.' I said, 'You mean grandsons?' She didn't know about that. All she could see was these two boys, one fair, one dark. She told Marjorie she saw her with palm trees—and of course Marjorie *is* in Monaco now, because of the tax. She hates it."

Their radio was tuned to their favorite FM station. None of them ever noticed how loud it was, probably because it was on all the time, and Minnie rocked in time to it unconsciously. It was part of them, like breathing.

Minnie said, in that dreamy voice she had when she was in her rocking chair, "My grandmother had six sons, and she was crazy about all of them. But when we grandchildren were there, she'd say, 'The interest's even better than the capital.'"

"My grandmother robbed a bank," Mickey said unexpectedly. "It's a fact. She was living with this guy who was a professional bank robber. Uncle Charlie—a freak, but she'd do anything he said. Gran was only given two years, on account of she wasn't armed, only looking out for them. In Flagstaff it was—Arizona."

"It's better to keep quiet about things like that," Ralph said.

Minnie usually stayed with them till quite late, and then they took her back to the hotel. "Sure you're all right?" they said as they delivered her over to George, the elevator man. George waited while Minnie stood and watched them walk away. They were off to spend their evening; they might go to a disco or a bar or drop in on a party—their evenings were unplanned but eventful and did not usually end before dawn.

When they were out of sight, Minnie said, "Okay, George," and entered his gilded elevator. He took her up to her floor. She stood for a moment outside the door of her suite, taking a deep breath. Quite often Tim was there. The best time was when no one was there. Once she found the sitting room empty and was relieved, but when she opened the bedroom door they were in there, two giant figures coupling on her bed. Half embarrassed, half amused, Tim shouted out, "Sorry, Minnie!" as she quickly shut the door.

One day, Sandra told her that she was pregnant. At first she said she was going to have an abortion, but then she didn't talk anymore about that. Instead, she began to drink milk and eat a great deal. She became fat. Tim teased her unmercifully about her appearance, but she walked around proudly with her stomach and breasts thrust out before her. She and Tim began to spend weekends with his mother in the country, and when they came back they laughed at his mother, who in her thrifty way had got some baby wool on sale and had already begun to knit. Minnie didn't do any knitting; she didn't know how anyway, and it was too late to learn. She guessed when the time came she would just go into one of the stores and charge up a whole lot of things. Sandra talked about her father; she hoped for his sake it would be a boy. They would call him Sam, which was a name that was coming back, she said. She couldn't understand why Minnie wasn't more enthusiastic. "Don't you want to be a grandmother?" she asked often. "A proper grandmother?" As though it were possible to be anything but a proper one.

(1980)

Aphrodisiac

KISHEN'S UNIVERSITY FRIENDS AT CAMBRIDGE COMpletely understood when he talked to them about the sort of novel that should be written about India—the sort of novel that he wanted to write. The thing was, he explained, to get the integers right, to be sure that these were sunk into the deepest layers of the Indian experience: caste-ridden villagers, urban slum dwellers, landless laborers, as well as the indecently rich of commerce and industry.

His own integers were sunk in a prosperous gated colony in New Delhi. Here he returned from Cambridge to live with his mother and his elder brother, Shiv, in the villa that his late father had commissioned in the International Style, which was prevalent at the time. During Kishen's absence, Shiv had got married—in a big, traditional wedding, which Kishen couldn't attend because he was in the middle of his finals. So he didn't meet his new sister-in-law until his return. He hadn't meant to stay in India. He'd wanted to go back to Cambridge and maybe study for another degree until he felt himself ready to start on his life's work. But then this happened, *she* happened: his sister-in-law, Naina.

It hadn't been an arranged marriage; Kishen's mother was too modern to arrange marriages for her sons. A respected economist, she had always been at the forefront of educated Indian women. Sometimes she and her elder son even served on the same committees, for Shiv was a high-ranking bureaucrat. He had met his bride at a reception in honor of her uncle, a member of parliament, who had brought Naina from her father's estate in their native province for her first visit to New Delhi. She was very young, shy, scarcely educated, though she had attended an elite girls' boarding school in Jaipur. After her marriage, her mother-in-law tried to encourage her to study at some New Delhi college, but Naina claimed to be too stupid—yes, even for domestic science.

Although Kishen couldn't help agreeing that she was, to some extent, stupid, she was the only person in the house with whom he was eager to discuss his projected novel. She took no interest in it at all, yet somehow she casually disposed of one of his greatest problems: how to communicate the nuances of Indian life in English, which was the only language in which he could truly express himself. Naina simply jumbled up her languages, English and Hindi. When he tried to talk to her about his work (because he wanted to talk to her about everything), she didn't even pretend to listen. Instead, she said, "I'm meeting the girls—coffee *pina hai. Aoge? Chalo bhai* we'll have some fun—*mazza ajaiga*."

She had formed her own circle of girlfriends, and Kishen soon became a source of entertainment for them. Naina was proud of the way he amused them and humored all their concerns. They valued his opinion in matters of style, and also of culture, though he laughed at their taste, which hadn't changed since they were schoolgirls. They held morning coffee parties in the smartest Connaught Place restaurants or watched pirated films together on the giant screens in their giant living rooms. When they cried at a heroine's onscreen plight, Kishen would murmur some remark into Naina's ear, converting her tears into giggles, which soon spread to all the weeping girls.

They liked attending polo matches and pretending to be in love with the contestants, who were princelings from the President's Bodyguard. These young women were all married, but mostly to rich, paunchy businessmen who in no way resembled the polo players. Only Shiv was tall and handsome (the opposite of Kishen), and Naina's friends sincerely appreciated her good luck. So did she, though she was, or pretended to be, critical of Shiv: of his absorption in his work, which didn't leave enough time for her; of his lack of interest in the romantic films and books she adored. She often laughed about him—she imitated his walk, the way his feet splayed outward, so busy, so important—and Kishen laughed with her. If his mother overheard them, she rebuked them but couldn't help smiling with pride in her elder son, which she knew Naina, for all her mockery, shared. Only Kishen's laughter was genuine.

Mother and Shiv, both busy with their work, were glad that Kishen and Naina were such good company for each other. But sometimes Mother would ask, "And your work?" For she was waiting for Kishen to become as successful in his field as Shiv was in his. "Coming along," Kishen answered, and he considered this to be true. He felt that, with Naina and her friends, he was immersing himself in his material. They were the integers with which he would build his world—the India that he knew, not what others thought he should know. The girls, too, were waiting for him to become published and famous. When they asked what he was writing about, he said, "You." That made them laugh, and they clamored for a percentage of the fortune he was going to make with their lives.

Meanwhile, he entertained them with stories, anecdotes from their New Delhi social world—hungry kites swooping over an open-air banquet, new, palatial apartment buildings without electricity or water, the Ayurvedic doctor poking his tented patients through their burkas, the dire results of a homeopath mixing up his aphrodisiacs with his laxatives. "You should write it down!" the girls exclaimed—and, at their urging, he began to do so. They snatched the pages from him and sent them to the editor of a leading English-language newspaper, who was a friend of all the girls and the lover of one. These writings—these tongue-in-cheek anecdotes—became the basis of his local fame. A magazine commissioned a weekly column; he was read everywhere. Mother returned from her meetings reporting the chuckles of her fellow committee members; Shiv quoted a cabinet minister who said that Kishen "had hit the nail right on the head." Everyone was proud of him.

That was during his first two years back in India. Then things began to change in the house. Actually, physically, they had begun to change soon after Naina's arrival. Mother had originally furnished the house with the newfound enthusiasm of the intellectual classes for indigenous Indian handicrafts—vibrant textiles from Orissa, village women's silver anklets turned into ashtrays. Now another layer was added, for whenever Naina went home to see her family—which she did often in those first years—she brought back precious objects of her own. These were not village handicrafts but something differently indigenous: the gaudy taste of the maharajas' palaces, which had drifted down to her own family of feudal landowners. She installed multicolored chandeliers, oil paintings of hunting parties and court ceremonials. Mother's bright hand-loomed rug was replaced by the pelt of a recently killed tiger. Naina was so proud of these acquisitions that Mother even allowed the head of a water buffalo to be nailed to the wall, though it had to be taken down when, having been improperly embalmed, it began to decay and disintegrate.

Then came Naina's first pregnancy, for which, in accordance with custom, she went home. When she reappeared, it was not only with a baby but with his nurse. This nurse, known as Bari-Mai, had been Naina's mother's and Naina's and was now very old. She spoke in a dialect that only Naina could understand, and she made it clear that no one in the house was of any importance to her except Naina, whom she called Devi (goddess), and the baby, Munna. But with Kishen Bari-Mai did establish a peculiar relationship. From the first moment she saw him, she wheezed so much that she could only point at him in derision—but for what? Naina said, "It's because she's never seen anyone like you."

"You mean, anyone so ugly?"

"*Aré*, gosh, darling, *yeh kya baat hai*? What are you saying?" She stroked his cheek, and, although he liked this affectionate gesture, it made him aware that he was short, squat, and balding: ugly, no doubt, to both her and Bari-Mai.

"*Dekho, Baba—Papa hai!*" Naina called out when Shiv came home from the office, and she thrust the bundled baby into his arms. Shiv held him nervously. No one in the family felt comfortable holding the baby. There was something disconcerting to them in the many little amulets he wore around his neck and wrists, each guarding him against a disease or the Evil Eye. He was also greasy from the oil that Bari-Mai smeared on him for the health of his skin and hair. And he had a peculiar smell, which was not that of a baby but more—though no one said it—that of Bari-Mai. For not only did she clutch him all day but she slept with him at night, on the floor of the nursery that Mother had furnished for him with a new white cot, a playpen, and a mural of Mother Goose rhymes.

After Munna's birth, Naina abandoned the outings with her girlfriends, and Kishen stayed home with her. She was very free in his presence, suckling the baby at her great round brown nipples, while Kishen sat near her, scribbling a piece for his column. He was a chain smoker, and sometimes she had enjoyed a cigarette with him. Now she returned to chewing betel, and one day she ordered Bari-Mai to prepare one for Kishen as well. "Open your mouth," she told him, and he was about to obey her when he saw his mother's cook making warning gestures at him from behind the door. "*Aré*—open—*kholo, bhai*," Naina said impatiently.

Ignoring the cook, Kishen allowed her to pop the leaf into his mouth. He disliked the taste and the feel of it. He asked, "What does she put in it?" Naina laughed. "*Khas cheez hai*—something very special to make you love Munna and me forever."

IT WAS KISHEN'S birthday, and Mother had a gift for him. She watched him unwrap it: a slim volume tastefully bound in hand-loomed cloth, containing reprints of his newspaper and magazine articles. Full of her own excitement and pleasure, she said, "It's all there. All your beautiful work." He thanked her, kissed her, but he thought, Is this all you expect from me?

They were interrupted by the cook, who burst in on them, wailing, "With my own eyes!" He had seen with his own eyes how she—the witch, Bari-Mai—had stirred a powder, a poison, into Kishen's birthday *pilao*. Naina came rushing in, shouting that Bari-Mai had wanted only to add her own touch with a pinch of saffron. "*Zaffran*," the cook repeated angrily. "As if I don't know *zaffran*." Naina had already turned from him to Munna, riding on her hip. "*Bolo*—Happy birthday, Chacha-Uncle!" She thrust him forward to greet Kishen with sticky caresses.

But later, when they were alone, she said, "It's all lies. Don't believe them."

"No," Kishen said. "I don't believe Bari-Mai is trying to poison us."

"They're all crazy. *Pagal hai sab*. They think she's a terrible witch."

"It's you," he said. "You're the terrible witch." Before she could say anything, he went on, helplessly waving his arms, "I'm twenty-seven years old today and I haven't done a thing. No! No, I have not written a beautiful book. Only Mother thinks so."

"Munna thinks so," Naina said, nibbling Munna's ear.

"When Munna grows older, he'll laugh at me as I'd laugh at

anyone who wrote this sort of rubbish. But what's the use of talking to you? You don't listen to anything I try to tell you."

"Oh, yes. I'm very stupid."

"You are—no ideas, no theories, thank God! If you had them, if you drove me crazy the way I drive myself crazy, thinking and theorizing and doing nothing all day but sitting here with you and all night thinking about you—it's you, you who's poisoning me. No, don't go away!" To keep her from leaving, he put his arms around her waist. At first too surprised to resist him, she then did so with ease. Not only was he shorter than she; he was overweight and breathless with lack of exercise. She gave him a push that sent him staggering backward to the floor, then stared down at him with angry, kohl-rimmed eyes. He stared back, partly in fear of her, partly in fear of himself and the sensation that had filled him when he touched her hot, soft flesh. The next moment, she put out her hand to pull him up; she was laughing, and he tried to laugh, too. It was all just a game between them.

WHEN A SECOND boy was born, Bari-Mai decided that only she could provide the nourishment her Devi needed to breastfeed two babies. She pushed aside the cook's stainless steel vessels for her own blackened cauldron, into which she stirred spices unwrapped from little twists of newspaper. Noxious cooking smells—asafetida, like a gas—pervaded the house. Naina moved around her urine-and-milk-soaked kingdom with one child on her hip and another sucking at her breast. Shiv's study was moved out of earshot of the rest of the house, and as far as possible from what had been his marital bedroom and was now inhabited by both children and Bari-Mai, who stretched out on the floor bundled in the single cloth she wore day and night.

Shiv began to come home later every night; Naina was always waiting for him. They spoke in low voices, but not intimately.

Naina's initial passion for her husband had changed into some other kind of passion, charged with resentment. Kishen, in his bedroom, willed himself not to hear, and he guessed that his mother was doing the same. When he went into her room after a restless night, he found her sitting up very straight, with her hands folded in her lap. Mother said, "Of course he comes home late—he's very busy with meetings and conferences with the cabinet, with the Prime Minister. He's important to the whole country." Her voice rose. "She should be proud!"

"She *is* proud."

"She doesn't understand. She understands nothing."

A modern woman, Mother had set herself against the stereotypical role of mother-in-law. She was determined not to complain about her daughter-in-law, or about the encroachments, the ruin of her ordered household. So she said nothing, not even to Kishen. Instead, she stayed out of the house at meetings of her own. Kishen suspected that she was no longer elected to the offices for which she had once been the unquestioned candidate. But still she forced herself to be present—trimly dressed, her short, stylishly cut gray hair brushed back, even a dab of lipstick and rouge applied to simulate an energy that was no longer required of her.

Meanwhile, the boys were growing up. They were no longer attached like limpets to their mother's body. And then they grew up more and were sent off to boarding school in the hills. Kishen had expected that Bari-Mai would be sent away, too, but that didn't happen. She still spent her nights rolled up at the foot of Naina's marital bed while Shiv slept on the couch in his study. He was at the height of his career now, and there were photographs of him in the newspapers, hovering beside the Prime Minister at the signing of an agreement that he had helped negotiate. However late he came home, Naina waited up for him. Her voice had become more strident and desperate; Kishen listened in spite of himself, and he knew that Mother, too, was awake and listening. During the day, he could no longer sit quietly writing his column by Naina's side. She kept interrupting him with complaints about Shiv; and when Kishen tried to defend his brother by saying that he was working late, she brought out the newspapers with photographs of Shiv and the Prime Minister and pointed to some female undersecretary in the background. It might have been a different woman in each picture, but Naina sneered in outrage—"Is this his work? Fine work!" Once, she dragged Kishen to the room where Shiv now spent his nights; she picked up his pillow and thrust it into Kishen's face. "It's *her* smell. Her dirty smell he brings home with him after he does what he does with her." She made a sound of disgust and Bari-Mai echoed it with a splutter of saliva. More and more it seemed to Kishen that Bari-Mai was not a person at all but an emanation of something in Naina herself: something that had been bred for generations in the stifling women's quarters of their desert home.

IT WAS JUNE, and the days were hot, cruelly hot. Kishen warned Mother not to go out, but one afternoon she said she had to—if she didn't, goodness only knew what those new committee members would get up to. An hour later, the driver had to bring her back, and she was an old, crushed woman. She lay on her bed and Kishen sat beside her; when he tried to get up, she clutched at his hand in a pleading gesture that she had never used with him before. She did it again, moments later, when they heard Naina's voice outside, with Bari-Mai's wild echo. "How do you stand it?" Mother whispered, and then he told her what he hadn't quite told himself—that he was thinking of returning to England.

At once, she rallied. She said that he should take another degree, or at least some sort of course. "What now?" he said, for he was almost forty. "A course in writing," she said vaguely, and he said, teasing her, "I thought you liked my writing the way it is." But he knew that she wanted him to leave for other reasons—in fact, for the same reasons that he wanted to go.

He looked into a writing school in Bristol, and Mother eagerly sent away for the application forms. She knew that it would take some time for these to arrive, but when six weeks had gone by she said that they would have to request them again. Although she and Kishen were alone in her bedroom, she lowered her voice: "I'll write for them today, this time by express mail." He nodded his consent, as though he, too, suspected that someone might be listening.

The next day, Naina invited him to go out with her. She drove with abandon, so fast that he feared for the rickshaws and the wandering animals that she kept missing by inches. His timidity amused her, so he tried not to show it and sat there tense and silent, his hands clutched between his knees.

She took him to an open-bazaar stall that was reputed to be the best for a kind of very spicy Delhi snack food. Kishen, with his delicate digestion, had never wanted to eat there, but Naina seemed perfectly at home. He watched her as she scooped up the little messes with her fingers in a trance of enjoyment; she soon sent him back for a second helping, which she finished just as quickly, and then—"I shouldn't!"—for a third. At last she was sated, spread out on a rickety little bench as a tattered servant boy with a rag wiped the ground underneath it. She seemed oblivious of the looks of urgent desire directed at her by other customers and passersby, and by the proprietor himself, perched up on his platform stirring a vat of fly-spotted cream; or perhaps she was used to them, as she was used to the way that Kishen was looking at her across the table.

She was almost middle-aged now, her body widened, fattened by pregnancy, by excessive eating, and by long hours of deep sleep in the hot afternoons. Yet he talked to her as he had done in her youthful years, though he knew she wasn't listening—not in the way his mother listened when he spoke of his work, or of himself.

And suddenly she interrupted him: "Why are you wanting to run back to England?"

He tried to explain it to her. He told her that it was better sometimes not to be too close to one's source of inspiration. And, as if he were talking about her as that source, she said, "But if I don't want you to go? If I say *mat jao*? Please stay?"

"Try to understand." And he repeated it all—about being detached, about recollecting in tranquility—everything that Mother and his friends in England understood and Naina didn't. But as he talked he thought of a painting by an elderly English painter who was a friend of his mother's; the painting depicted a giant hand caressing a mountain and was titled "I Have Touched the Breast of Mother India." It had always made him laugh, and now Naina was laughing as though he had said something just as ludicrous.

"When will you send off your application?" she interrupted.

"As soon as it comes," he said.

"It hasn't come yet? No? *Sachmuch?* Really?" She suppressed a smile as she opened her handbag and dug around in its messy contents. An envelope emerged; she held it out for him to see but not to take. He realized that not only did she listen at doors; she lay in wait for letters to purloin.

Now she smiled at him openly, teasing him—and how could he help smiling back at her? "Shall I?" she said. "Tear it up?"

She held it out, pulled it back, held it out again. It was a game now—one that he was determined to win. He leaned forward and snatched the envelope out of her hand, quite easily, because she let it go as if she knew what he would do with it: tear it in half, then in half again, all the time gazing at her for approval, which she gave.

The next time Mother asked him about the application forms, he told her that he had filled them out and sent them off. She seemed satisfied, but a day or two later she fell ill. Instead of going to her meetings, she lay in her bedroom with the curtains shut and the air conditioner on. Her face was drawn, and because her partial denture had been removed her mouth was sunken. The doctor came—he was a friend and contemporary who had worked with her on health-care reforms. He prescribed medicines, but when those didn't work Kishen and Shiv called in other, younger doctors. Still the sickness failed to subside, and now Mother mostly lay on her bed with her eyes closed.

Once, Bari-Mai, quick and agile as a monkey, clambered onto the bed and began to press down on Mother's legs. Mother cried out in shock and Kishen, too, cried out, so that Naina removed Bari-Mai and both left indignantly, protesting good intentions. Alone with Kishen, Mother apologized; she said she was aware that it was unfair to see anything but a poor old woman in Bari-Mai, sunk in the rites and superstitions of a backward part of the country.

But the cook saw more than that. He came into Mother's room and, whispering just loud enough for her and Kishen to hear, told them how all day he was on duty in the kitchen, and even at night he stayed up to watch. But who knew—worn out by his vigilance, he sometimes dropped off to sleep for a few moments, during which Bari-Mai must have insinuated her powders and potions into his pots. How else was it that Mother had been laid low by a sickness that the greatest doctors in the world were unable to cure?

"It's unhygienic," Shiv said, after, discovering the cook asleep in the kitchen one night. When Kishen and Mother told him the reason, he said that it was psychologically unhygienic to allow such thoughts to enter their minds. Still, they continued to feel uneasy, though they were ashamed to admit it, even to each other.

IT WAS THE summer vacation, and the two boys, Munna, now fifteen, and Chottu, fourteen, came home from their boarding school in the foothills of the Himalayas. It was the same school, modeled on Eton and Harrow, that Shiv and Kishen had attended in their time. Shiv had been very successful there, Kishen less so. Both Munna and Chottu followed in their father's footsteps, played all sports, were popular; Munna already had Shiv's confident voice and his pompous walk.

Naina couldn't stop petting her two boys, stroking their downy cheeks, though they frowned and pretended not to like it. They bullied her, told her she was getting too fat, and did she have to chew that disgusting betel? They made her play cricket with them in the back garden; she flew like a young girl between the wickets, flushed, her hair coming down, but they kept getting her out before she could make a single run. Bari-Mai was appointed fielder; she squatted, motionless as a stone, only her jaws moving in their perpetual mumble.

Shiv tried to come home from work earlier and, instead of shutting himself in his study, he sat with the boys to discuss their future. Munna wanted to join the Administrative Service, like his father, and Chottu was thinking of the Navy. Shiv considered their choices, the three of them serious together. Naina hovered around them with unwelcome interruptions—"Did you finish your milk, Munna?"—until he shouted at her that his name was not Munna but Raj Kumar. "Oh, big man," she said, her angry stare directed not at her son but at his father, who tried not to meet it. That night, for the first time since the boys' arrival, he and Naina fought again.

The older boy was especially affected by what he overheard, and the next day he sought out Kishen. Trying to answer Munna's questions about his parents, Kishen had to admit that he knew nothing about marriage—how could he? All he knew was that there were bound to be clashes of personality, especially between two people as different as Shiv and Naina. The boy nodded. "So you think they shouldn't be married?" he said. Kishen avoided a reply—not because he didn't have one but because he suspected that Naina or Bari-Mai might be listening behind the door. The boy repeated his question, and when Kishen was still silent, he gave his considered opinion, as judicious and balanced as his father's would have been: "Maybe they should get a divorce." The next moment, Naina came flying through the door. "Divorce!" she cried. "You dare say that in this house!" She abused him in her native dialect and then she raised her hand and slapped him. The sound of the slap echoed through the house, and remained there, ineradicable, even after the boys returned to school.

SHIV INVITED KISHEN to lunch at one of the new hotels, a grand palace with slippery marble floors and hothouse blooms in man-size vases. The prices here insured that only the richest Indians could gain admission. But the richest Indians were no longer the old style of businessmen, the ghee-fed descendants of milkmen and moneylenders: they were younger men, better traveled, almost cosmopolitan. Several of them came over to greet Shiv, with the respect that was due to him as a member of the administration that controlled permits and licenses. When they returned to their tables, Shiv informed his brother of their positions in the corporate world, the multi-*crore* companies over which they ruled. Kishen noticed his almost wistful glances at these men—and at the lively young women who accompanied them. He guessed that these were their secretaries, or perhaps their lovers, but Shiv said that they were their wives: yes, these slim, youthful women were wives, many of them mothers, too, and at the same time helpmeets, social assets to their important husbands.

Here Shiv changed the subject. He said that he had now reached the highest rank of the bureaucracy; his next posting would be as an accredited ambassador, and his success in that role would depend to a large extent on his social skills, and those of his wife. "Naina wouldn't be happy," he said.

"How do you know that?" Kishen said. "You don't know. You know nothing about her."

Shiv, too, grew more heated. "And she knows nothing about me. And cares nothing, about my work, my career—what sort of marriage is that?" He changed the subject again. "What about you? And if you don't mind my asking—you and the Great Indian Novel?"

"I thought you liked my little pieces."

"You shouldn't he hanging around the house so much. You should be getting out, meeting people. The middle classes. The new generation of businessmen. The entrepreneurs."

"And their suitable wives," Kishen said.

Shiv's voice became more intense, charged with suppressed anger. "She has this mad idea that I have some grand love affair going." He laughed without laughing, cut up his meat, chewed violently.

"And is it true, her mad idea?"

"Of course not! And, if it were, who could blame me? Living in that house, in that atmosphere—no wonder Mother's sick. We're all sick. The stench of those beasts alone is enough to poison the lot of us." He put down his knife and fork and stared at his brother, shocked at himself, though presumably he had been referring to the buffalo head, long since disintegrated, and the tiger pelt, which was going the same way.

ALONE WITH KISHEN in her bedroom, Mother whispered, "Have you heard from Bristol about your application?"
"They turned me down."
He lied without a qualm and was amazed by her reaction. She covered her face and rocked to and fro. When he caught her in his arms, she clung to him and wouldn't let him go. How thin she was, how worn away. When she released him, he tried to smile. "I didn't realize you were so eager to get rid of me."
She stroked his head, regretting perhaps all the hair he had lost. Then she kissed him. "Go to England," she said. "You'll have peace of mind there."
"And if I'm far away and you get worse?"
"When I know you're writing your book, I'll be well."
But the next day Naina told him, "Six months, that's all. Three months, six, a year. At home we can always tell. My uncle had a mistress, Mrs. Lal, *moti-taazi*, plump and nice—oh, he liked her very much! But Bari-Mai knew, and others knew, too. In six months, it was all gone, like a balloon, *psssst*, no more *moti-taazi*. It was God punishing her."
"Mother has done nothing to be punished for."
"She wants my husband to leave me. She's even set my sons against me! You think that such thoughts would come into my child's head if she hadn't put them there? I slapped him, God forgive me, but now God himself is slapping her—*aré, sunno*, where are you going?" He had got up to leave. She caught hold of his shirt, and it ripped in her hand. That made Naina laugh—her old playful, girlish laugh, like clear water running.
Kishen began to take Mother to various specialists. She

enjoyed driving with him from one clinic to another; he held her hand the way she had held his on the first day of school. Whatever the doctors said, she claimed to be perfectly well—a little pain here and there, but what was that at her age, compared with what others had to suffer? Still, she grew more and more gaunt, while Kishen looked on helplessly, and every morning Naina and Bari-Mai sat on the front veranda and watched them drive away.

Finally, Shiv decided to send her to England, to consult with a Harley Street specialist. Kishen would have to take her. If at all possible, Shiv would join them, but meanwhile he made the arrangements for his mother and brother—the plane tickets, the hotel, the appointment with the doctor.

Mother was glad to go and Kishen knew that it was for his sake. He wanted to leave, too, he thought, to be in a cool, green place, to collect and recollect everything in its complexity, which was impossible here with it all pressing down on him. Yet, at the same time, he felt guilty—maybe he had no right to go, maybe his place was here, even if he hated it.

"When are we leaving? Have our tickets come?" Mother asked Kishen so often that he began to believe there was some weakness in her mind. "Let them be sent by courier," she said, and then, every day, "Has the courier come?"

Kishen called the travel agent, who assured him that the tickets had been sent—yes, by courier. Kishen told him to cancel those and have duplicates sent to Shiv's office. Shiv brought them home and Kishen at once hid them in the inner pocket of his waistcoat, where he could check several times a day and know they were safe.

Naina had one of her great fights with Shiv. "Why are you sending them away? What use are your wonderful English doctors? It's written! Written here!" Kishen, listening from Mother's bedroom, imagined Naina drawing her finger across her forehead in the place where one's fate is inscribed.

"SHE WON'T LAST the journey," Naina warned Kishen. "And no one there will know the ceremonies. All they have is the electric crematorium; they'll give you the ashes and you won't even know whose ashes they are."

"Why are you saying all this?"

"If you go, that's what will happen. Did your tickets come?"

The way she was looking at him, through him, it was as if she could penetrate right to his heart. But he knew that she couldn't see even as far as the contents of his waistcoat pocket, and for once he felt he had the upper hand.

Maybe she felt it, too, for she said in a different, cajoling voice, "When you're gone, will you remember me? Will you remember me as I was?"

He looked back at her: no, she was not as she had been. She was heavy, her complexion spotted by the spicy pickles she consumed, her mouth stained red by the betel. Even her tongue was red—like a demon's, he sometimes thought when he was angry at her. But at this moment he was not angry; he said, "No. Now. I'll remember you as you are now."

She threw back her head and laughed with a deep-throated pleasure that could swallow him whole. "Will you write about me?" She took a newly prepared betel from Bari-Mai, and asked, "What will you write?"

"All the bad things you do."

"Yes, I'm a bad woman." She translated this for Bari-Mai, who broke into excited chatter. "Bari-Mai says she's making you a very special *paan*."

"Oh, yes? What's she putting in it?"

"You'll see—very special." Her eyes were dancing over his

face, looking to see whose turn it was to make the next move and win.

Bari-Mai handed her another betel, and Naina instructed him, "Open. *Kholo.*"

Kishen drew back slightly, and she said, "There's nothing in it that you haven't eaten a hundred times."

He thought, Well, whatever it is—an aphrodisiac or whatever—it's as superfluous now as it was all those other times. He opened his mouth and soon it was full of betel juices. "Good, isn't it?" Naina said, and he affirmed, "*Badiya.*" Superb.

She said, "Come on. Show. *Dikhao.*"

He didn't even pretend not to know what she was talking about. He took the tickets out of his waistcoat pocket. He handed them to her like a forfeit that he was called upon to pay.

She held them. "Shall I?" She waved them at him. "Or will you?"

"My turn," he said.

She pouted. "You did it last time." But she let them dangle loosely in her hand so that he could take them from her and begin to tear them in half—first his mother's, then his own.

(2011)

Acknowledgments

We want to acknowledge, first and foremost, our mother for leaving us with such a rich legacy of her writings. She was a prolific writer and wrote till almost the last day of her life, always encouraged and supported by our father.

This book is a collection of stories she published from 1957 to 2011 in various magazines and short story collections, many being written at the same time as some of her novels and screenplays. Some of these magazines are out of print, others unrecognizable versions of their past selves, but we do want to acknowledge their gracious communications with us regarding the short stories, especially *The New Yorker*, *The Kenyon Review*, *The London Magazine*, and *Cosmopolitan*.

This book was born with a note our mother wrote when she knew her life was coming to an end. She dictated this note to Renana (the eldest of her three daughters), saying the following:

> I would like all the papers relating to my prose writings to be donated to the British Library in London. This is in deep gratitude for my life (1939), the wonderful education they gave me, the English language itself, my great love of reading and trying to write, all of which have sustained me throughout my life.

She apparently kept copies of much of what she wrote, handwritten and in print (at a time when computers did not exist). These papers followed her to the United States, making their way from India wrapped up in careful bundles and stored in the deep closets so common in New York apartments. Upon her death, these bundles and an extensive amount of other material were shipped from New York to the British Library in London.

It turned out that our mother made a very wise decision. These papers could not have fallen into better hands. We want to thank the British Library archivists and staff, led by Rachel Foss, for accepting the papers and for the meticulous care they continue to bestow on those precious works. No acknowledgment of the Library's work would be complete without recognizing the scale of the task of archiving and cataloguing eleven large boxes of material undertaken by Dr. Pauline McGonagle. Over a period of seven years, Pauline assiduously opened, assessed, and recorded every piece of paper to emerge from the boxes, preparing an exhaustive list of Ruth's writings as part of her work for her PhD thesis. We would not have known where to start looking for many of these stories without Pauline's comprehensive list.

Finally, this acknowledgment cannot be complete without thanking our editor, Dan Smetanka, for encouraging us to choose the stories for this new collection and overseeing the whole process with so much care. Without his enthusiasm and guidance, this book would not have been possible.

Renana Jhabvala
Ava Jhabvala Wood
Firoza Jhabvala

RUTH PRAWER JHABVALA, born in 1927, wrote several novels and short stories, and, in collaboration with James Ivory and Ismail Merchant, won two Oscars for Best Adapted Screenplay (for *Howards End* and *A Room with a View*). She won the Booker Prize in 1975 for *Heat and Dust*. Her other numerous accolades include a Guggenheim Fellowship, a MacArthur Fellowship, and an O. Henry Prize. She died in 2013.